TRAVELING WITH THE WOLF

TALES OF THE ROUGAROU BOOK 5

JULIE MCGALLIARD

GOTH HOUSE PRESS

Edited by Shannon Page
Cover art and design by Julie McGalliard

ISBN:
978-1-951598-08-2

This book is for you, Mom

PART I

ATLANTA, GEORGIA

1

IN THE AIRPORT

In the crowded Atlanta airport, a young woman with bright red hair shows a passport in the name of Abnegation Asher. The agent at the podium glances from the girl to her documents, frowns.

"Abnegation? Is that French?"

"It's a family name."

"Traveling on your own then?"

"Just got out of school. Backpacking across Europe." She holds up her backpack, as if to prove her story.

He nods, frowning, makes a mark on her boarding pass. "Be careful. It's dangerous out there." He hands the pass back to her, welcomes the next person in line.

She exhales, a sigh of relief. The passport is brand new and not strictly accurate, as it proclaims her to have been born twenty-one years ago, when reality is closer to seventeen, and gives a name she has never used socially. She was called "Abnegation" for the first fifteen years of her life, but "Miss Asher" still sounds like someone she doesn't know.

She puts her backpack on the conveyor belt. She takes off her red boots and black denim jacket, puts them into a plastic tray, puts the tray onto the conveyor belt. The boots belonged to her grandmother, who the girl has never met, but her forty-year-old scent clings to them as a comforting phantom presence. The girl is anxious at being separated from them even briefly, and keeps glancing at them as she goes through the body scanner, making sure she knows where they are.

On the other side of the body scanner, she is reunited with her things. She puts the boots back on, returns her passport to the zipped inner pocket of the boot on the left. She carries the jacket. August in Atlanta and the outside air is a heavy, moist 95 degrees, but she has been moving through air conditioned indoor transit spaces and finds herself wanting the jacket sometimes. When she lands in London it's projected to be 65 degrees and raining lightly, so she will want the jacket there. She's looking forward to the weather. It should feel like Seattle, and Seattle always feels like home.

She makes her way to the international terminal an hour and fifteen minutes before her plane is supposed to start boarding. Outside the giant picture windows, the sun is low, a sullen red through a haze of pollution.

She scans the terminal for a way to pass the time. Should she take advantage of being officially twenty-one and get an overpriced beer at the fake British pub? She studies the outside menu for a while and decides to conserve her money instead. Abnegation Asher has some cash, a checking account, and a debit card, but is going to be overseas for an entire year without any source of additional income.

This doesn't worry her much. She knows she can safely "sleep rough" as the English put it. She knows she can kill her own food and eat it raw. But some things in life do require money, and she doesn't want to burn through hers too fast.

She fills her aluminum coffee cup with filtered water from a spigot, sips water that tastes lightly of coffee. She finds an empty seat near the gate and rifles through her backpack for something to pass the time. It takes her a moment to remember that she doesn't have her phone anymore. The old one was surrendered as part of this forced year-long severing of ties with her pack. She could probably buy a new one if she wanted, the kind where you pay up front and they don't need a permanent address to send a bill to. She's thought about it. But it would be an expense she doesn't strictly need, and it would present a temptation to seek out her old life, her old friends. And she isn't sure what would happen to them if she broke the terms of her exile like that.

Her father Leon told her that, in the past, when the pack had power struggles for the position of hunt leader, the losing faction was exiled permanently because "a divided wolf pack can't survive." But, since she was young, impulsive, and a faction of one, he gave her this alternative: a year to travel Europe, rethink her actions, come to accept him as her hunt leader.

Or not.

After a year traveling around Europe, will she come to realize that her challenge was misguided, even foolish? A moment of irrational paranoia, lingering effect of the black moon caused by her intensive trauma morph training?

Or will she decide that she was right the whole time? And, if so, what then?

Either way, she has a whole year to think about it.

She pulls out a mass-market paperback, bought used, a thick fantasy with a much-broken spine, and tries to work up an interest. But her thoughts seem lost in a dark fog. She reads the words but they don't echo in her brain to make a story. They're just words.

She closes the book and watches people making their way through the airport: bored faces, tired faces, intent faces, excited faces. Sharp-dressed businessmen walking briskly, ragged families with whining children, young and smoothly tanned backpackers who strike her as looking European, although she isn't entirely sure why she thinks that.

A blast from the air conditioning and she puts the jacket

back on. A dog has entered the space, a police dog, not a pet or a service dog. Why does she think it's a police dog? Some trace smell that clings to his fur? Something about the way he moves through the space? But she isn't worried yet. She knows her backpack doesn't smell like drugs or explosives, because she would have noticed that herself.

She takes out a different book, a travel guide to England, Scotland, and Wales, broods over the pictures for a while. She really does look forward to seeing the vast green fields and ancient stone monuments for herself. The tourist presentation can be a bit cheesy, but her friend Deena would be so envious to know she made it to Loch Ness and Stonehenge, if only she could send a postcard—

No.

Stop.

Don't think about it.

The dog is trotting past, pauses, turns toward her, sniffs her knee. He's large and dark, maybe a cross between a German shepherd and a Labrador retriever. He seems extremely happy to be sniffing her knee, as if he found something he was searching for.

She looks up at the two men in black who accompany the dog. They look less happy. In fact, they look very stern and intimidating, both tall and heavy with padding and weaponry. Cops of some kind.

"Could you come with us please, miss?" one of the men says.

The girl stands up, heart pounding. Something is wrong. What is it? She picks up her backpack. The man flinches as if he's afraid and barks out, "We'll take that, miss," as he grabs it roughly out of her hand. "Come with us please."

He takes her by the shoulder, to steer her, and she doesn't resist. She knows that's what you do in an airport. You need to cooperate with the cops. If the cops think you're trouble they can prevent you from getting on the airplane entirely.

What will happen to her, if they won't let her get on the plane?

She isn't sure. She doesn't want to think about it. So, she cooperates.

She inhales deeply and tries to stay calm, allows the cops to lead her away. Her questions bring terse answers.

"Where are we going?"

"Security."

"How long will this take? Am I going to miss my plane?"

"We'll make any necessary arrangements."

They lead her through a door marked "security only" and now they're outside and slammed with Georgia summer heat. She walks down stairs, feels sun-baked warmth coming up off the metal. The jacket is much too heavy now, but she's not taking it off. They might interpret that as a reason she's trouble, a reason not let her on the plane. Heck, they're heavily armed, they might even decide to shoot her. Sweat trickles down her armpits.

All things being equal, she'd rather not get shot.

She looks around the outside part of the airport, thinking about how she might escape. There aren't a lot of places to hide. If she just started running across the tarmac, she would definitely get shot with a lot of guns. Something like that might even be fatal.

The sun is well below the horizon and things will be fully dark soon. She takes a deep breath and continues on her present course, letting the officers herd her, even though a part of her balks at submitting to the authority of an enemy.

At the bottom of the stairway they steer her toward what looks like an unmarked police car.

"Get in."

"What? We're leaving the airport?" She is genuinely confused. She didn't picture them trying to make her leave the airport, this can't be right.

"Get in the car, Miss Asher."

"I don't understand. Am I under arrest?"

"Just get in the car." He gestures with his gun toward the back seat. "Otherwise you would be resisting arrest." He gives a nasty smile. "Which is a crime, miss."

"So I am being arrested?"

"Just get in the car."

She does. She still doesn't know what else to do, although she is starting to become pretty sure that whatever happens next, it does not involve her getting on a plane to London.

Her heart sinks. It's only now that she isn't going to London on a plane, that she realizes how much she was looking forward to seeing Europe. A part of her had been excited, in a tiny, cautious way.

Now that part has been crushed, replaced by a familiar sensation of fear and anticipation: *these men are going to try to kill me, aren't they?*

2

BUDDY

The dog jumps into the back seat of the police car, nudges the girl as if he wants to be friends. She absently scratches behind his ears and wonders if she can use the dog somehow. What is he trained to do? Locate her, or someone like her, obviously, but is he otherwise an attack dog? Or just a scent tracker?

The cops slam the door, locking it. They climb into the front seats, start driving.

"Where are we going?" the girl asks.

The men don't answer. Instead, the cop in the passenger seat makes a call on the car's radio.

"We've got her. We're heading out of the airport now."

"Good. Good. You boys know what to do." The voice is a man she doesn't recognize. "Now, I know you boys'll think she looks like a cute harmless little girl, but don't let her looks fool you. She's a killer. Don't you give her a chance. Use the hood, like I told you."

"Oh, don't worry, we won't be giving her any chances." The cop who's driving glances over his shoulder to give the girl a wicked, knowing grin.

She cringes, pretending fear. "Chances to do what?" She puts a quiver in her voice. The cops just laugh. They're human, and she wonders what makes them so confident. Is it because they know something she doesn't know? Or is it because they don't know something she does know?

The car pulls onto the highway, drives through the darkness for a while. She can smell the tension rising on the cop who's driving, but both men remain silent, following a map shown to them on a computer pad attached to the dashboard.

They pull off the freeway, drive down surface streets which are wide but dark and empty. Left turn into a business park which appears deserted, soaped-over windows and faded signs, grass poking up through the pavement.

They drive around the building and park the police car on the side hidden from the road. The highway roars distantly, an unseen river. Illumination comes from the dirty orange glow of urban lights reflecting off moisture in the atmosphere.

This is where they're going to try to kill her. That much seems obvious. But they still haven't put her in handcuffs, or a hood. What are they planning? How are they planning to do it?

One of the cops opens the door on the dog's side and he jumps out, eager, tail high.

Guns point at the girl's chest.

"Hands above your head."

She obeys, and doesn't fight them when they drag her out of the car, throw her roughly to the ground. She tenses, ready for the moment when they try to put cuffs or a hood on her, figures that's when the battle starts. But that's not what they do.

Instead, one of the men says, "Get undressed."

His partner frowns at him. "Ralph, no, not this time. You heard what Gutzman said."

"About her being a killer? Yeah, I don't buy it." He points the gun at the girl. She winces, looks away. "You're not a killer, are you, cutie?"

The girl shakes her head. No, she's not a killer, not really. The wolf is. Not the girl.

"See? Guts was just trying to scare us."

"But she's one of them. You know that. Buster found her."

"Yeah, okay, maybe she's one of them. But she's the mini poodle version. A little purse dog." He chuckles at his own joke. Gestures at her with the gun. "Hey, hon. I believe I told you to get undressed?"

"But why?" she asks. She really hasn't figured it out yet. She thinks he's asking her to shape shift, and can't work out why he would want her to do a thing like that.

The man makes a disgusted noise, and shoots her in the leg.

She drops to the ground, purely from the emotional shock. Her leg is already healed, but the pants now have a bloody hole in them. This lodges in her mind as the greatest injustice. *You ruined my brand-new pants you asshole*, she shouts at him in her head, but can't seem to make her voice work.

"Get undressed or the next shot hits something important."

All at once, she understands what he's trying to do. That he does this a lot. *Ralph, no, not this time.*

Tears streaming down her face, she stands up. Why is she crying? She doesn't know. She's more angry right now than she's ever been, why should that make her want to cry? It doesn't make any sense.

The man laughs. "What are you crying for? I'm not going to hurt you."

Not going to hurt me? You already shot me in the leg you asshole, she yells in her head, but still can't bring herself to say anything.

She takes off her denim jacket. She takes off her black and yellow V-neck women's T-shirt from Georgia Tech, a school she has never been to. She got the T-shirt in the same Atlanta sporting goods store where she got everything else. She takes off her black Performance™ sports bra, guaranteed to wick sweat away from the body and dry quickly after being rinsed out in the sink of a remote Scottish Bed and Breakfast. She takes off her grandmother's red boots. She takes off her cool-tech wool socks in neutral gray. She takes off her stretch comfort hiker's jeans with silver thread anti-grime technology. She takes off her black Performance™ underpants, companion to the bra.

She does this with rapid, assured efficiency.

Now she stands in front of the two cops, naked and pale in the light of the waning gibbous moon. The two men erupt into lust, a sharp green smell that tickles the back of her nose.

The cop gestures with the gun. "Down on your hands and knees."

She does this, suppressing a weird, maniacal giggle. Maybe unhinged laughter is better than crying? Her own emotional responses aren't making any sense to her.

Behind her, she hears the cop pulling down his pants.

He can't run like that.

It's time to summon the wolf.

But for some reason she hesitates. She doesn't know why. She doesn't understand her own reactions, not at all. Crying, laughing, freezing, none of that makes any sense.

He touches her, putting a hand on her waist as if to steady himself.

The touch jolts her out of shocked inaction, and half a second later, the wolf shakes herself, turns around, bites off the man's genitals. Meat, but the flabby texture bothers her and she spits it out rather than swallowing.

Blood gushes from his maimed crotch as the man screams in pain and fear. The wolf rears up on her hind legs, almost like a pet greeting an owner, but her purpose is to knock him off balance and she does. He falls backward hard, knocking his head against the fragmented pavement. The wolf positions herself on his chest, centering her weight so that he will find it hard to move, and hovers her mouth above his neck, so that he can see her teeth, inhale her hot predator's breath, feel the drip of saliva on his skin.

She wants him to be afraid of her.

But the human part of her hesitates to kill him, why?

We need to ask him questions. We need to find out who sent him after us and why they did that.

Explosion of pain rips through her chest. She knows this pain: bullets. The other man is shooting her with some kind of rapid fire weapon. She launches herself at him and bites into his neck, worrying it slightly as he falls backward, gun clattering to the ground. His neck is a bloody gash, a fountain that slows rapidly as his heart stops. She nudges the head, puts a little extra effort to remove it entirely from the body. This isn't strictly necessary, since the man isn't a wolf, but it still makes her feel better, reassured that he is truly dead.

The other man watches this happen. She feels his eyes on her. He's afraid and bleeding but hasn't given up yet. She braces herself, watching closely for his next move.

He calls out: Buster, ATTACK!

The little brother launches himself at her, snarling and barking like a wayward puppy. But his heart isn't in it.

She takes him gently by the neck, shakes. He whimpers, backs off, whining and releasing urine. She nods at him. His submission to her is noted. Now he's under her protection.

SHIT FUCK SHIT says the living man, his fear growing. His right hand starts flailing and she knows what that means: he is searching for his own gun and will shoot her when he finds it.

She bites the hand to stop it moving for the weapon. Her jaws are powerful and she's not being careful of him: she rips his hand all the way off, leaves a bloody, gushing stump behind.

She spits out the hand and steps away to consider the situation. Brother: surrendered. One enemy: dead. Second enemy: mortally wounded. Fight: over.

The girl sometimes called Abnegation rises to her feet, a couple of bullets popping out of her skin as she changes shape. The living cop watches her do this. He clutches the bloody, oozing, empty space where his hand should be and his eyes are confused, pleading. She remembers the time she lost a foot, the pain of that, the wrongness, the dismay. Of course, she grew a new foot before the next morning. The cop is human. He won't be growing a new hand. He won't be living much longer.

She asks him, "Who sent you to kill me?"

He shakes his head. "Please."

She makes eye contact, eyes flashing brilliant acid green. "Who sent you to kill me?"

His face relaxes, eyes unfocus. "My supervisor sent me," he says.

"Who is your supervisor?"

"Mr. Gutzman."

Gutzman? That's not a name she knows. "Who does Mr. Gutzman work for?"

"Homeland Security."

Homeland Security? She frowns. This isn't making any sense at all. "Why did Homeland Security send you to kill me?"

"New..." He seems ready to pass out. "New group... Extraordinary Threats Task Force. I..."

He passes out.

She considers trying to wake him up and get more answers, but finds herself reluctant to touch him with her naked human skin. Instead she gets dressed again and goes to the car to retrieve her backpack. Searches the interior, hoping for more clues about her enemies and their plans. Nothing interesting. Empty coffee cups, fast food wrappers. A book, *The Savage Way*, that looks familiar.

The radio crackles to life and a female voice says, "Davis? Jackson? You there? Come in please."

She needs to get away before more cops come.

Backpack over her shoulders again, she glances down at the damage to her jeans, the former wound in her leg. It doesn't look too bad. She can tell people she got scratched by a blackberry vine, mend it later.

A few steps into the darkness and a painful twisting in her gut sends her to her knees. She vomits up one of the bullets. She can feel several more working their way through her body. It's going to take hours to expel them all.

Beside her, a warm furry body, wet tongue on her face. The dog. He wants to be friends, part of her pack, ready to follow her. She considers this. She doesn't know where she's going, and it's probably dangerous for him. But if she leaves him behind, he might get blamed for the attacks, and executed. She doesn't want that. That seems worse than anything that might happen to him if he goes with her.

She stands up, slaps her thigh. The men gave the dog a name but she doesn't remember it, so she gives him a new one. "Come on, Buddy. Come on. I guess we're traveling together for a while."

He accepts his new name, comes forward to lick her hand, and trots close behind as she heads out into the night.

PART II

THE HITCHHIKING BANDIT

3

AFTER THE MOON

I wake up.

Morning after the full moon, instinctively look for my clothes, find one of those thin silk robes the Varger used to have by the dozens. It's hot. I have a vague memory that for several days now I've been wearing this robe and nothing else.

Things start coming back to me, in the dreamlike way of full moon memories. But there's more of them than expected. A lot more. Almost as if I spent more than one night as the wolf.

As if—

Atlanta airport, men who tried to kill me, and then—

"Buddy?" I call out his name, look around, don't see him. When the nights are cold we sleep cuddled up next to each other, but last night, after the hunt, he stayed with the kill. It didn't worry the wolf at the time, but it worries me now. I shoulder my backpack and head to the carcass of the buck we took down. Buddy is sleeping next to the buck's remains. His sides rise and fall, breathing. One fear relieved, anyway.

I kneel, place a hand on his warm black fur, inhale deeply, try to orient myself. Where are we? These mountains seem dry, full of long-needled pine trees and sparse underbrush. If we walked here from Atlanta, we should be somewhere in the Appalachians, right? How far have we come?

Images flash, memories falling into place, and I realize the wolf has been dominant for days. Weeks, maybe.

Inhale again, get a bitter tang of wildfire smoke. Cougars, coyotes, even wolves, not too far away. These dusty mountains feel like the ones in California or eastern Washington, but how could we have come so far?

Not important, it'll come back to me. There's something up with Buddy, a reason he's sleeping over here instead of next to me.

I touch his wet nose. "Hey, boy."

He wakes up and turns his big dark eyes to me, thumps his tail. Pleading gaze, sweat razor-sharp. He's in pain. Shit. He must have hurt himself last night during the hunt.

"Well, let's see what the problem is." I begin gently stroking his black fur, and he responds to the pleasure of the attention, but winces as I contact his many bruises and scrapes. Most of them are minor, but I feel a brief, intense guilt: I knew it was dangerous for him to follow me, I just thought it was less dangerous than leaving him behind. But also I liked having a companion. We've been a pack of two, and, I think we've been happy? Ish? A little trouble along the way, but nothing we couldn't handle together.

My fingers stroke his left rear leg and he yelps in pain, the most pitiable sound I've ever heard. Oh, no. It's much worse than I hoped. I think the bone is shattered. He's going to need professional medical care.

First thing is to prevent infection in the wound. In the backpack I have a few tools, hand sanitizer and a plain linen sheet I can cut up into bandages.

"Okay, boy this is going to hurt." I stroke him. He winces. But he trusts me. Bon Dieu, he trusts me so much it's terrifying. I wipe the wound clean as gently as I can. He shudders a few times, but stays quiet.

But when I put pressure on the swelling that I think marks a damaged bone, he howls in startled misery. Poor boy.

I have a flash of memory, standing next to a girl in a pink prairie dress, my older sister Chastity, handing her equipment as she tended to the broken ankle of a small boy, our little brother. She put sticks in to keep it straight, then wrapped cloth around it, to keep the bone together while it healed. But our little brother Righteousness limped even after the bone was knitted up again. It would have been better if we could have taken him to a real doctor. But outsider medicine was forbidden. Father Wisdom wouldn't allow it.

A familiar feeling of helpless anger briefly overwhelms me and I have to remind myself to take a deep breath. Father Wisdom is dead, everything's okay, there's nobody to stop me from getting help for Buddy.

I hunt around for straight sticks that seem they could do for a splint, then wrap the sticks and cloth around his broken leg. I hope I'm doing this right, going off those years-old memories of a girl who wasn't professionally trained herself.

As a child I didn't wonder about it, but now I do: where did Chastity get those ideas she used to have about outsider medical care? Splinting a broken leg, or giving CPR to our sister Sackcloth With Ashes? From a book, probably, but which book? Where did she get a chance to read it? The books in our cult library were pretty much all religious, plus a few educational primers, but nothing about medical care.

I wonder where Chastity is now, what she's doing. The meltdown of the New Harmony cult was about a year ago, although it seems longer. I know my stepmother Meekness and my brother Justice have been trying to keep the John Wise evangelical empire alive. I know this because I happened to catch them on a talk show, hawking a new book "by John Wise" edited by "Mercy Wise" and "Justin Wise." But they're the only ones I know anything about.

The younger children probably went with Meekness, but

the oldest kids, Chastity and Great Purpose, I don't know what they would have done. I hope they're all right.

I don't know how long it's going to take me to get Buddy to the nearest town big enough to have a veterinarian, so I pack up some of the buck's meat for travel. Get out my largest knife, stare at it for a moment, where did I get this? I know I didn't have it at the airport, because they don't let you take really big knives on a plane.

Right, that log cabin. Hunting lodge? Church camp? Weird place, full of bad taxidermy and calligraphied Bible verses. The front door wasn't locked, so Buddy and I went in to take shelter from a punishing rainstorm. There was a huge pile of dry wood and a big stone fireplace, so I built a fire, and that might have been a mistake. If the smoke was visible at a distance, that could be what drew those hunters to the lodge. Three men, all of them soaked through.

At first they seemed okay, grateful for the shelter, hanging their outer wear to dry, warming themselves by the fire, making small talk about the weather and the terrain. But after a while things started turning weird. The men became really interested in the fact that I was traveling completely on my own, except for Buddy. And they clearly thought I was stupid. The wolf part of my brain was dominant, as she had been for weeks, and so I was a bit slow to respond to things in words. The wolf found the men unimportant and not terribly interesting, but she wasn't angry with them. But I get angry now, when I remember what their mocking voices sounded like:

Hey, I've got an idea, why don't we all get totally undressed so we can dry our clothes by the fire?

Don't you worry, sweetie, we won't do anything to you.

You can trust us.

We did undress, because our clothes were soaked down to the skin, and even the clothes in my backpack needed a bit of drying by that enormous fireplace. We found a closet with some slightly musty blankets, wrapped up in the blankets like sarongs, sat by the fire. But the men were laughing at me the whole time. Laughing at me because they thought I didn't know what they were laughing about.

They offered a drink of warmed whiskey and I accepted. It smelled okay to the wolf, no drugs or weird ingredients.

We all drank and talked, but they talked mostly to each other, and I wasn't really listening to them. They thought it was funny, because they thought I was stupid.

The wolf continued to not be mad about any of this.

But I get mad when I think about what happened.

Because eventually, it went the way it was always going to go, the way any human could definitely see coming. All three men, stinking of lust and alcohol, reeking of the guns they carried, came into the room where I was sleeping with Buddy. They had a whispered conversation about feeding him drugged meat or possibly even killing him so that he wouldn't interrupt what they were planning to do.

Half-asleep and mostly thinking like a wolf, I got up and threw the men out of the room.

Literally, I picked them up and tossed them.

When werewolves do this to each other, it's often the *first* move in a fight, just a little something to get the adrenaline going.

But with these men, it was the last move. The first one hit hard against the stone fireplace, bones cracking. He collapsed to the floor, screaming and then moaning. The second man ended up impaled on the horns of a mounted deer's head. It was a little comical to see him up there, flailing weakly, as he bled. The third man flew into the kitchen area, colliding with a row of hanging cast iron skillets and a block of knives.

I remember having the thought, not really a wolfy kind of thought, that movies and television often show people with enhanced strength throwing other people across the room like it's no big deal, like it's something you do to get your enemies out of the way without really hurting them.

But these men were badly injured. They stayed where they were, not moving, for several minutes, while I made sure Buddy was okay.

When the men showed no sign of attacking, I started getting ready to leave, dressing and packing up my items. When they continued to show no signs of attacking, I went through their stuff and helped myself to anything that looked useful: cash, weapons, alcohol, seasoning salt, matches in waterproof containers. They had drugs too, a powder that smelled a little bit like berserker drugs mixed with cocaine, but this I burned in the smoldering embers of the fire.

Once I had looted their packs, I opened the door of the cabin to check on the weather: no longer raining, sky growing lighter with a clear pre-dawn. Seemed like a good time to leave.

"Are you guys gonna be all right here?" I remember the sound of my own voice saying this, and in my memory, it sounds sarcastic, but I don't remember intending to be sarcastic. Is the wolf even capable of sarcasm?

The man impaled on the antlers coughed. The one next to the fireplace groaned. The one in the kitchen made a weird little hitching cough noise before saying, "Bitch."

"Well, you're all still breathing," I said out loud. "Have a good day."

Again, it sounds sarcastic when I remember saying it, but I wasn't trying to be sarcastic.

With Buddy at my side I hiked out. The guns went into a ravine a bit later, but the knives went into my pack and stayed there.

All of this flashes through my mind while I go through the process of slicing off strips of deer meat, salting them, wrapping them in the butcher paper, putting the paper into a plastic bag so it doesn't leak. When the bag is full, I wipe off the knife, wipe off my hands. The carcass of the buck is still huge, but there are plenty of other animals around to eat it. Crows and cougars and other creatures.

I pull on my human clothes. Underpants and stretchy jeans that have a bloody hole in part of them, patched. Sports bra. T-shirt. Deep in the rattled contents of the backpack, I locate a brush and run it over my hair, long but not as matted as I was afraid of. Still, there are a few impossible knots, what my mother used to call witch knots or devil knots, and the only way to really get them out is to use scissors. I have scissors in the bag somewhere, but don't want to take the time for that level of grooming. Instead I corral my hair into what they call a French braid.

My face needs to be clean, if I'm going into human civilization. I pour out a tiny bit of water from my aluminum bottle into a cloth, rub the cloth over my skin, hope that does the trick. Then I drink. In my human skin I sweat and need a lot of water. I don't know what happens to a werewolf who gets too dehydrated, but in these dry woods, that is a concern. I stop drinking when I'm still a bit thirsty.

Inhale deeply, listen carefully. No traffic, so I can't be completely sure which way to go to get back to human civilization. We've been heading west and north, in a general way, so I'll continue to do that. Eventually I'm bound to hit something: a river, a marked trail, a road. I just don't know how long it will take. And I'm really worried about Buddy.

I touch Grandma's red boots, make sure they're still securely tied to the bottom of the backpack, but I don't put them on. They need to stay nice-looking for human habitation. My feet will heal, but these are the only shoes I've got.

"You ready, Buddy?" I ask the dog. He looks up at me with those big trusting eyes and thumps his tail and tries to stand up, the adorable idiot. "No, no, no, not on that leg, let me carry you."

I pick him up into my arms, and he thumps his tail wildly for a few minutes, thrilled beyond thrilled to have me carrying

him. Then I move him into the Jesus-carrying-the-sheep position, draped around my shoulders like a big awkward scarf.
I've carried him that way a few times on this trip, when the
terrain got difficult, or when he needed rest and I didn't. He
settles in happily between the back of my neck and the top of
the backpack.

"Okay, Buddy, hang on, we'll get you help as soon as we
can, okay? Just as soon as we can."

In spite of his pain he pants eagerly, excited for this new
adventure.

4

THE HITCHHIKING BANDIT

The hitchhiking is not going well.

It took me less time than I feared to locate a road, but it's taking me far too long to get anywhere. I managed to flag down one ride, from a young woman in a pickup truck who also had her dog with her, and our dogs got along well, so that was nice. And she was able to orient me on a map, so now I know where we are: eastern Washington a bit west of Spokane.

We really did come a long way, didn't we?

Knowing that, I pick Seattle as my next destination. Advantage: I know my way around there, and have confidence I can find a veterinarian for Buddy. Disadvantage: it's possible the people who tried to kill me in Atlanta will be looking for me in places like Seattle or New Orleans or Los Angeles, where I have friends. If the person ultimately trying to kill me is my father Leon, Seattle is probably the first place he'd look.

But I can deal with all of that later, after getting help for Buddy.

The woman who gave me a ride was heading south, on a camping trip. She dropped me off at a gas station service stop, where we could get fresh water and vending machine food. At first it seemed like a ride all the way to Seattle shouldn't be hard to come by.

But now the sun is setting, a small red ball through the pinkish haze of wildfire smoke, and I've been walking along this highway for hours with nobody stopping, and I'm starting to get cranky. Are people less likely to pick up a girl carrying a big black dog? Or is it me? When I used the gas station restroom, aside from being extremely freckled, my face looked pretty normal. But maybe there's something? Did I spend too long with the wolf driving, do my eyes do that flashy thing all the time? Maybe that wouldn't show up in a mirror.

Wait, that gives me an idea. The next time I hear a car roaring up behind me, I stop, turn around, try to stare down the driver. The car is a mammoth commercial truck and I see the driver, a big beefy man in a red baseball cap, frown at me. It's hard to tell through the glass if I made the right kind of eye contact. But it seems to work. He stops, anyway. He opens the passenger door.

"Hey, missy, need a ride?"

I'm not instantly inclined to like people who call me "missy" but suppress the slight annoyance and rush up to the door with what I hope is a pleased smile. "I do, thank you. My dog is hurt. I need to get him into town."

He nods. "Well, climb on in."

I've gotten rides in big trucks like this one, and know how to climb up into them. I don't think they're really supposed to pick up hitchhikers, but they get bored and lonely, spending weeks on the road, so they do it anyway.

I settle in, move Buddy to my lap, backpack to my feet.

"Thank you," I tell the man, as he pulls forward again.

"No prob," he says. "What's your dog's name?"

"Buddy."

"How'd he get hurt?"

"We were hunting and the buck got a little feisty." I tell him this with a conspiratorial air, because the fact that he's a trucker, and the red hat, have made me think he might be a hunter himself, and we'll have hunter camaraderie.

But he frowns. "Hunting? You were out hunting? All by yourself?"

"No, I was with Buddy."

"But—isn't that dangerous?"

"I guess it is, but I didn't know it. Poor Buddy, right?"

"No, I meant, dangerous for you."

This is not going quite how I envisioned. "What's your name?" I ask him.

"Howard." He points to a license on the dashboard. "Your name?"

"Ab—Abney," I spit out awkwardly, as multiple names fight for dominance on my tongue.

"Did you say Abby or Abney?" He frowns.

"Abney. Sorry." I cough, as if that will explain my weird stutter. "I've been out in the wilderness with just Buddy for a while, haven't used my voice much lately."

"A while?" He looks strangely appalled. "How long?"

"Oh, just for the summer." I grimace. This guy is definitely thinking I'm a weirdo and I'm not even sure what I'm doing wrong. "What about this wildfire smoke, right? Isn't it weird how it makes the sky all pink like that?"

He nods. "They say it comes up from California."

"Really, all that way?"

"But I think it's the government," he says.

"Oh. Okay." I don't know quite what to say to that, so I fold myself around Buddy for a moment, kiss him on the forehead. "How far to the next town? Someplace big enough to have a veterinarian?"

"That'll be Marysburgh," he says. "About thirty miles down the road. But I won't go all the way into town, I'm heading for Palouse Manufacturing on the outskirts, I'll drop you off there."

"Sure, sure. No problem."

We drive for a while in silence through the darkening highway, then he punches on the radio. A man's voice, shrill and angry, yelling about illegal immigrants "breaking in" to this country. His rage makes me feel really stressed out, but it's this guy's car, he's doing me a favor, I should suck it up. I sit for a long time, torn between the desire to ask him to change the channel and the knowledge of how much I need his help to get medical care for Buddy.

The man on the radio shifts topic finally, but then he says something about "lesbian bitches" and—

The girl turns toward him eyes flashing green fire and her voice rumbling in a low growl and she says TURN THAT SHIT OFF in a voice full of fang and claw—

Silence, as he obeys, face blank. Then he shakes himself, recovers. "I know Dick Manly is a little much sometimes," he says, as if he expects me to know who that is. "A lot of times out here talk radio is all you can get. Talk radio and maybe a little country."

"Dick Manly?" I goggle for a moment then snicker. "That's what he calls himself? Seriously? Dick Manly?"

The driver has the decency to look a little embarrassed. "It's really his name. I mean, Richard Manly. Dick is a nickname."

"Right. Sure. Of course." Long pause, while I think about it, suppress a giggle that comes out my nose. "But still. He really did that? On purpose? Called himself Dick Manly?"

"Why don't we try to find a country station?"

He punches a couple of buttons and soon some guy is twanging about how he's got "friends in low places," a catchy ode to dive bars that I've heard at karaoke, but never the original. I'm not familiar with country music, but I'm happy to hear any kind of music again. There are things about the human world that I missed a lot over the last few weeks. Coffee. Sleeping on a bed. Carbohydrates. Music. And this song seems so familiar, me and the driver are both singing along by the end.

The next song isn't familiar at all, another male singer, but this one with a twang so exaggerated that it sounds fake, singing about how much he loves the flag. The driver obviously knows it, singing along, thumping on the steering wheel in time with the music.

I stare out the window and absently stroke Buddy's head. We're moving into cattle country and the dry empty spaces give way to big ranches. Buddy is still in pain, I can tell that much. Pain leaves a raw, reddish signature in the sweat, like rusted razor wire, something sharp and unclean. Sometimes he whines, so softly that I'm not sure the driver can hear it.

The song ends. The DJ says, "And that concludes our old time trio, with Travis Trapper's 9-11 anthem, 'America the Red, White and Brave.' Can you still sing along with the chorus, friends?"

The truck driver laughs. "Do you remember that song or are you too young?"

"Too young I guess. I don't remember 9-11 at all." I think for a moment. Is that right? Would a current twenty-one-year-old remember 9-11? No, no, I'm good.

"Well. You kids don't know America the way it used to be. The way it's supposed to be."

"I guess not." I brace myself for a sermon, zone out, get ready to give the vague, noncommittal verbal responses that I learned during my childhood in the cult. Already lost my temper with this guy once, can't afford to do it again and lose this ride.

"After 9-11, people lost their damn minds. Do you know that's when we invented the Department of Homeland Security? A whole new part of the government, a third of the federal budget, just like that." He snaps his fingers. "And then all of a sudden we're taking our shoes off at the airport and they're making us get new IDs with computer chips inside."

"I don't like Homeland Security." The men in Atlanta, that's what they were from. Homeland Security, Extraordinary Threats Task Force.

The driver nods. "Yeah, yeah. And then they invent these smartphones, right? They're tracking you through those phones. You know? That same app you use to find your friend's house, that means the system knows where you are. Exactly where you are. It's a damned surveillance state and we did it to ourselves!"

"I don't have a phone," I say.

"Well." He pauses for a long time as if I have just let the air out of his favorite rant. "Good for you."

He falls silent and the radio goes back to playing music. I stare out the window, stroking Buddy, as the sky turns fully dark. No stars. That's probably the smoke. I consider his rant about smartphones as a surveillance state. He's not even wrong, technically, but he still ended up sounding like a crank.

Buddy starts whining again, softly, but a different tone, a different smell to his sweat: he's hungry.

"Okay, boy, it's okay." I pull out the knife and the plastic bag full of the salted meat, begin unwrapping, preparing to slice off something bite-sized to feed Buddy.

Beside me the truck driver explodes in alarm and anger. Slams on the brakes, a chaotic, noisy experience in a truck of this size. Metal shrieks and the truck drifts sideways, becoming unstable. Dangerous.

"I knew it! I knew it! God damn it you are the Hitchhiking Bandit! Just get out! Get out right now!"

I raise my arms in surrender. "Hey, Howard, it's okay, I was just getting some food for my dog, I told you we were hunting, right? It's just deer meat. That's all. The knife is to cut the meat into smaller pieces. That's it."

Buddy isn't sure what we're doing—surrendering or fighting—and makes a weird kind of half growl, half whine.

The driver calms down a tiny bit, but only a tiny bit. "I

don't care. Get out anyway. Whoever you are, whatever you are, just get out. And take that damned killer black dog with you."

I shove everything into my backpack, try to avoid threatening gestures. "Okay, okay, it's fine, thanks for the ride, everything's fine." I pick up Buddy and my backpack and scramble out of the truck, as careful of Buddy as I can manage. My feet have barely touched the ground when the truck pulls away noisily, leaving a sharp chemical smell of tire rubber and brake fluid.

Buddy, upset and confused, whines at me, a question, a plea.

"Yeah, Buddy, I'm sorry, I don't know what that was all about either."

I reassemble, putting on the backpack, draping Buddy over my shoulders, but leaving out the meat and the knife, so I can feed us both. With food, he seems to feel better right away. But I'm still confused. What did the driver call me? The Hitchhiking Bandit? Probably a criminal from one of those true crime podcasts. A "hitchhiking bandit" would certainly explain why it's been harder to get rides than I was hoping.

Where has the driver put us, anyway? He said we were twenty or thirty miles outside of Marysburgh when he picked us up, so we're obviously closer than that. But how far away is it?

I pass a highway sign. Marysburgh, 10 miles. Seattle, 117 miles.

Well, that answers that question.

"Hang on, Buddy." I feed him a slice of salted meat. "Hang on, we're almost there."

PART III

MARYSBURGH, WASHINGTON

5

NAUGHTY BUCKAROO

In the distance, beckoning, civilization in the form of a giant lit-up sign:

NAUGHTY BUCKAROO ESPRESSO
OPEN 24 HOURS

The logo looks like a 1950s retro pinup cowgirl, and the "24 hours" part flashes on and off. It's a beautiful sign, a wonderful sign, possibly the most wonderful sign I've ever seen. If I can just make it to that sign, everything is going to be all right.

I'll have coffee, and the coffee shop people will know where I can find a veterinarian.

(And how are you going to pay for a veterinarian, Abby? You know a vet's going to cost money, and you don't dare access that checking account, you know they'll find you that way.)

(Shut up. I'll figure something out when I get there.)

But getting there seems to be taking hours. I've been walking steadily for weeks, why should this particular ten miles seem so long? But it does. Exhausting, like it's wringing out the last little bit of my determination. Maybe it's the letdown. When that trucker first picked us up, I really thought we'd be getting all the way into town, not getting evicted ten miles away. I relaxed a little too much.

Maybe it's the smoke. Inhaling bad air is never good. Or the heat. The night hasn't cooled off nearly as much as it should have. Maybe I'm a little dehydrated, now that I think about it.

I drain the last of my water bottle, sharing it with Buddy, in the cautious faith that an espresso stand will have water, at least, even if it doesn't have all the answers.

I inhale deeply, tasting smoke and my own tears. Why am I crying? Emotional or is the smoke making my eyes water? Both, maybe. Tears of frustration and worry. Tears of dust and smoke.

The dry hills roll downward, finally, and I see a small hexagonal building painted red and styled to look like a barn, at the edge of a large parking lot. The entire area is well lit, welcoming. The lot is large enough to accommodate a commercial semi like the one that just dumped me off, but there's also a clearly labeled walk-up window.

Eagerly, I head to the window, where I'm greeted by a barista in costume: tight black sequined shorts and matching fringed bra, pair of bandoliers crossing her chest and really emphasizing the size of her breasts, low-slung gun belt, black cowboy hat over cascades of curly dark hair. She's heavily made up and gorgeous, and when she sees me approach, she winks and tips her hat.

"Well, hello there, I'm Antonia, what can I getcha?" She says this in an exaggerated Western accent.

Weirdly, I'm blushing, flustered and unsure of myself all of a sudden. This must be one of those bikini espresso bars I've heard about. The "naughty" part of the name should have clued me in, but somehow I didn't realize, and now I'm not sure I should be here, not sure what I'm supposed to be doing.

"Can I get some espresso?" My voice comes out sounding very small and timid. She laughs.

"Why, pardner, you shore can. That there machine is an espresso machine." She cocks her finger at a very nice looking espresso machine, all gleaming silver metal. "What can I do ya for? Mocha? Latte? Americano?"

"Uh, double shot please. Two of those?"

"Two doubles? You mean a quad, sugar?"

"Right, right, quad means four, yeah, sorry. But no sugar please. Over ice?"

She bursts out laughing and drops the accent. "Oh sweetie, you are really too much. One quad, over ice, on the house." She scoops ice into a small plastic cup, pours the four shots into it, swirls it around a little to melt the ice, adds a straw. She hands it to me, leaning way, way out of the booth while displaying maximum cleavage. Then she notices Buddy. "Oh my goodness, what are you wearing on your shoulders there, is that a li'l doggo?"

"He's hurt. This was the easiest way to carry him."

"Hurt! Oh, poor puppy!" She croons at him, making eye contact, and he pants toward her a little, wanting to make friends. "What's wrong? Can I help?"

"I hope you can. I think his leg is broken. I need to find him a veterinarian. Do you know this area well?"

"I do. Dolly? What do you think?" She calls over her shoulder at the other person working inside the booth, a tall person in Dolly Parton drag, who comes over to the window to peer out at me and Buddy.

"Oh no, my little ragamuffin, what's wrong?"

"Broken leg," Antonia says. "Her dog has a broken leg." She stops, does a double take. "Her?"

"Her, yeah. I'm a her. My name's Abney."

"Well, Abney." The person dressed as Dolly drops out of

persona for a moment and says, in a masculine voice, "Out of drag I'm Orville, he, owner of this establishment, and when ten a.m. comes around, we'll get your doggie to a vet. What do you think about that?"

"I think that sounds great. But what should I do until then?"

Antonia comes back, with food in her hands. "Eat a bagel breakfast sandwich we can't sell because we used an onion roll for somebody allergic to onions? Unless you're allergic to onions."

I nod, enthusiastic. "No, no, I'm not. That would be wonderful. Food would be wonderful." I laugh nervously. Bon Dieu, I've forgotten how to interact with people, I sound like such a dork.

She hands me the warm paper bag. Buddy smells it and strains toward it eagerly. "Just hang on, boy, you're getting drool all over my neck."

Antonia laughs. "He likes bagels, huh? Just a minute, I'll give him some with no onions." She puts a couple more bagels into a different bag, hands that to me. "Doggos shouldn't have onions, in case you didn't know that. So give him these, don't share the other sandwich. Okay, you see that area with the picnic tables?" She points, I nod. "There's a few larger wooden benches, you should be able to get Buddy settled on there, do you have blankets?"

"I have blankets. We've been, you know, we've been camping. I have all the usual camping stuff."

"Okay, there's water and a bathroom over there too. The door code is 1883, that's the year Marysburgh was founded."

"Thank you. Thank you so much for everything." Pause. "Do you, uh, do you know what time it is? I'm sorry, I don't have a phone or anything. I've been walking all night and it seemed like forever, but I think that's just because I was so worried about Buddy."

"Yeah, sure, it's four-thirty-eight." She points at a digital clock inside the booth. "Sorry you'll be waiting so long, but the vet won't be open until then anyway."

"Thank you. Thank you so much." I sip the espresso and for a moment I'm stunned. "Wow. That's good."

"Yeah, I'm the best." She gives me a wink. "My Italian ancestors smiled upon me."

I take Buddy, the espresso, the sandwich, and the bagels to the bench, lay down a few blankets, get Buddy settled. I give him all the plain bagels. Is bread good for dogs? I don't even know, but he loves it. Even more than the salted deer meat.

"You're a civilized boy, aren't you?" I tell him, and he thumps his tail at me, vaguely. He doesn't know what I said. But I'm thinking: I don't just need to find him medical care. I need to find him a new permanent home. Somewhere safe. He can't travel with the wolf anymore, it's way too dangerous.

After eating, we both droop, tired. Buddy starts doggie-snoring right away, and a little while later, I drop off to sleep myself, curled around my backpack, his warm furry side next to me. It's a light sleep, and I wake easily: when cars drive up and a bell inside the building goes DING!; when the sun rises in a pink haze of wildfire smoke; when some customers decide to have breakfast in the picnic area; when I need the bathroom; when I need to carry Buddy to a place where he can urinate.

Once, I'm awakened by somebody touching my shoulder, which sends me into combat mode instantly. But the person seems nice when I see them, genuinely concerned.

"Hey, I'm sorry, I just wanted to know if you...if you needed anything. A ride somewhere? That's my rig." They gesture toward a semi truck. "I'm going to Kirkland, you can get to Seattle from there if you want."

"Thank you. But the espresso stand people are helping me, I'm just waiting for their shift to be done."

"Oh yeah? That's great. They're good people here, I always stop by on my way through town."

The next time somebody wakes me on purpose, it's obviously a man and obviously a sexual come-on. "Hey honey, you need a place to stay? You can come home with me. I bet you clean up real nice."

I don't even have to growl at him, because Buddy saves me the trouble, fixing the man with a yellow stare and rumbling, deep in his throat, a reminder that even the fluffiest, friendliest dog you ever met is really just a few generations removed from being a wolf.

The man puts up his hands in surrender and backs away, never taking his eyes from Buddy.

I laugh and give Buddy a proliferation of smooches. "Good boy. That's a good boy. You're a very good boy."

As it gets later in the day, we shift benches to avoid the sun. By ten a.m. it's already getting hot. I'm dozing when Antonia comes by to touch my shoulder.

"Abney? Time to go, are you ready?"

I hop to my feet. "Ready."

She's wearing a loose cotton dress, bright pink, like something you'd wear over your suit at the beach, and she has taken off the wig, the hat, the bandoliers. Just behind her, Orville has also de-wigged, and is wearing a pair of jeans and a fringy Western style shirt under a tan cowboy hat, although most of his Dolly makeup is still intact.

Antonia laughs. "My goodness, you got to your feet fast, did you spend time in a combat zone?"

"Just my father's house." She gives me a horrified look and I laugh nervously. "Sorry, little joke. I'm just really worried about Buddy."

"Well, let's go, ragamuffin." Orville shakes his keys and I carry Buddy to the back seat of a vintage Cadillac painted a cool pink.

6

THE VETERINARIAN

Orville waits for me to get Buddy settled in the back seat before he starts driving. The Cadillac has been kept up well and the engine is smooth and surprisingly powerful.

He punches the radio and a voice twangs out, barely recognizable as music before Antonia turns it off. "No, Orv, no, not that country shit, not today."

He sighs. "Toni, dear, it is my car." He fusses with the radio some more and a song blares out:

YOU CAYANT GET A MAN WITH A GUN

"Country show tunes, a little something for everyone." He smirks and she sighs.

"Orville, you are really counting a lot on the fact that I'm too gay to want to say no to show tunes."

"I know you well, my dear."

After a few moments of silence, I speak up. "Orville? Antonia? There's something I have to tell you."

"You don't have any money for the veterinarian? Yeah, doll, we figured that out." Orville smiles at me in the rearview mirror.

"So what's going to happen?"

"Well, the way I figure it, we'll pay your dog's vet bill, and then—"

"You start working at the espresso stand!" Antonia inserts, breathlessly.

Orville gives her a slightly skeptical look. "Aren't you getting a little ahead of yourself, Toni?"

"She can sleep at the house, you know we've got that futon downstairs that nobody's using. Come on, we're down a person, that's why you've been my backup."

"We don't know that she's going to be okay making espresso in a bikini."

"Hey, Abney, are you willing to make espresso in a dumb Western-themed bikini?"

"I don't know."

And I really don't know. I like Antonia and I like espresso so I want to say yes, but I've never worn a bikini, I don't know how I'll feel about it.

As we get closer to central Marysburgh, Antonia makes a phone call. "Georgia? Are you free to look at a little doggie today? Uh-huh. Oh, right." She turns back to me. "Abney, what did you say was wrong with Buddy?"

"I think he broke a leg."

"Broken leg," she says into the phone. "Right. I don't know." Back to me. "How long ago?"

I think back, try to add up sunsets. "Two nights ago. I think."

"Two nights ago we think." She listens for a moment. "No, not that. Yeah? Okay, we'll be there in a few." She smiles at me. "Georgia's on it. We went to high school together. She became a vet, I became a bikini barista." Laugh. "But she's good, I always took my own dog to her."

The veterinary clinic is part of a strip mall and we're able to park right outside. The receptionist, a delicate-looking dark-skinned woman in a Muslim-style head scarf, smiles when we enter. But before she has a chance to do anything else, Georgia comes out. She's tall, broadly built, extremely freckled, curly reddish-blond hair. I can smell that she's not a rougarou, but she still strikes me as being extremely werewolf-like. Her presence dominates the space and this is very much her territory.

She zeroes in on me, makes serious, slightly frowning eye contact.

"How did your dog get hurt?"

"We, um, we were hunting together and the buck went down thrashing."

She looks taken aback, as if that's not at all what she expected me to say. "You were hunting? With a gun?"

"What? Bon Dieu, no, I never hunt with a gun, what do you take me for?"

"You hunt, but not with a gun?" Georgia frowns at me deeply. "What do you use?"

"Um…" Don't say claws and teeth, don't say claws and teeth, don't say claws and teeth. "A knife?" I pull out the knife. It's the same one that freaked out the truck driver, and Georgia recoils from it too, tension spiking, I put it away again immediately. "Sorry."

"I'm still confused. You hunt with a knife. How?"

"Um." I really was not expecting to have to explain all this. "I…run the prey down? Then I use a knife to kill them? I'm sorry, I don't hunt recreationally. Buddy and I were in the wilderness, we were hunting for our dinner."

Georgia gives me a complex look, dark and serious. "Why don't you bring Buddy into the exam room. Toni? Orville? I'll call you when they're ready to be picked up."

"Okay great." Toni hugs me. "Good luck, Abney. It'll be okay, Georgia really is the best."

We go back into the treatment room. Georgia gives me orders. Put Buddy here, hand me that. She's efficient. All business. Gives him a sedative, treats his wounds, sets his leg. Then turns around to give me a stern look and I'm half expecting her to come out with something like, "I know what you are, werewolf girl, and we have to talk."

Instead, she says, "He's been living rough, hasn't he?"

I nod. "He has."

"No rougher than you, I guess?"

I nod again.

She sighs. "You're homeless."

"At the moment."

"A drifter?"

"At the moment."

"And you took your dog?" She looks disgusted and that sparks my pride, a bit of anger.

"We are companions. We met along the way. I've tried to take care of him as best I could. We did okay until he hurt himself. But as soon as he did, I brought us back into human civilization to get him treatment. Which I know I can't pay for."

"Antonia's got you." She sighs. "You're lucky, she likes to take in strays." She clearly wants to be mad at me but she's sort of failing. She says, "Are you on drugs?"

"Well. Antonia made me a quad, so, technically yes."

"You know what I mean."

"No. I'm not homeless because I'm a drug addict. Next question?" I don't quite know why we're so hostile to each other, but it feels a lot like when the wolves have a dominance staredown. We both want what's best for Buddy, maybe that's the point of contention.

"Okay then. Why are you homeless?"

"Is that really any of your business?"

She looks guilty for a second, then rallies. "I'm not being nosy. I'm asking for Buddy's sake."

"I ran away from home. Home was bad." It seems simplest to rewind my life story, more or less, to the point a year and a half ago when I first left New Harmony.

"How did you meet Buddy?"

"Some cops were, um, they were hassling me. And they were, um, they were, you know, they were trying to, you know." My voice trembles and I take a big, long breath. I thought I could say it. I thought I could say the words. But somehow I can't.

"They sexually assaulted you?"

"They tried. Buddy protected me. He disobeyed them to protect me. But he, um, he hurt them physically and I was worried that he would get in trouble for that, so I took him with me."

She nods thoughtfully. "Good call. So he's a police dog."

I nod. "He's extremely well trained. But I think he was trained to be a scent tracker, not an attack dog. That's probably why he ended up…on my side instead of theirs. I guess. Is the best way to explain it."

She sighs. "Okay. So. You fought off the cops and took their dog and then you decided to…take up cursorial hunting?"

"I don't know what that is. But we did hunt for food. Buddy is basically just a few generations removed from being a wolf, he didn't think it was weird. Until he got hurt, he was having a great time." I sound defensive. Was Buddy having a great time? Really?

"Cursorial hunting is when you run the prey down with your body." She sighs. "I'm a vegan, I have a lot of issues with hunters. Human hunters, anyway. It's natural for dogs like Buddy."

"It's natural for me too." Bon Dieu, I sound pouty. "I'm a predator, he's a predator. That doesn't make us evil."

She frowns for a moment, many different expressions chasing themselves across her face. "Humans are omnivores."

"That means we take what we can get. In the wilderness, hunting was what I could get. Bears are omnivores, do you get mad at a bear for eating a salmon?"

She shakes her head, sighing. "Okay, why did you go into the wilderness?"

"To avoid people."

She looks startled, laughs. "Yeah? Okay, that part I get."

"To avoid cops specifically. I was worried after the attack that me and Buddy would be on some kind of hit list of cop killers."

Her jaw drops. "Killers? Buddy *killed* them?"

This is really getting out of control. "No. Yes. I don't know." I close my eyes. "I'm sorry, I don't mean to lie. I'm pretty sure they're dead. But that wasn't our intent. They shot at us. We fought them off. But when we left, they weren't moving."

She shakes her head. "None of this is going where I expected it to. But I admit, you seem a lot more focused and rational than I expected."

"You thought I was lying when I said I wasn't on drugs."

"It's a thing people lie about."

"Maybe that's true. But you know as well as I do that people end up homeless for all kinds of reasons, and deep down it's mostly about money." I spit this out, a little more angry than I meant to be, but she relents, seems a little chastened.

"I didn't mean anything by it, Abney, honestly. I just want to protect the animals who can't speak for themselves. Is living your kind of life really what's best for Buddy?"

"Obviously not. That's why we're here."

A moment of silence. Then I say, "I know you're concerned about him. I am too. And if I have to leave town again, I'll try to make sure I can leave Buddy here. Probably with Antonia. They seem to like each other."

"Antonia is a good choice. She lost her own dog of old age, just a few months ago." She shakes her head in exasperation. "But why would you have to leave town again? There's something you're not telling me."

"There's a lot I'm not telling you. You don't need my whole life story in order to treat Buddy, do you?"

She turns self-righteous again. "Tell me the truth. How did he really get hurt?"

"It's exactly what I told you. We were hunting and he got injured during the hunt. Herbivores are a lot more dangerous than people think."

She laughs. "That's true. You do not want to piss off a horse."

A long pause, then she sighs. "All right. I have your word that you're not taking Buddy with you into any future…adventures. Is that right?"

"That's right."

"Here's the sheet of instructions. Please call me if you have any questions about how to take care of him."

7

THE GLITTER RANCH

Orville and Antonia pick up me and Buddy from the veterinarian and take us to downtown Marysburgh, which is nice, historic, but small. We stop outside a large, well-kept Craftsman-era home, painted in shades of lavender and gray.

"Welcome to the Glitter Ranch," Orville says, with a sweeping gesture toward the house. "It belonged to my grand-parents, then my parents, then me. I don't live here anymore. When I got married, we moved into his spiffy modern town-house. But I still rent out the rooms here. I'm attached to the place. I keep it in good repair, and I won't rent to just anybody."

"It's a college town," Antonia says. "There's a high demand for short-term single-room rentals, so he can afford to be picky."

"All the proper rooms are taken right now," he says. "But there's a kind of half room in the basement, semi-private. You can sleep there while Buddy recovers and you figure out what you're going to do next." Pause. Then he says, "Well, you can sleep there as long as you can sleep through a bunch of drunk queers watching the Tony Awards."

"I can sleep through just about anything."

I follow them into the house and down into the basement. The entertainment area is defined by a large sectional couch arranged in a U-shape around a projection TV screen.

One person is sitting on the couch, all wrapped up in a fuzzy peach-colored bathrobe, hair in curlers like a 1950s housewife, watching a drag contest show. I get a wary look. "New roommate?"

"New roommate," Orville says. "Her name is Abney and she's just staying here while her dog recovers. Abney, they're Sin."

It takes me half a second to parse everything and realize he's giving pronouns and a name. "Uh, hi, nice to meet you, Sin."

"Likewise." They take my hand in a prim, mannered way that matches the old-fashioned curlers.

"We'll get you set up over here." Orville leads me to a dark corner behind the main viewing area, where a futon is set up behind a folding Japanese-style paper screen. "This little futon, folded up, used to be the couch down here. We moved it but didn't get rid of it when we got the big sectional. Is it going to be okay?"

"Better than okay." I sit down, testing the surface. Luxurious, even. An actual mattress.

"Do you want Buddy sleeping on the futon with you? Or is that bad with his broken leg?"

"Georgia said he should sleep by himself while he heals. I'm kind of a restless sleeper anyway."

"Do you think Buddy would be okay on a used doggie bed?" Antonia asks, pulling one from another corner to place it near the futon. "This belonged to my dog Princess until she died of old age a couple of months ago. She was a big dog who looked a lot like a Neapolitan mastiff but she was a rescue so I've never been sure. Anyway, it's for a large dog as you can see."

"It looks perfect. Georgia mentioned that you lost your

dog recently. I'm sorry. But I do think Buddy will be fine with a used bed, he's friendly with other dogs." He wakes up slightly as I settle him on the bed, but goes right back to sleep.

Orville hands me a stack of sheets and blankets. "You can use these while you're here, but you're responsible for washing them yourself. The household is a community. You contribute. Clean up after yourself. Basic courtesy on things like when you make noise."

"No practicing the drums at two in the morning, got it," I say, and they stare at me for a moment until I smile. "It was a joke, I don't play the drums."

Antonia laughs, while Orville gives me a courtesy smirk. "Follow the house rules. No homophobia, transphobia, biphobia, racism, misogyny, or any other kind of asshole behavior. No smoking or vaping indoors. And no hard drugs. If you have a drug problem, we'll get you into rehab, but we can't deal with that here. It just makes trouble for everyone else. All of these house rules also apply to any friends, lovers, dates, or one-night stands you bring over."

"I can do all that." We make eye contact. We shake on it.

He says, "You've been through a lot just to get here, so today you and Buddy can sleep as long as you want. But tomorrow we'll need to figure out what kind of a job you can do to earn your keep here."

"Don't you worry about the vet bills." Antonia kisses Buddy on top of his head. "That's on the house."

"The house?" Orville says, skeptically. "Girl, you mean it's on you."

"I'm part of the house." She shrugs. "I just don't want her to worry about Buddy."

"I'm not. I mean, I'm still worried about him, but—" Antonia and I make eye contact and it's a little intense. I look away, down to Buddy's sleeping form. "He's in good hands here."

Antonia yawns and gives me a brief, busty hug. "Welcome to the family."

Orville gives me a somewhat more stiff hug, and they both leave. I sit on the futon feeling surreal. Am I really here? After all that happened, is this where I am?

A voice behind the screen shouts out, "Hey, new kid, are you all done back there, can I go back to Dragster Speedway All Stars Marathon?"

"Sure!" I call out, then emerge from behind the screen and sit on a different part of the couch. "Do you mind if I join you? I need to relax a little before I can get to sleep."

"Knock yourself out." Smile, brief curler adjustment. "I'm Sinnamin with an 'S' and people often call me 'Sin' as you heard. You're Ab-something?"

"Abney."

"Welcome to the Glitter Ranch, Abney. Want some no-alcohol frosé?"

"Frosé?"

They hold out a pitcher and a plastic cup. "Frozen rosé. But no alcohol. It's better than you might expect. I have a migraine."

I accept a cup and it is pretty good. "I'm sorry you have a migraine."

"That's why I'm staying home all day watching the Dragster marathon. And why I look like crap."

"I think you look good."

"Well, aren't you sweet." They unpause the TV. I watch for a while, getting a running commentary on who the contestants are and what techniques they're using for clothes, hair, and makeup. Eventually I start feeling tired and go back to the futon, check on Buddy who is still sleeping with his little doggie snores. I dump the contents of my backpack onto a chair, sort through for the oversized T-shirt I brought to sleep in, change into it, put everything else back. I don't want the people here to see all the knives and freak out.

Climb into bed, lying down on a proper mattress for the first time in a month. And I'm out.

Standing. Looking up into Sinnamin's frowning face, my body tensed in a combat ready crouch.

"Sorry." I make a point of relaxing and looking down at the floor. "I guess I was having a nightmare."

"I guess you were," they say, with a wary look. "You were making a lot of noise over here. It was annoying. Also I was a teeny bit worried. But mostly annoyed."

"Sorry. I guess I'm doing that thing again."

"Again?" Raised eyebrows. "That thing?"

"I used to have night terrors and sleepwalking sometimes, but I haven't done it for a while, I thought I was over it."

"Well." Long pause. "More no-alcohol frosé?"

8

BELLE STARR

My grandmother sits down next to me, looks at her red boots. "You're taking good care of them, aren't you?"

"As good as I can, Grandma. As good as I can."

She nods thoughtfully. Puts on a pair of reading glasses, takes out a small notebook and a pen, writes something on a page of the notebook, rips it out.

"Don't read it just yet," she says. She rolls up the paper and puts it in my mouth. Unexpectedly, it tastes good, sweet, like honey. "When the time is right you'll know what it says."

She wraps her arms around me, which is warm, comforting, except now the paper is stuck in my throat, a lump that won't go down. My throat works and works, swallow-muscles churning pointlessly, paper stuck, scraping against the sides of my throat, making my throat feel raw and aching. A panicked feeling rises up, choking me. Nothing in the world except this struggle to swallow the paper, trapped, darkness closing in around me and if I can't swallow I'm going to drown, I'm going to die, I'm going to starve—

I wake up.

Panicked, sitting up already. Cough out a single strand of

dog hair that had somehow become lodged in the back of my throat.

Really, brain? A single dog hair and that's what you do to me?

I rush to the bathroom, get water from the tap, swallow and swallow until my throat starts to feel free. Now I'm a little sick to my stomach. Is the tap water no good here? It tasted fine.

No, wait, I think I'm just hungry. That makes me feel sick sometimes.

Wait, where am I again?

Right. Marysburgh. Glitter Ranch. Antonia. Georgia. Orville. Sinnamin.

Buddy?

I find him in his inherited doggie bed, but not sleeping, watching me eagerly. He needs to go outside to relieve himself.

The basement has an external door into the lower half of the garden. I put on pants and carry him out through that door, making note: external door could come in handy on the full moon.

Buddy does well until he tries, instinctively, to use his broken foot to chase after some smell that interests him, yelps when it hurts.

"Poor boy," I tell him. "Come on, we'll get you some breakfast." I lean down to pick him up but he gives me a look of defiant refusal and instead starts limping back to the house on three legs.

"Well, okay then, good for you, Buddy."

Although he's able to get back into the house on his own, he's not quite ready to make it all the way upstairs on his own, so I carry him up there.

Antonia and Orville are sitting at the dining room table, drinking coffee. Pour-over style, and it smells amazing. But Antonia is making a scowling face. "Well, I've tried it, and I hate it." She puts her cup down, then notices me, gives me a big smile. "Abney, hi, you want to try some coffee with whipped olive oil in it?" She pushes the cup toward me.

"Olive oil? Is this like that thing where people put butter in their coffee?" I sniff the cup. It smells okay. Like the coffee, which smells amazing, and like the olive oil, which smells pretty good.

"You got it. Last year I guess the trendy new thing was butter, this year it's olive oil." She rolls her eyes. "I ask you, if olive oil belonged in coffee, don't you think the Italians of all people would already have been putting it in there?"

I laugh, take a sip. "It's not terrible, but it's not better than milk. Maybe if you're lactose intolerant?"

"See?" Orville says, with an air of having proved something. "Try the one with coconut oil."

He pushes another cup toward me and I take a sip. "Same. Not bad, but not better than milk. What about coconut milk? You know, like in a curry? Or coconut water? I had a sports drink once that was coffee and coconut water, that one was pretty good."

Antonia gives me a horrified look, but Orville looks thoughtful. "A sports drink you say?"

"Yeah, I guess caffeine helps you recover after sports, or something. I don't know. I got it on discount at a convenience store."

"Interesting." Orville gives Antonia a pointed look. "See, there's a lot of things we can do with this concept."

"Look, Orv, I'll put anything food-safe into their coffee if the customers are willing to pay. But I don't have to be happy about it." She goes back to drinking her pure, unadulterated coffee. "Anyway, good morning, Abney, help yourself to whatever kind of coffee you'd like, and if you want regular cream that's in the refrigerator."

"Thank you. Breakfast?"

She waves a hand. "Help yourself to literally anything in the refrigerator."

"Nobody has anything private?"

"That's the other refrigerator."

I nod, yawn. "Like the public house, sure."

"Public house?" Orville looks intrigued.

Shoot, I wasn't thinking at all. Because I meant the public house at Bayou Galene, the Cajun werewolf town. I smile, nervous and brittle. "Um, the, you know, the religious compound where I grew up? There was a public house."

"Religious compound?" Antonia looks horrified. "You mean like in a cult?"

"Yeah, a cult." I take a deep, shuddering breath, prepare to tell the story I've rehearsed in my head. "It was one of those situations where the girls aren't allowed to leave until they get married, even when they're over eighteen. I didn't get a driver's license or a bank account or anything like that. But then they got me a passport because I was supposed to go on an overseas mission trip with my, uh, my soon to be husband. Once I had the passport in my hands, I took off."

I pull out the passport. Orville studies it thoughtfully. "Twenty-one? That's good, you could work in the bar. I assumed you were a bit younger." He takes a sip of his olive-oil infused coffee. "How long were you planning this escape, doll?"

How long?

How long *was* I planning my escape?

It seemed completely spontaneous, an idea that first occurred to me during the funeral for my sister, Sackcloth With Ashes. I counted the number of us standing vigil and we were thirteen, the Devil's Number. But if I left they would only be twelve. It seemed so obvious. I had to leave. I was the problem. I was the Devil. Without me around everything would be fine.

But was that really what I was thinking? Or was it just what I told myself I was thinking?

I remember in the cult, the way it sometimes felt like my

mind was running along on two different threads. The thread at the top, bright and obvious, like embroidery, shown to the world, always ready to give the right answer when Father Wisdom interrogated me, ready to obey his commands, ready to follow all the rules that I had learned to follow.

But underneath ran a different thread, darker and stronger, hidden, but this was the thread that really held everything together. This thread hated Father Wisdom, hated his god, hated myself, hated my life, wanted to leave, wanted to die, wanted him to die.

"I don't know," I admit, finally. "At the time I left, leaving felt like a brand new thought I'd never had before, triggered by the sight of the passport. But I think until I was ready to leave, I had to hide that part of myself from everyone, even myself."

"I'm a gay man who grew up in a cow town, so I do know a bit about that." He nods, sympathetically. "So, you got your hot little hands on a passport and then you just took off? No plan? No destination?"

I nod. Of course, in the real timeline, I took off without a passport. Without a wolf. Without anything. Sometimes I think it was brave. The other werewolves in the Varger pack tended to see it as brave, and they respect that kind of courage, so I never worked very hard to give them a different interpretation. But sometimes I think it was suicidal. Self-destructive. The thing that gave me the guts to leave was the hopeless feeling that it didn't matter anymore, that I didn't care what happened to me.

"That's it," I say. "No plan, I just took off."

"So, how did you end up here? It's a long way from Louisiana to Marysburgh."

"Without a plan, I drifted. You know. Hitchhiking and odd jobs? But I was heading north and west in a general way. I knew people were less religious there, in the northwest. That's what I was looking for. Someplace where I felt safer. Like people wouldn't return me to the cult."

"You're over eighteen, legally they can't do that anyway," Antonia declares. Then looks worried. "Can they?"

Orville shakes his head with a sigh. "Girl, I don't know. Ten years ago I would have agreed with you, but with everything that's going on in Florida…"

"Why? What's going on in Florida?" I don't know much about Florida, but I know it's where Flint Savage is from, so I have a possibly unfair negative opinion.

"I don't want to talk politics right now," Antonia says. "It'll just make me mad at a bunch of people who aren't in the room right now, so I can't yell at them. Anyway, they're horrible everywhere, maybe a little better in Seattle, so you weren't wrong in your instincts."

Long thoughtful pause. We drink our various kinds of coffee. Then Orville asks, "Abney, were you ever a sex worker?"

Antonia reacts angrily. "Orville! Why would you ask her that?"

"I'm not being offensive, Toni, I just wanted to know. A lot of young women who run away from home end up doing sex work, and there's no shame in it."

"No." I make eye contact. "I have never been a sex worker."

He smiles. "Well, what kind of jobs have you done, child?"

"Things I've been paid for? Bartending and dangerous animal control."

"Dangerous animal control?" Toni looks intrigued. "What was that like?"

"Mostly rats, but I did have to deal with some really big spiders."

"Well, we don't need anything like that," Orville says primly. "Why don't you tell me about the bartending. How did that come about? Given your hyper religious background."

"It was a private event and I was hired to do more general catering support, but the bartender showed up late so I ended up mixing drinks." I pause. "They said I was good at it."

"Did they?" He nods thoughtfully. "Well, I happen to run a bar called the Pink Pony, in addition to the espresso stand. Do you think you'd want to work as a bartender?"

Antonia wilts a little. "Don't you think she can work at the stand?"

"Toni, does she even want to work at the stand?" To me, "Hon, do you want to work at the bikini espresso stand?"

I look down, feeling hot and nervous, like there's too much blood in my face. "I don't think so. I've never done anything like that before. I've never even worn a bikini." True, I have been entirely naked in public a lot, but that's different. Usually, when I'm naked in public, I'm trying to become un-naked as rapidly as possible, I'm not just standing around letting people look at me.

Orville says, "I know you're from a super-religious background, hon. You probably internalized a lot of those taboos, you really can't help it. There's no shame."

I laugh. "No shame in having shame."

Toni frowns. "Are you sure you're not willing to even try it? I mean, we're not wearing regular bikinis, you know? We're wearing Western-themed costume bikinis."

"Toni darling, don't push. If Abney isn't comfortable working in a bikini, she's not comfortable working in a bikini."

"No." I frown, feeling weirdly like a failure. Shouldn't I be willing to push myself? To overcome the taboos and shames of my youth? "Anyway, I have scars on my right shoulder, they're pretty severe." I say this, as if that's the reason. Oh, no, I couldn't possibly. Scars.

"Scars!" Both of them look alarmed. "What kind of scars?"

"I'll show you guys, okay? Just so you know." I turn away from them, lean over, slip out of my oversized sleeping T-shirt, hold the shirt in front of my boobs, turn back around. They gasp. Toni reaches out as if to touch the scars, then pulls her hand away.

"It's okay, you can touch them if you want."

"I'm sorry, I didn't mean to—do they hurt?"

"Not usually. But sometimes they feel kind of weird? Overly sensitive? I don't know, it's hard to describe."

"How did it happen?"

"I told you I grew up in a cult, right? My father was really into physical punishments, it was a huge part of his religion. This idea that you needed to break the spirit of a child in order to make them righteous."

"Break the spirit?" Orville looks properly horrified. "My goodness, is that as bad as it sounds?"

"Worse. I'm kind of, I don't know, naturally feisty I guess, so I was always getting in trouble. Also, my cult father wasn't my biological father, so I think he targeted me in a special way. Anyway, one time I got beaten very badly and the wounds got infected. For a while they thought I was going to die. It was the nicest my cult father ever was to me." My voice trembles, threatening tears. All of this stuff still bothers me, as much as I try to pretend it doesn't.

"Obviously I got better, but the wounds left scars. Because of the infection, probably. Most of the time the physical chastisements didn't leave scars no matter how painful they were."

"Oh my God," Toni says.

"It's okay. It was a long time ago." I turn away from them again, put my T-shirt back on. It wasn't really that long ago.

"You know, if you did want to work at the espresso bar we could put you in a costume with a cute jacket," Orville says. "We've got a little sheriff's outfit in silver and white that would look great on you."

"Wait, I thought it was Toni who was trying to get me to work at the espresso bar?"

Orville shrugs. "I just happened to notice that, objectively speaking, you have the perfect body for it, and I would be foolish if I didn't at least try to get you on the roster."

"See, I told you," Toni says, folding her arms with a smug air.

"Okay, let's say that I agreed to do this, what am I agreeing to?"

"You'd be my partner," Toni says. "We always work in pairs, even during the less busy hours, and that's for safety. We're down a person right now, so Orville has been backing me up as Dolly Would, but he's got a ton of other stuff to do. Don't you?"

"That's right. With Rodeo Days coming, I don't really have the time to work the espresso stand."

"We work six-hour shifts. Most of the time, Monday through Thursday, I work four a.m. to ten a.m., the busiest shift. On Fridays I work four p.m. to ten p.m. Our schedules are posted online, so—"

"No." I spit this out abruptly and they turn to look at me, surprised. "I'm sorry, it's just that I can't be too…public. Like, my name or photo on a website, I can't do that."

Orville looks suspicious. "And why is that, exactly, hon?"

Shoot, I didn't rehearse this part. I reach back to what I told Georgia. "Did you hear about how I met Buddy?" Head shakes. "Okay. He's a police dog. Ex-police dog. I told you I've been, you know, drifting. There was a point where some cops were hassling me and they—they wanted to hurt me—in a particular way. You know?"

"Oh my God," Orville says quietly. Antonia says nothing but her nostrils flare and her sweat starts smelling of rage.

"Buddy disobeyed them to protect me. But he hurt them physically and I was worried he would get in trouble for that, and that's why I took him with me."

"Hurt them physically?" Orville looks both intrigued and appalled. "How badly did he hurt them?"

Deep breath. "They might be dead. The two cops. I didn't stick around to make sure."

Orville sucks in his breath, shocked. "Well. Okay then. So what you're saying is that you, and possibly Buddy, are on a list of cop killers?"

"Maybe. I don't know."

"Oh, you know." He nods, sighs heavily. "You don't want to know, but you do know. You're smarter than you pretend. I'm not saying what you did was wrong, but…"

"It wasn't wrong," Antonia declares passionately. "It was not wrong."

"They were trying to kill me," I say, as if in my defense.

"I'm sure they were." Heavy sigh and Orville thinks deeply for a while. "All right, I think I get it. They probably saw your passport in the name of Abnegation Asher?"

I nod. "They did. At the beginning of the encounter, I thought I'd just show them my passport and then they'd let me be on my way. I wasn't actually used to being hassled by cops, you know? I wasn't prepared for it."

He nods, knowingly. "And how long ago did this happen?"

"Um, I'm not sure, a little more than a month?"

He closes his eyes, looks pained. "A month? Dear lord." He sighs. "Well, I don't want to tell a person of your extremely young age that you're fucked forever, but…shit. Okay. You need to become someone else. Not Abnegation Asher. That's way too memorable anyway." He thinks and thinks, then brightens. "This could be good. Working at the stand, you're heavily made up, wearing a wig. You just need a different name."

"And a mask," Antonia says. "Maybe she needs to be a bandit too."

He nods, thoughtful. "You're right. Do we have two bandit costumes?"

"That part is easy." She waves her hand dismissively. "So what's your bandit name?"

"Um. Black something? Black Bart, Black Betty…"

"What about Belle Starr? She was a famous cattle rustler," Orville suggests and we all collectively think about it for a moment, then nod.

"Sure. Belle Starr. That's my bandit name."

"Okay, it's Friday, you can work with me tonight as your training shift." Big smile. "Before then, we'll change your look."

"Change it…how?"

"Hair, clothes, makeup."

"But I don't wear makeup."

"So any kind of makeup will be a change, right?"

Orville stands up. "Well, Toni's the best at this, you two don't need my help at this point. Feel free to get any clothes you like from the used section of Outlaw Outfitters. That's my western wear emporium." He hugs us briefly, then leaves.

Toni turns to me, clearly excited. "My friend Cassidy can do your hair and makeup, she's really good. Oh, we need to make sure Buddy has a sitter when we're gone, don't we?"

As she starts making detailed plans, I start to feel a little—

Maybe—

Railroaded?

I started out not at all sure that I wanted to work at the bikini espresso stand and now somehow I'm doing exactly that.

9

ITALIAN GRANDFATHER SWEARING

"How does the outfit feel, Abney? Sorry, Belle?" Toni tucks in a strand of my hair, which has been bleached to a pale straw color and coiled up on top of my head, festooned with feathers and beads.

We ended up making me more of a dance hall girl than a bandit, and I'm wearing a partially deconstructed corset with a short, flouncy skirt. Corsets I'm okay with. They remind me of the breast bindings we used to wear in the cult, and no matter how sexy they're supposed to be, they don't make me feel naked and exposed in the same way as a bare midriff. My first shift is, as promised, the Friday night shift. We left Sin babysitting Buddy, and we're out here at the Naughty Buckaroo.

"Pretty good." I take a deep breath, just to make sure I can. "Yeah, all good."

"Great." She glances up at the video display. "Looks like that car's gonna turn in here, let's do some real-time training with customers. You ready?" I nod.

We hear the first ding, and Toni points to one of the video displays. "First ding shows on that camera. If you recognize the car as a regular, you can start prepping for the interaction.

But either way, when you hear the ding, tits up and smile on."
She demonstrates. I attempt to imitate her. She laughs.
"You're not a smiler, are you?"

"Maybe not?"

"No problem, just try to...frown in a sexy way? Okay,
they're here, just follow me."

A big white truck pulls up, the kind with an extended cab,
and it's stuffed full of young men. Very young, seeming like
high school students, giddy and laughing. Toni's eyes narrow
slightly and I can see that she thinks she has their number, but
I don't know if they can see it.

At them, she smiles big. "Well, howdy, and how can I help
you boys?"

The driver starts laughing. "Yeah, uh, we'd like to order
some, uh, some—"

A boy in the back seat pipes up. "We want some T and
A!" and the others explode in laughter.

"What you see on the menu is what you can order, fellas,"
Toni says, gesturing at the menu.

They laugh some more and then the boy in the passenger
seat says, "Four Milky Way Mamas"

"Coming right up, pardners." She glances at me. "Since
we're doing four at once, you can help. Notice how there's two
of everything? Just try to do what I do.

"You're going to make two shots at once, right? Use this
basket with the two channels. For a double, you'd drip them
into the same cup, but these boys look like single-shot dudes to
me." She cocks out her hip and turns to wink at them, and
they explode into laughter again.

"Unless the hopper is full, run the grinder for a couple of
seconds. Put the basket here, flip the lever twice, tamp it down,
screw it into the machine. Yes boys, I did just say screw, I'm
training our girl Belle Starr here. Press the button, it forces the
water through and the espresso drip-drip-drips out, yes boys
you see that right. Now steam the milk. You want to use whole

milk for flavor unless they request two percent or nonfat. We also make lattes with soy and almond milk but they don't foam up properly, they basically just get warm. The actual cow milk gets warm and frothy." She winks. "Real warm and frothy.

"So you dip the wand in a few times—yeah, boys, dip the wand, that's it. You want to get the milk heated up, but not boiling. Boiling is bad. You know what boiling liquid does?"

"It, uh, it boils?"

"That's right. It boils out onto your hand. So, to get the proper foam—yes boys, nice creamy foam, mmm, so good— you want the steaming wand, yes, I just said wand again, you want the tip of it—oh, yeah, just the tip—just under the surface of the milk, and you want to get the liquid swirling around in a little whirlpool. And now, Belle, here's the part you've got to pay attention to, because when the milk is right, the sound changes. Listen—listen—listen—there it goes. Did you hear that? Okay, now you try it with this other pitcher."

She watches me closely while I imitate her actions, then smiles broadly. "Excellent, I think you got it. Now, by the time the milk is steamed, the espresso will have finished dripping into the pitcher, so you get a paper cup—you want the *big* ones, don't you boys? Of course you do. That's this size right here. Now, all of our drinks go together in a certain order. If it has a flavor, like chocolate for a mocha, or the Milky Way, you squirt that in—yes, boys, you squirt it all in there—first, so you can see how much you're using. Usually you fill it to about there, unless they request double flavor—boys, do you want double flavor? I know you do. You want it all don't you? With double flavor you fill it to about there. Then the espresso. Stir, to make sure everything is dissolved. Then, you pour in the milk. Not too fast. And if you steamed it right, and you pour it right, at the end, see how the foam is mixing with the color of the coffee? You can make a little picture, usually I do a heart. See?"

She watches me pour and gives me a pat on the shoulder.

"Well, you didn't quite get the heart, but it looks like you did steam the milk right, good job. Now, depending on the drink and the customer request, there might be a topper, or a bunch of toppers. We'll give these boys the works, what do you say?" She winks at them and they explode into laughter again. "You put the whipped cream on in a little pyramid like this—only so high, so the lid will go on it—oh, you'll like this one, the Milky Way gets a special dark chocolate with glitter syrup, and you swirl it on like this—and then we have this little shaker of silver sprinkles, like stars. Isn't that pretty? You try it. Perfect! Now, you sort of—display a very special drink like this to the customer before putting the lid on, because the lid messes it up a little bit. Like this. See that boys? Don't you want it boys? Of course you do. Now the lid—and one of these straws, the one labeled for hot drinks, through the hole in the top. And there we have it, our first perfect Milky Way Mama." She holds it out, leaning forward to give a little extra cleavage, and the boy driving reaches out as if to grab it, the drink or her chest, but then, with an abrupt change of demeanor, she steps back to bring both the drink and her chest well out of reach.

"Now, boys, four big Milky Way Mamas, with tax, is thirty-six dollars and forty cents. Will that be cash, credit, or e-payment?"

The car explodes with laughter again. The driver says, "Uh, yeah, well, the thing is, we don't have any money."

Toni's smile turns steely. "Oh, I think you do, boys. You see, dine-and-dash—what you're trying to do here, ordering food or drink with no intention to pay for it—is considered petty theft, a crime in Washington State, punishable with a fine of up to $5,000 and up to 364 days in jail. And, of course, your automobile and its license plate are clearly displayed on our security camera." She points. "So, if you don't pay for these delicious espresso concoctions, the cops will get the owner of that license plate reported and a warrant will go out for their arrest. And I have a feeling we'll find out which one of your parents owns this fine vehicle? And all of you boys will get the distinct pleasure of trying to explain to your parents why you took their nice truck to the Naughty Buckaroo when, I imagine, you told them you were taking it—where? The library? The rodeo? Football practice?"

As she's speaking, I smell the panic put a yellow spike into their sweat. "Shit, man!" one of them says.

"What about that cash your grandma gave you?"

"Aw, man, that's my birthday money."

"Just give it, asshole!"

The driver throws two twenties into the window. "Keep the change!" he yells, and drives off.

"Don't you boys want your drinks?" Toni calls out as they drive away. Then she bursts out laughing. "Damn, I had no idea that was going to work."

"What just happened there?"

"Well, it's a small town and teenagers get bored. So, sometimes they get it into their heads that it would be a real hoot to go someplace—a diner or a fast food joint—and order a bunch of stuff then run off without paying for it. Sometimes they think it would be hilarious to do this at the bikini espresso stand. You can usually tell because they're young, dressed well or driving a nice car, something that tells you they're not just poor and hungry, and they can't stop laughing. They're not cool at all. And they like to order the most expensive thing on the menu, especially if it's got a goofy name. Anyway, usually I peg the type pretty well and get cash up front before even making the drink—at which point they either drive off or pay up—but this time I figured it would be a good training exercise."

"So is that true about it being illegal? With jail time and everything?"

"It is, but I've never heard of anyone actually going to jail for it. Usually we can't get the cops to care because the amounts are so small. You heard that, even four of the most expensive drink on the menu was less than forty bucks. And, yes, it is also true that we take pictures of all the license plates for security reasons. Not that it's ever come up. But if it did, we've got 'em."

She holds out one of the Milky Way Mamas. "Have a sip. You should know what all our drinks taste like."

"Whoa, that's sweet."

"It is, isn't it?" She takes a sip herself. "I don't usually drink this kind of thing either, but they are the basis of our business. The way Orville explains it, we create a discreet environment for heterosexual men to safely order a giant whipped cream sugar and caffeine bomb without a threat to their masculinity, and that's even more important than getting to see a half-naked girl working an espresso machine. Like, if they ordered this kind of thing at Starbucks, all the other bros in the office might see them, right? But here at the Naughty Buckaroo, you can order whatever you want in privacy and we'll never tell. And you can always tell the other bros you were here for the half-naked girls."

Ding. Another car drives up. A lone man in a business suit.

"Why hello there pardner, it's your lucky day. You get a free Milky Way Mama along with your order." She winks, and hands him one of the untouched drinks.

Soon, we settle into a rhythm, how we respond to the customers, how we hand off tasks, how we take money, make espresso, flirt with the customers. She's obviously better at every aspect of this—the flirting, the espresso, the up-sales, even the math. She always tells them what the final price will be before I've finished entering everything into the computer program, and she's never wrong. There's a point, just after we've had a mild slam of six cars right after each other, that I turn and tell her, "You're really smart."

"What?" She gives me a perplexed look.

"You're really smart. You do all that math in your head, and you know so much about how the machine works, and the chemistry of the milk, and how to get those dumb boys to pay their bill, and—all of it. You're just really smart."

She flushes with a kind of pleased embarrassment, looks down. "Wow, I can honestly say that's the first time in my life anybody's ever told me that."

She continues to look down, blushing, distracted, touches the wrong part of the espresso machine, burns her hand and bursts out swearing. "Manaja!" she shouts.

"Toni! Are you okay? What did you just say?"

"Yeah. Sorry, that was Italian grandfather swearing."

"What does it mean?"

She laughs. "You can't explain swears, chica bella. But manaja is like 'dammit'."

"Manaja?" I repeat and she laughs.

"No, it's more like, manaja."

"How do you spell it?"

"You know, I don't actually know, I learned it by hearing it."

We use her phone to look it up online and it turns out the word is spelled mannaggia, and by the end of our shift I'm almost pronouncing it right.

It's around three a.m. and things are getting slow. Toni is showing me how to do end-of-shift routines like inventory checks and cleaning. Then we get a customer. A man who gets the wolf's hackles up so instantly that I actually have to suppress a growl. I blink, fighting back the urge to give him a predator stare. Toni glances from me to him with a slightly perplexed look, then takes over the interaction.

"Hey there Darren, would you like the usual Peppermint Love Mocha?"

He nods, very slowly, not blinking. Toni gives me the gesture that has come to mean, "you make the espresso, I'll deal with the money." But when I reach for the filter basket, the man barks out a hard "No." He stretches out a hand to point at Toni, and holds it there, trembling slightly. It doesn't get anywhere near her, and yet, it still feels like he's crossed the line, like he's touched her when he's not supposed to. "I want to watch her make it." His voice is flat, demanding. I suppress another growl, even while Toni shrugs and starts making the drink.

"That's six fifty-two, please," I tell him, trying for the chipper tone we're supposed to have, failing utterly. He doesn't seem to notice that. He give me a twenty. "Give her the change," he says. Again, he points at Toni, with that weird, trembling, possessive hand. "Don't add it to the general tip pool. I'll know."

"Of course. Sir." I run it through the cash till and make a show of rolling up the bills and tucking them into the black gun belt that circles Toni's hips.

She hands him the mocha. The man's fingers brush Toni's, briefly, in a way that might simply be a natural side effect of a hot beverage changing hands, almost identical to something that has happened dozens of times in the last six hours. But it doesn't feel the same. It feels slippery, slimy, dangerous.

But nothing happens. The man drives off and I wait, holding my breath, until I hear the second ding that means he's driven out of our space again. Then I turn to Toni. "Does that guy creep you out?"

She looks thoughtful for a moment, then shrugs. "I guess a little. He's a regular, though. And he's never actually done anything, or he'd be banned already. I think he's just awkward. Shy."

"I don't think that's it. Did you ever have a dog who just didn't like somebody who seemed okay at first, and then it turned out that person wasn't okay at all?"

She looks confused. "He's never met Buddy, has he?"

"No. But I like to think I've learned something from Buddy." I pause. I don't even know how to characterize my worry. "It's just, when Darren is the customer, I think we should keep the bear spray handy."

10

NEW MOON

After just a few days, I'm starting to feel settled into life at the Glitter Ranch, it's starting to feel like home. Maybe I can really stay here for a while. Not just until Buddy is healed, but until the end of my exile?

No, that's ridiculous. I shouldn't daydream about things like that. What if those men from Homeland Security come after me again? What if Leon comes himself? He might hurt other people to get to me. He might hurt Antonia. What if I have to leave to protect her?

Toni tries hard to make me feel like a part of things. She notices that I am, in her words, "shy." Which I am, I guess, but there's so much more to it than that. She takes me to karaoke night at the Pink Pony and she invites me along to her dance studio. "You've got to do something to stay fit, now that you're not hiking all day every day, right?" Together we do pole dancing, modern dance, yoga, hip-hop, middle eastern, even ballet.

"You're a really good dancer," Toni tells me, after we've been at it for a couple of weeks. "And you pick up choreography just like that. Are you willing to perform in public?"

"I don't know. I've never done it before."

"It's just, for Night of a Thousand Dollys I'm putting together a performance of '9 to 5' for the people who work at the espresso stand and the Pink Pony. We're going to hassle Orville a bit since he's our boss. So I thought you might want to be a part of that."

"I might. What is Night of a Thousand Dollys?"

"Orville does it as part of Marysburgh Rodeo Days. There's Dolly Parton drag, some karaoke, some dance, even a little comedy. Super fun."

"Sure, I'll be part of that."

Then, all of a sudden, it's the new moon.

I tell everybody I'm cranky on account of premenstrual syndrome, which isn't strictly accurate, since my period usually comes a couple of days past the full moon. I make sure I'm not scheduled for a shift at the espresso stand, make sure Sin is okay watching Buddy, and decide to explore the town.

Wandering around, not paying much attention to where my feet are taking me, I find myself in a neighborhood full of newer houses, the kind my aunt Vivienne used to sneeringly call McMansions. Big and obviously expensive, but ugly and cheap-looking at the same time.

"For people with money but no taste," Viv would sniff, with boundless disdain. She was a sharp, prickly, sarcastic, demanding person, and I always thought she kind of hated me, and I really miss her. I hope she's all right.

When I challenged Leon for the hunt leader position, I accused him of killing her to clear the way for his power grab. But I'm not so sure about that part now. I don't think he had to kill her. I think he just had to talk her into it. Viv said it herself, Leon could always talk her into doing things against her better judgment.

I take a deep breath, realize that I was following a scent trail, if not consciously: one of the prankster boys, my first customers at the stand. Now I'm standing outside one of those McMansions: large, ugly, disjointed, pathetic little yard, giant white truck parked in the driveway in front of an enormous three-car garage. I know that truck. I've seen it on the espresso stand security camera. The bumper stickers jump out at me:

CRUSADER FOR TRUTH

ARE YOU ON THE RIGHT PATH?

MY KID IS AN HONOR STUDENT AT MARYSBURGH
HIGH SCHOOL

I don't really know why I'm here, and don't think about it too much, just walk up to the house and ring the doorbell. A maid answers, in a uniform and everything. She's dark-haired, dark-skinned, and has a strong accent when she asks, "Can I help you?"

"Yeah, I, uh—I don't know. I think I have the wrong house maybe?"

"Are you looking for Robbie?"

"Robbie?" Something about the way she says the name makes me think he's the young man, maybe she guessed my business based on age. "Yeah, I am, is he here?"

"He's at the pool, please come this way."

She gestures. I follow. At the pool? Fancy. But the interior of the house doesn't seem well designed. Everything is subtly wrong. Ceilings high, but then suddenly low in one place for no obvious reason. Columns that serve no purpose and don't match each other. Windows all different sizes and shapes. Beige interior, dull artwork. One of the nonsensical columns is damaged, and I can see the styrofoam core under the stucco crust. Definitely a McMansion.

"Wow," I mutter under my breath, staring at the damaged area.

The maid notices and gives me a very small, knowing

smirk, then goes back to her neutral work face. "Robbie had a little accident there," she says.

We enter a stark, unpleasant courtyard, all beige gravel and paving stones, completely lacking the lived-in charm of New Orleans courtyards. Robbie, definitely the driver of the truck, is floating in the middle of the pool on a lounge chair, drinking a can of soda doctored heavily with vodka. He startles when we approach and makes a gesture as if he's going to hide the drink. Then he does a double take.

"You," he barks out. "The dance hall girl."

"Me." I say it with a bit of a growl.

The maid seems to notice the tension in our exchange and frowns. "Mr. Robbie? I thought she was a friend of yours?"

"It's okay, Consuela, you can leave us alone."

She nods, and goes back into the house.

"What are you doing here, lesbo bitch? Decide you wanted some dick after all?"

"Ew, why are you so gross? Actually, I don't know why I'm here. I'm just having a bad day and wandering around town, recognized the car, decided to talk to you."

I sit down on the side of the pool, remove shoes, stick my feet in the water.

"Do you want money or something? I don't have any. I mean, my dad has money, but that doesn't mean I get to use it for anything. Did you see that hole in the column in there? That happened when we had a fight about whether I would get access to my father's money for anything other than rancher college."

"I did see that hole in the column, yes. I also noticed the column appears to be made of styrofoam."

"Yep, that's my parents. They have a lot of money, and they spend a lot of money on stupid shit. Like, that big white truck out there? My mom's truck. She's at her book club right now, did she take the truck? No, she took her car. Because she has a truck *and* a car." He guzzles the drink, looks up into the hazy pinkish sky. He's allowing the float chair to drift and my paddling feet are getting it to drift toward me.

Huh. I just realized: I don't really know how to swim. I've been in the water before, lakes and rivers and even the ocean, but that was just splashing around, not real swimming. I have this sense that I would figure it out somehow—dogpaddle, haha—but don't actually know what would happen if I fought somebody in the water, especially if my opponent did know how to swim. I try to picture it. Would I drown? Is it possible that even with the wolf and her gifts, I'm just as vulnerable to drowning as any regular person who doesn't know how to swim?

Today, on the new moon, that's something I might have to worry about.

The sun seems intolerably hot on the top of my head, burning down like molten syrup, dripping. The only part of me that feels good is my feet, the part in the cool water. "I'm getting in the pool," I tell Robbie. Strip down to my underwear, enter the water in a graceless hop that splashes him.

"You're going swimming now? Okay." He shrugs, takes another long swig of the drink.

"I don't think I know how to swim. That's what I'm testing out. Just a moment." I try imitating what I've seen real swimmers do, paddling their legs, swooping their arms, turning their heads to breathe. I feel like I'm flailing, and I'm sure it looks ridiculous. But I do manage to move through the water, and I don't instantly drown, so that's good. I spot another pool float, grab hold of it, use it to float my upper body while I kick my feet to steer closer to Robbie, who gives me a baffled look.

"So are you flirting with me or what?" he asks.

"Why do you think I'm flirting with you?"

"I don't know, you took off your clothes and got closer to me, that kind of looks like flirting."

"Does it? I'll keep that in mind. Actually I was trying to figure out how easy it would be for somebody to drown me."

"Drown you? Shit, why would somebody want to drown you?"

"I don't know. People are always trying to kill me for some reason. I guess I'm just annoying like that."

"Yeah, but killing somebody is serious shit. I don't think I ever met somebody who was so annoying that I literally wanted to kill them."

"No? Maybe we should spend some more time together, see how you feel then."

He frowns for a moment, then laughs. "You're actually kind of funny. Are you really so annoying though?"

"Well, you said it yourself. I'm funny, people don't always like that in a girl."

He laughs again. "You're not Jewish, are you?"

"What? Why would you ask me that?" I feel weird about the question. My grandmother, who I never met, but admire greatly based on what I know about her, was Jewish. But I have a bad feeling that if people ask, "are you Jewish?" it's not a harmless and well-meaning question. And I don't know how to answer. I wasn't raised Jewish. I was raised in a type of cultish, fundamentalist Christianity that I emphatically don't believe in anymore. But if I say I'm not Jewish, is that me denying my own heritage? And if I say I am Jewish, is that me claiming an identity falsely?

Robbie answers, "I dated a Jewish girl for a while. She was also short, hot, and funny, so I thought maybe…you know, my family freaked out a lot more than I thought they would."

"About her being Jewish?"

"Yeah. My mom's kind of resigned to the fact that I don't go to church with her anymore, but it still seemed to freak her out that I was dating a Jewish girl. She kept asking if Rachel had converted to Christianity and I had to keep reminding her, 'Mom, I'm not a Christian anymore, so what's the deal?' It wasn't even that serious, we only dated for a couple of months before she went off to college."

"It's just interesting that you'd ask me that, because my grandmother was Jewish but I never met her. And my mom was a weirdo Christian. So I'd rather embrace my grandma."

He laughs, holds out the drink in a kind of cheers gesture. "Hell yeah! Here's to the cool grandmas!" He drinks. "I used to have one of those, until she died." He drinks. "It was just a few months ago, you know? It hurts more than I was expecting. You think when somebody's really old that it won't bother you when they die, because it was, like, their time and all that? But it does."

"I know. I lost my grandfather a couple of months ago."

"Yeah? Did you like him?"

"He's one of the best people I ever knew."

"Well, yeah, okay. You get it. Cheers to the cool grandparents." He raises the drink again. "You know, it's kind of weird since the way I know you is that I tried to dine and dash your bikini espresso stand, but I'm glad you're here, I was so bored before you showed up."

"So bored you snuck your mom's vodka?"

"You noticed that, huh?" He chuckles. "She never does. I can water a bottle down about a third before she starts wondering what's wrong with it, and by then I've got a replacement lined up. I've refilled her Grey Goose with the cheapest no-name brand so many times. It's vodka, right? Unless you're drinking it straight, which she never does, nobody can tell the difference."

"She doesn't notice it on your breath?"

"Not vodka. How did you notice, anyway?"

"Well, I can smell it, probably because I haven't had any."

"Huh. You want some?"

"Not right now."

"How did you know it was my mom's?"

"Educated guess based on stereotypes."

He laughs. "Stereotypes. Yeah, that's my family all right. We're just a bunch of stereotypes." He gives me the clearest, most honest look I've seen from him. "Including me, that's what you're thinking, right? The douchey rich kid who makes an ass of himself at the bikini espresso bar?"

"You said it." I continue paddling around the pool. I'm not sure if I like swimming in a pool. The chlorine from the water goes right up my nose and makes it hard to smell anything less obvious than the vodka.

He takes a sip from his drink. It's very strong, based on how much I smell it even through the chlorine. Stronger than what somebody floating in a pool should probably be drinking.

He says, "I'm supposed to be getting ready for college in the fall but I didn't turn in any of the paperwork and my parents got so mad when they found out. They just about kicked me out of the house. I told my dad I got scared of college because it was too liberal.

"I don't really care about that shit but my dad does. So he said he understood. Then he told me maybe college was like that back in the old days but it's different now. Anyway it was too late for fall quarter but I'm supposed to be trying for spring. They got me a college coach. Almost like a tutor. He fills out all the boring paperwork and stuff, helps me write the essays. But I still don't want to go."

"Why don't you want to go to college?"

He's silent, drinking, for a long time. Then he says, "They picked out a college for me. The local one. I'm supposed to major in ranching."

"You can get a degree in ranching? Wow."

He shakes his head. "I don't know, that's not exactly what they call it, it's some kind of business major with an animal husbandry focus? But basically it's ranching. Inherit the family business." He makes a grunting noise. "I don't know why they don't focus on my little sister if that's what they have in mind. She's a real horse girl, she loves all that ranching shit. But they're so...I don't know, old-fashioned I guess. They think their oldest son is the one who's going to carry on the family tradition. But I'm a filmmaker. I want to go to film school in Los Angeles. I got accepted too! My parents just don't want me to go there, and it's their money, so…"

He takes a large swig from the can, nearly finishing it. "It doesn't matter anyway. I don't always know why I do stuff." By the tone of his voice, I think he's crossed some threshold of drunkenness, and we're about to move into blubbery true confession time. "That stuff where I'm mean to people. Even my parents. They're okay really, but sometimes they make me so mad. Everything makes me mad. Because it all seems so pointless, you know? Like what's the point of anything?" He takes off his sunglasses to look me in the eyes with his blood-shot ones. "What's the point of this stupid life?"

"Are you asking me?"

"I don't know. You got an answer?" He tilts back the can and drains it with a few gurgling sips.

"Life doesn't have a point. It's just a bunch of stuff that happens, then you die."

"Life's a bitch and then you die." He laughs. "Just like the bumper sticker, right?" He tosses the can toward the edge of the pool, misses, nearly falls out of his float chair, which makes him laugh harder. "Life's a BITCH and then you DIE!"

"Right, bumper stickers. Dude, I'm thinking, maybe you should get out of the pool and lie down on a bed or something? What do you say?"

"You want to go to bed? Okay."

"Not that kind of go to bed—never mind. Come on." I start paddling, dragging his float chair to the edge of the pool.

"I never had sex before," he says. "You can't tell anybody, okay? This'll be my first time. You can't tell anybody."

I ignore him, continue dragging the float chair to the edge of the pool.

"I lie to my parents about it sometimes…tell them I need money to go on dates…I make up all kinds of dumb shit." His voice is fading as if he's ready to pass out. "I just want them off my back...leave me alone...I...just...want...leave me alone..."

And with that he rolls himself off the chair into the pool and just floats there.

Not trying to swim. Not trying to breathe.

I move around to the other side, push him toward the edge of the pool, scramble out, drag him up onto the ground, turn him over to his side, check for breathing.

He starts coughing vigorously. Up comes pool water, vodka-laced grape soda, and, yep, there we go, bit of vomit.

Reassured, I thump his back. "That's it, get it out, get it out."

He coughs some more and says, "I don't know why I did that."

"You're depressed and you're drunk, that's why you did it."

He seems slightly more alert already. "I'm not depressed. My mom is depressed. She does all kinds of shit. Goes to a counselor, takes these pills. She's not supposed to drink when she takes the pills but she does anyway." He gives a low burbling chuckle, coughs up some more liquid.

"If your mom is depressed it might run in your family. Maybe you should talk to her about getting help."

"Hmph. Help." He makes a scoffing noise. "Nobody ever helps anybody."

"I just helped you not drown."

"Huh, you did. Why did you do that? I thought you hated me. But you were going to sleep with me too. Or was that a dream?"

"That was a drunk fantasy, dude. I'm not sleeping with you. But I did pull you out of the water."

"Yeah. I guess you did that."

"Which is weird because I think I came here to beat you up."

"No shit." He laughs. "You came here to beat me up. You?"

"Well. I wanted you to start it so that I could feel like I was the one in the right. But coming over here in order to beat you up kind of proves that wrong, doesn't it? Like, if I come over here to taunt you hoping that you would throw the first punch so that I would get to throw the second punch, that doesn't really make me in the right, does it?"

"No, dude, seriously, I'm still kind of stuck on the first part of that. You came over here to beat me up? You? Beat me?"

"You don't think I can?"

"Well, I don't see how. You're like half my size."

"Just a second. I want to show you something." I kneel down, get under him with my arms, stand up with him still in my arms. I've done this with Edison before, and Edison is taller and heavier than Robbie. It's a little awkward because of the way he dangles, but, yeah, even on the new moon I can deadlift a guy considerably more than my own weight. I stand for a moment to let him take that in, then toss him into the pool.

He makes a huge splash, fights his way to the surface, swims to the edge. "No way, you did not just do that, did you?"

"I can do it again."

"No, that's fine. Once was kind of fun, though." He smiles. A friendly and genuine looking smile. "That was wild, how did you do that?"

"I'm a power lifter. And I study martial arts too. I really could beat you up, I'm not bullshitting. It's all about leverage, right? Leverage and training."

He laughs. "Okay, I believe you." A long pause. Then he says, "Why don't you throw me into the pool again? I want to see if you really can do it a second time."

We end up doing that over and over. I throw him into the pool. Then he throws me into the pool. "Dude, you are way heavier than you look. Muscles, I guess." Then I throw him into the pool. Then he throws me. Then his mom comes home. We hear the car and all of a sudden she's in the court-yard, looking very concerned.

"Honey? What is going on back here? There's water everywhere."

"Uh, hi, Mom, this is Belle, she just came over to go swim-ming, and, you know, we were swimming."

His mother frowns at me. "Are you—what kind of a swim-suit is that?"

Which is when I remember that I'm wearing my under-wear, which isn't technically any more revealing than a two-piece swimsuit, but is kind of obviously made out of under-wear material and not swimsuit material, so I get embarrassed and say "oops," grab a towel, wrap it around myself. Robbie and I look at each other and burst out laughing.

His mother gives me a stern look. "You can go on home now, young lady. Grab your things. You can keep the towel."

"Sure, fine, okay. Thanks for the swim, Robbie!"

"Any time."

I walk, barefoot, drying in the late afternoon sun, back home to the Glitter Ranch.

11

NIGHT OF A THOUSAND DOLLYS

"I'm glad you're over your bad mood from a couple of days ago." Toni strokes glitter onto my eyelids.

"Yeah. Yeah, I told you it's severe PMS? That makes it kinda predictable."

"Oh, I'm sorry. Did you find the ibuprofin, the hot water bottles, that sort of thing?"

"I got what I needed, thanks."

"You must have a real regular period."

"I guess I do."

"I don't," she says. "Mine is on this wild elliptical orbit or something, anywhere from twenty-eight days to thirty-six days. It's a good thing I only sleep with women, otherwise I'd have to be taking a pregnancy test all the fricking time."

"I'm sorry."

"It's okay, I'm used to it." She smiles. "There, what do you think?" She turns me around to see myself in the mirror. I look very sparkly and unlike me, even unlike Belle Starr.

"It's good. Thanks."

"You really don't like wearing makeup, do you? By the end of our shift, you've always rubbed most of it off. Good thing your skin is perfect to start with."

I blush, look down. "I guess when I'm not paying attention it starts to feel like there's dirt or something on my face and my instinct is to rub it off."

She laughs. "Well, this only has to last a couple of hours. Let's go."

We leave the bathroom and pass Georgia, who is babysitting Buddy tonight. "Hey Georgie, you're really okay just missing out on the show? I bet we could take Buddy to the Pink Pony, he's really well-behaved."

She sighs. "You know I love you girl, but I just can't support any part of Rodeo Days."

We take our bags and walk the few blocks to the Pink Pony. Antonia starts circulating, greeting people, introducing me, giving a bunch of names I won't remember later. It reminds me of the one time Edison and I went on a "proper" date, to a kebab place, which turned out to be the official "Husky football team made it to the Rose Bowl" celebration. They never got to play that game. It was canceled after a full moon outbreak of bitten-wolf chaos caused a public health scare in the Los Angeles area. But during the celebration, he knew everyone. And even though he went out of his way to include me, I still ended up feeling overwhelmed and out of the loop.

Antonia and I go backstage to freshen up our costumes and do a quick dress rehearsal where we step through the "9 to 5" routine. I feel more sure of myself there, because I have a purpose: remember the steps of the choreography and do them at the right time.

"We're going second, right after Orville does 'Mule Skinner Blues' as the opener," Toni announces.

We hear Orville's number from backstage: he's not a singer and he lip syncs the song as sung by Dolly herself. None of the people who introduced me to modern outsider music were big country fans, so I don't know much of Dolly's catalog, but this song is catchy and features yodeling. I'm somewhat reassured that "mule skinning" seems to mean herding the mules instead of literally skinning them.

Applause, and Orville-as-Dolly says, "And now, my friends, I'd like to do a song I'm sure all y'all know quite well, don't be afraid to sing along."

The opening chords start up, as if he's going to do "9 to 5" without us. But this is how we rehearsed it, and those of us in the number shuffle rapidly onto the stage, led by Toni. It's intended to be humorous. The joke is that we, his employees, are hassling Orville for being a bad boss. Toni confronts him directly, lip synching lyrics like "they use your mind and never give you credit" and "you're just a step on the boss man's ladder" with vehemence, while the rest of us back her up with our choreography. Orville, for his part, keeps feigning exaggerated innocence, "who, ME????"

The audience laughs, so I think we must be doing it right. I haven't performed in front of an audience before, and the laughter and applause go to my head a little. Ah! I made these people laugh!

Then it's over and we're taking our bows, then rushing backstage to make way for the next number.

Toni hugs me. "That was fantastic, Belle. I can't believe it was your first time on stage. Now, I have another number to do, will you be okay on your own?"

"Of course."

"When I do this particular number, I like to direct it at somebody in the audience, is it okay if I pick on you?"

"Sure, you can do whatever you want to me." I stop. "Uh, you know what I mean."

"I know. Thank you."

I venture out to the audience and one of our fellow performers, a guy named Kilian, has already snagged a table near the front. He notices me and gestures toward an empty seat.

We watch through the next few performances, then Toni

comes out again, dressed like a very unglamorous 1950s housewife. Oversized housecoat, hair in curlers, face covered in some kind of white cream, mop in hand. Her housecoat doesn't entirely obscure the fishnet stockings and high-heeled dance shoes, so it's pretty easy to guess where this is going.

Still, she's a good actress. She looks timid and sad when the music starts up. "Jolene," one of the few Dolly Parton songs I already know, but it seems like a remix, music and cadence of the vocals different from what I expect. When the song goes: "I'm begging of you please don't take my—man" there's a little pause right before the word "man" that I'm almost sure isn't in the original version.

Antonia takes a step toward me, pretending to sing about my "flaming locks of auburn hair" and "eyes of emerald green." She runs her fingers through my hair and everyone laughs, even though my hair is dyed blond at the moment. But it does have magenta tips. My natural hair is, more or less, a flaming auburn. She walks away from me as if she's very sad, starts wiping the cream off her face, but keeps glancing back over her shoulder at Kilian, with a contemptuous look, as if he's the man in the song who's obsessed with Jolene

The music changes abruptly, stuttering into a different tempo and beginning to sound like modern electronic dance music, with repeated phrases and a heavy-hitting beat. She dances to the new tempo of the song, wiping off the face cream, applying lipstick while mouthing, "Please don't take my" and not completing the phrase, as if she's forgotten about the man. She struts into the audience, right toward me, removes the scarf from her head, drapes it around my neck.

One by one, in time with the beat, the curlers come out of her hair and get tossed into the audience, each one greeted with a cheer.

Curlers removed, her hair is long, dark, curly, gorgeous. She turns away from me again, mouths over her shoulder,

"The only man for me." and a long pause before she delivers: "Jolene," as if now "Jolene" is the only man for her.

The music stutters again and changes tempo, to something you can do a kick line to. She opens the housecoat, dances, teasing the moment when she finally throws it off and reveals the fringed and spangled leotard underneath. Couple of high kicks as the crowd cheers, and the vocal, even more distorted, begins again. She struts toward me and seats herself in my lap. Lip-synchs, "Begging of you, begging of you, begging, begging, begging, begging, please don't take my—"

She caresses my head.

"Jolene."

The music stops and she gives me a big juicy kiss that leaves my mouth smeared with red lipstick. The audience goes wild with applause. She goes up to take a bow, says, "And that, my friends, is for anyone who has ever listened to that song and thought the singer and Jolene should be the ones who ended up together." She blows me a kiss. "Thanks to my co-worker Belle Starr for being a good sport, and also for having beautiful green eyes."

I look down, blushing, shy all of a sudden, uncomfortable, feeling like too many people are staring at me. I decide to go up to the bar for a drink, watch a couple more performances from the bar.

Something is bothering me. Nothing I can consciously characterize as a smell, but, I know from experience, uneasy feelings sometimes come from there. Etienne would call these vague scent-based intuitions "hunting after ghosts" and I think of him with a gut-punch of melancholy and panic, a visceral memory of what happened the night he died, the horrifying smells of the chemical weapons the New Orleans mayor deployed to use against the bitten wolves, to reduce their numbers in a project called the cull. It mostly failed, because of interference from me and Babette, but it still killed Etienne. He had been injured for several years before that, the kind of severe head injury they call Arda's Wound, which prevents transformation. If you go without becoming the wolf for long enough, the gifts of the wolf start to fade. He never lost his wolfy sense of smell, but his healing abilities were not much better than a normal human.

Before he died, I told him that sometimes a bite from a transforming wolf calls the wolf back and starts the transformation again, and I offered to bite him as I had once done for my father. And he said, oh, Bon Dieu, he said no. Because he thought we needed him as he was, a person with a wolf's sense of smell who stayed human on the full moon. And because he wasn't a trauma morph, he saw that as his only path.

All of this tumbles through my mind, a cascade of terror and sorrow, a loss I never had a chance to process. Etienne was killed, then Steph's father, then I went out to Bayou Galene and found Pere Claude and Vivienne missing, assumed the worst, accused Leon of a deadly coup, lost my fight, agreed to this exile, got attacked in Atlanta. Everything happens all at once, collides in my head, making me feel trapped, sharp chemical smell all around me and I'm drowning, drowning—

Suddenly I need to get outside, so badly that I exit through the first door I see, a fire exit that promises "alarm will sound." But it doesn't. It never does.

I tumble out into an alley full of restaurant dumpsters and odd broken furniture, smell food trash, rats, and the sharp chemical bite of explosives, so powerful and overwhelming that for a moment I think it's a hallucination, a memory of the night of the cull.

Then I spot two young men crouched and furtive. Clear my throat and say loudly, "What are you doing?"

They startle, staring up at me in shock. One of them stands. "We're just—"

I interrupt. "Hold on." Grab them, casually, by their collars, drag them out toward the main street. They could probably get out of this light hold if they really wanted to, but shock, or maybe guilt, gets them to comply.

Out on the main street there's a small anti-drag protest and a growing counter-protest. I make note: Robbie is part of the counter-protest. He has a homemade sign that reads TRY MINDING YOUR OWN BUSINESS and gives a little wave when he notices me. I nod in his direction.

One of the anti-drag signs jumps out at me:

GOD SEES AN ABOMINATION

At first glance I think it says ABNEGATION and have a weird disorienting panic, is anything real at all?

Determined, I tighten my grip on the collars of the two young men. They gasp and struggle.

"Hey, you. Christians." The protesters all turn toward me.

"I caught these guys trying to light the building on fire."

I shove them forward and they stumble, fall to the ground.

"Oh no, no," says the ABOMINATION woman, "No, they wouldn't do that, we wouldn't do that, we're peaceful, very—"

One of the boys, rises to his feet and a small mason jar full of liquid falls out of his pocket and shatters.

"That wasn't gasoline," the woman says.

"Really. Then it's okay if I light a match." I reach toward my pocket as if for a match and they all flinch, the young men scurrying away.

Behind me, Toni comes out of the club. "Abney, what's going on, you just ran out like you were sick...do I smell gasoline?"

I gesture at the young men who fled my imaginary match. "These two members of the protest were trying to light the building on fire."

Toni looks indignant. "Cody? What the hell is wrong with you, I sell you a mocha nearly every week."

The ABOMINATION woman turns toward him. "Cody, is that true? Do you go to that slutty gay espresso store?"

He turns flame-red and mumbles. Obviously the answer is yes.

She turns her wrath on Toni. "You let children, children go to that filthy, filthy—"

"He's eighteen, Mrs. Wright, and it's a bikini espresso stand. He can see a woman in a bikini just about anywhere, don't you think?"

"Children," she says, voice trembling in rage. "You take the children, you take them away. That filthy show." She points at the Pink Pony.

Orville comes out the front door. "What on earth is going on out here?" He takes the whole scene in. Steps back, drawing himself up with a stern look, haughty but wounded. "Ms. Wright? Ms. Roberts? Why are you all out here trying to shut down Night of a Thousand Dollys?"

"Orville James Thompson, I knew your parents, what you do is a disgrace."

He shakes his head. "Ms. Roberts, we've been doing the Dolly show for years, why are you getting upset about it now?"

"It's different."

"Different how?"

Her lips tighten and she frowns more deeply, the way people get when you ask them a question they don't know how to answer.

Another woman speaks up. "It was on the Dick Manly show. He was talking about how the gays are recruiting children into their pervert cult these days."

"You listen to a guy who calls himself Dick Manly and you think gay people are the perverts?" I say this, incredulous, disgusted.

Orville gives me a smirk, but grabs my hand in a way that clearly signals that he wants me to be quiet. And I get it. He knows these people, I don't. I nod and step back. He addresses them in his powerful announcer voice. "My friends. Why are you here trying to disrupt the show honoring the great Dolly Parton? This show that we've done every Rodeo Days for the past fifteen years? You know me. You know us." He makes a gesture that includes me and Toni and a couple of other people who have come out of the Pink Pony to stand with us.

"What you do isn't honoring Dolly, it's a, it's a parody," says one of the men holding a DRAG IS UNGODLY sign.

I notice that most of the protesters have signs that were pre-printed, as opposed to the counter-protesters whose signs are homemade. This seems to indicate something about the nature of where the protest comes from. And I know organizations just like the ones Father Wisdom used to belong to, they would get the word out to little communities like this, their churches would get the message that they should go to a particular place at a particular time to protest a particular thing. Churches are structurally a great way to convert people to your cause, whatever it is: because there's a church in every town, no matter how small, and a lot of them get their materials from centralized national suppliers. Pre-packaged protest. I feel a rush of shame, thinking about how often as a child I was one of those protesters, holding a sign that was too big for me, for a cause I knew nothing about.

"Now, Mr. Martin," Orville says, to one of the men. "I know you like our espresso, why are you doing this?"

Mr. Martin looks embarrassed. "It's…it seemed like…"

"Friends and neighbors," Orville says. "It seems to me like maybe you've gotten caught up in something—you've been listening to people who aren't even a part of our community, people like your Mr. Manly, who runs a national talk radio show, and you've been letting them fill your head with a lot of East Coast nonsense."

"East Coast?" One of the protesters seems really unsure of herself all of a sudden. "What do you mean?"

"I mean what I said, Ms. Everett. Don't these men broadcast from the East Coast?"

"Florida," Mr. Martin says, scowling. "Dick Manly is out of Florida."

"Well," Orville says, drawing himself up into his Dolly persona. "The last I heard, Florida was definitely on the East Coast."

"He broadcasts out of a place he calls Frog Bucket." This information is volunteered by someone out of the crowd who I can't see, and it's hard to tell if it's meant to be pro-or-anti Dick Manly, but it inspires a smattering of cautious laughter.

The crowd's energy has been diffused. The tide has turned, they're starting to feel silly, the counter-protest has begun to outnumber the protest. The window in which things might have escalated into violence has passed.

Sirens. I hear them in the distance, grab Toni, whisper, "Toni, I hear the cops, I'm going to take off."

"What? Why? I'm sure the show will go on after they get everything sorted out."

"I don't want to be around the cops. Remember?"

"Oh. Right. Sorry." She kisses my cheek. "Do whatever you have to do."

I take off. But in spite of being a little panicked about the cops, I feel pretty good about my role in the conflict. I just helped protect my people without any violence, and without any obvious wolf stuff.

12

RANCHERS AND WOLVES

"It's good to see you happy."

Toni says this to me during our morning shift at the Naughty Buckaroo, a few days after Night of a Thousand Dollys. It catches me up short, feels almost like an accusation. Happy? Who says I'm happy? What was I doing that would cause anyone to say I'm happy?

Dancing around with the espresso basket, singing a dumb song I made up about espresso, with a tune cobbled together from the various blues, soul, and rock songs that rattle around randomly in my head. Does a person doing that look happy? I guess maybe so.

"Thank you," I say. "I mean, thank you for caring. For taking care of me. If I'm happier than I was before, it's because of you."

"When we started working together—" She stops. "Never mind." But she's already revealed more of herself than she might want. I can smell her flicker of sexual interest. I noticed her take a tiny step toward me, almost as if she wanted to embrace me, then step away. She goes back to working, but remains tense, keyed up. She turns back to me. "It's just, I could see you had a lot of trouble. I could tell you were sad.

You know, the kind of sad where it feels like you could live the entire rest of your life and never be happy again?"

I swallow over a lump in my throat. Gosh, was it that obvious? "I guess so."

"And I know that kind of trouble doesn't go away in a few weeks. But, for you to be happy even for one moment, that just seemed so precious to me. I can't—I don't—I'm sorry. Never mind, I made it weird. I called it out and I wrecked it."

We hear the ding and serve a customer. She seems to consider a lot and then says, "I need to tell you something and I don't know how else to tell you other than just spit it out—"

"You have a crush on me?"

Her face goes pale. "You knew? Was I—I mean, was I inappropriate? I really tried not to be—okay maybe that Jolene number was a bit much—"

"No, you were fine, a perfect gentleman." I stop, think about what I just said, laugh. "I'm sorry, that came out wrong, I wasn't trying to misgender you. But if I said you were a perfect lady, that wouldn't mean quite the same thing."

She laughs, giddy now that the biggest hurdle is over with. "Is there such a thing as a lady gentleman? Maybe I want to be that."

"Same. I want to be a lady gentleman." I inhale. "Do you want to kiss me?"

"You know I do. Is it okay if I want that?"

"It's okay."

"Is it okay if I do that?"

"Yeah. Yeah, I think that would be okay. If you kissed me."

We move together, her taking the lead, and she's only the second person I've kissed romantically, so I'm not sure what to expect. Her lips seem so small and delicate compared to Edison, and her cheeks are so lacking in beard stubble. She's not much larger than I am, and I feel wary of crushing her. But there's a point where I start to get into it, and actually lift her off the floor, and she gasps like that's the most amazing thing and then

DING

Customer

We break apart, hot and nervous and fluttering, and the guy in the car can't possibly have seen anything, and yet, he seems really extra excited just to be here getting espresso, and tips us a twenty.

"Oh my God, that was amazing," Toni gushes, as soon as he's gone. "You're amazing. Is it okay? Are you—would you do that again?"

I would.

For a couple of weeks our relationship is pure magic: kissing and holding hands and cuddling on the couch. We take Buddy for short little walks, we go out dancing, we go to the movies, we go out to dinner. Actual date-date stuff, which Edison and I barely ever got a chance to do.

Orville notices the change in our dynamic, tells us, "I don't know if I have to tell you girls this, but, at the espresso stand, no matter how much money the customers offer you, do not make out in front of them, okay? They could be cops and that could be considered sex work and that could get us all sent to jail." Then he smiles. "Other than that, you crazy kids have all the fun."

But then, on the day of the full moon, Toni is very put off that I want to do something alone and can't tell her what it is.

"I just don't know why you can't tell me. Do you have to kill a man or something?"

"Toni. If you knew what it was, you'd know why I can't tell you. Don't you trust me?"

"Of course I trust you. I just—I mean—I don't care what it is, I just want to know. Are you killing a man? Meeting with your secret family? Part of a coven? I noticed it is the full moon tonight."

"You noticed that? Good for you."

"But why won't you tell me?"

"If I told you why I can't tell you, that would basically be the same thing as telling you." I shoulder my backpack, planning to spend the night in the eastern foothills of the Cascade mountains.

"But you're going camping," she says. "You hate camping."

"I was camping for several weeks in between leaving my old home and showing up here with Buddy."

"Right. And you hated it. That's what you said. You made it sound like you never wanted to go camping again."

I sigh. "It's complicated." This was a terrible idea. I can't date somebody who doesn't know about the wolf. I have to tell her. But how do I tell her?

And, shit, what if it's dangerous for her? The Varger generally believe that wolves and outsiders can't date, but is that about secrecy or the potential for physical harm? My father Leon dated a lot of non-wolves and as far as I know the worst thing he ever did was impregnate them with future werewolves like me, but now that I'm thinking about it, do I know that for sure? Do I know he never hurt any of those women physically? And why am I suddenly thinking about all this now? I never worried about hurting Edison, did I? Am I being sexist?

No, that's not true, what am I thinking? I used to worry a lot about hurting Edison, until after I bit him and he came back with partial wolfiness. But I did stop worrying about him at some point.

Maybe it's nothing. Just me being nervous.

Antonia intercepts me, takes my hands. Gives me a serious, eye contact look. Bon Dieu, she's beautiful. Like a young Isabella Rossellini. "I'm sorry. I have to be serious about this. I don't believe in secrets, when you're dating. Secrets are bad. Secrets mean you're dating someone else on alternate nights, or that you have an STD you never mentioned, or that you're gambling away every paycheck and deeply in debt and some very bad people are going to come and try to collect." She blows out her breath, nervous, slight laugh. "That one might be a little personal. My mom. She was a, she was a gambling addict. A single mom, not that most married women could afford a gambling addiction, not unless she's married to Jeffrey Epperton or somebody like that." Nervous, quick laugh. "But it was bad. You think being addicted to alcohol or meth or something is bad, but a person can be addicted to gambling, and it's just as bad. Sometimes worse."

"I'm not a gambling addict. Anyway you already know my biggest dark secret, I told you and Orville right off. About how Buddy and I met?"

"Oh. Oh, that." She looks horrified. "The dead cops. But now it makes even less sense. If you already told me about that, why can't you tell me about this?"

"Fine. You really want to know? I'm a werewolf."

She rolls her eyes and makes a scoffing noise. "Okay, don't tell me."

I consider proving it, showing her the wolf, but just as I'm considering this, Sin enters, senses the tension in the air, asks, "Hey are you two okay?"

"Abney has to kill a man tonight and she doesn't want me to come along," Toni says, sighing.

"Well of course you don't want to be a part of that, it would make you an accessory." They pat Toni's shoulder. "You just let her do whatever she has to do and when the police come by, you saw nothing, you heard nothing."

"Thanks, Sin," I say.

"Thanks for what? I heard nothing." They pick up a bag and leave again, making a little lips-zipped motion.

I hug Toni, awkwardly, wearing the backpack. She hugs me back, reluctantly, stiff.

"Buddy's going to miss you," she says.

"I know. I'm sorry."

Hiking up into the mountains for the next few hours give me plenty of time to think about my dating relationships and really wish I had an older female werewolf to talk to about this, Vivienne or Babette or somebody like that. But I can imagine what they would say. Vivienne would say, "You can't date a human, don't be ridiculous." And Babette would say, "Go for it, cher, she's almost as hot as me."

Imagining Babette's voice saying this makes me want to laugh, which immediately makes me want to cry. It's the full moon, I shouldn't feel like this, this crushing despair, but it just seems to crash over me again and again, like a tidal wave. I'm not home, this isn't my home, these dry hills, these cattle ranches, these people who don't know about werewolves.

I like the people here. I like Antonia a lot, obviously, I wouldn't kiss somebody I didn't like. I like Orville and Sinnamin and Kilian and Robbie and so many others. But the place isn't right. It's not where I belong.

Exile.

I haven't really felt the weight of it before. Numb, maybe, after everything that happened. Going through the motions. But it hurts. Like a dagger stuck into my heart, sharp and hard, keeps me from taking a full breath. Shame and self-loathing overwhelm me, the memory of fighting and losing, being expelled, cast out, and now I don't belong anywhere.

I weep for a while, but keep hiking and eventually stop crying.

The amazing healing power of walking.

That's what got me started in Atlanta.

Right now I'm following a trail map I got from an outdoor goods store near the college campus. Deep into the woods, far from the main trails, I set up camp in a little clearing.

I don't build a fire. The woods are dry and the last thing anybody needs around here is more wildfires. Anyway, it's warm enough that I shouldn't need a fire while the sun is up, and the wolf doesn't get cold.

I eat some pre-cooked steak and vegetable skewers I bought at the grocery store. I'm a little worried about the wolf going after somebody's ranch cows before I can stop her, and want to make sure she's not too hungry. I hope I'm far enough into the mountains that the wolf will find a deer or something first, before she heads all the way to somebody's cattle ranch.

But when the moon comes, the wind is blowing in exactly the wrong direction for that. The wolf gets enticed by the smell of what seems, to her, like an entire herd of cows just hanging out, waiting to get eaten. She makes a wolf-speed run in that direction, while inside I'm screaming at her.

Idiot! Fences means humans claim these animals! Get away from there!

She doesn't want to listen to me. It's an all-you-can-eat buffet! How could it—

Human smells. Human noises, hey you! Explosion, sulphur smell, pain searing into her side. She howls and runs back into the hills, annoyed that I was right.

Of course I'm right. This is human stuff, the part I know about. You've gotten awfully cocky just because I let you drive the whole body for a few weeks.

She tosses her head in annoyance and runs down a wild deer. Fine. We'll do this instead.

We eat, sleep.

I wake up curled in my own clothes.

Find a bullet on the ground, obviously expelled from my body sometime in the night, pocket it. Lonely, waking up without a pack around. My first couple of moons were like that, lonely. Spending time with the Varger, my father's people, got me used to having a pack. I got so used to it that I challenged my father for the hunt leader position.

What was I thinking? Me, as hunt leader? Did I really want to lead the people, or did I just want to stop Leon from doing it? And why did I think it was so important to stop him?

He warned me that trauma morph training might cause

what he called a permanent black moon, meaning, it lasted every day until the training was over. He found the black moon to be so bad that it kept him from ever truly mastering his trauma morph.

Wait.

That was still true, decades later. He never did learn to call his wolf purely at will. So how did he call his wolf before I did, during our fight?

I remember, maybe, was there a smell in the room like berserker drugs? Can a trauma morph use berserker drugs to call the wolf? And if so, how did he administer those drugs so quickly? He must have been prepared for a challenge, expecting it.

And another thing. Leon must have had help for the attack in Atlanta, somebody with Homeland Security connections, and who could that have been? I helped Leon confront the Veneray, the anti-werewolf secret society that murdered his mother forty years ago, but the very next day the New Orleans mayor's office carried out the cull, a scheme to lure werewolves to City Park and murder them with phosphorus weapons. The two events seemed unrelated, but what if they weren't?

What if Leon was getting in way over his head, when he confronted the Veneray the way he did? Vivienne seemed to think he was. She thought the Veneray parent organization, the Azphokites, were extremely bad men to get on the wrong side of. What if Leon sold me out because he was threatened? And, if true, does that make things better or worse?

Sigh. I don't know how to answer any of these questions, and even if I did have the answers, I'm not sure what to do about any of it.

Instead I go through the usual post-moon motions, get dressed, pack up, while nearby some crows chatter about me.

"Goodbye crows," I tell them, as I finish packing and walk away. After I've gone far enough, the crow noises change, and

I glance over my shoulder to see them going nuts ripping meat from the carcass of the deer I killed.

Back at the house, I try to be quiet as I enter from the secret back way, collapse onto the futon.

Much later I wake up to find Sinnamin watching the local news.

A woman with a microphone is outside talking to a cattle rancher who was menaced by a wolf last night. He must be the one who shot me.

I head toward the television, feeling surreal. "Morning," Sin tells me. "How did the murder go?"

"Fine. Is Toni still mad at me?"

"I doubt it. She's not really the grudge-holding type."

Security camera footage, spooky and green-tinged, shows wolf me menacing the cows, getting shot, and running away. It's very dramatic. You can't see that the wolf's fur is bright red, but you can see that she is very large and ferocious looking.

Toni comes downstairs, carrying a mug of coffee. "Abney."

"Toni."

A moment of awkwardness, then she smiles, holds out the cup. "Coffee?"

"Uh, I don't want to take your coffee."

She places the mug in my hands. "It's your coffee, mine is still upstairs. Sin?"

Sinnamin considers for a moment and then shakes their head. "No, I think I'll skip the coffee this morning, but thank you so much."

Toni heads up to get another cup of coffee, then comes down again, this time carrying the entire carafe in her other hand. We sit down on the couch, next to each other, coffee in hand. She smiles and squeezes my shoulder. "It's okay," she says.

"Yeah? Thank you."

On the television, a talking head is chattering about how the local ranchers object to wolves in the Cascades because of this, because they menace the cattle. But then a different talking head, a young woman with long blond braids, says, "Look, this particular individual wolf was obviously turned away by the security procedures and no cattle were lost. The system is working."

The argument turns more and more contentious.

"Why is everybody so into this wolf, it's ridiculous," I say.

Wow, somebody sounds defensive. In a werewolf movie, that would definitely signal who the werewolf is.

"It's a small town, people are bored," Toni says.

Right. A small ranching town. No wonder I feel ill at ease here. Ranchers and wolves are a bad combination.

13

RODEO DAYS

"Well, it looks like this good boy has made a complete recovery," Georgia declares, kissing Buddy on the forehead. "Take him for walks, but be ready to carry him if he starts to seem like he's tired or in pain."

"You hear that, Buddy?" Antonia says. She kisses him on the forehead. "You're going to Rodeo Days." Georgia frowns, but doesn't say anything. She still doesn't approve of Rodeo Days.

I kiss Buddy on the forehead myself, because that seems to be the thing we're doing right now and he obviously likes it, but I'm troubled. Why am I troubled? I already know that if I have to leave again, Buddy's staying here with Antonia. I guess that's what's bothering me. I feel like I'm going to have to leave here soon, but I'm not entirely sure why.

A big group of us goes to Rodeo Days together, Glitter Ranch residents and employees of the the Naughty Buckaroo and the Pink Pony, so Buddy has a babysitter when needed. Antonia and I go on a few rides together. The Spider. The Devil's Wheel. The Hurricane. The Music Express. The Zipper. It's my first time doing carnival rides. Fun, but awfully expensive for something that lasts, at most, a couple of minutes.

We share something called a "funnel cake" which is basically a giant donut.

"Thanks for splitting, I know I can't eat a whole one. Do you like it?"

"It's fine."

"You don't like it, do you?" She laughs. "I guess that's good, considering you work at a bikini espresso stand. I wouldn't like it all the time, but it's a Rodeo Days tradition. You want to watch actual rodeo stuff?"

"I don't know. I don't know anything about rodeo stuff."

"The calf roping semi-finals are happening right now at the main stadium. We can get Kilian to watch Buddy, they don't let pets in there."

"Okay, sure."

We find stadium seats close to the floor right away, in between rounds of competition. A couple of people nod in our direction as if they recognize Toni, but nobody says anything.

A couple of rodeo clowns are performing. A man dressed as a cowboy runs after a man dressed as a cow, throwing a lariat around the "cow's" neck, then struggling to tie his arms and legs together. In this comic performance, the cow performer always comes out ahead, to much laughter, wriggling out the lariat and roping the cowboy instead, or allowing himself to be roped only to run around the stadium dragging the hapless cowboy behind him.

The clowns exit, to much laughter and applause. The announcer lets us know the semi-finals are about to happen and gives names and stats, but the audio is distorted and I don't know what any of the stats mean anyway.

A loud mechanical noise and a calf comes tearing out into the stadium, running at top speed and obviously terrified. The fear comes off her in waves. Wolf-me gets a little excited by this, because it smells like dinner, but Abby-me is disturbed.

The cowboy emerges, on horseback, chasing after the calf. He throws his lariat around her neck, yanking it sharply to get her on the ground, on her back, eyes wild and rolling, making distressed bleating noises. But the crowd cheers. He gets off the horse with a jaunty hop and goes to tie up the limbs of the calf.

Even the wolf is starting to feel like this is wrong. You don't go out of your way to terrify the prey like that, you're just supposed to kill them and eat them.

When the calf's limbs are securely tied, the cowboy raises his arms triumphantly, the announcer gives some more stats, and the audience applauds.

Then it happens again.

And again.

And again.

"I need to go," I say. Try to sound casual, but my voice comes out shrill and tight.

Toni nods. "It is a bit much, isn't it? Anyway, we've got the late shift at the stand tonight. We can go. Kilian can get Buddy home, I'll let him know."

"Thanks."

We head out, not really saying anything until we're in her car driving home.

Toni asks me, "Are you okay? You seem really thrown by the calf-roping."

"It was just a lot more viscerally upsetting than I expected."

"I get it. I grew up here so I kinda take it for granted. But if you're not used to it, it looks pretty brutal. That's why Georgia won't go."

"It was torture. That calf was terrified."

She nods. "I guess so. You okay to work?"

"I'm okay."

One of our first customers of the night turns out to be Robbie, who has become a regular. "Hey, Abney, I just wanted to let you guys know, my parents changed their minds, I'm going to film school after all."

"What? That's fantastic, Robbie. Have a Super-duper on us!"

"What's a Super-duper?" Toni frowns at me.

"I don't know, I'm just going to make it up."

He continues: "We had a long talk after the Dollys protest, and it's funny but I think the protesters there helped put my dad on my side? Because he was all, like, 'those puritan biddies were really out of control. Dollys is an important Rodeo Days tradition.' And it wasn't too long after that he told me film school was a go."

The Super-duper ends up being something I would drink myself: a dark chocolate quad mocha with no whip and a glitter star pattern shaken onto the foam. Robbie takes a sip. "Whew, that's potent. You guys really do make the best espresso in town, I swear to God, it's not just the bikinis and lingerie."

"I know," Toni says, with a wink.

"Well, I'm not starting school until winter quarter, so if you guys ever want to just hang or anything…" He holds up his phone and Toni nods, holds up her own phone, they exchange numbers. He drives off.

"I'm glad you and him made friends," Toni says. "I don't know how you did it."

"I saved his life and then threw him into the pool."

"I'm sorry, what?"

"I went over there to yell at him, but he was depressed and drunk and at one point he kinda rolled out of the chair and was floating face down in the pool. I don't know for sure that I saved his life, but I did pull him out of the water and make sure he was breathing."

"Wow." She gives me a little half-laugh. "You definitely saved his life. But then you threw him into the pool?"

"Well, he didn't believe I could do it."

Interrupted by a ding, we make a bunch of festive drinks for a car full of people leaving the Rodeo. For a while we're busy with a steady stream of people leaving the Rodeo. There's no trouble, except for one time when I'm pretty sure the driver's had a little too much to drink, and we use free food to persuade him to sit in the picnic area while he eats it and sobers up. It starts to get late and the customers slow to a trickle, stop for a while.

Then. Darren.

I've seen him a few times since that first night when he creeped me out so much, but just as promised, he's never crossed the line. Tonight he seems off, though. Like something's on his mind. We go through the usual routine, me doing prep work and taking money while Toni makes his espresso drink, but this time he slips me something in addition to the money.

"Give her the note," he says.

"I can't do that," I tell him.

Anger, pure seething rage, blazes in his eyes for just a second, then subsides. "It's just a note," he says. "Just give her the note."

"I told you I can't do that, Darren."

"Darren, please." Toni comes over to the window and takes on the patient, slightly exasperated tone of somebody explaining something to a toddler. "I've told you before, we can't look like we're doing illegal sex work here. Private notes and things, that could get us shut down by the cops. You don't want to get us shut down, do you? Do you?"

"No," he answers, sullenly.

"Right. You don't want us to get shut down. So you have to follow the rules. And if you can't follow the rules, then we can't let you be a customer anymore."

He looks down, mouth and eyes tight, body trembling. His rage and lust exude in a miasma, foul, the sick purplish color of a bruise. He breaths in a shallow pant, as if in pain. Then he blurts out "My name is Darren Torrenson, send me a message."

He drives away without his mocha.

Toni is a little scared, it's her face, her sweat. She frowns. "Well. That was weird even for Darren."

"He's escalating. We should ban him."

She nods. "I guess so. I'll talk to Orville about it."

The next few hours pass normally. It's getting toward closing time, and she yawns. "You know what I've never done? I've never made you a proper lasagna feast."

"Are you even allowed to do that for people who work in bikinis all day? Orville talks like we're not allowed to eat any carbohydrates at all."

She rolls her eyes. "He doesn't know what he's talking about. I'm Italian, without enough pasta my body ceases to function entirely."

DING

A customer. Late, during the usual dead hour. I glance at the security camera.

"Toni, I think that's Darren's car, we should get out the bear spray—"

But he's already here at the window and I smell a sharp sulphur reek: gun. Movement. He's getting ready to fire.

I don't stop to think about what I'm doing, just get my body in the way of the bullet aimed at Toni, reach into the car, grab his arms, force them into position where the gun is pointing back into his own mouth, making his hand pull the trigger.

The back of his head explodes.

Blood, skull, brains, all splatters, most of the gore inside his car, but some of it sprays into the espresso booth, hits me and Toni. Darren's body falls limp. Hope I did it right, hope Toni isn't hurt, hope there's no trouble, hope hope hope.

The whole thing took about ten seconds.

14

FIVE BULLETS

Chaos paused, I take stock. Three bullets I can feel in my gut, maybe more. Blood everywhere. Fragments of skull caught in my hair along with the feathers and beads. I rip it all out, throwing it onto the floor.

Toni's face is blank, splattered in blood. Her hands go up to her face, as if making sure it's still there. She brings her hands down, stares at them for a moment. They're covered in blood and gray fragments of brain tissue.

"What." She breathes, shaky. "What. What was. What happened?"

"Toni, I'm sorry. I just needed to stop him as quickly as possible, the gun was in his hands, I didn't plan for what to do with it, I just went on instinct, okay? I made him shoot himself. I was trying to protect you, that's all I wanted. Just to protect you."

Her face is blank. "We need to call the cops?" She says it as a question.

"Okay. Okay, I'll do that. Your phone?" She hands it over. I punch in 9-1-1 and get a dispatcher. "Hello, this is the Naughty Buckaroo espresso stand, we just had an incident where a man tried to shoot us, there was a struggle for the gun, the man got shot and is badly hurt, maybe dead, I think we're both fine, please come."

"Your name?" asks the dispatcher.

I panic and hang up. How did I forget I can't talk to the cops? That was a dumb move. Maybe it'll be all right. I need to take off, leave town right this minute. But Toni's pretty traumatized, I can't do that to her. I need to stay with her.

A moment of discomfort in my gut reminds me that I have bullets trapped in there. I look down. The corset is torn and bloody in several locations. I need to cover up. I put on my robe.

"Toni, do you want your robe?" She accepts it, blankly.

We don't have long before the cops arrive. Blurp of a siren, knock on the door. I recognize the two young male officers as customers here, out of uniform. Shoot. Somehow that particular risk never even occurred to me. I've been very stupid, thinking a fake name and a costume would protect me.

"We have a report of an incident?" one of them asks.

"That was me. I called."

"You are?"

"Belle Starr. I work here with Antonia. There's this guy, Darren—he told us his last name—Torrenson, that was it, anyway, he's always been a little creepy, obviously has a crush on Toni, and earlier tonight he tried to give her a special note. She wouldn't take it, and we told him if he tried anything like that again he'd be banned as a customer. Then a couple of hours later he comes back, he's got a gun, he's aiming it at Toni. I tried to take the gun away, but it went off and hit him. See?" I point into the car, an absolute horror show.

One of the cops looks ill. "Jesus." He covers his mouth and I smell the bile.

The ambulance arrives. I watch as they extract Darren's body—clearly that of a dead man—from his car.

Leon tried to kill himself this way. Shot himself in the head. They thought he was dead, whoever found him. There was nobody more shocked than the people who went to put him in a body bag and realized he was still breathing. Or maybe he wasn't breathing. Do we ever do that? When healing a particularly bad injury, go into a kind of hibernation where we don't give any ordinary signs of life, but give us enough time undisturbed and a few hours later, we're breathing again? Apparently back from the dead?

Then it hits me like a hammer: my grandmother was probably still alive when the men from the taxidermy shop took her. She had been shot in the head and wasn't moving, probably appeared dead. But they knew what she was and they knew not to give her a chance to heal. They sliced her open, started removing internal organs before the morning came.

Bon Dieu, what a grisly murder.

I double over, kicked in the gut by the bullets moving into my digestive tract.

"What's wrong? Were you hurt, miss? Were either of you hurt?"

"Not by the bullets. I don't think. I'm just—"

"You might be going into shock," says one of the EMTs. "Let her sit down, get her a blanket or something. Both of them."

"Right, yeah, okay," says the more functional of the two cops. They seem so young, and this is a small town, it's possible they never have done this before. Soon Toni and I are both sitting on the outside bench, wrapped in our robes and blankets, giving statements to the police.

The cops want to take us down to the station. I don't know how to say no without making things worse, so I agree, but with every new cop encounter the likelihood goes up of running into somebody who knows somebody who knows somebody who wants to kill me.

Or, so I think. I don't even know for sure that a random police department in a random town will have any connection to the people trying to kill me. I have to fear the worst. But maybe that's all it is. Me fearing the worst. And the worst doesn't always happen. That's still possible, right? That the worst doesn't happen?

The station is downtown and there aren't a ton of people working right now. But when they take my statement I have to show them my ID and now they know my legal name and that's going into a database somewhere.

Toni gives her statement in a separate room from me. To make sure our stories match? I get nervous, is she going to tell the story differently in a way that makes me seem suspicious? But suspicious how? I don't know how anything I've done makes me look guilty, or like a werewolf, but I feel it. I'm caught. It's just a matter of time. How much time though?

Orville picks us up at the police station.

"Oh my goodness, my girls, my poor girls." He envelops us both in a big hug. "Oh my goodness. What a thing to happen. What a terrible, terrible thing. Do you think it's connected to the—the unpleasantness at Dollys?"

"I don't think so," I tell him. "Darren obviously had a really unhealthy fixation on Toni, but I don't think he was connected to that other group. Oh! Toni's car is still parked out there."

"Of course. Don't you worry. We'll go out and get it." He nods. "You just get some rest, okay?"

Back home, Toni collapses onto the bed.

"Is it okay if I sleep next to you?" I ask.

"You'd better," she says.

A couple of hours later, I'm awake, run to the bathroom and vomit bullets into the toilet. Five of them. I didn't realize I got shot so many times. His gun must have been an automatic of some kind, to get five bullets into me so quickly. When the police examine the espresso stand, they're going to wonder where those bullets went. Down the drain, is where. I take off the tattered remains of the costume, put the robe back on, go back to bed. Buddy follows me into the room this time, seeming concerned, and I go back to sleep with his warm, furry body in between us.

Dreaming. Running and running and running, under a full moon, never able to stop running. Hunt never ends, because the prey is never caught.

I wake up.

Lie curled around Buddy and Toni for a long time, letting my mind drift, trying to think about where I can go next, what I can do. I don't want to leave here, but I can smell trouble coming, and trouble for me means trouble for all these people I've come to care about in such a short time. Buddy will be okay with Toni. I know he will. She loves him. They all love him. Poor puppy.

Toni wakes up.

Startles, squirms out of my arms, sits up. "You," she says, in an oddly accusing tone. "You got shot, I saw you."

"Really? Are you sure?" Oh. Great. Good answer, Abby. That'll really put her mind at ease.

"I saw the bullets go in." She reaches out and lifts up the hem of my robe, runs her fingers across my abdomen. Which, um, actually feels really good and I wish she'd keep doing it. I hold my breath.

"Blood," she says. "The blood is still there but not the holes. Your skin's perfectly smooth." She continues rubbing, widening out into bigger circles, as if looking for where the bullets could have gone, but I'm very—um—turned on? I think that's what this feeling is. This trembling nervous excitement swirling around, centered in my lower body but shuddering out into my everything. "Perfect," she says. She takes her hand away and I feel bereft. "What are you, Abney?"

"Um. Werewolf? I think I told you that already."

"But I thought you were joking. I mean…you're not especially hairy."

I burst out laughing. "No, we're not especially hairy. Not when we're in human form, anyway."

"How did you get bit?"

"I didn't. I was born this way. But we don't start changing until young adulthood. Everything I told you about the cult, that was all true. I ran away. Then I turned out to be a were-wolf. Father Wisdom always talked about how I had a terrible beast inside of me, but I thought he was being metaphorical."

"Wait." Her jaw drops open. "The cops that were killed. You killed them. Didn't you? As a wolf."

"I did. That's why I was afraid Buddy would be punished for the deaths. And it wasn't a random attack, either. The cops I mean. They knew who I was and they had been sent to kill me in particular."

"Oh my God. Why? Who would want you dead?"

"I'm not sure. Maybe my father. We had a conflict for leadership of the pack and he sent me away, maybe he figured it wasn't far enough. But the cops were part of some Homeland Security sub-group, the Extraordinary Threats Task Force, so there might be something bigger going on. Toni, last night the cops put my name into a database or something. Whoever is trying to kill me is going to know exactly where I am. I need to leave town, basically, now, and I need to leave Buddy with you."

"Of course." She brushes my hair away from my fore-head. She looks sad. "Do you mean right now? As in, now-now?"

I nod. "Ideally, I'd leave in a car, so there's no scent trail."

"No scent trail?" She goggles at me. "You mean they have, like, bloodhounds they can send after you?"

"Yep." I kiss Buddy's forehead. "That's how Buddy found me. He had obviously been trained to scent track people like me. And they might even have werewolves they can call in."

"Werewolves." She looks blank. "Werewolves tracking werewolves."

"Yeah. It's a thing we do. Wolf nose, human brain. We're like the ultimate bloodhounds."

"Oh my God." She sits down on the bed, cuddling Buddy. "How is any of this real?"

"Would it help you to see the wolf for yourself? Or would that make it worse?"

"See the wolf?" She looks stunned. "You can show me the wolf?"

"I can show you the wolf."

Breathe out, little half laugh. "Well. Yeah, if that's a choice. Hell yeah. What's the fun of dating a werewolf if you don't get to see the wolf part?"

I nod. Kneel down. Take off the robe. Inhale, reach for the wolf. The air sizzles with a slippery feel and a smell like pepper and lightning. Buddy reacts, sneezing, shaking his head, then recognizes the wolf as his friend and gets excited briefly, going into play and greeting mode, nuzzling and licking, jumping up.

It's hard to say goodbye to a dog. They don't have much concept of future. But he picks up on her somber mood and goes from excited play to dropped tail and whining. The wolf nuzzles him, trying to give comfort.

"Belle? Abney?" Antonia says. She drops to her knees and reaches out to touch the wolf's head, cautiously. "Is that really you?"

The wolf dips her head, dips further, gives the body back to me as the air in the room goes hot and slippery again.

I rise. Naked. Put on the robe, go back to petting Buddy's head.

"But you looked just like a big dog," Antonia says. She takes my hands. "Just like a really big, really pretty dog. Like a dog I'd say hi to in the park."

"When a wolf isn't hunting or angry, that's what she's like. That's what she is, basically. Big dog."

"But wolves are…I mean…around here…the ranchers

talk like wolves are cattle-crazed supervillains." She stops and starts laughing. "Oh my God. This is real. This is real." She throws her arms around me and laughter turns to tears, wet on my neck. "You're really leaving."

"I'm sorry. I really am."

"I'll call Robbie, he can drive you out of town. It would look suspicious if I did it." She gives me a long, serious kiss. "I don't know if we'll ever see each other again. I hope we will. But no matter what happens, you'll always be the girlfriend who took a bullet for me."

"Five bullets. But who's counting?"

I'M READY TO GO. DRESSED FOR TRAVEL, WEARING MY backpack. Kissing Buddy and Antonia goodbye, both of them crying in their own way, Antonia silent and eyes glossy, Buddy whining very softly.

It makes me feel sad but in a weirdly good way, because there is something perversely comforting about realizing that you will miss people, that you will be missed. It means you mattered in the first place.

I gather them both into a group hug.

"I'm so sorry. I hope we'll meet again. Take care of each other."

Nodding. Weeping.

I step out into the evening, brutally hot and smoke-tinged, as so many of the days and nights have been. If the air is dangerously polluted with smoke for three days, you might stay inside the whole time, but when it goes on for three weeks, you start to act like everything is normal. You just cough a little more than you used to. And maybe somewhere down the road, twenty or thirty years from now, you die sooner of something that may or may not be obviously tied to inhaling all that smoke.

Depressing thought.

Outside on the sidewalk, I spot Robbie's big white truck. Well, his mom's truck.

Also I spot a police car. In between me and Robbie's truck.

Two cops get out. One of them is a bitten wolf.

Okay. This is really it. There's no way they would send a bitten wolf after me if they didn't know.

"Officers." I nod at them, try to stay neutral.

"Are you—" Checks notes. "Abnegation Asher?"

"I might be."

"We'd like to ask you a few questions. Would you come down to the station with us?"

He takes a step forward. I take a step backward. "Oh, I think you already know I'd prefer not to do that."

The werewolf cop speaks up, gruffly. "Abnegation. Come with us."

Eye contact. Flash. "No. Stop. Leave me alone. Get back in the car."

He goes blank for a moment. His non-wolfy partner looks from him to me in confusion and I fix the non-wolf with a green stare.

"Stop. You have the wrong person. Get back in the car."

They both get back in the police car.

It won't last long. I rush past them to Robbie's truck. He's watching me closely and opens the passenger door as I approach. I climb in, slam the door. "Drive!"

He grins. "Yeee hawwww!" he shouts, as he makes a U-turn in the middle of the street, tires screeching, as we roar out of town.

15

LEAVING

"What the hell was that thing you did back there?" Robbie asks, smiling, as he pulls his mom's truck onto a dark, empty highway.

I'm cautious. "That…thing?"

"You told those cops to leave you alone and they did. And your eyes did that thing! I thought maybe I was imagining it before, but they did it again, it's definitely real."

"My eyes did a thing?"

"They glow bright green for a second, just like when you shine a flashlight into the woods and something out there has eyes that flash it back at you?"

Wow. He noticed the eye flash. It's rare for anyone who isn't the direct target of a dominance stare to notice the flash.

He continues, "They were glowing like anything when you confronted those protestors outside Night of a Thousand Dollys, but I thought it might be the light hitting your contact lenses weird. But it happened again just now. So what is it? Are you a superhero or something?"

Different responses tumble through my mind. Deny, deny, deny. Wacky made-up explanation involving…cataracts? Maybe tell him I'm a trained hypnotist?

Then I decide: screw it. He's an ally, allies get to know the truth. "What do you think it would take for you to believe in the existence of werewolves?"

He bursts out laughing. "I knew it!" He slaps the steering wheel in excitement. "I knew you weren't a power lifter. You're a fucking werewolf, that's how come you're so freaky strong. I knew it."

"You knew it? Really? Because most people would find the power lifter story a little more plausible."

"Most people are boring."

Surprised, I choke out a laugh. "You might be right about that." Pause. "Okay, so where are we going?"

"Well, I figure we have about four hours before my mom freaks out about her truck being gone. Which means we can go anywhere that's two hours or less. Your choice."

"Seattle's about two hours away, isn't it? No, wait, I can't go there. They'd look for me there. Salt Lake City?"

"Sure." He punches some things into his phone, displayed up on the dashboard, gets a map. "Why Salt Lake City?"

"Because I have no reason to go there, so I hope nobody would look for me there."

Pause, while he changes direction according to the phone map. "Who's looking for you? I mean obviously those cops back there, but…"

"I think it might be my father. Werewolf stuff. We had a fight for pack leadership, I lost, got exiled for a year. He told me he would leave me alone as long as I left the country, but then some Homeland Security guys tried to kill me in the Atlanta airport."

"That's harsh. Why would he do all that though? I mean, why bother pretending he was going to let you go if he just wanted to kill you?"

"I don't know. I have guesses. But I don't really know anything. I don't even know for sure that my father is the one trying to kill me."

"So you're just gonna keep lying low?"

"I guess."

"You're gonna run forever?"

"What?" I startle, stare at him. "What do you mean?"

"Whoa, okay, don't flash your eyes at me, dude. I'm just looking at the logic of it. Somebody is trying to kill you, okay. You're lying low to avoid them, okay. Moving from place to place, changing your identity and your appearance, always one step ahead. Great series premise. But how does the series end?"

"Shit. I hadn't thought that far ahead. Beyond the year in exile, I mean. I was mostly planning how I'm going to survive until next summer, I wasn't picturing these guys maybe chasing after me for the rest of my whole life." Both of us sit with that for a moment, then I say, "The attack in Atlanta really messed me up, I think. I kinda went into reactive survival mode."

He nods. "Understandable. Nobody's ever tried to kill me, I don't even know how I'd react."

"Actually, people have tried to kill me a lot, and it's pretty upsetting, but what made it worse was that these guys tried to —I mean, they made it pretty clear they were going to—mess with me—before they killed me, you know?" I hear the nervous trembling in my voice, the about-to-cry tightness.

He glances at me with a sympathetic frown. "You mean they were going to try to rape you?"

"I…" My throat is trying to close shut, and my next words come out in a whisper. "Yeah. That's right."

"Well, shit. I'm sorry. I don't know what else to say."

"Thank you. That's really all you can say, I guess."

"You shut 'em down, though," he says. "Right?"

"I killed them, if that's what you mean."

"Whoa. Wow. I guess that is what I meant, but…you just killed them? Just like that?"

"I went to wolf form first."

"You can do that? Just go to wolf form whenever?"

"I can." I nod. "Not all werewolves can do it. But I can. And before you ask, yes, it does come in handy."

Silence for a good long while. Then he says, "I'm sorry if this is a rude question, but, can I see it?"

"You want to see me change into the wolf?"

"Is that okay?"

"Sure. Just find a good place to pull over, away from the highway. I'll show you but I don't want to show everyone."

We find a place. I start undressing and his eyes get wide. "I'm sorry, you—of course you have to take off your clothes first. I just didn't, um, I didn't picture that part of it." He covers his eyes with his hands. "Sorry, didn't mean to make this awkward. Go ahead."

A moment later, in wolf form, I nudge him with my nose and he actually yelps. "Holy shit." He looks down at me. "You're actually a whole-ass goddamn wolf." A pause. He seems unsure of himself, then holds out his hand for a sniff the way you might do when meeting a dog.

After sniffing his hand, I take a few steps backward and go into pretend attack mode, head down, growling, nose pulled into a wolfy sneer so he can see all my teeth.

He gasps and his sweat shows startled fear. More fear than expected. I move into a more friendly and doglike posture, sitting upright and attentive, slight canine smile, ears twitching.

He gapes at me, eyes wide, unable to say anything.

As myself I stand up again and he gasps, covers his eyes, but not before a little green shoot of lust. "Holy shit," he says. "You're totally naked."

"Dressed," I tell him a minute later.

He looks at me with an expression of shocked awe. "That was real," he says. "Goddamn, that was real."

"You said you wanted to see it."

"I did. Yeah. I did say that. But why did you, uh, why did

you seem for a moment like you were getting ready to attack me? Because that was actually kind of scary."

"It's part of the package. I thought you needed to see it. That wasn't even real attack mode, it was pretend attack mode. Like if I was play fighting with another wolf who was my friend."

"Well. Holy shit." He takes a deep breath. "That was pretend attack mode?"

"Yeah."

"What is, uh, what is real attack mode like?"

"I don't know for sure. Nobody who sees it gets a chance to talk about it later." I smile, to show that I'm joking. Sort of.

"Holy shit." He breathes heavily for a moment, then starts to calm down. "You were, is your wolf the same size as your human self?"

"That's right. Conservation of mass."

"Because as a human you seem pretty tiny, but as a wolf you looked enormous. Like, you could have eaten my whole head with your jaws."

"You're not wrong. Even a small human like me is pretty big for a wolf, and it just goes up from there. You should have seen my grandfather's wolf." My voice tightens in grief, as I remember. Am I ever going to see Pere Claude again? Is there a chance he's still alive somewhere? Wherever hunt leaders go when they retire?

"Holy shit." Shaky laughter. "I know, I keep saying that. But this is intense. I didn't picture it being so intense."

"Good intense or bad intense?"

"Good, I guess. I mean, you didn't eat my head. Even if you could have." He takes a deep breath. "Okay, I think I'm ready to drive again. Let's go."

PART IV

RETURN OF THE HITCHHIKING BANDIT

16

RETURN OF THE HITCHHIKING BANDIT

Seems like I've been here before.

Not here, exactly. Somewhere like here. Dry rolling hills, mostly empty. Nowhere.

Robbie dropped me off a few days ago in a random location in southeastern Washington. Since then, I've been meandering vaguely in the direction of Salt Lake City, taking whatever rides came along, but it hasn't been an easy journey.

The last time I tried hitchhiking a significant distance, I was already sixteen and did have my wolf, but I was a couple of inches shorter and the people who picked me up in their cars treated me like a little kid. They were kind, sympathetic. Even the jerks were usually trying to save me in some obnoxious way, like take me to a shelter or their church or something like that.

But now, it seems like half the cars that stop are single men who assume I'm a sex worker. I wouldn't think a young woman in ratty jeans and a denim jacket and battered cowboy boots looks like a sex worker, but then again, I'm not a lonely, horny dude.

Most of the men are nice about it when I say no. They act slightly embarrassed and drop me off somewhere well-lit. But

some of them get mean. Drive off in a huff, even threaten
violence. Usually a brief growl and a glare sends them on
their way again with no trouble, but I'm getting mighty sick of
this.

I've lost track of time. A couple of days but less than a
week. The sun is getting low, and after dark it gets even harder
to find a ride.

Finally, a car. Another single man. Of course. Big, toothy
grin at me through the window as he pulls over to the side of
the road.

The window purrs down, releases cold air-conditioned
smells of a man who's been traveling in this car by himself for
a while: farts, alcohol residue, old fast food, sour sweat.

"Can I give you a ride, my dear?" he says with exaggerated politeness, exhaling spent-alcohol breath right into my
face. "Where are you going?"

"Salt Lake City."

He nods thoughtfully. "Well, my dear, I can take you there.
Get in!"

The passenger door pops open and I climb in next to him.
He pulls the car back onto the empty highway. "I'm Ronald."

"Tina." On this trip I've cycled through "Tina," "Tori,"
"Shawna," and "Gail."

"Nice to meet you, Tina. And how old are you?"

"Twenty-one."

"You don't say?" A skeptical, knowing smile. "You seem
young for twenty-one. Tina."

"I'm just short. How old are you?"

He laughs. "Old enough! Old enough, my dear."

"My guess is that you're fifty-five."

He startles and glowers for a second. "I'm forty-seven,
girl." Then he composes himself again. "But of course, you
young people think that everyone over thirty is equally
ancient, don't you? Why are you going to Salt Lake City?"

"Just going back home."

"Really." He says this in a skeptical way. "You're from Salt Lake City?"

"No, I'm from Baton Rouge Louisiana, but in Salt Lake City I can get a bus."

"Of course. Of course." He licks his lips, nervous and excited. "Baton Rouge, yes."

Why does the name Baton Rouge excite him? This guy is really creepy. Good thing I'm a werewolf and don't have to worry about it too much, but how do regular girls deal with it?

"How far is Salt Lake City?" I ask out loud, wondering how long I'm going to be sharing a car with this weirdo.

"Oh. Not too far." He waves a dismissive hand. "Maybe an hour."

"You don't know? Don't you have a phone or something?"

"Yes, but I never get any coverage out here."

"You drive this route a lot?"

"From time to time." He smiles, as if he's keeping a very big, very exciting secret. Guy who cheats on his wife? Gambling addict, maybe? Nevada's right there. Mormon who likes to go out of state and do non-Mormon stuff?

"Mormons don't drink, do they?" I ask out loud.

He glowers. "Who says I'm a Mormon?"

"I don't know, you live in Utah, it was just a guess."

"Who says I live in Utah?"

"Assumption based on your license plate. Fine, you're not a Mormon from Utah."

"No, I'm from Salt Lake." He sighs. "But you're from Baton Rouge. How did you end up all the way out here?"

"I went to Seattle for a while. Now I'm going home."

"Do you have family or friends around here?"

"Not around here, no."

Excited panting, and his skin flushes with a burst of over-ripe lust. He licks his lips, as if struggling to keep all the saliva contained. In a breathless hiss he says, "Nobody around here will miss you?"

Oh. That's where he was going with all this.

Inside me, the wolf tenses up, preparing for battle. Outside, I smile. "No sir. Nobody around here is going to miss me at all. What about you? Are there people in Salt Lake City who will cry if you don't come home?"

He exhales, excitement growing. "My children are adults, out of the house," he says. "My wife is frigid. My paycheck is all she cares about. Does that answer your question?"

"I don't know. Paycheck, what do you do for a living?"

"I'm an insurance salesman. I make good money." Dripping smile. "If you want to go to a hotel or something, I can buy us a nice room. A real nice room."

"A hotel?" I look around at the dark emptiness, the stars in the sky. "You mean in Salt Lake City? Or out here?"

"I know a place."

"Out here you know a place?"

"It's like a resort hotel. You want to go?"

"No, I want to go to the bus station in downtown Salt Lake. I was just surprised there even was a hotel out here. So, you're not a Mormon, do you know any Mormons?"

He frowns. I just poured cold water on his lust, somehow. "Why do you want to know?"

"I don't know, I've never known any Mormons. I was just curious."

"About what?"

"Are Mormons Christians?"

"Of course." He pauses. "Well. We think so."

"You said 'we.' So you are a Mormon?"

"Around here you kind of have to be." He laughs. "It's just part of doing business."

"That whole thing about getting your own planet after you die, is that real?"

"Um." Very uncomfortable. "We don't really talk about that part of it very much. It's more about how to live a righteous life in the eyes of God."

"Is it true that Mormons believe men are saved through their faith but women are only saved through marriage and childbirth?"

He frowns fiercely at me. "Where did you hear that?"

"I don't remember now. But it's kind of what we believed in New Harmony, so I wondered."

"New Harmony?"

"Christian patriarchy cult. It was briefly infamous, but, because we didn't all kill ourselves, we weren't in the news very long."

He shrugs, not interested. "You're so young, Tina. Don't you want to learn about the real world?"

Give him a weary look. "Sure, Ronald. Why don't you teach me about the real world." To myself I sound sarcastic, but he doesn't appear to notice.

He says, "First I have to take a piss."

Abrupt right turn into a side road, guns the car, and we arrive quickly at a ruined structure that might once have been a nice motel.

He knew this was here. He knows this stretch of road. He's done this before.

A chill down my back, as I sense what's coming.

Engine off, he gives me a studying, appraising look. "You're not beautiful," he says. Small, satisfied, nasty smile. "Your features are too strong, masculine almost. But your body is good."

"You're not beautiful either. You're a pudgy middle-aged guy with a potato nose and no fashion sense."

He glowers, sweat spiking in a black anger. "What did you call me?"

"Oh, I thought we were just giving random opinions about each other's appearance. You know, I have red hair, bleached blond at the moment, and a lot of freckles, you have graying hair that you dye to a fake-looking reddish brown and a spray tan that's way too orange, I thought they had better spray tans nowadays but maybe that's just in Los Angeles."

"Humph." He grunts, angry but also satisfied. He antici-pates getting a chance to put me in my place. My uppity smart-mouthed little place. "You think you're pretty hot, don't you?"

"I thought you had to pee?"

"I do." He gets out of the car, leaves his door open. "You can get out of the car too, let's have a drink." He waggles a one-liter bottle of Diet Coke in front of me briefly, then opens it. Smells like it's half rum. He swigs from it, waits for me to get out of the car, hands it to me over the top of the car. I pretend to take a sip, wipe my mouth with the back of my hand, pass it back.

"That's good," I say. "So I guess you do drink."

"I drink. And I fuck." He slams his door shut as punc-tuation.

"That's fine, but I'm not a sex worker."

"That's okay. If you don't want any money for it, I won't give you any money."

A gun has appeared in his hands.

"Let's stop playing games, bitch, I know who you are."

"Oh yeah? Who am I?" I'm genuinely confused. I was tensed for battle and now he's thrown me a curve. Is he another assassin? How on earth did they find me out here?

"You're the Hitchhiking Bandit."

Shoot. I'd forgotten all about that. But it comes back to me now, that trucker who freaked out when he saw my knife.

Ronald continues. "You seduce men, rob them, drive away in their cars, leave them stranded by the side of the road naked, then abandon the car."

"You've got the wrong gal, buddy. I have never, ever done anything like that."

"Oh yeah? Let's see." His face twists into one of the most

purely evil grins I've ever seen, and he gestures with the gun. "Take off your clothes."

"You first."

"What?" He looks confused, when I have the gun, and he doesn't anymore. "Wait, how did you move so fast?"

"Just a gift I have. Why don't you take off your clothes?"

He drops his pants, steps out of them, stands in his underwear with a leer.

"Like what you see?"

"Step away from your pants." I gesture with the gun. He leers harder.

"You won't shoot me." He taunts, smug.

Why does he say that? Am I holding the gun wrong? Steph's brother Morgan taught me how to use a gun and I was a pretty good shot when I concentrated on it. I had a gun as part of my standard equipment when I was on the track and chase team. I've never enjoyed using guns. They're noisy and I don't like the explosive feeling in the hand when they go off, but I think I know how to use them.

"I won't shoot you?" I say out loud. Testing it. "Why won't I shoot you?"

My moment of hesitation gives Ronald a moment of confidence. He grins smugly, takes a step forward, hands reached out as if he's planning to take the gun away from me.

I shoot his right foot. He screams and collapses to the ground.

"You shot my foot, bitch!" He clutches at it, moaning.

I have a brief, startled impulse to laugh, then I do laugh. Consider saying something else, then just keep laughing. It seems to bother him.

Laugh while I rifle through his pants, which reek of semen and sweat, pocket his phone, wallet, keys, toss the pants as far as I can out into the field.

He moans. "What did you do that for?"

"To keep you busy." I drop the bullets out of the gun,

pocket the bullets, throw the gun into the field in the same trajectory as the pants. "Goodbye, Ronald."

He stares at me blankly, from the ground.

His car is just sitting there. Can I drive it? I don't have my license yet, but I was practicing to get one and I do know, in a general way, how to drive. Might as well give it a try, right? I have his keys.

Doors closed, start the engine, put my hands on the wheel, put my foot down on what I assume is the accelerator. The car moves forward. Victory! I turn the steering wheel to point the car in the right direction, accelerate a little more, and before long I'm driving back down the highway in a stolen car, exactly what he was afraid the Hitchhiking Bandit would do.

It's so funny. He thought I was this Hitchhiking Bandit person, but he still didn't expect resistance, did he? Apparently some guys really can't get it through their heads that a woman can be a physical threat. At least, I think that's their problem. They've heard I'm dangerous and they believe it, but only in an abstract way. They take one look at my little five-two self and can't make it stick in their minds.

It's good, I guess. It's probably saved my life. But for one moment it makes me so angry that I'm glad I killed those cops in Atlanta.

Then I feel guilty. Ashamed. I hear Pere Claude's voice in my head: *We should never find it too easy to kill.*

After I've gotten used to the car, I start trying to get into Ronald's phone, but it's face-locked, and eventually I give up and toss it out the window, let it shatter on the pavement. The moment it shatters is very satisfying and I wish I had more breakable things to toss out the window. He has a pair of sunglasses in the glove compartment, but they're nice, Ray-Bans, and I pocket them instead of shattering them.

This road is so deserted, it seems safe to go through his wallet while driving, toss everything out the window when I'm done with it. License, credit cards, punch cards, business cards. Finally, nothing in the wallet but a few receipts and cash. I pocket the cash, and the wallet itself goes out the window.

The car probably has some kind of navigation system, but I don't know how to use it. And it's night, so I'm not sure what direction I'm heading.

When I see the next city listed as "Boise" I know I must be going north again. I don't want to go too far north and get back to Marysburgh, so I take the next highway going west. Check the gas gauge. Nearly full. Check the sky. Full dark. What if I just keep driving west until I run out of gas? Abandon the car in a rest area or something?

Decision made, I keep driving. Punch in some tunes, satellite radio, find a station called "Fierce Females" which seems way too on the nose, but I do like all the songs, from artists like Garbage and Alanis Morisette and Aretha Franklin. I sing along loudly, probably out of tune. Nobody has ever told me I'm a good singer.

Dawn approaches, finally. The car is running low on gas and my brain is running low on alertness. I seem to be near Portland, Oregon. Pull off the highway to a little park on the Columbia River, leave the car unlocked with the keys on the dash. With any luck somebody else will steal it and confuse the trail even further.

Yawn, stretch, count my cash, decide if I can afford a hotel room, try to think of my next move. It's already getting hot. People have been talking about the incredible heat wave in the west, which has been going on for a couple of weeks now, rendering even places like Seattle and San Francisco as blistering, dried out, used up, haunted by smoke. Nothing feels right.

The sun rises in a pinkish haze.

"I just want to go somewhere it's rainy and nothing is on fire." I murmur this out loud, shading my eyes to stare at the blood-red sun through my brand-new polarized sunglasses.

A very fit young man pedals a sports bicycle into the park, nods at me in a neutral way, puts down his feet to anchor the bike while he stares at the same bloody sun, sips water from an aluminum bottle, eats an energy bar. Glances at me, frowns.

"Is that your car?" He gestures toward the one I just abandoned.

I shake my head. Shrug. "No, it's not mine. I don't know who it belongs to."

"Oh. Because whoever it is, they left their keys inside."

"Yeah? Huh. I wonder where they went. That car was there when I got here."

"Are you on foot then?"

"On foot. Yeah. Trying to pick my next destination."

"Do you have an ultimate goal?"

"Not at the moment. But I think I want to go somewhere it's rainy and nothing is on fire. Also somewhere without a lot of people around. No cops."

He laughs. "No cops. Why no cops?"

"I don't know, they hassle me sometimes, I don't like cops."

He nods, knowingly. "I get that. If they think you're home-less they'll treat you like absolute shit." He thinks about it for a long time, then says, "It's none of my business, obviously, but I think I've been to the kind of place you're looking for. Out on the Olympic Peninsula, along the coast. A whole bunch of these unbelievably small towns, and it really feels like the ends of the earth. Beautiful though."

"The Olympic Peninsula, huh? And the rainforest isn't on fire?"

"Not yet," he says, ominously. "The Green Bus system will get you out there, they take cash and they have a pickup spot in this park." He points to a sign that clearly says:

GREEN BUS GATHERING SPACE

"That sounds exactly like what I was looking for. Thanks for the info, random bicycle person."

He laughs. "I'm Carl."

"Jennifer."

We shake. He pedals off on the bicycle and I prepare to wait under the sign, hoping I don't have to wait too long, hoping it's not some really elaborate trap, hoping that, in the time between now and me arriving, the rainforest won't have caught on fire.

While I'm waiting, an obviously homeless person pushes a shopping cart full of miscellaneous items into the park. He notices me, and seems about to ask for a cash donation, then notices the car. The car, with its keys on the dashboard. He moves closer, looking around as if waiting for a trap to be sprung.

Then he comes to a decision. Makes his move. Opens the back door, shoves all his stuff inside, gets into the driver's seat and takes off.

Good luck, dude. Good luck to both of us.

PART V

THE OLYMPIC PENINSULA

17

THE SURLY LUMBERJACK

"Hey, Shawna, there's a guy out here who says he knows you." Joe Halsey, owner of the Surly Lumberjack, comes into the kitchen, speaks to me in a low voice. "You went to the same church or something as kids?"

"Yeah?" I put down the cleaver, try to stay casual in spite of my thundering heart. I already know who's here. And I know what he is. "Did he give a name?"

"Justin Wise."

"What does he look like?"

"Kinda sketchy." Quick grin, displaying a missing canine tooth on the left side. "But then, you looked kinda sketchy when I first saw you, I'm sure he'll clean up all right. Tallish, blond hair in need of a haircut, thin face. Intense blue eyes."

I nod. "I know him."

"He ordered a Lumberjack Pile, extra surly, if you want to bring it out and take a few moments to chat."

"Thanks. I'd like that."

The Lumberjack Pile is hash browns covered with melted cheese, steak, sausage, ham, smoked venison, and a couple of fried eggs. Extra surly is topped with salsa and fresh jalapeños.

I came up with it myself. Halsey thinks I'm a good cook.

He knows I think that's funny. In New Orleans and Bayou Galene I was not considered a good cook. There, I rarely even did the cooking because there was always somebody around who was way better at it than me. In fact, I got to hang out with one of the best North American cooks there's ever been, the famous Charlaine Quemper of New Orleans.

But I guess hanging around such an elevated caliber of cheffing rubbed off to the point where I'm the best cook in Timberland. Maybe the best cook *ever* in Timberland. And I'm still not that good.

I take one of our nicer plates, blue, undamaged, scoop the pile onto it, add salsa, jalapeños, and finally a sprinkling of habanero Tabasco. For that extra surly kick. Deep breath. Walk out of the kitchen.

Justice sits at the bar hunched over a pint glass of light lager, black raincoat damp from the drizzle outside. His hair falls into his eyes and he has a day or two of stubble. Was he old enough to be growing a beard when I saw him last? How old is he now? Eighteen, nineteen? He's taller than I remember, broader shoulders, but thin. He always looked more like Father Wisdom than any of my other siblings, and that resemblance leaps out at me right now. He wears the same unhappy, brooding look that Wisdom used to get. I learned to dread that look. It usually meant our father was about to share some new and horrible revelation from God about the ways we should be tormented in order to bring about our greater salvation.

I slide the food toward him. "Justice."

He looks at me, nostrils flaring, twists his mouth into a slight half smile. "Abnegation," he says. "It's good to see you."

"Is it?" I pause. "Good to see you too."

A slightly more genuine smile. "You don't have to lie. You're shocked to see me here. And to see me like…" He gestures at himself, his body, his clothing. Worn jeans, T-shirt, jean jacket under the raincoat. T-shirt faded black with a stylized skull on it. The last time I saw him on television he was with Meekness on some kind of religious talk show, and he was still very clean cut, pressed slacks and sweater vests and a wide-eyed preacher smile.

I make a guess: "You're not with the church anymore?"

"No." He shakes his head. "My stepmother and I had a difference of opinion about how to steer my father's legacy and I...lost."

"I'm sorry." I pour myself a beer. Move around to sit next to him. He starts eating. "Maybe not that sorry. You know I would just as soon nobody keeps that legacy alive."

He nods. "It's possible I'm coming around to your way of thinking, sister."

"Right, and that's not the only way you seem to have come around to my way of thinking."

He barks out a short laugh. "Of course you noticed that right off."

I tap the side of my nose. "We can always spot each other, Justice. How did it happen?"

"I went to New Orleans looking for you." He takes another bite of the Lumberjack Pile. "This is good, did you make it?"

"I did. Why were you looking for me?"

"For guidance. How to cope with the outside world. I thought about trying to find Great Purpose, we were close once, but with him I didn't even know where to start looking. But you—because of that *Teen Mode* article—I knew you had been living in New Orleans. I had a place to start."

"But you didn't find me there."

"No. I asked around. Showed your picture. Found some people who knew you."

"Some people who knew me?" All the people I know in New Orleans dance through my head with a powerful jolt of painful nostalgia. Who's still there? Do they think of me at all? Do they worry? Or do they imagine I'm safe, having fun, backpacking around Europe, touring ruins and drinking wine on the Riviera?

"Not close friends of yours," he says. "I don't think they knew you personally. They knew *of* you."

Knew *of* me? This is sounding more ominous. He could have been sent here by my enemies. And it would be clever, sending an assassin who I won't want to kill.

Carefully neutral, I ask, "What did they tell you about me?"

"Only that you had a falling out with your family, and left town. But my search put me there on the night of the full moon."

"Ah. So you got attacked?"

"I did." He pauses for a long moment, face troubled, remembering. "It was the strangest thing. They had a curfew. Whole town. Sunset to sunrise, everything locked down."

"New Orleans had a curfew? The actual city of New Orleans? As in, nobody selling booze for a time?"

He nods. "That's it. But I didn't take it seriously. I didn't stay indoors like they said. I was out wandering the streets. The thing that attacked me, it was like a demon. The size of a man, and it walked upright like a man, but hunched over. Furry, all teeth and claws, the shape of a monster." He imitates it, looking like a wolf man from an old-school horror movie.

"Some new wolves are like that. Even in wolf form they keep trying to walk upright or move like a human. It can look creepy. But usually it's harmless."

"Well. This one wasn't harmless. I think he would have killed me, except he got interrupted. A group of men came by, soldiers or cops or some kind of paramilitary group. Anyway, they were heavily armed. They shot him, which slowed him down but I don't think they killed him. While they were fighting I ran away. Left town. Drifted, I guess. Not sure what to do with myself. Worked a few odd jobs, slept in doorways,

scrounged out of dumpsters. And twenty-eight days later..."
He shrugs. "I guess you know the rest."

"I guess I do." I consider for a moment, then ask the thing
that's really on my mind. "How did you know to look for me
out here?"

I raise a hand to the back of my head, check to make sure
my hair is still tucked up under a baseball cap. The whole time
I've been here, I've worn nothing but baseball caps, giant
blocky T-shirts, plaid wool flannel overshirts. Halsey thinks
I'm a dyke, but he's cool with that. Really I'm just trying to
look as different as possible from both my usual self and also
my bikini barista self.

I thought I was successful, at hiding. There's been no
trouble here for months. But maybe it wasn't success at all,
maybe it was random dumb luck.

Justice says, "It was a video, posted online. I saw your face.
A chance thing. And I couldn't be sure until I was here."
Smile. Big. Fake. "I wanted to be sure."

"Justice." I finish my beer. Think about pouring myself
something stronger. "Justice, who sent you out here? What did
they tell you?"

"What? Abnegation, you're paranoid, nobody sent me."

"No? Justice, look at where we are on a map. Timberland,
Washington, rough coast of the Olympic Peninsula, population two hundred and forty-eight. Basically the ends of the
earth. You don't come all that way just for chitchat."

"No, sister, no." He seems sincerely wounded. "I just
wanted to talk to you. I just wanted to connect. That's the
only reason I'm here. We're family. And if you're estranged
from your other family too, you and me, maybe we're the only
family we've still got."

I shake my head. I'm pretty sure he's lying, and I could
probably flash him right now and get the full story, but I want
to take all that wolf stuff out of town. There's a huge and

sparsely populated forest out there for us to fight in, if it comes to that. Right now, I'll play along.

"All right. Let's talk." I go behind the bar again, get out the large mason jar full of cocktail concentrate I mix up ahead of time in order to make a "Rusty Chainsaw." Halsey gave me free rein to invent fancy cocktails and sell them to tourists at Seattle prices. If I were serving this to a regular customer, it would get diluted with a lot of crushed ice and soda. For myself I pour it straight into a pint glass.

"That smells good," Justice says.

I pour him his own glass. "Go for it. It's wolf strength."

"Alcohol," he says, nostrils flaring. He takes a sip. "I never even had a drink until after all this happened."

"Me neither. It's hard to get one of us drunk, you've probably figured that out by now. But we still get hangovers. I don't know if you've figured that out yet. If we drink this whole jar together, you might." I clink glasses with him. "How's the whole werewolfing thing working out for you, bro?"

"I don't know how to answer that," he says. "Good in some ways, I guess. But sometimes I get so hungry. It's ridiculous." He shovels more of the Lumberjack Pile into his mouth, chews angrily. "I couldn't stay vegetarian. You couldn't either, I'm guessing?"

"No. Not that I didn't try."

"It's just too powerful. The urge. To feed, to hunt, it's like —I don't always like that part of it. Feeling so overwhelmed by, you know. Animal urges."

"Yeah. We were raised to see meat as a moral failing. So there's a part of me that feels like a failure, every time I eat some."

"Exactly." He sips the drink. Gives me a serious, complicated look. "You know, I've been wondering something. Is the wolf why you left New Harmony? Or did it happen after?"

"Justice, you were there when Father Wisdom tried to

shoot me with silver. He already knew what I was. We just don't start changing shape until we reach adulthood."

"So the wolf is why you left. Okay. Do you think that's why you had so much trouble in New Harmony? Why you were so rebellious? Why you could never really submit to his authority?"

"How can I know that? There's not an alternate me who's exactly the same in every way except not a wolf. Whatever I am, I was born this way."

"Yeah? I don't know what I was born to be. I used think I knew. I thought I had the truth. His truth. Jesus, I mean. But now I'm not really sure about anything."

"But that's good, you not being sure." I say it casually, but he recoils. "What? What is it?"

"I, I'm sorry. I just— " He downs the drink, slams the empty glass on the counter. I pour him some more. He takes it, hands trembling. Drinks it. Then says, "Maybe you don't understand. What it used to be like for me."

I shrug. "Maybe I don't."

"I used to know. I mean, really know. All the way down. I knew who I was. I knew what I was expected to do. I knew how to be good. I knew how to be sure of heaven. Do you understand what it's like to have that? And lose it?"

"I guess I don't. Because I never had that same kind of certainty."

"You always were too rebellious," he says, nodding in a way that strikes me as smug. Like, it's coming back to him, that old role, Justice my older brother in the cult, pious and favored, lecturing his rebellious little sister about how to be good just like him.

"Right, because you were always daddy's perfect little boy." My voice comes out low, growling, angry. "That was never even an option for me, Justice. And you know why? Because I wasn't his. Because I was a *girl*. I worked as hard as you, I tried as hard as you. Harder. Because everything was stacked against me from the beginning.

"Wisdom had already made up his mind that I was especially wicked, tainted by the substance of my conception. So he made it true, by singling me out for even more abuse than all the rest of you got."

He frowns. "You really think that? You think Father treated you worse than the rest of us?"

"I know he did. Especially after my mother died."

"But he was trying to—he knew you had that wolf spirit inside you. You were in need of extra guidance. Extra discipline. He was just trying to steer you right."

"Well obviously it didn't fucking work." I growl, rage spiking so red for a moment that Justice draws back, startled.

"You have a lot of anger still," he says.

"You don't know the half of it." I drain the remainder of my drink, pour another one.

There's a moment of awkward silence, while I smolder, seething over old hurts that will never really heal.

I look away from him, study my drink. Keep talking. Reminiscing, I guess, but that makes it sound like we're talking about something pleasant, something fun. "After my mother died, everything was different. Different because she was gone, but everything in my head was different too. Chastity and I had to step up to take care of the younger children, that's where most of my time went. But in my head, I started to have doubts. Doubts about our faith, and doubts about my doubts, and doubts about that. I agonized over everything. Why didn't God save my mother? Was it just like Wisdom said, and my faith wasn't strong enough? Or was God not there? Not listening? Maybe not even real? I started trying to prove things to myself one way or the other. I would pray to God for revelation. Show me you're there, show me you're real. Then, when nothing happened, I would get frustrated and curse him. Pray to the devil instead. Show me you're there, show me you're real. But nothing happened then, either.

"By the time Ash died, I had pretty much stopped seeking answers from God or the devil. Until leaving, I went through the motions of our faith, because I didn't have much of a choice. But I didn't feel it in my heart. Except, I was always afraid I was wrong about that, too. That it was all real and I was just missing it somehow. That God was there, but he had turned his face away from me."

Justice looks down at the plate, takes the final few bites of the pile. "You know, there are things about growing up in New Harmony that only a few of us can really share. The kids younger than you, they all went with Meekness. She's married again, they're growing up in the outside world, they won't even remember it later. You, me, Chastity, Purpose. We're the ones who remember."

"I guess we are." A pause. "Chastity, Purpose, do you know what they're doing?"

"They were living together in Austin, Texas, last I heard."

"Were they doing okay?"

"I guess. As well as anyone." Long pause. Then he says, "You know, it sounds ridiculous, but if you put another Lumberjack Pile in front of me, I would eat that one too."

"Yeah? Why don't I do that, hold on."

"No, please, you don't have to."

"On the house, bro. Grill's already hot, won't take more than ten minutes. Hang on."

I head back into the kitchen, find Halsey fumbling around trying to make a grilled cheese sandwich for a different customer. He wipes his hand on his apron, which has somehow become filthy, as if he's the one who was cooking all day.

"Oh thank God," he says. "Shawna, can you make the grilled cheese?"

"Sure, but I'm also making another Lumberjack Pile for

Justin. He was being a little coy with you, he's actually my stepbrother. We grew up together. Remember how I told you I was raised in a super religious household and got kicked out?"

"Yeah, I do remember that." He gives me a brief one-armed hug. "I'm sorry."

"Thanks. Well, when I left, my brother Justin was still there. But now he got kicked out too."

He shakes his head. "Man, these holy rollers, I just don't know. They say they want everybody to join their church, but then they're always kicking their own kids out."

"Yeah, it's kind of funny, isn't it?"

"You know, I keep reading about how young kids, like you, they're just not religious anymore."

"No." I think of my Seattle friends and my peers in the Varger track and chase teams. "We're not, mostly."

"That's probably fine." He nods. "You know, religious folks, they talk pretty big, but they're not really any better than other people. And they're lousy tippers."

"They are, aren't they? The after-church crowd are the worst tippers."

We laugh together.

But by the time the second Lumberjack Pile is ready, Justice is gone.

I eat the pile myself, work the rest of my shift, but a current of uneasy anticipation runs just under my surface thoughts about orders and money and food and drinks.

At the end of the night, Halsey pays me out of the till as usual, saying, "Here you go, all cash, no feds."

I count it. He's honest, but not great at math. The amount is correct. "Halse, I'm sorry to do this to you, but I have to leave town, basically, now." I open the door to the storage closet where I sleep on a cot, start gathering up my things. Halsey watches me pack.

"Right now? But Shawna, you're such a good cook."

"Carlos has learned all my dishes, he's a smart kid, he'll

get good at making them eventually. Anyway, it's getting late in the fall, your business is going to drop off a lot real soon as winter takes hold. Right?"

"True." Sigh. "Your brother, stepbrother, is he why you're leaving?"

"Yeah. Family stuff. Too much to go into."

"He's another werewolf, isn't he?"

"Uh…." I sit down on the cot, for a moment unable to say anything more. "What did you say?"

He laughs, steps all the way into the storage closet, shuts the door behind him. He's a big man and this makes it feel very crowded. "Don't worry, Shawna, I'm not going to turn you over to the feds. It's just that I know about your people. I used to know a guy from the pack that lives out on the Quinault Reservation."

"Quinault? There's a native wolf pack?"

"Native? No, I think they just live out there. This guy, he wasn't Quinault himself. He was a white guy. But he said their pack had moved there a long time ago, that they had an old agreement with the Quinault people." He pauses. "Looked a bit like you. Reddish hair. Freckles. Only his eyes were a kind of golden brown color, not green like yours, but just as striking. Not tall, but real tough, you could see it in the way he moved." His face takes on a nostalgic air and his sweat just a hint of sexual interest. "He moved real good," he says. Wistfully. Shakes his head, shutting it all down. "Anyway, I don't know what happened to him, he went off to the city or something, but I never forgot him. Sometimes if the wind is right I hear the wolves howling out on the rez and I wonder where he is. I wonder if he thinks about me."

"He probably does. Wolves have good memories. We think a lot about people we've known."

I touch my grandmother's boots, which smell like Grandma Leah Evangeline, and like my Aunt Vivienne who used to wear them until she grew too tall, and like Grandma's perfume which reminds me of Aunt Charli who gave it to me and Babette who loved the scent and wanted to make her own version of it. So much history in a single pair of boots. And now there's one more piece: the silk scarf Antonia draped around my head during her "Jolene" performance is folded up in one of the zipper pockets.

"How did you know what I was, Halsey? I'm just curious. What gave me away?"

"Well, like I said, you remind me of this other werewolf I knew. Small, fast, tough, a lot stronger than you should be, amazing sense of smell. Plus, you've only taken two nights off work this whole time, and they were both on the full moon."

"Yeah, I guess that would be a bit of a giveaway, wouldn't it?" We hug. "Thanks for everything, Halsey. You've been very kind to me."

He laughs. "Not all that kind. You really are the best cook we ever had."

"Halse, you cannot believe how sad it makes me to know that's true."

I shoulder my backpack and take off into the night.

18

BERSERKER

My own scent trail from the last full moon leads out from Timberland into the forest. During previous moons I didn't notice scent traces or howling from other wolves, so the Quinault pack must be a ways off, even though part of the reservation is nearby. I pull out my paper map of the area, orient myself. The main Quinault territory is triangular, wide along the coast, reaching back to a point where it hits Lake Quinault. I'm guessing the pack is farther inland, and I decide to follow the Quinault river back toward the lake.

Sometimes I wonder how many other wolf packs exist in the world. We know each other instantly by scent, but scent tracking is chaotic, intimate. It happens on the ground, it happens on foot. It's old-fashioned. In the modern world, you can track people by their cell phones, find a dot on a map, get in a car and drive there. Scent tracking isn't like that at all. If I stumble across your trail I can follow you anywhere, but I have to find your trail first.

New Orleans is just one city, thickly inhabited by the Varger, but even right there, deep in their own territory, there were bitten wolves they'd never tracked at all, like my father's reclusive ex-girlfriend Lunora.

This country as a whole is vast, and it's mostly empty space. There might be wolves all over. And I did pass a few, when I walked across the country after the attack in Atlanta. I didn't think about it much at the time, because I was letting the wolf drive, and her thoughts on the matter were simple: other wolves, their territory, act polite and get out. Her instincts assume other wolf packs are friendly-ish, unless proven otherwise, and I hope those instincts are correct. Otherwise things could go pretty badly for me if I do find the Quinault pack and they're hostile. One of the few things a werewolf really does have to fear is a bunch of other werewolves.

Hiking through these woods would be pleasant, if I weren't tense about what's going to happen with my brother Justice. The rain finally let up, leaving the forest glistening in the light of the gibbous moon. Lush, full of life, thick green smells of wood and ferns, trees heavy with moss.

The sky darkens, clouds obscuring the moon, silver glow in their ragged edges. Justice is coming. Rushing up behind, reeking of berserker drugs and madness, disturbing the peace of the forest with his unhinged grunting and growling.

He attacks from behind, tries to bite me on the neck like some cheesy movie vampire. I flip him easily to the ground. This doesn't stop him for long, and he hops up again to come after me. I step aside and he collides with a tree instead. We do this a few more times, him attacking in a way that's brutal and ferocious, but not well-considered. It's almost like bull-fighting.

Is this typical for a wolf on berserker drugs? A pure unstoppable will to rip things apart, but no strategy, no planning?

Justice isn't as strong against me as he expects to be, that much seems clear. Every time I repel his attack, he acts confused, and comes back again in pretty much the same way. He's not consciously evaluating my strengths and weaknesses and adjusting his strategy accordingly. It's almost like he's not conscious at all.

He attacks, fails, attacks, fails, attacks, fails. He doesn't speak except for growls and yelps and howls. I don't think it's ever been easier for me to fend off an attacker, and that includes purely human attackers without weapons.

This is the famed berserker rage? Maybe a human would be terrified, but to another wolf, it's nothing. Dull.

And it seems to go on forever, me leading him deeper into the woods, as he attacks and attacks. Eventually he starts to get tired. Wrecking himself against me, like a boat flailing on a rocky shore, and when the drugs wear off, he collapses. Falls over into the ferns and decaying cedar logs.

I kneel down to check his breathing. He's still doing it. Breathing. Good. Going through his pockets, I look for clues to show how he found me out here. He doesn't react. The berserkers of old must have had sober brothers to look out for them, otherwise they would all have all been killed while they were sleeping it off.

There. In the back pocket of his jeans, a much-folded sheet of paper, screen captured from a video. Me, my face in a brutally clear close-up, as I'm shoving a customer out the door.

Shoot, I remember that guy. He was some kind of neo-Nazi jerk, a Faith Keeper or something, and once I realized that, I kicked him out. I even remember exactly what I said. "The Surly Lumberjack has a strict no fascists policy." But I was mad. I probably showed more of the wolf than I meant to. And somebody I didn't even notice at the time filmed it and put it online.

Title: Faith Keeper Kicked Out of Bar by Crazy Strong Girl

Based on the stats in the screen capture, the video went viral. Of course it did. Judging by the comments on this one screen shot, some of the people sharing the video were on his side, absolutely outraged by my behavior. But other people shared it because they were on my side. Some of the comments debate whether the girl in the video is "hot" or "dog ugly but with a good body," as well as suggestions that there's no way she really is that strong, it's a fake.

Oh, internet, how much I haven't missed you.

But wait. Back when I was still working with the Varger track and chase teams, they had a whole computer group that worked to scrub videos like this one. Are they not doing that anymore? Or, has Leon changed their mission, got them specifically looking for me?

Justice scrawled all over the paper with a red fine point pen. His handwriting is familiar, neat and cramped. I've seen it so often in the margins of church bulletins. Practical information, like a phone number with a New Orleans area code, and the bus sequence to get from Seattle to Timberland, but also a lot of deranged rambling. Almost like a poem, or scripture:

Beware the treacherous She-Wolf
The degenerate World of Men
Shall end in fire and flood
Ragnarok is coming
The God of Sheep devoured
The God of Wolves shall rule
The Brotherhood of Olvenar will triumph

Okay.
It's a cult.
A cult sending people to kill me.
Figures.

19

THE BROTHERHOOD OF OLVENAR

I keep looking through Justice's pockets until I hit the jackpot: his phone. Does it unlock with a face? His face is unconscious, but it's right there.

The phone doesn't unlock right away. I try different things. Forcibly open his eyes. Put my stolen sunglasses on him.

Bon Dieu, that worked.

Okay, now that I have phone access, what am I looking for? His battery is depleted, I don't have much time.

Start with email, text messages. Who has he been talking to? What has he been saying? But it feels like a dead end. The messages seem old, from before he was estranged from his stepmother. It's actually kind of sad, reading him and Meekness going back and forth about the schedule for some Christian book event they were going to do back in September.

Email is worse. Way too much junk from Christian organizations and Republican politicians. It would take me forever to wade through it all.

Back to the main screen, I notice a red logo with a starfish, an app called 5-Ray.

Click.

Bon Dieu.

The first thing that comes up is a discussion board called Bitches Must Die, entirely dedicated to me and Babette, and how we are bitches, and how we must die.

The board has a pinned message at the top, with a video. Do I dare watch it? How do I not? If these are some of the people trying to kill me, don't I need to know everything I can about them?

Click. The video begins. First: a familiar-to-me shot of Babette, covered in blood and stark naked except for a contraband ruby choker, gesturing defiantly at the security camera outside the New Orleans mayor's office. Her nipples are obscured by a black bar which somehow makes the shot look even more provocative.

I think about the night of the hurricane, when the mayor reportedly ordered a "cull" of bitten wolves that ended up killing our mentor Etienne. Well, to me he was a mentor. To Babette, he was even more, a loving parent substitute when her own parents failed her. She set out to kill the mayor in revenge, and since the mayor was dead the next day, I can only assume she succeeded.

The brief clip of Babette gesturing at the camera stops and music starts up. Ominous. Her eyes are made to appear glowing red.

Text appears, slashy red letters:

THE BITCH

The words drip blood like cheesy horror movie credits. Flames start up, eventually overwhelming the image of Babette, as the text displays in a series of screens:

THE BITCH RUNS A MOTORCYCLE GANG
OF VICIOUS SHE-WOLVES
THE RUDE BITCHES
THEY OPERATE IN THE SOUTHEAST

RIDE INTO TOWN LIKE VALKYRIES
BURN SHIT DOWN
BUST SHIT UP
KILL MEN WHO GET IN THEIR WAY
LAST SPOTTED IN HOUSTON
BROTHERS
YOU KNOW WHAT TO DO

The text stops.

Crude animation: a wolf man (wolf head pasted on top of a very ripped, muscular male body) takes an axe, cuts off Babette's head, holds it aloft triumphantly while blood drips down from her neck and fountains up from her torso.

It's almost too ridiculous to be disturbing. But it's still disturbing. And, honestly, if any of it's true, it sounds awesome and I'm ready to ride with the Rude Bitches myself.

Now the image dissolves in flame. Look! It's the clip where I'm kicking a neo-Nazi out of the Surly Lumberjack!

The video stops on a moment where I've got my head down, eyes up, fierce look as if I might have been flashing somebody, but the flash doesn't always show up in a photo or video. The video compensates by giving me the same glowing red eyes Babette got.

The text slams on:

THE ABOMINATION
LONE SHE-WOLF
SMALL BUT DEADLY
LAST SPOTTED IN TIMBERLAND WASHINGTON
BROTHERS
YOU KNOW WHAT TO DO

The same weirdly ripped wolf man appears to remove my head from my body.

Now he's holding both of our heads while the blood drips from our necks. The video text shows:

OLVENAR BROTHERHOOD VICTORIOUS

Under that, a pair of crossed hammers which is almost but not quite the Hammerfit logo.

The end.

The video was posted by a user called "Lupercius." I scroll down through the other content, skimming, torn between so many conflicting emotions: disgust, morbid curiosity, pragmatic desire for understanding. A lot of the content reminds me of other extreme online anti-feminist spaces, although this one has been given a strong spin into werewolfing and half-baked Norse mythology. Also that very specific obsession with killing me and Babette.

Online misogyny always reminds me a little bit of the Christian patriarchy I was raised with in the New Harmony cult. They convey the same ideas about women being lesser than men, inherently corrupt and foul, not even human in the same way men are. But in New Harmony everything was filtered through high-minded piety and flowery Biblical language about perfection and redemption.

The 5-Ray stuff is much more low-minded, crude and disgusting. Open talk of killing and torturing women, weird sexual fetishes based around humiliation and forced breeding. They call female werewolves "she-wolves" and have some really peculiar ideas about the ways we supposedly differ from male wolves.

Did you know that most of the negative stereotyping of werewolves as wild, animalistic and inhuman is based on she-wolves and not male wolves? Well, I sure didn't!

Did you know that female werewolves are much more violent, but also weaker and stupider than male wolves? No, I did not know that!

Did you know that she-wolves are hyper-sexualized sluts who want to sleep with all men, even though they hate all men, and act too much like men, and also have nothing in common with men? Yeah, I absolutely did not know any of that.

Lupercius seems to be host of the board, but also seems different from the others. Most of them give off a strong "teenager living in mom's basement" vibe. But Lupercius seems older, alludes to having an ex-wife and children he doesn't get to see. He also seems to know what he's talking about in the werewolf sense, which a lot of the others do not. He cautions against relying on silver weapons, for example, and reminds them that she-wolves have a sense of smell stronger than a bloodhound, even though he still gives it a misogynistic spin: "They use sense of smell to make up for their weakness in other areas."

He cautions about using the berserker drugs, mentioning two of the things I noticed—that you need a sober brother watching over you afterward, and that the berserker rage is less effective against another werewolf, even a she-wolf, than you might imagine.

Some of the other posters are obviously werewolf wannabes, daydreaming about being given the "gifts of the wolf" if they serve the Brotherhood well. Give them my head, for example. Others seem to be actual werewolves, bitten, and they allude to the Hammerfit chain, as if they got to this board from other boards related more specifically to Hammerfit.

Justice has a few posts, under his full name, Always Seeking Justice in the Service of the Lord. It doesn't look like he shared with his brothers the fact that he was going to look for me in Timberland. I hope that means he doesn't have any backup coming.

Another thing I'm starting to wonder: do the Olvenar get together in person? It seems like they would have to. Otherwise, where do they get the berserker drugs? And if one of them did manage to remove my head from my body, where would they go to deliver it?

Scrolling down rapidly, looking for information in this area, I run into a post from Lupercius that causes everything to snap into focus:

> We intended Hammerfit to be an all-male gym, but were convinced that we had to allow females in order to be profitable. But now we're successful enough to split off: "Fierce Females" is going to be the new female-only gym and the existing Hammerfit Clubs will transition to male-only and rebrand as "Savage Fitness."

Damn. Lupercius is one of the twins, Roman or Rufus. Rufus, I think. The wording sounds more like him, and also, it's easy to imagine Roman telling Rufus, "Hey, bro, can you start an online discussion board all about killing our sister Abby and her friend Babette?" but a little hard to imagine it going the other way. The twins have a weird relationship, close but fraught, as Rufus obviously envies his brother's highly dominant wolf, and Roman envies his brother's fully mastered wolf.

It must be Leon trying to kill me, otherwise, why get the twins involved?

Still, it's hard to imagine Leon knows much about the content of the Bitches Must Die 5-Ray. Leon has a lot of flaws, but misogyny has never been one of them. Unless Leon himself got radicalized online somehow? No, that doesn't feel right, and none of the posters seem to be him.

He probably asked for something generic, like, "See if you can widen the search for Abby, maybe take it online." And then the extreme misogyny came from Rufus, with his coiled-up resentments of his more dominant brother and his woman-hating extremely divorced guy energy.

Rufus was always polite, when he was helping me train to control my trauma morph. He never acted like he hated me personally. But sometimes I could tell he hated that my wolf was more dominant than his. He would make little jokes-that-weren't-jokes about it. But I thought it bothered him because I was young and small, not specifically because I was a girl.

The whole thing is very disturbing. Just a few months after creating a discussion board all about killing me, he's roped in seemingly dozens of men eager to do just that. Men I've never met, who have no rational cause for a grudge against me. Their murderous hatred seems to be driven by the simple fact that I have the audacity to exist at all.

And I know, sometimes, men like this are all talk. But why even talk like that? Why is imagining elaborate and unhinged ways of torturing and killing me something they consider recreational, a happy fun way to spend their leisure time?

As I'm scrolling through the messages, I accidentally click on a link that takes me back to the original video of me kicking out the Promise Keeper. It's only about a minute long. I scroll through the comments, not entirely sure what I'm looking for. But then something jumps out at me: a comment from BDog13, one of Barney's internet handles. Barney was one of my track and chase colleagues, part of the online team, wolfless, a computer expert, one of the people who used to scrub incriminating wolfy videos like this from the internet.

BDog13
A, I don't know if you'll see this, but we know why you did it now. He's running track and chase through the Hammerfits and selling off the traditional maisons, most of the old team quit, everything is in tatters. Find us if you can. Austin.

The comment is dated Halloween, a few weeks ago now. But it seems to confirm everything I suspected. Leon is making a mess of things and has repurposed the traditional track and chase teams to be chasing after me and Babette, rather than trying to contain new wolf outbreaks. Apparently, this is not popular with the traditional track and chase teams.

But I don't have much time to follow up any of this before the phone goes dark. Battery out.

Now what do I do with it? I've been wary of using the internet, even out in Timberland, because I know it leaves traces and sometimes people who know what they're doing can track you that way. I'm not especially tech savvy, but I am especially paranoid. And I know you can use smartphones to track people, because on track and chase we used to do exactly that.

All right. I decide to smash up the phone with a rock. Sorry, Justice.

Wait just a damned minute. Why am I sorry? This freaking loser was here to kill me. He's lucky it's his phone and not his face that I'm smashing up with a rock.

I think about scattering the plastic remains here in the wilderness, but littering makes me feel gross, so instead I put all the pieces into one of the plastic sandwich bags I have in my backpack. I try to make sure the little electronic bits are too smashed to be fed into any kind of chip reader. I'm not a hundred percent sure I recognize the part they call a sim card, but if I make sure none of the little bits are intact, that should do it, right?

Bon Dieu, I really don't know anything about technology.

I take a look at my brother's sleeping face. Should I leave him? Kill him? Watch over him? If I just leave him, he'll come after me again. But I still can't bring myself to kill him. Not even after he literally tried to kill me. He's just sleeping now, I can't do it.

Anyway, I need to ask him some questions. Find out who Leon's working with, or for. Is it the mayor's office? Extraordinary Threats Task Force? Some other group I never heard of?

It's late and I'm tired too. I get out a couple of my most prized Timberland possessions: a blanket and a poncho, each with a slick waterproof side and a warm fuzzy wool side. The blanket goes below, waterproof-side down, and the poncho drapes over me. Once set up like that, on the soft forest ground, I'm fairly comfortable and start drifting off right away. But I want to wake up as soon as Justice stirs.

Move myself closer to him, drape the poncho over both of us. It's not quite big enough for that, so I'm less covered than I was. But, his body is putting out a lot of heat. My brother Nicolas tells me that werewolves tend to run a little hot, our base body temperature closer to 99.1 rather than 98.6. But I don't know if that stat is just for born wolves. Maybe bitten wolves are different. Maybe they run even hotter.

I'm thinking about warmth, fire, sun, hot springs, as I drift off to sleep. Dreaming. Nicolas is trying to explain something to me, he says, according to my calculations in ten years everyone will be a werewolf who's related to you and I say, wait that's not how genetics works? And he says, that's why the numbers are so disturbing, it's the apocalypse, causality will start running backwards.

I wake up.

The sky is hinting at dawn and Justice is already on his feet in a defensive crouch. But he seems confused, gaze darting around rapidly, nostrils flaring.

I don't get into a defensive posture myself. I stay seated, just observe him. "Justice?"

"Abnegation." He rubs the back of his head. "I think I was supposed to kill you."

"You think? How is that something you're not sure about?"

"I don't know, my memory is messed up." He shakes his head. "Nothing seems real."

"That's the berserker drugs. Who are the Brotherhood of Olvenar?"

"No. No." He gets very upset, sits down, covers his head with his hands. "It's not my place to share the secrets of the brotherhood."

I stand up, take him by the shoulders, hard green stare into his pale blue eyes. "Justice. Tell me the secrets of the brotherhood."

His gaze unfocuses and he goes under entirely, no resistance. He speaks in a soft voice. "Every man is a wolf or a sheep. Are you a wolf? Then become a wolf. Step up to meet your destiny, become who you were always meant to be. But beware. If your brothers bring you over and discover too late that you're a sheep after all, they will rip you apart."

Okay, that tells me what their philosophy is, but it's not very useful in a practical sense. "Justice, why do the Brotherhood of Olvenar want to kill me?"

"Enemies of the brotherhood must die."

"The brotherhood considers me an enemy? Why?"

"You killed two of our brothers in Atlanta."

"Justice. The two brothers in Atlanta, who sent them after me?"

A blank look. He genuinely doesn't know. I try a different angle. "Justice. How did the brotherhood recruit you?"

"They found me when I was in New Orleans. I went to the Hammerfit. That's what people said to do, if you were bitten by a werewolf."

"Why did you come after me alone, Justice? Why didn't you post your plans on the Bitches Must Die board?"

"We don't post detailed plans on that board. We have no idea who's reading it. There could be spies, loyal to you."

Hmm, that's a somewhat reassuring thought. "Where do you share your plans?"

He looks at me like I'm insane. "Hammerfits. We meet at the Hammerfits. Private workouts. Brothers only." He blinks, shakes his head. "Where's my phone?" He starts checking his pockets, seeming a little more alert. My stare is wearing off. I decide to let it.

I hand him the plastic bag full of fragments. "Here you go."

He stares at it. "You…destroyed it? Why?"

"So you couldn't use it to track me, of course. Or, call your brothers here? Or, whatever it is you were planning to do."

"But without a phone how do I get home?"

I make a scoffing noise. "Listen to you, an actual werewolf, wondering how to get around without a silly phone. Look at me, do I have a phone? Where's home for you now anyway? New Orleans?"

He frowns, briefly angry, growls. "She-wolf. Maybe you can live like an animal, but I can't."

"No? That's a weakness, Justice. I don't know what lies your so-called brothers are telling you, but being able to 'live like an animal' is one of our gifts. You can and maybe you should. Don't go back to them. Stay here in the woods with me, I'll teach you how to be a real wolf."

For a moment he seems incredibly sad, like he's about to start weeping, and I have a flare of hope that maybe I've gotten through, opened up a crack in his fanaticism.

But just as quickly, he hardens. "Why didn't you kill me when I was asleep?"

"I thought about it. But you were asleep, it seemed wrong. I guess that's my weakness, Justice. Report that back to your brothers. Deep down the abomination herself doesn't actually want to kill anybody."

He stares at me for a long time, intent, occasionally opening his mouth as if he wants to say something more, but closing it again, keeping his silence. Eventually he says, "I guess this is goodbye then."

"I guess it is."

He takes a small step toward me with open arms, almost as if he would give me a hug, but when I don't respond in kind he steps back. He looks troubled for a moment, then says, "I can't betray my brothers."

"But you can betray your sister. All right then. You made your choice. This really is goodbye. I hope, if we meet again, that you will have made some better choices in the meantime. But I doubt it."

Each of us turns to follow our path. I go deeper into the woods, looking for the Quinault pack.

Justice goes back the way he came.

20

QUINAULT PACK

The moon is full and we're on the hunt, me and the wolf, together. Hear the other pack howling in the distance, follow the sound until we start to encroach on their territory. Instinctively, we know the protocol. A howl that means: hello, here, guest, please?

Wait for a response.

We get it. A howl that means: come here to this place, hunt leader will give welcome.

We follow the sound. Find the hunt leader, bow to her. Hunt as guest? She places her head on top of our head. Yes. Guest, follow me. She howls to the pack. Guest hunts with us tonight.

The pack howls in return. Welcome good guest.

Affirmation but also warning: a good guest is welcome, a bad guest will face consequences.

We howl in acceptance. We know. We accept. We will not offend against their pack.

We run together.

We hunt together.

The hunting here is very good, deer and elk big and plentiful.

After the main hunt, where senior pack members get most of the meat, the wolf and I lead a secondary hunt of younger pack members. We bring down a tremendous bull elk, eat, then fall asleep in a warm pile.

Dawn.

Wake as wolves, instinct to return to where we started. Behind us, the hunt leader of the pack makes sure there are no stragglers.

Back to my clothes, I return to human earlier than most, stand up as a human, stretch, while most of my guest pack is still furry.

Except their hunt leader, an older, heavyset woman.

I nod in her direction and she nods in response. But then she frowns and rushes to push me hard against a tree, thick hand to my neck, brown eyes flashing gold.

"What are you doing here, roug?"

"You accepted me as a guest in your territory last night," I manage to squeak out.

She drops me abruptly, makes a disgusted noise, but doesn't lose focus. "Last night the wolf ruled. Today I rule. And I ask again, what are you doing here, roug?"

"Why do you call me roug?"

"You're a born wolf not of our pack. Are you saying you're not a roug?"

"Well, it's complicated. My father, he was one of the rougarou, but my mother was a human religious fanatic, and I was raised far away from any of my father's people until after my wolf came. So I don't know, I guess I am one of the rougarou by some ways you could reckon it, but in other ways I'm not. I wasn't raised by them."

Her eyes widen. She seems, somehow, to tense up and relax at the same time. Shakes her head. "Shit. Of course. You're not just a roug, you're *that* roug."

"What do you mean? That roug? You know who I am?"

"Abby Verreaux. Leon's daughter. You challenged him as hunt leader and lost."

"Oh. I guess you do know who I am."

"Aren't you supposed to be in Europe?"

"Well, I thought so. Turned out that was a trap. Leon had some cops try to kill me in the Atlanta airport as I was about to leave the country."

"Hmmph. Sounds like him. Well, I'm sorry for your troubles. But you can't stay here."

"I didn't intend to stay long, I just wanted to meet you all. Hunt together."

She folds her arms, suspicious. "Really? You came all the way out here just to hunt with us for one moon?"

"No, I was in the area already and heard about you. From Joe Halsey in Timberland?"

"Halsey." She obviously knows the name, smiles. "Surly Lumberjack, haven't been there in years. How's old Halse doing, anyway?"

"Pretty well. He takes things a bit slower after the heart attack, but he's still engaged in the business. And he was very good to me."

"Heart attack? That's too bad. I should go visit sometime soon. We used to go out there on the regular, I'm not sure why we stopped."

"Well, if you get out there soon enough, order a Lumberjack Pile, you'll get some of the venison that I personally caught and smoked, which I have been told is very good."

She nods, seems to finally accept me, starts getting dressed. I follow suit. The rest of the pack is waking up now, and some of them come up as humans to welcome me, give handshakes, even hugs. Their leader welcomed me last night, so I'm assumed to be an ally.

"Back to the longhouse." The hunt leader taps me on the shoulder. "The wolfless should have coffee going. Most of us don't eat much after the hunt, but if you want some human-style breakfast food, it'll be there."

The longhouse feels similar to the public house in Bayou Galene, although it's made of wood, not concrete. Built to withstand constant rain, not occasional hurricanes.

"Thanks. What's your name, by the way? I mean your human name."

"Oh, right." She laughs. "Maggie Williams. And you're Abby."

We shake hands.

Breakfast in the longhouse is similar to the post-moon breakfasts in the Bayou Galene public house, everyone chattering excitedly, children too young for wolves asking about the hunt, adult wolfless smiling but a little sad.

But if this is their whole community here, it's obviously much smaller than Bayou Galene. Maybe a couple of hundred people, no more. Even smaller than Timberland.

Everyone other than the hunt leader is very friendly to me, asking questions and engaging in chitchat. Some people have heard about the shakeup in rougarou land and ask me about it in a vague way. I respond in a similarly vague way, and they seem satisfied. There was a conflict, I left, now I'm looking for a new place to be. Is that new place going to be here? Probably not, but it's always nice to meet other wolves. All packs should be allies, even if we each have our own territory, don't you think? Oh, yes, certainly. It's a big country. Lots of space for all of us.

Maggie taps me on the shoulder, makes a follow-me gesture. I follow, carrying a cup of coffee. Into a private room obviously used as an office. Feels very much like the room Pere Claude used to use, the one Leon took over. Clunky old computer, papers everywhere.

She gestures, sit down.

I sit in the chair across the desk.

She sits in the desk chair.

I flash back to the moment when Leon kicked me out, we were sitting in Pere Claude's office almost exactly like this, and he—

"You just got really upset, why?" Nostrils flaring, she looks thoughtful.

"Flashback. When Leon exiled me, he was sitting in a desk chair and I was sitting across the desk. Just like this."

She sighs. Shakes her head. "Of course, you have to make this hard."

"It's fine that you're kicking me out, I never intended to stay. I really did just want to meet you. Remember, I wasn't raised by the rougarou. All wolf people are... I mean, I'm curious about you." I pause. "Unless you're doing worse than kicking me out of your territory? Are you planning to kill me or something?"

She looks up at the ceiling. "Of course we're not going to kill you, Abigail Verreaux. Don't be ridiculous. And I have a lot of sympathy for your situation, I really do, but I'm the hunt leader here and I have to look out for my own people first."

"I get it. And the name is Abnegation."

"What?" She frowns deeply.

"Abby isn't short for Abigail. It's short for Abnegation. That was my name in the cult. Self-Abnegation in the Service of the Lord. I tried being Abigail Marchande for a while, but it didn't really stick. So my name is Abnegation. Abby's fine. But not Abigail. That's not my name."

She nods. "Abnegation. Very well. You're young and you weren't raised as a wolf, so there's a lot you don't know. And what you do know, it was the rougs who told it to you, yes? So when you heard about their history, you got the version of it they wanted to tell."

"The pere diaries," I say.

She nods. "We keep our own story here. We split off from the New Orleans pack in 1938. There was a fight for the hunt leader position. My grandmother challenged Jean-Claude Verreaux and lost."

"Jean-Claude Verreaux? Was that Pere Claude's father? Grandfather?"

"Grandfather. When a challenger loses, the challenger and their people get exiled. Your exile was a little unusual, from what I hear."

"I was a faction of one, and it was supposed to be temporary."

"So you might not know. In the usual exile, called a ghosting, the exiled group is sent out on pain of death. If the rougarou know where you've gone, if they're reminded you exist, they will kill you. The rougs tolerate no other wolf packs. So you have to act like one of the dead."

"But that can't be right. We've allied with other packs, with the Lobos, the Los Angeles pack."

She smiles tiredly. "I hear rumors, things might have changed under the leadership of Pere Claude. He discovered the Los Angeles pack and let them be for a long while, then partnered up with them to try to stop a bitten wolf outbreak. So now they consider each other to be allies. But it wasn't always like that. And maybe Claude made friends for a practical reason: the Lobos are a large pack, almost as big as the rougs. It would be foolish to try crushing a pack of that size. Our pack is small. We can't assume we'd get the same treatment. And we really can't assume we'd get the same treatment from Claude's son. He's different from his father. Everyone's holding their breath, waiting to see what kind of a leader he's going to be." She shakes her head. "Early signs are not encouraging."

"Pere Claude was special," I say, nostalgically. "He was the longest-running hunt leader the Varger ever had."

"I never met him, of course, but that's what I hear. That he was incredibly fierce, absolutely formidable, but also kind and generous. Forward-thinking. Open to new things. They say it was the influence of his wife Leah Evangeline. A Jewish liberal from New York."

"You're talking about my grandmother," I say, heart pounding, voice coming out in a tight little growl.

She makes a placating gesture with her hands. "Sorry, I meant no offense."

I make an effort to calm down. This is her territory and in one way I have no right to get mad about anything. But I know that even otherwise decent people can be pretty conservative out in these little rural enclaves, and I know that when they say "a Jewish liberal from New York" that means something to them, something that isn't always good, and I'm going to shut it down, I don't care if it's my territory or not.

I say, "I never met my grandmother in person, but I have read her diaries, so in a way I know her very well. And I've never known anyone I admired more."

She says, "I really meant no offense."

I stand up. "I should leave."

She stands up too. "I don't want us to part on bad terms, Abnegation. I think all this tension, it will blow over soon. Leon will either settle down to become a good hunt leader, or the pack will rend him. You know about rending?"

"I do. It's in the pere diaries. It used to happen fairly often."

"Rendings and exiled splinter packs, yes. The rougs were prone to that until Pere Claude. With him gone, it might become more common again." She gestures toward the main room of the longhouse. "This pack, I'm their hunt leader. If I lead well, we thrive, if I lead poorly, we suffer. My leadership is important to the people who depend on it. But it doesn't mean anything in the larger world. Nobody's going to fight me for control of this pack.

"The New Orleans pack is different. Bigger. Older. Richer. Well-connected. It really matters who leads it. So there are struggles for that leadership, like the one between you and your father. What happens to the losers? They disappear. Or else the power of the rougs gets turned against them. My advice to you: disappear. Make a little pack of your own somewhere. You're young. Healthy. Resourceful. And you're a survivor, I can see it in your eyes. Find a nice boy, somewhere the hunting is good. Forget about all this rougarou business. And they'll forget about you."

I nod. Politely. "As you say."

"Find my grandson James, he's fifteen and not a wolf yet, but getting antsy about it. He'll give you some dried meat for the path ahead. I don't want you to think of me as your enemy. I just don't want my pack involved in this conflict at all. You understand?"

"I understand. And I really didn't come here to make trouble for you."

"I believe you." Pause. Sigh. "I don't know what possessed you, child. To try to become hunt leader of such a large pack at your age. You're barely a wolf yourself. But I think, if you start a much smaller pack of your own, you will lead them well."

"As you say." Then a thought strikes me. "Maggie Williams, you say this pack isn't important, that nobody will fight you for control of it? That's not right. People will fight you for control of anything. Anything at all, if they get it into their heads that they should."

I remember the piece of paper in my jeans pocket, unfold it, hand it to her. "This is what I'm talking about. This kind of thing."

She reads it, a sour look on her face. "What the hell is this?"

"I found it on my former cult brother, now a bitten wolf, and also apparently a member of some weirdo misogynistic werewolf cult that calls themselves the Brotherhood of Olvenar."

"I don't understand."

"The brotherhood sent him to kill me."

"The brotherhood is working with the rougarou?" She looks confused.

"I think so. I think my father started it, maybe accidentally. But I need to warn you. You think you're safe out here, but nowhere is safe. You think you're gonna be okay because you're the hunt leader, but there will be somebody who starts the idea that women can't be hunt leaders. And people will believe that idea. And then somebody will fight you for this thing you have that you don't think anybody else wants."

Emotions chase each other across her face, brief and fleeting. One of them looks like fear, but she quashes it.

"The young are so melodramatic," she says, smiling slightly. "It's going to be all right, child. Remember what I said. Forget about them and eventually they'll forget about you."

FORGET ABOUT THEM AND EVENTUALLY THEY'LL FORGET about you.

Her words echo in my mind as I hike deep into the wilderness. If Leon doesn't hear anything about me for long enough, would he assume I was dead? Stop actively sending people after me?

Take the fight to them. Don't let them make you their prey.

The words pop into my mind in that alternate voice I hear sometimes, the same voice that originally told me to leave New Harmony. And I think that voice has always been correct. Is that what I've been doing? Letting my enemies make me their prey?

Is Leon my enemy? He must be. But I might have other enemies too. In fact I probably do. I have a feeling that Leon is trying to kill me at the request of some other enemy.

Wait. Leon has been an assassin. Assassins kill for money.

Is someone paying him to kill me? Are the Varger short of money now, after Hurricane Pax basically flattened the entire town? The post from Barney said they were selling off the traditional maisons, that definitely suggests money troubles.

But who wants me dead, if it's not Leon? And why do they want that? It must be the New Orleans mayor's office, or somebody connected to it, otherwise, why go after Babette too?

My thoughts spiral like that, never reaching a firm conclusion. It feels like there's got to be an answer, something I'm just not seeing, but the answer never comes. Just the frustration of not quite knowing what to do.

For a few more days I walk, think, eat the food the hunt leader's grandson packed up for me. But it's getting late in the year. It's misty, damp, chilly. I'm not sick of trees and ferns and moss, exactly, but I would prefer to look out at them from behind a window, in a heated lodge, with a fireplace, holding a hot chocolate.

I told Leon once that I don't much like camping, because it reminds me of New Harmony. I think about that day and get angry. We were connecting that day. We felt like a father and daughter. Like family. Like friends. And he betrayed me. Made himself my enemy.

Maybe I should kill him.

The words sparkle across my mind, and instantly I run away from them. I don't want to kill Leon any more than I wanted to kill Justice. But it's not just about what I want, is it? These Olvenar, they're not just a danger to me, they're a danger to all of us. The poisonous, hate-filled ideas I saw on the Bitches Must Die board aren't going to be confined there. Poison spreads. Bad ideas catch on, replicate, get worse, like a virus.

As I'm hiking, it grows darker and colder rapidly. Snow begins to fall.

I have never been in a snowstorm before.

At first, it's kind of exciting. The snow itself is a beautiful glittering white, cold but soft, and seems to deaden the sound, bring a hush to the forest like nothing I've ever experienced. It feels like everything has stopped except the snow.

But as I keep walking, I realize that my habit of walking barefoot, like a hobbit, is making my feet so damn cold. But Grandma's boots aren't built for terrain like this, they wouldn't be much better than bare feet. I have wool socks I could put on, but they'll get wet and icky very quickly.

I could go to wolf form. The wolf is thickly furred, she never much feels the cold. But my wolf can't carry the backpack.

I think, briefly, about the logistics of designing a backpack that could be carried by either a human or a wolf, but it's not like I could make one right now. I need shelter.

A shallow cave near a waterfall still smells of bear, but not too recently. I move in, spread out my wool blanket and poncho, take off my wet clothing, call the wolf. Warmed by her thick undercoat, we snuggle under the blanket and go to sleep.

We wake, late, with the sun, venture out into a thick, brilliantly white world of new snow. She loves it and I let her play, rushing madly through the drifts, hopping and pouncing and rolling around. Neither one of us has seen snow like this before, but somewhere deep in her mind, the part that runs on instinct, the part that once came from the Norse lands, she knows snow, and believes winter snow to be correct. The world operating as it should.

She hunts in snow, eats a fat marmot.

Howls in snow.

Runs in snow.

Returns to her cave, sleeps again.

If she weren't lonely without a pack around, it would be the best time of her life so far.

THE HALL OF VIOLETS

I wake up.

Me, not the wolf. New moon. I'm not sure how many days I let her simply revel in the snow, almost a full half moon, but that's over now. The wolf is sleeping and the snow is dirty, crusted over with ice, melting into a soggy, dreary mess. We're not high enough in the mountains to stay snowy all winter, apparently. Or maybe that comes later in the season. What is it, November? The Varger have names for all the moons and the one in November is the Wet Moon. But I think they're based on the expected weather in southern Louisiana. It's wet here, too, but the thing I notice most is that it's dark. The cloud cover is heavy, the days are short, the sun is far to the south.

The wolf, for her part, thinks this is all entirely correct, just like the snow. She remembers the Norse lands. There, the sun disappears almost entirely in the heart of winter.

But today I'm me, and it's the black moon, and everything seems impossibly dreary, dripping and muddy and generally unpleasant. I venture from my cave a few times, first for water, and then because I don't want to piss inside my own cave. I'm not hungry, yet, because the wolf had so much fun hunting in the snow. But then I get cold and bored and go out hoping to find dry firewood. I feel like I've become a very dull nature program.

The hunt for dry firewood is pointless. But as I return to the cave, I notice the fresh trail of a familiar bear. Heading to my cave, which was once her cave.

My first reaction is annoyance. Wave my arms and start yelling. "Hey! You! Bear! Didn't you smell the wolf piss outside? This is my cave now! Aren't you supposed to be hibernating?"

She cranes her head to look at me curiously, unconcerned and slow. She weighs five hundred pounds, she doesn't care what I'm doing. Human or wolf, I'm no threat to her. Then she moves to sniff my luggage.

Shit, if she gets really into my luggage she might tear it all up, looking for food, or just out of curiosity.

She might ruin Grandma's boots.

"Hey! Hey, bear! Get away!"

I run toward her full tilt, shouting, howling, waving my arms around. I seem to vaguely remember hearing that you can scare away a bear by seeming large.

When I get close, feel her size and heat, I have a moment of pure apprehension, a thrill of fear, a conviction that this is a terrible idea and she's about to rip my head off.

She regards me with mild annoyance, rushes to chase me away. I circle around behind her. She's stronger and much bigger, but I'm faster and more agile. It's almost the same equation as when I fight a large werewolf like my brother Rufus, except, he's got a human brain and she's only as smart as a bear.

We rush at each other a few times. In human form I'm not much of a threat to her—no teeth, no claws—but she still recognizes when a fight isn't worth having. Seems almost ready to back away, leave me alone, look elsewhere for shelter.

KAPOWWWWWWW

A gunshot goes off, loud but not too close, and she startles, roars, swipes at me with her claws.

It looks so casual. She's barely using a fraction of her enormous strength. But it slams into me with tremendous force, knocking me backward to the floor of the cave, guts raggedly opened by thick, dirty claws.

Body on fire, I clutch my abdomen, pant, reach for the sleeping wolf. Nothing. Right. New moon.

Adrenaline is what gets me to my feet, head down and howling, as I head-butt the bear. She's practically the size of a small car, but a thick human skull knocking hard into her tender little nose still shocks her with pain. She whimpers, once, and gives up, lumbering away, looking for somewhere else to spend the night.

I collapse onto my blanket, panting. I just fought a bear, I think, giggling. And I won. Sort of. I got her to leave, anyway. But I'm the one left helpless. I tip my hat to you, madam bear. You put me and my kind to shame. If there ever really were any bear shifters, you would have kicked our mangy wolf asses.

The pain is intense, healing slow, and I black out a few times.

Am I dying? I might be dying.

When did it get so warm here in this cave, did I manage to light a fire after all?

(Infected, the wounds are infected, bear claws are filthy)

This is how people used to die, in the wilderness. Germs.

(Just like what happened to the wounds on my shoulder, the ones that left scars)

Slipping into darkness, rising, as if I'm smoke. The world below spins, wheeling, so far away. Eyes of the raven become my eyes, open up a vast landscape beneath me, infinite in time and space. I can see what every wolf in the world is doing.

I can see what Leon is doing.

Rushing toward a focused target makes me feel dizzy and

nauseated, but I see him, much as he was when I saw him last: in the office that used to belong to Pere Claude, with papers piled up all around and a distracted frown on his face. But I see him from above, behind, as if I'm hovering somewhere around his right shoulder. It seems, if I focus hard enough, I'll be able to read the paper he's staring at.

He looks up, expression changing to confusion as he sniffs the air, as if he senses me.

Suddenly I'm tumbling down into red darkness, a moment of fear, am I going to fall forever? Am I going to hell?

I cry out, reaching, "Grandmother, Grandmother are you there?"

A slightly annoyed voice as she takes my hands. "I'm always here, child."

"Grandmother, am I going to die?"

"Eventually? Yes. Right now? No. But you'll feel like hell until the moon comes back. You already know all this. Come along with me."

Into the woods, I follow her. Smoke tickles my nose, promising warmth and cooked food.

"Where are we going, Grandmother?

"Hall of violets."

"Violets, why violets, are there violets in winter?"

"That's just the name, kiddo. It's warm there. I'll intro-duce you to the ancestors."

"More ancestors than you?

She laughs, a wolf laugh, tossing her head. She is human and wolf at the same time, shimmering between two forms, both of them small and red and fierce. Like me.

"Yeah, kid, you take after me." She smiles, but it turns sad. "Your path is gonna be even harder than mine. I'll try to help you with that, but I'm sorry. There's no way forward that isn't hard."

I knew that, I think. *I always knew that.*

The hall of violets is a living building, made from trees

coaxed to grow together so they make a shelter. Winter, so the flowering vines that twist up around the trunks are bare. But the trees are evergreen. In the center of the hall is a stone fire pit, vast and warm, exuding the smell of roasting meat. Ancestors are gathered round the fire pit, pulling meat directly off the carcass of a sheep. My grandmother says to them, "This is my granddaughter, Abby. She's been through a lot to get here."

They all look at me. "We know her many deeds and trials," says a golden-furred female wolf, nodding. "We know her spirit to be the true spirit of hunter and protector. Welcome to the hall of violets."

A black male wolf sniffs, giving me a skeptical look. "She's the one? A bit small, isn't she?"

My grandmother bristles and her eyes flash green. "You're gonna judge a wolf by her size, Blackfur? That's human bullshit and you know it."

He laughs. To me he says, "Show me your teeth, then, small one."

I don't like his attitude. "Why should I do anything you ask?" Pause. "Asshole."

He laughs again. Makes hard eye contact with me and his eyes flash gold, while I feel mine flash green in answer. As the will of our wolves clashes, the rest of the world becomes gray and distant, until only the two of us are here together, eyes locked. Me and Blackfur. We speak without noise.

You should kneel/roll over before me, youngster
No. I will not kneel/roll over before anyone
I am the oldest and strongest wolf you have ever met
So what?
So you should kneel/roll over
Bullshit. You should be the one to kneel.

A long, drawn-out moment while we continue to stare at each other, and then, the rest of the dreamworld comes rushing back. Blackfur starts laughing. Just laughs and laughs and laughs for a ridiculously long time. "Somebody get this little wolf her summer mead!" he shouts out and now there's a mug in my hand, full of a sweet drink, like wine, but it tastes of flowers. Golden flavor, goes right to my head, which becomes fuzzy, light.

Everyone starts congratulating me as if I won a fight, but I'm confused. "I didn't win the challenge."

"But you didn't lose," says a male wolf, white-furred. "Against Blackfur himself, you didn't lose."

"But what does that mean, exactly?"

Blackfur thumps me on the back, laughing uproariously. "It means you have a chance, small one. Not much of a chance, but you've got one. And that's more than most can say."

"A chance to do what?" I ask. But nobody's paying attention to me anymore. They're watching a new wolf enter the hall, eyes bright, and I know: this is Grandmother Wolf, not my own grandmother, but the grandmother of us all, both like and unlike my own grandmother.

A red wolf, but so old she has hints of gray in her fur. Her shape is different from the modern wolves too, something prehistoric about her. Oversized paws and head, teeth long as daggers. Her human look is different as well, older, it's in the angled shape of her eyes and cheekbones. She comes from the very far north. Her skin is pale and freckled, her hair is red, her eyes are as green as the underside of a glacier.

She stretches out her arms and points to a hot spring that starts bubbling up out of the ground, filling the hall with warmth, moisture, and a faint but not unpleasant sulphur smell. Some of the wolves get into their human skins and hop into the warm mineral pool which has now appeared.

"Get in," says Grandmother Wolf. "We need to talk."

Ease myself into it. Bon Dieu it feels so real. It's probably just the warmth of fever, or who knows, maybe I pissed myself, but it feels just like sinking into a hot tub and right away all my muscles unknot.

Grandmother Wolf says, "Your father Leon leads the people falsely. He cheated to win the challenge you brought against him. Used berserker drugs, not will alone, to call his wolf before you called your own."

"But what does that mean? If he leads falsely, do I have to kill him?"

Gasping and shock from some of the wolves, but others nod thoughtfully.

"I will not say kill," says Grandmother Wolf.

"I will," says Blackfur. "Leon is dangerous. The only way to be sure of him is to chop off his head when he's not paying attention." He pantomimes using an axe.

"No!" my own grandmother exclaims, a look of horror on her face. "She can't do that." She turns to me. "Granddaughter, you can't do that. A hunt leader can't take power by assassinating the previous hunt leader. You can't."

I nod. "Sure, that makes sense. Otherwise you'd have dominant wolves offing each other all the time, like deranged medieval kings."

She looks sad. "But it's even worse than that, kid. If you assassinate Leon, after that you would have to exile yourself from the Varger forever. A real exile. A wolf who assassinates a hunt leader is an abomination."

Abomination. That word again. It's following me around like a message from the universe. But what is the message supposed to be? That it's my destiny to kill Leon and become such an abomination?

Another wolf speaks up, "Bad hunt leaders are subjected to the judgment of the pack, a rending, why are we talking about overriding this? If Leon is truly such a bad hunt leader, it's the pack that renders judgment, not any single wolf."

Grandmother Wolf shakes her head. "Haven't you been paying attention, Sharpnose? Leon is compromised. His bad deeds as hunt leader are hidden from the pack." She points at me. "He has been sending proxies to kill her, after telling the pack that she was sent only into temporary exile. He has been squandering territory and sharing the gifts of the wolf with the unworthy."

My own grandmother says, sorrowfully, "I don't know all of my son's heart. He doesn't reach out to us the way you do. But to me it feels like he's unhappy. Trapped. Like things aren't going according to his plans, either. He might not be your real enemy, kid."

"I thought as much. But then who is my real enemy?"

Another wolf jumps in to say, "He's still a bad hunt leader. A bad hunt leader needs to die, end of story," which starts a period of lengthy bickering.

I fold my arms, drink the mead, sift through the arguments. Three main ideas: I should gather my allies and challenge Leon on the full moon according to ancient law. Or, I should gather my allies, but we should be encouraging the people to rend Leon as a bad hunt leader, according to ancient law. Or, screw the ancient law, I should just chop off his fricking head and let everything else take care of itself.

Grandmother Wolf turns away from all the bickering, and toward me. Her face is sad, compassionate. "Child. No matter what you do next, things are set in motion. Turning, change, upheaval. We call such a time Ragnarok. Ride the storm or be consumed by it."

"Ragnarok." The word resonates, echoes, like a noise dropped into a very deep well. Ragnarok rok rok rok rok rok. A flash of rapid-fire visions: apocalyptic destruction, storms and earthquakes and lightning, flames and battle, bombs and chemical weapons and every kind of ruination. And then a small and sudden hope as a single green shoot pokes its head up through the blasted earth.

I shake my head, feeling dizzy and strange. "A dream

within a dream," I say. "What's going on? Where am I? Is any of this real?"

Grandmother Wolf gives me a sympathetic look. "Visions can be confusing and difficult to sort out, child. Many of our people reject them, for that reason. But they can be a great gift as well." She takes my hands and clasps them together inside her hands, a gesture Pere Claude used to make, which meant something like solidarity. "The young have mostly forgotten, but if you act with us, we are there also with you. When even the strength of the wolf fails you, the strength of the ancestors remains."

"All-Grandmother," I say, seized with a sudden urgency. "My brother Justice spoke of Ragnarok, and he spoke of the Olvenar Brotherhood, do you know about them?"

"Olvenar?" Blackfur frowns. "That's an old name for the wolf-berserkers. You think I'm an asshole, small one, you should've met those guys."

More bickering ensues:

"Berserker means bear, there's no such thing as a wolf berserker."

"You know what I mean, don't be so fucking pedantic."

"They were an elite brotherhood of warriors. The fiercest."

"Not elite, just hopped up on drugs. Sent out to die first. The opposite of elite warriors."

"Pfft, they weren't warriors at all. Young, aimless wolf shifter men who did a lot of drugs, made complete asses of themselves, and got us all driven out of the Norse lands."

Grandmother Wolf howls once, a short barking howl that means: everybody but me, SHUT UP. Everyone does.

"The Úlfhéðnar, the wolf-warriors, changed over time," she says, giving the word its proper old Norse intonation. "In the beginning, the human kings valued our kind, and treated us as elite warriors. But warriors for hire. We accepted money, goods, land, political influence, to kill enemies who were not our own enemies. We became mercenaries."

"Hit men." I pounce on the concept excitedly, as if I've just picked up an important scent trail. "That's it. That's our original sin. The family curse. The family business. Killing people for money. And we keep getting pulled back into it. Mercenaries in the Norse lands, hunters of people in Louisiana, and Leon was an assassin in Los Angeles."

My grandmother winces. "Yeah, he did that for a little while, but he didn't feel so good about it."

"No, but he did it. Maybe he would do it again. Maybe all of us would always do it again, if we get desperate enough. Because killing is the one thing we're all really good at, right?"

"You got that right," says Blackfur, making a kind of cheers gesture toward me with his mead. "As you know very well, small deadly one."

Grandmother Wolf gives him a glance that shuts him up, then says, "This business of hunting and killing for others was lucrative. So lucrative that it began to dominate our own culture. We devoted more and more of our resources toward producing these wolf warriors. And the families that specialized in producing these warriors, they became our richest and most influential families."

"The Verreaux." I'm still on fire with the excitement of discovery. "That's us, right? We started out as one of those families that specialized in producing mercenaries?"

"Yes, although the name Verreaux came about long after the exile. Your family line can be traced back to a wealthy and influential family that specialized in producing wolf mercenaries.

"But over time our people became corrupted. They encouraged war, so that they could profit from it. Our young men, raised to be killers for hire, became arrogant, cruel, casually violent. And, worst of all, we began to make bitten wolves for this purpose. Always young men, and not always chosen with any great thought to what it would mean to give the power of the wolf to such a man."

"That sounds like the Olvenar all right."

"If someone is bringing any of that back, it's bad." She frowns. "More than bad. Following this path once got our people exiled from our home. And if it ends in disaster again, where can we go? The world is so much less free than it was."

Murmuring, consternation, more argument. For a moment all the ancestors turn away from me, converse in a low hum that I can't understand. Then they turn back toward me.

My own grandmother folds her hands around my hands, and Grandmother Wolf folds her hands around both of us.

"And though she be but little, she is fierce," says my grandmother. She smiles nostalgically. "Claude used to say that about me. It's from Shakespeare. I'll say it now about you, kid. And though she be but little, she is fierce."

"He's alive," I say, realizing suddenly. "My grandfather. He's not here. He's still alive."

"He's got one foot in the living world, yeah," my grandmother says, her face becoming sorrowful. "But he won't be able to help you. And I'm so sorry about that, kid. You've got no idea."

Grandmother Wolf says, "We charge you now with a deed. Stop these Olvenar before they ruin our people once again."

"Stop them entirely? Stop all of them?" I gape at her. "I mean, it's not that I don't want to, it's just a lot to ask of one wolf, don't you think?"

Blackfur chimes in. "Oh, well, small one, if you're not up to the challenge—"

"Shut up." I flash him and he laughs. "Fine, you made your point. It's just, I don't really know how to do that, you know? I can fight a particular Olvenar, but how do I get rid of their entire death cult? Where do I even start?"

"Start at the beginning," Grandmother Wolf says.

"New Orleans," I say. "Right? That's where I have to go next. Back to New Orleans."

But the dream world is already fading, tattering, turning dark and far away. I wake up mid-dream, confused. There was a party. I'm supposed to kill Leon, but also somehow not kill him? And I have to stop the Olvenar. Pretty sure about that one. And this requires going back to New Orleans.

Maybe it makes sense, as a destination. Sure. If by some chance Leon isn't the one trying to kill me, he ought to understand. And if he is my enemy, well, I should start practicing my axe moves.

I wake up entirely. I don't know how long I was asleep, one day or several, but the moon is back, the wolf is back. I'm a little worn out, but fully healed.

I pack up my cave and venture forth, looking for a road.

PART VI

THE BETTER ANGELS

22

COLD

Back to hitchhiking, and after a nice couple drops me off at the Tacoma bus station, I go up to the counter and show the clerk a decent pile of cash saved from working at the Surly Lumberjack.

"Can I get to New Orleans with this?"

"Probably. Let's see what the computer says."

Turns out it is possible, but it's going to take five days and the list of cities I need to pass through is enormous:

Seattle
Spokane
Billings
Fargo
Minneapolis
Milwaukee
Chicago
Indianapolis
Louisville
Nashville
Atlanta
Mobile
And, finally, New Orleans.

As the clerk hands me a pack of tickets, I have a strange feeling, almost like a premonition, that I won't make it all the way to New Orleans. But I don't have a better plan, so I shrug off the premonition of doom. Things might not work out? Yeah, story of my life.

It's a strange journey. Turns out, the named cities are just the ones where the bus parks for a while, or we have to change buses. But we actually stop briefly, to drop off and pick up passengers, in many smaller towns along the way. So many that I start to lose track.

Somewhere on the edge of Wyoming, we have a full two-hour gap before the bus leaves again. I climb off the bus stiff, blinking in the sharp, cold sunlight. Two hours is enough time to maybe get some real food, after surviving for days on what they have in bus station vending machines.

I walk rapidly away from the bus station, toward what looks like a downtown business area. It's an unexpectedly nice day for the middle of winter, the air crisp but still. Directly in the sun, it feels almost balmy. But the decor tells me it's Christmas season.

Christmas. Almost the new year.

My official term of exile is half over. This is both encouraging and depressing. I'm starting to feel like I've been wasting time. Hiding from my problems and responsibilities. The exile was a weakness. I should never have let it happen in the first place. Maybe I really shouldn't be the Varger hunt leader after all.

I pass an attractive older brick building, which is running some kind of holiday market, and venture inside. It smells strongly of cinnamon and apple cider. It's nice. Festive. But there's something sad about it. People are here, but not quite enough people. The vendors call out to me, making me very conscious of the cash I have stuffed into Grandma's boots. I feel so bad that I end up buying a Christmas-themed scarf, handmade, red and green stripes.

Most of the food booths are sugar-related, selling cookies and cinnamon rolls, but one booth is selling cheese balls and crackers, while another booth is selling homemade venison jerky, and it turns out it's not really so different from eating out of the vending machines after all.

I leave the slightly sad holiday market to walk around while I eat, discover a small waterfront park on the river, next to a boarded-up factory that still stinks vaguely of whatever industrial activity they used to do here.

The weather is becoming nicer by the minute, and I notice quite a few people enjoying the park. Head down closer to the river, but the closer I get, the more I become aware of something off, a wrong smell, something chemical. It reminds me of my childhood in some way. Is it something from the old factory, leaking into the river?

It's the smell of…the smell of…

"Gasoline," I say out loud.

I see a dark mass in the river, realize it's a young man floating, face down. Dead? Or not quite dead?

Panicked, I wade into the water without kicking off the boots, make my way toward the young man. Get my arms under him, turn him around so he's facing up, drag him to the bank, climb up onto the bank, start dragging him out of the water—

And then

The river

Explodes

Flame

Burning

Can't breathe

Can't see

Can't move

Agony

Drop to the ground instinctively. When the fireball has passed I roll, putting out the fires that smolder on my clothing, in my hair. Healing abilities working hard, racing itchy tingle up and down my body, but it hurts it hurts so bad…

Darkness.

I WAKE UP.

Claustrophobic, frantic, clawing at things that bind me, trap me, ropes, cords, chains, hell, it's hell, I've been sent…

Inhale. Hospital. Misery and disinfectant, sterile white walls and tile floor, splash of blood where I ripped a needle out of my flesh. The nightmare fades a little and I start to make sense of my situation. I was strapped to that hospital bed. The straps are in tatters now. The floor is covered in gauze wrappings and a thick layer of my own skin. Everything stinks.

The newly revealed skin of my arms is reddish, unfreckled, patched with scars. My arms look thin, muscles stringy.

I can guess what happened although I don't remember it. Badly burned, I was wrapped head to toe in sterile gauze and taken to this hospital. Werewolf healing abilities mean I recovered from otherwise deadly injuries in—hours? Days? Weeks? I don't even know.

Why was I strapped to the bed?

Were they having trouble keeping me still?

Do they know something about me?

Are there Olvenar waiting outside that door?

I have to get out of here. The last thing I need to do is to show up on somebody's list of "miracle patients."

Also, if I stick around they might want to get paid money and I'm pretty sure the cash in my boots is not enough to pay for hospital care.

Cash in my boots, right, are Grandma's boots here? Did they survive the fire? I sniff around, find a locked cabinet that smells like it might have my things inside, break the lock, pull out my things.

Crispy and fragmented. Some clothes, unwearable, but no backpack and no Grandma's boots. Shit. I shove everything back into the cabinet, close it.

A young male doctor comes rushing into the room, does a double take.

"My God. You're…you're walking around. How is that… my God."

"Where are my things?" My voice comes out in a low, clogged rumble. I cough, spit something like thick phlegm into a tissue.

He shakes his head. "It's all in there. Everything you were wearing."

"My boots?" I croak out.

"No, no shoes or boots."

"Damn." I sigh heavily and sit down on the edge of the bed, overcome with a moment of despair. The Olvenar probably have my boots now. They can track me by scent. I need to get out of here.

"Miss, I don't—you seem almost completely healed, I don't understand."

I don't have time for this. I flash him. "Doctor, give me your clothes."

He looks confused. Shakes his head. "I don't understand."

Damn.

If I'm too weak even to flash this guy, I'm gonna die.

Okay, focus. I can do this. I've done it so often. I've done it without even meaning to.

I make note of the name on his badge. Catch his gaze. Hold it. Pour everything into it. "Doctor. Ryan. Everest. You need to give me your clothes. Right now."

"Okay, but I don't understand." He leans down to take off his shoes, hands them to me. "You were in a coma." He takes off his belt, jeans. Hands the jeans and belt to me in a unit.

He's not a huge guy, but they're still too big. If I roll up the cuffs and put the belt on the smallest hole, I can manage it, I think. Shoes much too large, but I'm used to that, when I was a child in the cult we always wore shoes that were too big and stuffed paper into the toes.

"You had third and even fourth degree burns over most of your body."

White doctor coat comes next.

"You were going to be in the hospital for months if you recovered at all. We thought you were going to die."

Blue button-down shirt, no tie. He's wearing a T-shirt underneath.

"We hoped you would die, honestly, nothing personal, but a Jane Doe requiring expensive long-term care is a nightmare for any hospital. They cut the amount of national support we get for that kind of thing, and it was never enough in the first place."

Untucked, his shirt hangs halfway down my thighs. I have no idea what I look like. Ridiculous, I assume. I hope the white doctor's coat covers it up a bit.

The back pocket of his jeans has a slim wallet inside, minimal, just a Colorado driver's license, single credit card, some cash. Not much cash. Probably not enough to get me all the way to New Orleans.

I pocket the cash and put his wallet on a table. He's a doctor, he can afford it. Probably.

He shakes himself, seems to wake up a little. "Miss? Why are you wearing my clothes?"

"You gave me your clothes." My throat clogs up with that phlegmy substance again and I start coughing, gurgle it up into a tissue. Gross. I grab a large handful of tissues and stuff them into the pocket of the white lab coat.

"I…gave you my clothes?"

I find his gaze again. Think about him saying, *We hoped you would die, honestly, nothing personal.* "Doctor Ryan Everest, you are tired and you need a nap." I yawn, just to get the point across. He yawns in return. Slumps into a chair.

"I've been on duty for almost ten hours today already," he says. He yawns again. Eyes droop. "We're understaffed. There's just so much going around these days…"

A quick snore and I slip out of the room.

Outside in the corridor I see a digital clock that tells me it's eight p.m. Late but not too late. Dark. Nobody in the halls. I head to the end of the hall, the stairway, fire exit. At the bottom, one of those doors that claims an alarm will sound.

I push.

No alarm. There never is.

Outside. Bitterly cold in just the white doctor's coat. Damn I miss my wool poncho. I shiver and try to stay out of the wind, move away from the hospital as quickly as possible in case somebody's looking for me. I need to swap this doctor's coat for something warmer and less conspicuous.

Where am I, anyway? The driver's license said Colorado and this is obviously a big city, not the small town I got burned in. Denver?

How am I going to get from Denver to New Orleans without an ID or money? Hitchhiking? I guess. Or, if that whole Hitchhiking Bandit thing makes it too weird I can…I guess I could walk. It'll take a while to get there, but I already walked across the country once, I might as well do it again.

Okay, that's settled, if all else fails, I'm walking to New Orleans. Wait, that's a song, isn't it? Which reminds me of Steph's dad, which reminds me of Steph, which reminds me of all my friends I might never see again, Varger or not, and my eyes start welling up with tears and I just want to stop moving for a moment, sob until I'm done sobbing, but…

I can't stop moving.

I can't.

I'm hungry, though. I don't think I can make it all the way to New Orleans without a meal. Healing the burns really depleted me. I need meat protein. Without it, I could enter what the Varger call a death spiral: a feedback loop where you're too weak to hunt, so you keep getting weaker, and less able to hunt, until you die of starvation. It rarely happens in the modern world, where ready-to-eat food is plentiful if you're not too picky about scavenging, but it can still happen. According to the pere diaries my great-great grandfather died that way.

Well. I'm not too proud to dumpster dive.

The wind picks up and it gets colder. Sharp, like tiny knives stabbing at my skin. In the mountains, to escape the cold, I went to wolf form. That's not an option right now. It takes energy to shift, and I'm spent. Feels like the new moon. Dark. Hopeless.

I spot a convenience store, head inside. A heater blasts warm air on the threshold and I stand basking for a moment.

"Hey, you, get out of the doorway." The clerk is gruff, angry. I step fully into the store.

"Sorry," I try to say, but my throat fills up with that gross phlegmy stuff and the word comes out all strangled and weird. I cough.

"Are you sick? If you're sick you've got to get out of here."

"I'm not sick."

I go to the coffee station, pour a large coffee and empty a hot chocolate packet into it.

"Hey, I saw that!" the clerk says. "You have to pay for both the coffee and the hot chocolate."

I turn around, make eye contact, nod. I don't have a lot of (stolen) money but I do have enough for that. I bring the coffee and chocolate up to the hot food case up front. Jackpot, they've still got chicken tenders warming under the heat lamp. They look a little sad, like they've been there all day, but they're boneless, exactly what I need.

I point at the case. "Chicken, please?" My voice goes all

rumbly again, but I'm pointing and he seems to understand me.

He glares. "You want chicken? You got the money?"

I pull out a twenty, hold it up.

His scowl intensifies, as if somehow he's more mad that I can pay for it. As if he was really looking forward to kicking me out. But, with no ready excuse to do otherwise, he sells me the items, gives me change, deliberately avoids contacting my hands. I guess my hands do look a little weird, covered in scars and kind of gnarly. But it doesn't hurt you to touch somebody's scars. No open wounds or anything. I'm really not sure why he's acting so weird. I'm reminded, all of a sudden, of Old Testament Bible verses about leprosy.

Turning to go, food and drink and change all gathered in my hands, he blurts out, "Was it a meth lab?"

I turn back around. Give him a confused look. "Huh?"

"Did your meth lab catch on fire? Is that what happened to you?"

I try to think of a bitingly sarcastic response that can be expressed in less than five words, give up and shake my head with a sigh. "Church camp fire." Take my food and leave in a bad mood.

Damn I forgot how cold it was outside. Am I in real danger of freezing to death? I don't even know. I'm not used to this level of cold, but maybe it's just unpleasant, not deadly. I've spent most of my time in more temperate climates. I don't know how to evaluate the risks of extreme cold.

I drink the coffee and hot chocolate mixture first. I'm hoping the coffee helps me stay awake until I can find a safe place to sleep, but even though I like it, coffee never seems to do much to keep me awake. Werewolf metabolism. The sugar from the hot chocolate does make me feel a little more perky.

Now the chicken tenders. And when I bite into the first one, I have the weirdest experience. Part of me is so gratified, shaking with relief to be getting meat protein. But part of me is instantly terrified. Horrified. Overcome with shock.

Because when I start to chew—

My teeth feel kinda loose.

They don't fall out, not right now. But they're tormenting me with a visceral sense that they could fall out, that part of the death spiral might include losing teeth.

When I first saw Leon, his wolf was maybe twenty years gone by that point, and he was dying of cancer. He was missing several teeth.

Goddamn it.

I saved him by restoring his wolf and now I probably have to kill him.

Keep walking. It feels warmer when I'm walking. But I still haven't seen a place to spend the night. What am I even looking for? Abandoned building? Homeless shelter? But I don't know this town, and I don't have a phone or anything, I don't even know how I'd find a homeless shelter.

What about a highway, a place I could hitchhike? I probably won't freeze to death in somebody's car. Or maybe a bus station? A soup kitchen? A church? I've really never been in a situation like this before. Alone, in the winter, with the wolf severely depleted. It's scary and depressing.

What I really need is a kind person. Just a person who's nice enough to look on their phone, find out where the shelter is, point me in the right direction. When I left New Harmony, it was Steph who saved me. I didn't even have my wolf yet. I just ran away and straight into the path of a woman who took me in, helped me.

Damn it. Other people have helped me since then, other people might help me in the future, but nobody will ever help me quite as much, for as little reason, as Steph did. I simply crossed her path, entirely at random, and she saw I was in need, and she helped me.

I wipe away unexpected tears. I hope she's okay. If Leon has hurt her in any way, I really am going to kill him, no joke.

I bite into the second chicken tender and something else happens, even weirder than the loose-feeling teeth. It's almost like my tongue has forgotten how to chew, my throat has forgotten how to swallow. The first bite of chicken tender seems to catch high in my throat and I gag on it, start choking as if I'm going to throw up.

I rush to a planter full of dead flowers and start gagging up half-chewed pieces of chicken and a thick, viscous liquid that might be my own saliva, plus more of that white-gray phlegmy tissue. It feels almost like my throat has stopped working, as if I'm choking on the scar tissue.

Pant, pant, pant, make sure I'm still breathing. Okay. I'm not going to suffocate immediately.

But damn it. If I can't even swallow a few bites of chicken, I'm going to enter the death spiral sooner than I thought. This is bad. This is really bad.

But what can I do about it? Healing takes time. So I do my best to clean myself up, and, not knowing what else to do, start walking again. It's dark and cold, not many people on the street. When I do pass other people, either they don't seem to notice me at all, or their faces twist in repulsion and they look away.

What the hell do I look like?

I get the feeling it can't be good.

I rub my hands over my head, realize how cold my head is, how weird my hair feels, much of it burned off. I should get a hat. Maybe a hat would make me look more normal and also keep me from freezing to death.

I don't know where a person would get a hat this time of night. Or a sweater. If I had a warm enough sweater, another layer of socks, maybe I could make it through the night. Then, in the morning, things will be different, more clear.

Are there late night thrift shops?

Without thinking about it, I've been following something: recent scent trails of people. Maybe a section of town with nightlife? People still awake, who probably have phones, maybe know the city, where a homeless shelter might be found?

Then, like magic, I'm in a hipster part of town. Historic buildings, pubs with clever names. Music venues, cocktail bars, night spots. People.

Nobody wants to talk to me. I get it. They're used to weird, shabby people asking them for money, and if you don't want to give to panhandlers, it's simplest to just act like you don't see them. It can be exhausting to interact with every random person in an urban environment who wants to talk to you. Just saying "sorry, no" over and over gets to be such an emotional burden. Before the wolf, sometimes I would even get harassed and threatened by panhandlers.

But now, from this side of things, I feel how frustrating and dehumanizing it is to have people act like you don't exist.

And I don't have a good solution. Because if I ever get out of this, if I'm ever on the other side of things again, I'll probably go back to just ignoring most of the people who approach me randomly on the street.

Then, a miracle: thrift store with a "FREE" box outside. Among the thrashed paperback bestsellers and chipped coffee cups, I strike gold: a hooded sweatshirt commemorating that time the Denver Broncos played the Seattle Seahawks in the Super Bowl (Seahawks won), and a big mustard-yellow wool sweater.

Hoodie, then sweater. The white doctor's coat goes into the free bin. With the hoodie snugged up around my head I feel almost warm. Can I keep this up all night? Just wander around aimlessly until the morning? Do I have the strength for that? I'm already feeling kind of worn out, like the thing I really want to do is curl up somewhere warm to sleep. But there isn't anywhere warm to sleep. Nowhere safe.

Wait.

Smell of male bitten wolf. Three of them. I'm being followed. And they remind me of Justice, that faint residue of berserker drugs lingering in the sweat.

Olvenar. They're here. And they're tracking me.

23

TRAPPED

No. No way. Not Olvenar, not right now. I'm too weak to hunt, let alone fight other werewolves. I don't have any weapons. I don't have any allies. I don't have the wolf. I don't have anything.

When even the strength of the wolf fails you, the strength of the ancestors remains.

These words dance across my mind, tantalizing, like the lyrics of a song I can't place. The strength of the ancestors? What would that even be?

Well, whatever it is, right now, I need it. Come on, wolfy ancestors, are you more use than the Christian god? Help me out now.

I turn a corner, dark alley, dead end. Turn around to face my enemies, make as much of a stand as possible. Go down fighting, at least.

Three Olvenar swagger into the other end of the alley. Dressed a bit like Justice was, in black T-shirts and long black coats. One of them holds up a plastic bag with my burned clothes from the hospital.

"Abomination. We've got something of yours."

"If I wanted that shit I would have taken it." I try to sound defiant but my voice comes out in a weird gurgling rumble. I cough and spit more of that white, phlegmy substance. The Olvenar don't have my boots, which probably means somebody else does. Who?

"You look a wreck," one says, with a smug smile. "Are you even up for a fight? This is going to be way too easy."

I close my eyes for a moment, gathering my will. Ancestors, are you there? Grandmother, are you there?

Movement on the air, half-glimpsed scent, echo of a memory

When all other strengths fail you we are there

And suddenly it all seems so clear. When all else fails, a dominance stare. And behind me, the will of the ancestors.

Open my eyes, make hard eye contact with one of the Olvenar, the one in front who's acting like their leader.

"Stop," I say. "Go away."

He blinks, confused, and I find the eyes of the second one. "Stop. Go home."

The third takes a step forward, growling. "Abomination, those witchy she-wolf tricks won't work on me—"

"Stop. Go."

He shakes his head in confusion and turns away from me. All three turned away, now, in a crucial moment, but how do I fight them, where do I go now?

Half a breath of weird dark quiet, and something, like a voice but not a voice, coming from behind me:

Duck

Drop to my knees, and there it is, a hole in the wall of an abandoned building, big enough for me to scoot through, maybe too small for them.

All the way to the ground, in a position like the one the Varger call alligator, using only hands and feet to move, I enter the hole into the derelict building. They'll smell where I've gone, so I have to keep moving.

The building is undergoing renovations of some kind, interior gutted out. I move through empty, dusty spaces until the back exit dumps me out into another alleyway.

I need to find a large group of regular people. I don't think the Olvenar will attack openly if I'm surrounded by civilians.

Sounds of live rock music reach my ears. Live music means crowds, and I head toward the sound. Spot some men outside a medium-sized brick building, gathered near what looks like a side door of a theater. Black leather and denim, huddled, smoke fumes hovering thick in the cold air.

As I approach, one of the men, a medium-build Black man in his forties or fifties, says, "No change, kid, sorry." He pauses, looks me over, gets an expression of pity. "I've got half a tuna sandwich, you want half a tuna sandwich?"

I nod. "Yes please." My voice still has that weird, rough, phlegmy sound, and I'm not entirely sure I'll be able to swallow any food, but I hold out a hand. He drops the half tuna sandwich into it. I chomp down hungrily. It's not the best tuna sandwich I've ever had but it's far from the worst. It's soft and the small pieces seem to go right down without any of those chewing or swallowing problems. I make eye contact with the guy who gave it to me.

"Thank you." I'm learning to talk around that weird feeling in my throat. It kind of hurts to talk, and my voice sounds weird, not like my own, but I can form words. "Can I see the show?"

"Sorry kid, it's sold out." He shrugs. "It's almost over anyway."

"Okay. Thanks."

I turn to leave, try to find somewhere else to be.

Then a lot of things happen all in the same moment.

One, I'm not eager to leave. So, in leaving, I move slowly.

Two, movement catches my eye. One of the smoking men

has been leaning against a stacked pile of boxes, and when he moves, the pile becomes unstable.

Three, one of the suddenly unstable boxes is about to land on the head of the guy who gave me a sandwich.

Four, with a short burst of wolf speed and strength, I catch the unstable box and place it on the ground, then make sure the other boxes get stabilized again.

All of this takes a few seconds, tops. But sandwich guy notices. He nods thoughtfully at me. "Thanks for saving the back of my head."

"Thanks for the sandwich."

He laughs. "Payback, right? You must be a lot stronger than you look, kid."

"I'm not sick."

"No? Who said you were?"

"People think I look sick. But these are just scars."

"What's your name?"

"Ab—" I start to say Abby, but break down in a coughing fit. He nods.

"Abe. I'm Luke. Nice to meet you." He shakes my hand. "Do you want a job, Abe?"

I nod. I don't know what kind of job he's offering, but Luke is one of those people, like Steph, who inspires instant trust. And I still believe my best chance of escaping the Olvenar involves keeping a lot of regular people around.

Luke escorts me into the backstage area of the venue, which seems about the size of the Paramount in Seattle, which seats close to 3,000 people. I don't recognize the band, but they sound like 1990s rock. Maybe a legacy band, old school? The men on stage don't look young, except for the dark-haired guy playing saxophone.

Luke brings me into a small room, hands me a knit cap with the band logo on it: The Better Angels, logo reminiscent of the one for the rock musical *Jesus Christ Superstar*.

"Your head looks cold, if you want to wear the cap. Do you know the band?"

"Sorry. No."

"You might be too young. The Angels were pretty big in the nineties, but they broke up for a while. This is a revival tour." He holds up a tour T-shirt, where the back has all the cities listed. "We're here, in Denver, see? Next, we're going to a bunch of smaller cities, and we end with a festival in Las Vegas."

I run my fingers over the slightly raised ink of the printing. It seems perfect. Time to recover and I'll be in a different city just about every single day, plus, routinely surrounded by large crowds. It's almost too perfect. Like a gift. From the ancestors? Is that the kind of thing they can do?

"I'm in."

"Okay, Abe, that's great. Except, first, I gotta ask. Do you have a drug problem?"

"No. Sir. I don't."

"Figured." Slight smile. "That's why you're getting this job right now, because your predecessor had a drug problem. He was unreliable. Tonight he took off to get dinner, supposedly, and he never came back."

"You don't think he was attacked? Or had an emergency?"

He shakes his head. "Sadly, no. He's pulled this before, flaking out on the second part of his shift, only to show up in the morning at the motel, thinking he's still on the crew. And we keep letting him back in, just docking his pay for the hours he was supposed to work and didn't, because otherwise we were even more shorthanded. But if he pulls that tomorrow morning, I'm going to tell him he's off the crew." Smile. "If you're still with us after tonight, anyway. If you've never done this kind of work before, maybe you'll hate it. Now, what we're gonna do is, we both go watch the rest of the show from the sidelines. I've got this headset, here's one for you. I'm your

immediate—well, I don't want to say boss, I'm not your
boss—"

"Leader." Barely stop myself from saying "hunt leader."

"Yeah." He smiles. "That's right. Oh, do you have problems climbing ladders or stairways? Vertigo or anything similar?"

"No."

"Okay, good. Now, you operate the headset like this." He demonstrates, does a sound check, and, satisfied, leads me to an area off to the side of the stage, where we get to watch the last forty minutes of the concert. During this time, I am mostly doing band member support: water, towels, quick blast of air with a little handheld fan, sometimes fix makeup or clothes. Sometimes Luke wants me to haul something.

I've done this kind of thing for Edison's band, mostly when they were rehearsing, and it feels easy and kind of fun.

The band mostly doesn't seem to notice me, until the point when I'm toweling off the face of the lead singer after the last song of the regular set list and before the first encore. The singer frowns at me, and Luke says, "New junior roadie I hired when Gareth didn't come back after his dinner break. Name's Abe."

The singer nods, and I wipe the sweat from his face, which comes off with a good deal of medium-toned foundation. I hold up the towel, not sure how to phrase my question.

He frowns. "Mirror?"

I hold one up and he studies himself or a moment. "No, we can leave it. I don't want to be wearing that heavy stage makeup when we exit the venue. Maybe a little powder?"

I dust his face with a light color-correcting anti-shine powder, while he sips enhanced water drink through a straw. He looks at Luke. "Timing?"

Luke glances at his watch. "Forty seconds."

The cheers grow and grow. The singer inhales and exhales deeply, with conscious effort, like someone doing yoga, his eyes on Luke, who finally nods. The singer ventures back out onto the stage to raucous cheers.

"That's Matthew, Matt," Luke tells me, gesturing at the singer. "You'll want to remember him. He's not bossy or anything like that, but he is the boss, if you get me." I nod.

For the next few songs I don't have as much to do, so I start really paying attention to the music. The crowd reaction tells me these are some of their most popular songs. And now I'm starting to get an uncomfortable vibe.

Lyrics about faith and redemption. Gospel song. Johnny Cash number where he talks about God.

I'm very nearly sure of it: this is a Christian rock band.

Part of me wants to run away screaming in horror. But I'm too worn out. Right now I really need this gig. I need shelter, food and a safe place to sleep. And Christians aren't always terrible. Steph is a Christian, pretty much, and Luke seems like a genuinely nice guy.

I can stick it out for a few weeks, can't I? Right at the moment I don't have a lot of other options.

The concert ends and the crowd starts leaving. Luke gestures at me and we begin breaking down and moving out. We communicate so well through hand gestures, most of the time he doesn't bother using the headset. I don't speak formal sign language, but I recognize that he is signing, and even though I don't get the full nuance of what he's saying, the wolf part of me is very attuned to meanings conveyed through gestures and body language, so overall we communicate pretty well.

After we get everything loaded onto the bus and the trailer, he taps me on the shoulder, pulls me aside.

"That was good work, Abe. You speak ASL?"

"No. Body language."

He nods. Gets sad for a moment, taps his ears. "After thirty years in the rock biz, my hearing is kinda shot." Then he brightens. "But we can teach you ASL. What do you say? Are you in for the next few weeks?"

I nod. "Yeah."

"Great. Now, we're going to drive this bus out to the motel. And you have a choice. You can sleep on the bus, it's pretty comfortable. The seats in the back fold down to make a bed and there's a little bathroom and a propane space heater. Or you can share a hotel room with me."

"Bus."

He laughs a little. "Well. You answered that pretty quickly, Abe. Are you worried I snore?"

No, I'm worried the Olvenar can scent track me if I get out of the bus.

What I say is, "Night terrors." This isn't even a lie.

"What? Is that like nightmares?"

"Yeah. Sometimes I wake up screaming."

"You don't say." He frowns. "Is that—"

"After the accident."

Long pause, then he says, "Okay, Abe, I get you. Bus it is."

We head out to the bus. He introduces me as "Abe, the new junior roadie" to anyone who seems curious. Mostly they nod and go back to whatever they were doing. But the lead singer of the younger band, a dark-haired guy named Andrew, gets a bit hostile. "You're not a druggie, are you?"

"No. Just a burn victim."

He has the decency to look slightly embarrassed, and leaves me alone after that.

We drive the bus, and its trailer, to a plain-looking motel on the outskirts of town. Maybe Christian bands don't believe in spending a lot of money on hotel rooms.

Luke shows me how to fold down the seats, gives me a pile of blankets, turns on the space heater, shows me where the weird little bathroom is found. Easy to miss, because it looks like part of the rear exit.

And now I'm cocooned in blankets and everything is warm and cozy and my eyelids start drooping.

"Thank you," I tell him. "I'm okay."

"See you in the morning, Abe," he says. "God be with you."

Oh. Yeah. Right. I'm surrounded by Christians.

Maybe I can't stick this out after all.

24

THE BETTER ANGELS

I wake up.

Morning, early, cold, where am I—

Bus, right. I spent the night on the tour bus for a couple of Christian rock bands. The drummer for the younger band, The Stones Rolled, is on the bus, staring at me, obviously startled. He holds out his hands in a placating gesture.

"It's okay, buddy. You spent the night on our bus instead of freezing to death, no problem. You can just pack up and leave and I'll pretend I didn't see anything."

Instinctively I raise the blanket as if to cover myself, but I'm not naked. I shake my head. "I'm your new roadie. Luke hired me last night." I cough.

"You're Abe? But I thought—are you, uh, are you…a girl or a boy?"

"Why does it matter?"

He gets really uncomfortable. "It's just. I mean. We're a Christian band. Two Christian bands."

"Yeah?"

"We can't have…immorality. On the tour."

"Immorality?" Shit. Last night, Luke thought I said my name was Abe and I guess he thought I was male. But in the cold light of day, I probably look like a girl again. Or, like a trans boy. Lord knows these Christians can't have that. Well, I'm not about to make it easy for them. If they're going to fire me right away because of anti-trans bigotry, I'm gonna make them say it out loud. "What kind of immorality?"

He gets really uncomfortable. "You know. Sexual immorality?"

"Sex? You think I want to have sex with you? Why would you think that?" I cough harder and some of that weird phlegm bubbles up in the back of my throat, I find a tissue to cough into.

He recoils. "No! No, I mean. I'm sorry. You're not a girl, now that I hear your voice it's really obvious. What happened to you?"

"What do you mean?" I know what he means. I'm going to make him say it.

"I mean…uh…why do you look like that?"

"I was in a fire."

"Oh. I'm sorry. That sounds…bad."

"I was in a coma. They didn't think I'd wake up. But I did."

He brightens. "So it was a miracle!"

"If you want to see it that way."

Luke steps onto the bus. "Morning, Abe." He holds up a hotel key card. "I thought you might want to shower before we leave. Room 218."

"That's nice of you, but I don't have clean clothes to put on after."

"I got you." He holds out a plastic bag. "These sweats were kinda cheap, I guess, anyway they shrunk up a lot the first time I washed them. I was going to donate them to the Goodwill, but if you want them, they're yours. I figure they'd just about fit you."

"Thanks." I take the bag, recognize the smell of his detergent.

"When you're done, you can find me in the lobby or out here."

The drummer seems to have decided I'm okay. "Abe? Nice to meet you. I'm Philip."

He shakes my hand in a hearty way. I already know I don't have particularly feminine hands even when they're not scarred. I give the squeeze a tiny bit of wolf strength, just to be annoying, and he winces, but also seems reassured. Because a grip-off is very much a guy thing.

Other members of the bands and road crew are starting to show up, pack things, move them around. We don't talk much. Andrew, lead singer of the Stones, seems hungover. He walks on wearing dark glasses, grunts at everyone, plops into a seat at the front, starts snoring right away.

Luke counts heads. "Okay, we're all here, let's start getting the equipment secured."

But several people aren't on the bus, including Matthew, the Angels singer.

"Where's everyone else?" I ask.

"Matt, his wife Joanna, and their daughter Marta take their own van. Talitha and Mary, backup singers for the Angels, and Jordan, the other singer for Stones, are on the women's bus along with Maggie and Liz from the crew."

"There's a 'women's bus'?" The disgust in my voice is obvious.

Luke grimaces. "I know what you're thinking, Abe, but it's not like that. The women's bus is a motor home. It's smaller than ours but much nicer. Joanna used to ride on the women's bus, before she and Matt were married. It was her idea. She didn't like how…crude…we could get over here. And it prevented the appearance of immorality."

If I hear the word "immorality" one more time I'm gonna run away screaming, I don't care how badly I need this job.

Peter, saxophonist for the Angels, reaches out to tap me on

the shoulder and I flinch. "Oh, sorry," he says. "Do your scars hurt?"

"Sometimes. I don't mean to be rude, but, please don't touch me when I'm not expecting it."

"No problem." He frowns. "Now I forgot what I was going to ask you."

"Why don't you go get your shower, Abe," Luke says.

I nod and take off. The motel turns out to be low end, the kind of place where the surfaces seem perpetually damp and the toiletries smell like despair. But it's nice to have a shower. Hot water and a towel and clean clothes to wear afterward.

I'm thinking about all this, about the levels of deprivation that were commonplace in the cult, that became commonplace again after I was exiled. Really basic things like food and shelter became incredible luxuries. So how can I be snobby about the toiletries?

But I am. I can't help it. The wolves on the track and chase crew always favored scent-free but very fine toiletries, French soaps and things like that. That's what I got used to.

This makes me think of Babette, who was, among other things, an amateur parfumer who had spent time in Paris. She was the best scent tracker I ever knew except for our mentor Etienne.

Is she really out there running a motorcycle gang called the Rude Bitches? It seems so unlikely, except Babette did always have a kind of lawless, wild quality. She was a good time party girl when I knew her. But Etienne getting killed changed her, maybe forever.

Switch off the shower. Hope Babette is all right. Towel off, wrap another towel around me, get out into the steamy bathroom, wipe the steam off the mirror.

Bon Dieu.

I almost forgot, right now I probably look like some kind of half-melted horror movie monster. This is my first really good look at my own face after the accident, and it's so much worse than I imagined. Red, raw skin, criss-crossed with white scar tissue, stretched across my skull in disturbingly gaunt lines. It looks so bad, I wonder how long it'll take me to heal. Some of these scars might even be permanent.

My hair is the worst. That's what really makes me look like a freak. It's nearly all burned off, but not to a clean, bald look. It's patchy and weird, with random longer bits and shorter bits and entirely gone scar-tissue bits. Like a horror movie monster, Virginia Madsen at the end of the original *Candyman* movie, when she shows up in the mirror. Maybe even worse.

Luke left his electric razor plugged in and I decide to use it on the remainder of my hair. It does a great job. My head looks instantly less weird with all the longer hair shaved down to a fuzz. I make faces into the mirror, fascinated by the way the scarring and lack of freckles make me look so much not like myself. Grotesque, but, maybe I kinda look like Deadpool?

Not that I would expect a couple of Christian bands to notice that. They're probably not allowed to watch *Deadpool*. It was rated R and had a lot of...immorality.

Still, there are advantages to looking so incredibly not like myself. Nobody's going to spot me in a random online clip and think, "that's the abomination right there."

I get dressed in the gifted sweats. Clean, oversized, unisex. I wish I had a sports bra or something. After the accident I'm a lot smaller than usual on top, so I'm not sure anyone will actually notice boobs under bulky men's clothing. But it would get awkward if they did.

Am I really going to do this? Actively pretend to be a dude? Maybe I should just run. Take cash for a single night's work, explain it all to Luke: I didn't realize you thought I was male, and I'm not about to ride on the women's bus, thanks, see ya.

But then I remember how it felt to be at the end of that alley with the Olvenar on the other side. How it felt to be really worried that I would lose a fight, even against as pathetic an enemy as that. I remember what it felt like to be scared I was going to die. A strange nervous anticipation: whatever death is, whatever really happens, pretty soon I'm gonna know. But also despair and a sense of wrongness.

I don't want to leave the fight. It's not time for me to leave the fight.

I rub my chin. It's pretty obvious I can't grow a beard, but with all the scar tissue there, maybe that's not so strange. If you look really close at me, you might see me as a girl. But you'd have to look close. And right now, I don't think anybody wants to look that close.

Outside, I find Luke drinking a large coffee. "I like the hair," he says.

"Thanks." I rub the fuzz self-consciously before replacing the knit hat. "I borrowed your razor, was that okay?"

"It's fine, Abe. You can borrow my razor any time. I guess I'll go finish getting out of the room, and then we'll be ready to go."

25

APPROXIMATELY THE SIZE OF PRINCE

My first day on the tour bus goes pretty smoothly. Luke gets me coffee and a breakfast sandwich. The sandwich prompts a couple of panicky moments where I think I'm getting a return of the can't-swallow thing, but it passes, and with the coffee to wash it down, I manage to eat.

It's warm on the bus and I drop off to sleep again before we've even pulled onto the freeway. My dreams are vivid but disjointed, nothing I remember upon waking, except for a vague sense of having been somewhere far away.

During our first rest area stop I have a close call when, out of habit, I start heading toward the women's restroom. But I catch myself in time and go to the men's instead. It's a single-occupancy restroom anyway. Why bother gendering a single-person restroom? The only difference is that this one has both a urinal and a sit-down toilet.

If I'm going to be a man for a while, I wonder if I need to figure out a way to urinate standing up. Or maybe I can just always make sure to use a private stall? I have other reasons to want a private stall, so maybe it won't make people too suspicious.

Back on the bus for a few more hours of driving, and I mostly sleep through that, too.

Now here we are in a new town, Oklahoma City. A couple of hours moving stuff, then a dinner break. Luke tells me, "Go ahead and explore the city, but make sure you come back by five thirty."

"Do you have a watch I can borrow?"

"You don't have a phone?"

"Sorry, no." I shrug, show him my empty hands. "I kinda don't have anything."

"Oh. Right." He thinks. "Well, you need a phone. For while you're on the tour, at least. Just for today, take mine." He hands it over. "The lock code is jesussavedme, two esses, all one word. The numbers of the rest of the crew are all programmed in there already if you need help."

"Thanks, Luke." I put the phone in the pocket of my sweatshirt, although I wince a little at the idea of typing his passcode. I guess I don't need to unlock the phone to use it like a pocket watch. "See you at five thirty."

"Oh, and, I know I paid you cash for last night, here's the rest of your pay for the next two weeks."

"All cash, no feds," I say, as I pocket the money next to the phone. But he frowns.

"No feds? You mean, no federal taxes? I pay my taxes, Abe."

"Sorry, it was something an old employer of mine used to say."

The frown deepens. "Did this employer pay his taxes?"

"I don't know. I wasn't his accountant. He wasn't dishonest. He was just paranoid and hated paperwork."

Small, reluctant smile. "All right, Abe. I think I get you. But we do things above the board here. We're Christians, we have an example to set."

I glance away, hiding my automatic eye-roll. "Thanks. I need to buy a toothbrush."

Oklahoma City surprises me for how large it seems, given that I've never really heard much about it. It's not famous for anything, I guess. But it's large enough to have Indian food and cheap clothing stores. With my head shaved and the hat on, people don't have quite such an extreme reaction to my appearance. Some people give me a second look, or an expression of distaste or pity, but most people don't seem to notice me at all.

When it comes to clothes I hit the jackpot: a hipster vintage shop where I'm greeted by a mannequin dressed in a sharp-looking three-piece suit of dark gray that looks small enough to fit me.

I stroke the fabric. It's much finer wool than I have any right to expect and I start to get worried I won't be able to afford it, even vintage. But when I find the price tag, I see it's still well within my budget.

Suddenly the clerk is standing behind me. "I heard Prince wore that," she says.

I'm pretty sure he didn't, although I don't know what Prince smelled like, so I can't be sure. I turn around to look at her. "Are you trying to upsell me?"

She laughs. "No, I just figured your next move was going to be a lowball offer. It's kinda expensive compared to our other stuff. But it's real Italian wool, so it's, like a thousand dollars new. Two thousand maybe. You are getting a real bargain there."

"Hmm." I take the jacket portion off the mannequin, start examining it closely for damage.

"It's just, we don't get a lot of men in here who can wear a suit this small." She laughs again. "That's why I said that about Prince. He was only five foot two, you know?"

I'm not sure if I did know that, but I nod. "Can I try it on?"

"Of course." She helps me take it off the mannequin and points me to the dressing room. It fits, a bit large. The man who wore this was small but not quite as small as me (or, apparently, Prince). He didn't wear it often. It smells more like the store than a person.

Perfect.

I emerge from the dressing room wearing it and the clerk gets all excited to "complete my look," runs around finding me a vintage fedora and a pair of shoes that look like classic men's business dress shoes, but with a thick two-inch platform sole on the bottom.

At a certain point, she stops, gives me a serious, eye-contact look. Glances around as if to make sure we're alone and not under camera. Drops her voice to a whisper.

"Hey, um, do you want a binder?"

Binder? Oh, breast binder, that's probably what she means. In the New Harmony cult, all of us old enough to have boobs wore them, but in the outside world, it's often trans men who wear them.

I nod. "Thank you. Yes. Please."

The combination of binder and suit vest works well to make my torso look fundamentally dude-shaped. I think I've got Abe's ideal look. Slouchy sweatsuits are too unisex, somebody could see me as a sloppy, ugly girl. But in a real tailored men's suit? Women don't much wear those. Even men hardly wear them anymore.

"Well?" I stand in front of the clerk, turn around for inspection.

She claps. "Oh my God, you have no idea, it's always been my dream to get someone a whole new look. It's fantastic."

I think for a moment, picture myself climbing around the stage rigging in this, laugh slightly. "I need more casual clothes too. Something I can do physical labor in."

"I got you, hold on," the clerk says. "There's some good stuff we haven't even put on the floor yet. We just don't get a lot of men's wear customers who are looking for anything that small." She grins. "It's Oklahoma, right? The guys around here are built like their trucks, all—" She makes a gesture indicating both tall and wide.

Seemingly on cue, a male-female couple enters, woman leading, shopping bags in hand, large man in trucker cap trundling along behind her with a sour "I'm sick of my girlfriend dragging me to all these dumb stores" air about him.

The woman's eyes fall on me and light up. "Oh my God that's a great suit, did you get that here?"

"I did."

"See," she says, punching the man lightly in the arm, as if this supports her side in an argument they were having. Then she strokes my arm. Just reaches out and strokes it.

I frown at her hand and she snatches it away like she touched a hot stove.

"Sorry, I just wanted to feel the fabric. It's nice."

The man glares at me, like this is all my fault. "You're short," he says, voice sullen.

"Yeah?" I try to keep my voice neutral, low, but I tense up, ready to flash him if I need to.

"A real little guy," he says. "You know that?"

The clerk tries to lighten things up again. "Yeah, just like the singer Prince, I was telling Mister, wait, I didn't catch your last name."

"Abernathy." I say the first name that pops into my head, no idea where it came from. "People call me Abe."

"Right. I was telling Mr. Abernathy that his suit used to belong to Prince." She laughs. It comes out a little forced. "But he didn't believe me."

"Prince." The big man frowns. Thinking about it. It's almost like I can see the wheels in his mind turning, as he's trying to figure out whether me being Prince-like should make him more or less mad about the fact that his girlfriend stroked my arm. I almost want to shout, hey, did you notice I look like Deadpool over here? How can you be jealous of this?

The clerk jumps in again. "Hey, will you two be okay on

your own for a few minutes? I was just about to show Mr. Abernathy some more clothes in his size that we have in the back room."

"Oh, sure," the woman says. "I'm gonna look at your jewelry over here, that's what caught my eye in the window."

"Great. Look at whatever you want, and if you want to see anything in the locked case, just let me know."

I follow the clerk into a back room, crowded and chaotic, stuffed with clothes and other items. But she seems to know exactly where to find what she's looking for, snatching things from here and there, handing them to me until I have a tidy pile. "You can try them on back here, okay? I'll go out and deal with the other customers. I'm Indigo, by the way, Abe."

"Indigo. Nice to meet you. Thanks."

She nods, disappears into the main store. With a rush of discomfort, I realize that except for the binder I have no underwear. I'm going to need boxers or something. But that's one thing I don't want to get at a secondhand store.

About twenty minutes later I have my items picked out and Indigo returns. "Are you good back here?" she asks.

I nod. I have a "yes" pile and I'm wearing my favorites from the more casual items: a pair of slightly stretchy black jeans, white T-shirt, white button-up shirt, and black leather jacket in the style of a sport coat. But my shoes are still the platforms, I'm going to need some sneakers. It's complicated to be a man. Well, I guess it's complicated to be anything at all when you woke up in a hospital room a couple of days ago with your old life entirely burned away.

"I think I have enough things picked out," I say. "Were these all owned by the same man?"

She nods. "Estate sale. You can usually get a good bargain buying all the clothes in a single lot, but then you have to do the work picking out the good stuff." She looks sad for a moment. "I'm sorry about that…that guy. He was just in kind of a bad mood. He wasn't really out to make trouble for…

people like you. He felt bad about it later, I think, he bought his girlfriend one of our nicer bits of estate jewelry and they both left happy."

"Thank you for distracting him at a crucial moment." I smile.

"Any time." She looks troubled, like she wants to say something more, then just smiles at me, a chirpy clerk smile that doesn't quite reach her eyes. "Well, let's get that stuff all packed up for you."

She ends up giving me several of the items for free. "If it doesn't have a tag, it's not part of our inventory."

I collect a bouquet of plastic bags and hand over a shocking amount of the cash Luke gave me. Guess I'm committed to working for him the next two weeks at least, given that I spent half the money and haven't even bought a toothbrush yet.

I leave the store with my bags and think about walking in a masculine way, do men hold bags differently than women? I never really thought about it. I look around at the people on the street.

Men and women do have somewhat different body language, generally speaking, although certainly not all men or all women. Men tend to move in a way that seems larger, more forceful. They walk with longer strides, swing their arms more. But is that because they're men, or because they're dressed differently from the women? In high heels you can't walk the same way.

Thinking about shoes reminds me that I have a pair of stolen shoes. The doctor could probably afford it. And I really did need the shoes when I took them. But I still don't feel good about it. What if he really liked these shoes? What if they were special to him in some way? They're pretty nice shoes. I've been wearing them with tissues stuffed into the toes, but maybe they fit him really well.

I try to push it out of my mind but it starts to nag at me

and won't go away. I'm here in a city, they'll have a post office or something, I have enough cash right now, I could mail them to the hospital.

This is silly. It's just a pair of shoes.

But I still remember his name.

Doctor Ryan Everest.

I remember him saying: *We hoped you would die, honestly, nothing personal.*

I was kind of mad at him when I took the shoes, I guess. That wasn't why I took them. But it gnaws at me.

I walk past a small shop that advertises itself as:

BUSINESS SERVICE CENTER.
Mail! Photocopies! Internet!

Okay, fine. I march inside and emerge minus one pair of shoes that don't fit, and even more of the cash.

Twenty minutes before I'm supposed to be back at the venue, Luke calls me on his phone.

"Hello?"

"Hey, Abe, how are you doing?"

"I'm okay."

"Do you need me to pick you up from anywhere?"

"No, I'm almost back. See you soon."

Luke whistles when I arrive in the new clothes. "Looking good, Abe. I can see where you spent your first paycheck."

I tug on the jacket, a little self-consciously. Does he think I'm trying to be way too cool, wearing black leather? "Found a thrift store with things in my size."

He claps me on the shoulder. "Used clothing. Very resourceful."

After the show, Luke escorts me to a hotel room of my very own.

"I didn't think it was right, to make you sleep on the bus,"

Luke says. "You're a really good worker, Abe, and the tour's doing well, we can afford it."

He leaves, shutting the door behind him, and I have that weird feeling I get sometimes, when I'm all alone in a room, where it feels luxurious and lonely at the same time. I'm not accustomed to having a room all to myself, nothing bigger than a closet, anyway, so it always feels like a special occasion.

I explore all the little hotel room accoutrements. Glasses wrapped in paper that says FOR YOU in old-fashioned brush lettering. Tiny wrapped soap. Plastic ice bucket. Coffee maker, so I make coffee. Drawers that seem like a great way to lose something by putting it in a drawer and then forgetting about it.

One of the drawers has a Gideon Bible inside it. I know about Gideon Bibles, in a general way, but I don't know anything about "The Gideons" who put them in hotel rooms. Has anyone ever read a Gideon Bible, because they were bored, and then had a genuine conversion experience?

I flip through it, curious, wondering if the once-familiar words will trigger a panic attack the way hearing them spoken out loud during sermons will sometimes do.

> Then the LORD put forth his hand, and touched my mouth. And the LORD said unto me, Behold, I have put my words in thy mouth.

No. It seems like I can read the words without a problem. Good to know.

I dump out all my plastic bags, inventory my stuff. From the vintage store: the very nice suit, two pairs of jeans, three white button-up shirts, black leather sport coat, brown suede sport coat. Jeans and shirt from the doctor (I'm not mailing those back to him, I'm just not). Oversized sweatsuit and Angels knit cap from Luke. Seahawks sweatshirt and ugly sweater from the free box. From a variety store, boxers and T-shirts, toothbrush and toothpaste, cheap electric razor. From a hipster soap store that was having a sale: deodorant, black soap, exfoliating wash cloth, and a product called SCRUFFY that was advertised as being a treatment for beard dandruff. Active ingredient: salicylic acid. I'm shedding my outermost layer of skin rapidly as I continue to heal, and I don't want to leave gross skin flakes all over the place, so I hope this'll help with that. Scruffy also has a strong, but not unpleasant perfume that smells like cedar with a hint of tobacco, wood smoke and bourbon. Possibly the most stereotypically mascu-line-smelling thing I've ever put close to my nose.

I think about Babette again. She could probably break down all the perfume ingredients and tell me five different commercial scents that are similar to it.

I blew through an entire two-week's paycheck buying all this stuff, even though I was very budget conscious. But I think I'm set for a while. I hope so, anyway.

Coffee made, I drink it while flipping through TV chan-nels. Stop short when I see, on the television, me.

Well, not me. Not exactly. An actress who looks like me. Specifically an actress who looks like I did in the Atlanta airport: denim jacket, backpack, jeans, long red braid, freckles. Her T-shirt is tighter than mine was, and she's wearing a padded push-up bra, not a Performance™ sports bra. She's also wearing obvious makeup, which I almost never do. But still: me.

I turn up the volume. The show is *American Bounty Hunters*, and they're talking about the Hitchhiking Bandit. I wonder. Is this yet another scheme cooked up by my enemies? Or just random bad luck that I happen to strongly resemble a real hitchhiking bandit who isn't me?

No, this version is definitely supposed to be me. Because it's a "part two" and it's specifically about that guy in Utah.

The one I shot in the foot. It's surreal to watch "me" go through the motions of something I did, but all changed around. The man, in real life a jerk who pulled a gun on me first, is framed as an innocent victim, while the "me" character is literally described as a "pint-sized seductress."

Pint-sized? Come on, I'm not that short. I mean, I'm apparently the size of Prince, and that man was an absolute legend.

And yet, even though I'm clearly intended as the villain of this piece, I end up kind of liking me. I'm funny! I make quips at the guy I'm robbing. Not quips I actually did make, but they're quips I might have made, if I'd thought of them. And the guy comes across as kind of pathetic, standing there by the side of the road in his underwear while I drive off in his car. Big smile on my face, gleefully tossing his cell phone out the open window while my scarlet hair blows around.

A 1-800 number appears on the screen and stays there while the visual landscape fades to a fake Western set. A woman and a man, both very attractive and dressed in Western gear, trade off dialog.

"Now, pardners, if any of you-all have information about the Hitchhiking Bandit, call this number. Cash awards for useful information."

"Remember, Bounty Hunters, you gotta bring 'em in alive to get your cash."

The camera pulls in close on the woman, who shakes her finger at the camera with a big, flirty smile on her face. "No taking the law into your own hands, pardners. You could get in trouble for that and we sure don't want no trouble."

It goes to a theme bit where the two attractive people lasso sexy "bad guys" and reel them in. Then there's some yee-hawing and shooting into the air, a weirdly catchy theme song, and that's it.

So. That's the Hitchhiking Bandit. That's why it's been so

much trouble to get around by hitchhiking. Obviously this is something my enemies are doing to try to find me, but it seems unrelated to the Olvenar. This is not at all reassuring. How many different groups of people are after me?

At least, right now, I could not possibly look less like this Hitchhiking Bandit person.

26

A HOMELESS DRIFTER

Things with the tour settle quickly into a pattern: drive, load, dinner break, more loading, concert, unloading, sleep.

Sometimes when the guys on the bus get bored, they get it into their heads to talk to me, even though I'm never very talkative in response. At first, it's because my throat hurts when I talk, and fills up with that weird phlegm. But as I heal a bit more, I start to become worried that if I got involved in a really animated conversation, I'd forget to drop my voice into that low, damaged rumble that apparently strikes people as masculine.

They don't mind. They just want to talk, it doesn't seem to matter what I say.

Luke is teaching me ASL, which is cool, and Mark, bass player for the Angels, gives me one of his guitars and a book, so I can start learning to play. That's fun.

It's less fun when they want to talk to me about Jesus. Philip in particular appears to have a special burden on his heart for me.

"Don't you think maybe your suffering is all part of God's plan? Everything that happened led you here, and maybe here's where you were meant to be."

"Maybe so," I say, neutrally.

"I'm serious," he says.

"I know you are."

"But you don't believe it?"

I shrug. "I don't spend time worrying about it."

"But why not? Don't you want to know God's plan?"

"Sure. And if God himself decides to come down here from heaven and tell me exactly what that plan is, I'll be sure to take notes."

He looks confused, then a little half smile. "You're kidding around."

"Little bit. Yeah." I inhale, deeply, and then do something that kind of makes me hate myself. I speak as if I'm actually still a believing Christian. "Phil, I know you mean well. But I don't think it's right to second-guess what God wants us to do."

He looks shocked. Says, "Oh." in a small voice. "I just, I never thought about it that way before. When we talk about God's plan, we might be doing it wrong, what we're doing might be—" He pauses, as if searching for the words, and I decide to dig in a little with the knife he just handed me.

"Divination. That's the word you're looking for, Phil. Trying to map out what God's plan is. Same as fortune telling."

He nods, looking really, really sincere. Christian sincere. So sincere I can hardly stand it. And he shakes my hand. "Thank you, Abe. I didn't even realize."

I give him a little wolf strength in the shake, but I'm smiling. "It's okay."

He goes away, back to his own seat, and for now we're done.

But a few days later he knocks on my hotel room and says, "Hey, Abe? You awake?"

I open the door a crack. I am awake, but not very. I yawn. "Yeah?"

"It's Sunday. Some of us are going to church in town before we drive off, do you want to come?"

"No thank you," I say.

"Are you sure?" he says.

"I don't like going to strange churches." Which is true. Of course, I don't like going to familiar churches either.

"I know, some people don't, but it's kind of a bonding experience for the crew. When we go to church together. Matt likes to be seen doing it. You know. Just a regular guy going to a regular church. Not some out-of-touch rock star."

"And not a heathen who's lost his faith?"

He winces. "Okay, you're on to us. There are rumors in the press that he isn't a Christian anymore. And it's not true, but you know how people are."

"Sure, I'll go." A chance to wear my fancy suit, anyway. The last time I was in a church I had a panic attack, but that seems like ages ago now. I didn't understand some things about myself very well yet. I don't think it'll happen again. But if it does, I know what to do.

Relieved smile. "Okay, I'll stop back in about half an hour."

I'm getting efficient with the razor and the exfoliating, so I'm ready to go and smelling vividly of cedar and bourbon in twenty minutes.

"Wow, nice suit." Phil is surprised. He's wearing a suit too, hair slicked back, but his suit isn't as nice as mine to start with, and he definitely did not use one of those little hotel room mending kits to give it a bit of tailoring to make it fit better.

"Secondhand. Lucky find."

"I guess so." He smiles. "No Christian should be ashamed of wearing secondhand. It's resourceful. The people who say it invites demons…"

"People who say it does *what?*"

He grimaces. "It's something that's been going around.

This idea that items you get in a thrift store might be inhabited by demons from the previous owners."

"You believe this?"

"No! No, not me. I just thought... Never mind, it's obviously ridiculous."

"Uh-huh."

The crew going to church is sizable, but since we don't have any equipment, we can all pile into Matt's family van. Apparently it's okay for men and women to ride in the same van to and from church.

The church itself is nice, historic building of gray stone, large stained glass window in front, two banners hanging on either side of the window. I recognize the banners from some of the churches that operate on Capitol Hill, Seattle's main gay district: a white dove on a blue background that says PEACE and a cross on a rainbow background that says LOVE.

Maybe it's different in the Midwest, but in Seattle the rainbow banner says "We're one of the few Christian churches that welcomes LGBTQ people and won't try to tell you that you're demonic merely for existing."

If true, huge, and completely changes my understanding of the kind of Christians I'm traveling around with. But on the sidewalk outside, I see a handful of protesters. Some of the signs look familiar from Night of a Thousand Dollys, as if they were purchased from the same place. They say things like

AN ABOMINATION UNTO THE LORD

And

REPENT OR PERISH

We press our way through the gauntlet, heads down. But

one of the women gets directly in Matthew's way, points a trembling finger.

"Shame," she says. "Shame, shame on you, Matthew Fisher! Leading all these little ones astray. Thou shalt be crushed under a millstone! Millstone!"

Matt delivers an obviously rehearsed response, booming it out so that the entire crowd can hear. "I'm sorry if some of my fans feel upset by my view of how we should live our lives based on the teachings and example of Jesus in the Gospels."

The crowd jeers in response. The shame lady keeps pointing at him, spittle flying from her mouth. "Millstone! Millstone!"

She's really getting on my nerves and I find her gaze with my own, flash her. "Put a sock in it, lady." She gets a dazed look and steps back, reeling.

Luke frowns at me. "Abe, that wasn't very nice."

"Sorry."

But Andrew and Jordan from the Stones are both smirking in amusement.

Now we're inside the church. Our crew fills a whole pew and part of a second. The confrontation outside made me think I'm going to be okay here, but now that I'm actually inside the church, it doesn't feel so okay. The familiar geography, the pews, the pulpit, the arched roof, it all triggers something dangerous, a feeling like I'm being swallowed up. Churches have a distinctive smell, maybe the smell of a building that isn't lived in every day, and that smell makes me tense up inside.

But I don't want to freak out here. Not in a church that's maybe on my side.

A female priest walks out.

Priest? No, that's not right. Priest means Catholic and the Catholics don't have female priests. I don't think? So she must be…Episcopalian? Lutheran? Methodist? My knowledge of other Christian denominations is sketchy and filtered through

Father Wisdom's scorn for the less conservative varieties that would have such a thing as a female priest.

"Good morning," she says. The congregation responds: Good morning!

"Some of you have noticed we have a celebrity worshiping with us this morning." She gestures toward our rows and everyone laughs, as if it was a joke.

"And, this is probably what increased our other guests outside." She gestures toward the outer door and there's an angry crowd reaction, a kind of moan or rumble.

"Remember, do not let them provoke you to violence. Some of you have heard about the incident in Seattle a couple of weeks ago." She pauses, as there's more rumbling from the crowd. "Nobody was seriously injured, but it could easily have been much worse. You cannot fight hate with hate or violence with violence. Now, turn to page 132 of your song book, we're going to sing 'Great is Thy Faithfulness.'"

The rest of the service proceeds in a way that feels familiar. A few songs, a few Bible readings, nothing that triggers a strong reaction. Even the "stand up and greet the people around you" part of the service goes okay, because I deliberately make eye contact with a person who doesn't exist and pretend I'm shaking their imaginary hand.

The music is pretty good, although I can't sing. The attempt makes me cough and spit some of that weird phlegm into a tissue.

The topic of the sermon isn't something that annoys me, although it hits a little close to home right now. She's talking about the nation's growing homeless population through a Biblical eye, urging the congregation to recognize the humanity of the homeless.

"We can't agree on a solution, and that's okay. It's a big, complicated problem. But when we harden our hearts against homeless people, when we help secular society demonize them as nothing but criminals and drug addicts, that's us making the problem worse when, as Christians we ought to be making it better. We corrode our own souls through that kind of cruelty. And we should all recognize one thing: If Jesus our Lord walked among us today, he would be seen as a homeless drifter. No permanent residence. No fixed income."

The eyes of the crew all turn toward me. I feel their gaze. Homeless drifter you say? No permanent residence you say? No fixed income? Hey, we know someone like that.

I smile at them vaguely, look away. I do not want to encourage this line of thinking.

Or maybe I do? That's right, Christians, I'm the second coming. Your lord walks among you as a freakishly strong, badly damaged, sexually androgynous werewolf.

This thought amuses me so much that it becomes difficult to control the urge to start laughing. In New Harmony, if I had an uncontrollable fit of the giggles I would sometimes fake "holy laughter" to cover up my real laughter. As Abe I turn it into a coughing fit, excuse myself and rush out of the church, through a side door into a little courtyard.

One of our group is already out here, Jordan from the Stones Rolled, vaping with a furtive air. She notices me and startles, coughing, puts the vape away.

"I'm not smoking," she says. "It's vape. Not smoke."

"We're outdoors, I don't care."

"No? Okay, good." She pulls it out again, exhales a cherry-scented puff of vapor, gives me a thoughtful look. "You're not a smoker are you?"

I shudder, as I remember being literally on fire, bark out "No" with more passion than I meant. I try to soften it with a smile, but honestly, I don't know what it looks like to have Deadpool smile at you. Maybe it looks like a horrific grimace.

She turns apologetic. "Sorry, I didn't mean to upset you. Oh! It's because of the accident, right?" I nod. "Sorry. Luke told me about it when we were introduced, but I sorta forgot. We haven't really talked much. You and me, I mean."

"No. You're on the women's bus."

She rolls her eyes. "Yeah. Tell me about it."

There's a pause, and I take the opportunity to ask something that's been bothering me this whole time. "Jordan. Are you and the other women really okay being on the women's bus?"

She grimaces. "Okay? Yeah. Okay is the right word. I don't love it. I don't hate it. The RV itself is fine, and I think there's too many of us to ride on the same bus anyway. So we'd be divided up somehow. Why not along gender lines?"

"Why not? Because it reinforces inequality?"

She rolls her eyes with a weary, cynical air, takes another puff on the vape. "Yeah, okay. But doesn't everything? I mean…" She sighs, draws in the vape slowly, blows it out slowly. "I got into this whole thing when I was only sixteen. Andy too. We were going to a place called Maranatha Christian High School. We won a talent contest, then a bigger talent contest, then a bigger one. Then we were on the short list for the new band to tour with The Better Angels, one of our heroes. Then it happened. We were on tour. Dream come true, right? But that was three years ago. Now we're both nineteen. And I know it's only three years, but it feels like forever. Andrew and I write all the songs together, you know? I actually play the guitar too, I just don't play in concert because I never figured out how to play and sing at the same time. The Stones Rolled is our band, the other guys are just studio musicians for the tour. But I feel like the press always treats us like we're Andrew's band. Like I'm just the singer. Eye candy. Completely interchangeable. And the Christian press is the worst of all."

"You want to strike out on your own?"

She gives me a sad, weary look, takes a long drag on the vape. "I don't know. I really don't. The industry is so male-dominated, secular music too, and everybody seems to want to keep it that way, you know? I'm thinking I should just bank the money from the tour and go to college, get an office job or something. And sometimes I wonder about…"

After a moment of silence I prompt, "You wonder about what?"

"About the Angels of Rock festival. What's going to happen when we do that."

"The Angels of Rock festival? What is that?"

"Vegas. The Vegas date is Angels of Rock, a festival Matt started way back when, but they haven't had it since 2001. It was meant to be a Christian Lollapalooza. Matt showed us a documentary when we started the tour. It was pretty interesting. Angels was very popular for a while in the 1990s, even bigger than Lollapalooza. But then there was The Incident. This was 2001. Right after 9/11. I don't know, I guess people were all keyed up. And there was this country artist—not a Christian artist. Maybe the guy, Travis Trapper, was personally a Christian but he wasn't part of the Christian music scene. But he had done this super patriotic 9/11 song called 'America the Red, White and Brave.' It's cringe as hell when you listen to it now. But it was so big that he got added to the lineup at the last moment.

"I don't know what he was like as a person, he might have been a decent guy, but that song was so big, riding on this kind of 9/11 fever, he brought in all these people who wouldn't normally have been at Angels of Rock, and they weren't all decent. There were some issues that came up. Overcrowding. People got hurt. One guy died when he climbed on stage and knocked over a stack of speakers."

"Somebody literally died?"

"Four people died. Actually." She looks embarrassed. "There was drug use. Not typical for Angels of Rock. A couple of overdoses and one person died of dehydration. It was a warm day and they had too many people there, so they were running out of stuff to drink."

"They ran out of *water*?"

"Drinking water." She frowns. "I think that was it. Anyway, right from the start there were a lot of people who were, like, 'That wasn't Angels of Rock, that was just the Travis Trapper fans.' And they wanted to do another festival the very next year. But they lost out and now it's been twenty years. Matt told us the Vegas tickets are selling really well. We might even sell out. And nothing that went wrong last time could possibly go wrong this time. It won't be hot, we won't be outdoors, we won't have a secular country star as a last-minute headliner, and they'll have a strict cap on attendance numbers. So I think it's gonna be okay. Yeah."

She looks troubled for a moment, then takes a final hit on the vape and puts it away. "Nice chatting with you, Abe." She goes back into the church, leaving me here in this garden sitting there with that story.

The last time they had an Angels of Rock festival, four people died. That seems like a bad omen, and I feel a clang of foreboding, a sick sense of dread, that feels almost like a premonition.

I go back inside and finish out the rest of the service quietly, distracted by the story Jordan told me, and the fear that I'm going to be part of something very, very bad.

PART VII

WELCOME TO FABULOUS LAS VEGAS

27

GOLDEN HOUR

We pull into Las Vegas at sunrise golden hour, park the bus and the RV in the median of Las Vegas Boulevard so everybody can get out and get their picture taken under the famous "Welcome to Las Vegas" sign.

"It's cold," Andrew says, zipping up his coat. "I thought it was warm in Las Vegas."

"It gets cold here in the winter," Luke says. "The hotel pool is going to be closed for the season."

"Oh, no, really? I was looking forward to the pool."

Shadows are long, stretched out. Up toward the rest of the strip, the famous Vegas lights are starting to fade in the growing daylight.

We're behind another tour bus, its passengers already formed into an orderly line. One person hands their phone to the person behind them, goes to stand under the sign, poses, then retrieves their phone and gives the next person a chance. We join the line. Everyone is very efficient but we're still highly conscious of the ephemeral nature of the light. When our group gets our turn, Matt's wife Joanna takes all the photos. She's been the main tour photographer, and I made a joke about her being "the Christian rock Linda McCartney." Luke got it but I'm not sure anyone else did. They laughed politely, though.

We get to the end of our part of the line and she says, "You can go up, Abe."

"No, thank you. I can get your photo, though."

Joanna stares at me for a long time before nodding. "All right then. Thank you." She gestures at Matt and they pose under the sign together. It looks awkward. As I'm taking the photographs, Jordan sidles up to me, doing that furtive vape thing she does. "It is weird, isn't it?" she says, voice low.

"Excuse me?"

"Matt and Joanna. They're an odd couple. She's his second wife, you know, and much younger than he is. That was controversial at one time. I think he's gay myself. Or maybe ace? There's a lot of ace Christians but they won't admit it."

"By 'ace' you mean asexual?"

"Yeah." She nods, tries to blow vape away from me, almost succeeds. It smells like strawberries. "What do you think?"

"I don't think it matters."

She laughs. "Yeah, probably not."

We get back onto the bus and continue driving up the Strip into the portion where the big casinos are. As we drive, the sun finishes rising.

Phil has a tour booklet and keeps reading little tidbits. Such as:

"According to this, the Strip isn't in Las Vegas proper, it's in Paradise."

"Paradise!" Andrew says, like it's a joke. "I thought it was sin city."

"'Sin city' is right," Luke says. He has a troubled expression. "I've been here before, and 'sin city' is a very accurate description."

"What sins?" I ask it as if it's a joke, but suddenly I'm

thinking about New Orleans with a powerful jolt of nostalgia. Memory of pushing my way slowly through a raucous Mardi Gras crowd, caught behind one of those Christian groups with their big signs, a list of "sins" that always seems to include things like "football" or "loud mouth women" that I'm pretty sure aren't mentioned in the Bible.

Luke grins a little. "Well, I'd say the big ones are sex, gambling, and booze."

"Not to mention rampant criminality." Phil waves a brochure for something called the Mob Museum in front of us. "Apparently the Mob built Vegas."

Andrew says, "So, can we go into a casino?"

Luke sighs. "It's more or less impossible to avoid them, my friends. Every hotel, every restaurant, every kind of entertainment, if it's in Las Vegas you get to it by going through a casino."

"Divorce!" Phil says. He's reading from a different tour book. "Nevada had lax gambling laws, but people would also come from all over to get married or divorced, back when it was harder to get a divorce in other parts of the country."

"Divorce is a sin, right?" says Peter.

Everyone falls silent and stares at him for a moment, until he reddens. "Sorry, I really didn't mean anything by it."

Mark, one of the original Angels members, looks grim. "Matt knows what people say. But read the book more carefully. Jesus condemns male-initiated divorce, and their split was Susan's idea."

Silence in the bus as we roll past the gaudy, fabulous casinos. We pull into the parking lot of our hotel, the Safari Oasis, under a giant flashing electronic billboard:

Clean Skies Arena
Angels of Rock Revival
Friday Jan 28 - Saturday Jan 29
with
The Better Angels * The Stones Rolled * Randy Greenstone *
Sister Mary Travis * The Old Time Gospel Revival Chorus *
Daughters of Men * Many others!
CleanSkiesArena.com

We park the bus and the RV next to each other in the parking garage and enter the vast lobby of the hotel all in a big group. Once we're in the lobby, Matt is pounced on by a serious-looking woman in a suit who draws him into a private room for conversation.

"She's the coordinator for the Clean Skies venue," Luke explains, seemingly in response to my look of curiosity. "They're going to make sure everything's set up okay, then the rest of us will take a couple of hours to get familiar with the venue."

He turns to the rest of the group and says, loudly, "We have a nice block of rooms in the Camel Tower, wait here and I'll check us in and get everybody's keys. We're doing the walk through and initial setup at two, and that should take about three hours. But after that, there's no show tonight, so everybody can go out and have a little fun in Las Vegas. But not too much fun." Laughter. Luke heads to the front desk.

The rest of us mill around aimlessly with our luggage, stretching and yawning. Andrew sits down at one of the video gambling stations and feeds it a twenty. Jordan says, "Don't be an idiot."

He ignores her and starts punching the buttons. It seems to be a video facsimile of a slot machine, the old-fashioned kind with three physical wheels that would spin to show different symbols, and you would win money if the symbols lined up in the right way. Andrew gets a match. Three wolves.

The machine howls briefly and the amount of money goes up by two dollars.

"See?"

"I'm going to time how long it takes you to lose it all." Jordan taps her smartwatch.

"I smell tobacco smoke," I say out loud. One of the older crew members, Joe, nods.

"They still allow smoking in the casinos," he says. "Only on the casino floor proper, but you know how it is with smoke."

It occurs to me that Las Vegas must not have the same strict twenty-one-and-over laws about casinos that New Orleans does. Because I know for a fact that Andrew is only nineteen.

"How old do you have to be to gamble here?" I ask.

"Twenty-one," Joe says.

Jordan says, "See, Andy, you're not even supposed to be doing that in the first place."

"Don't distract me," he says. He punches the button again, the video display "spins." He gets a match but it's not as exciting, no wolf howls. But the money goes up again. Still, overall, he's losing. His original twenty is down to sixteen dollars and twelve cents.

Matthew's wife Joanna meanders away from the larger group and inspects a jewelry kiosk. Marta, her daughter, and the two female backup vocalists with the Angels, one who plays violin and the other who plays keyboards, follow her. I've never met them, but I know their names are Talitha and Mary. They're Black, and I sometimes wonder how they feel about being on this tour with mostly white people and being forced to ride on the women's bus.

Andrew stands up. "Okay, I'm out of money."

"Twelve minutes and forty-three seconds," Jordan says. "That's how long it took you to lose twenty bucks."

He rolls his eyes but doesn't have much of a chance to say

anything, because Luke comes back and hands out our room keys. He gestures and we follow him down along the side of the casino floor, passing several restaurants and bars, then up an escalator, past a few more restaurants and bars, and then down a very long, enclosed glass hallway. Maybe it's passive solar heating, but the hallway is stiflingly warm, seemingly ten or twenty degrees hotter than the rest of the hotel. At the other side of the hallway is another lobby, set up to host conferences, although nothing is happening at the moment.

Up to floor 22, and out into a kind of lounge area, couches and seats and an impressive view of the airport.

Luke gathers us all together for a kind of huddle.

"Okay everybody. Here's the schedule. We meet here today at two for the walk through and initial setup, and I expect everyone to show up for that. After that, free time for the rest of the night. Tomorrow is the first day of the festival, but we're not expected to support that. You can work if you want the money, see the festival for free if you want, or take a vacation day. If you want to work, meet here at nine a.m. No matter what else you do, we're all meeting right here, in this seating area, at nine a.m. sharp on Saturday morning, sober and ready to work. Otherwise, have fun. But, like I said, not too much fun."

My hotel room seems weirdly huge. Take everything you would have in a normal hotel room, the bed and the end tables and the dresser and the desk table, and put an extra two feet of empty space around it. I guess Vegas has the empty space. Nothing but desert all around.

I crash onto the bed for a while but don't get much sleep, possibly because I spent so much time sleeping on the bus. I decide to take a shower. It's large, with a deep tub that can be turned into a jet spa, and the hot water gets blisteringly hot. My Scruffy supply is getting low, but that's okay, my skin has mostly stopped flaking off randomly. From now on I can probably get by with a regular soap.

Shave my head down to about half an inch, notice that the random scarred patches are mostly gone. I have a full head of hair again. It's nice to see you, hair. I didn't know how much I would miss you until you weren't there.

Hair gel, which I think makes my hair look more like a dude's. Sleeveless cotton undershirt, then the binder. There's a lot more boob to bind, which I find annoying more than welcome. But it also means I'm nearly healed, right? Anyway, the binder just has to keep doing its job for another few days until the tour is over. Surely it'll hold out that long.

White T-shirt on top of the binder, white button-up shirt on top of that. Brief consideration, what outfit should I wear for the walk through? I don't want to have to come back here and change clothes before I go out exploring. Maybe the three-piece suit? No, not today, maybe if I go to a really fancy restaurant tomorrow. Jeans and the black leather jacket. Put on my indoor sunglasses, lightly tinted in a smoky greenish color. They were super cheap at a truck stop but I liked the way they looked, and the way they helped obscure my appearance.

Memory: Leon helping me pick out lightly tinted glasses to wear into the Baton Rouge capital, explaining that tinted glasses help hide the werewolf eye flash.

A nervous lurch in my guts. If I am healing, it's almost time for me to go back to New Orleans and confront my father. And I'm a little scared. I can admit that now. I'm scared because I don't know what to expect. I don't know what's going to happen. I don't even know if this is a good idea.

But I'm going to do it either way. So I guess that's it.

All dressed, I survey myself in the mirror, shocked at how un-obvious the scars have become. At a casual glance I look almost normal, hardly like Deadpool at all. In fact, more than ever, I look like my father did when he was young. I hope that's a good sign. A sign that when I confront him, things will go well for me.

Pocket my room key, cash, and the pre-paid cell phone Luke got me for the duration of the tour. The leather jacket has an amazing feature typical of men's clothing: inner breast pockets. There's something weirdly satisfying about the gesture involved when reaching into the breast pocket to remove something. Not merely a classic dude gesture, a classic cool-dude gesture. If you're James Bond that's how you retrieve your gun. If you're the Devil, that's how you pull out your soul contract and awesome fountain pen.

It feels so secure to put something there too. Close to the chest, which is probably where that saying came from. Nothing is likely to fall out, not unless I get literally dumped upside down and shaken vigorously.

There. I'm ready to hit Vegas.

With only a couple of hours before the walk through, I decide to explore the Safari Oasis itself, but that turns out to be underwhelming. Everything seems to be closed off, like the pool, or undergoing renovations, like the hotel's other tower. And it's one of the smaller resorts, so it doesn't take long to map out pretty much every inch. I try exploring things that are nearby, but there's not much there either. I manage to find a couple of even smaller hotels, a liquor store, and a diner, before it's time to head back for the walk through.

The Clean Skies Arena is close enough that I could walk to it, if I wanted to trudge my way through a big sandy lot that's still in the process of being made into a parking garage. We take the big tour bus with the trailer, since we have all the equipment, and for once everyone's crowded onto the same bus. It's just a few blocks, so I guess they're not so concerned with the "appearance of immorality." A few people on the street wave at the bus, Matt waves back.

From the outside, the arena looks like a typical covered stadium, with a seating capacity of maybe 30,000 people. But from the inside, it looks like an outdoor multi-stage venue. The illusion is fairly convincing to the eye, even if the fake grass smells all wrong. The roof is particularly impressive: a video display that looks like a bright blue sky dotted with clouds. The clouds move. Sometimes there's a bird.

We're shown around by the same woman who talked to Matt earlier, the one in the serious-looking suit, Ms. Abigail Larson. I never really called myself "Abigail" but I still feel a little sense of kinship with her, which makes me slightly more tolerant of her corporate-speak introduction about the arena's "commitment to the future of carbon positive buildings" and their "goal to be the most responsible and sustainable entertainment venue in the United States." She does a demonstration of the extensive environmental controls, which are genuinely impressive, taking us through a simulated sunset in which the air gets slightly colder and more windy as the sky darkens and the lights turn purple. Then, she demonstrates the fantastical side of the ceiling: realistic constellations of stars turn into animations, and the sky becomes entirely psychedelic, wheeling us straight into the heart of a pulsing, brightly colored nebula as many of us gasp.

Then the blue daylight sky returns. "And we can do so much more," Ms. Larson says, with a big smile. "The possibilities are literally infinite."

Suitably impressed, we explore the rest of the venue. There's a stadium within the stadium, about 15,000 seating capacity, where the main stage is being set up. Outside of the stadium, there's a children's play area with a wading fountain. Two colorful circus tents, for speaking events, and two smaller stages, one of them built to mimic a natural amphitheater. The walkways are lined with merchandise and food booths.

After we've toured the entire arena, including all the emergency exits, restrooms, water spigots, electricity outlets, emergency phones, surveillance cameras, hidden speakers, and medical stations, we get to work unloading and setting up the equipment. We're doing a kind of pre-setup, since there are several other bands playing on this stage before the Stones and Angels come on. We need to make sure all the necessary equipment is placed where it's not in the way of the other bands, but we can easily get to it on Saturday.

Everything goes smoothly, and, as promised, after about three hours, Abe is a free man.

"Do you want a ride somewhere Abe?" Luke offers. "Some of us are going to dinner at The Spaghetti Emporium."

"Thanks, but I want to walk."

He nods. He has come to accept that Abe is a person who likes to walk around on his own. "Okay. But be careful. This is Las Vegas, remember?"

"I remember. Have fun."

Outside is colder than I was expecting, even though I remember it being cold when we got out to photograph ourselves under the Welcome to Las Vegas sign. But while I was in the arena, I started to kind of forgot that I wasn't outside. Everything in Las Vegas is designed to look as if it's supposed to be warm, clear skies and palm trees and outdoor swimming pools, so the actual cold temperature shocks me. It's good though. Feels refreshing somehow. If it weren't cold I don't think I'd be enjoying this very dry air, but right now it has a sharpness, a clarity to it. The sun is low in the sky, and the casino lights are starting to come on. It feels like something exciting is about to happen.

I start out exploring with high spirits and curiosity. Even though my pop culture knowledge is limited and quirky, I have heard about Las Vegas. And there's a maison here, some-where, although I don't know what part of town. Used to be a maison, anyway. I'm not quite sure what I'm going to do if I run into a werewolf who knows me. Of course, anyone from the Las Vegas maison isn't going to recognize me by scent, they've only seen me on video. So it probably won't come up.

Still, there must be werewolves here, and I do have to know what I'm going to tell them.

I think about this, as I walk, and there's a lot of walking to be done. Casinos on the Strip are laid out like the furniture in my hotel room: surrounded by lots of empty space. Just to get from one casino resort to the one right next to it can be as much as a mile of walking. I walked across the entire country, and I was prepared to walk from Denver to New Orleans, and this still seems like a lot of walking.

In the shopping promenade, under Caesar's Palace, where the roof is vaulted and painted to look like the sky, bright cerulean with fluffy white clouds, a low-tech version of the arena ceiling, it hits me: Las Vegas is like a space port. Or, maybe it's the other way around: space ports in movies and TV are based on Las Vegas. A totally enclosed artificial environment with flashing lights and hucksters and a constant soundtrack of upbeat pop hits from different eras.

After a couple of hours walking through these spaces, I'm starting to get cranky. Everything looks different at first glance, but deep down it's all the same. The same high end shopping chains, the same slot machines, the same little design touches.

Which resort am I in now? The Roman one, the hipster one, the pirate one? It just goes on and on. Fake Egypt? Fake Rio? Fake New York? Fake Paris? Fake Venice? The fake Paris just reminds me that I was supposed to be traveling right now, maybe seeing the real Paris, and, briefly, I get so angry that I almost want to punch something.

Maybe I'm just hungry.

I've heard that Vegas has legendary buffets and decide to look for one. A werewolf still healing a major injury can do serious damage to a good buffet. Where to find one? I've been hesitant to use the phone for anything other than time keeping and communicating with the rest of the crew. Based on my vague understanding of how cell phones work, I'm afraid that if I start getting online and doing anything that signals "Abby is here" a swarm of Olvenar will descend upon me. Like locusts.

But I brave the phone's internet connection to look up "Las Vegas buffet" and get a hit from a casino called the Mesopotamian, "famous all-day buffet with a focus on Mediterranean and Persian dishes."

Sounds perfect. The problem, as I have learned from the last couple of hours navigating the Las Vegas Strip, is that a dot somewhere in the middle of the giant footprint of one of their casino resorts can be quite hard to find.

The Mesopotamian is about a block off the Strip proper. The base is similar to the Luxor pyramid, but cut off flat at the top, and the surface has a rustic stone look, as if it really is some ancient ruin found in the desert. The base structure surrounds a golden-hued high-rise tower with a jagged top. The signs seem to indicate that the base is called "The Ziggurat" and the tower is called "The Spire."

Inside the Ziggurat is an impressive indoor greenhouse with a tiered garden. And, the distinctive scent trace of born wolves.

I decide to follow the wolves first, hoping maybe they know where the buffet is. It's an interesting journey. Up one escalator, down another, through a series of twisting hallways, and then a long, dark hallway with no businesses, which makes it feel like I'm leaving the resort entirely and going who knows where.

Then, I turn a corner and behold: the buffet.

The entrance is set up with a switchback line, but that isn't needed today, with only a handful of people waiting. The food smells good, but I don't see the price listed. I don't want to wait in even a short line if the price turns out to be more than I want to pay. While I'm still looking for the price, a born werewolf girl of around fifteen comes out to talk to me. Lobos, I think. She has the dark coloring and strong features I associate with the Los Angeles pack, and she's wearing a T-shirt from the Disneyland Haunted Mansion.

"My grandma sent me out here to talk to you," she says, with a slight eye-roll. "You're just here for the food, right?"

"Of course."

"Yeah, figured." She shakes her head. "Everybody's so on edge these days after what happened in New Orleans, but it's stupid, why would anybody come to a Las Vegas buffet just to make trouble?"

"I'm not here to make trouble."

She nods. "I'm Camilla, by the way. You are?"

"Abe. Nice to meet you." We shake.

She says, "What pack are you from?"

"Quinault. Washington State."

"Oh." She nods thoughtfully. "What brings you down here?"

"I wanted to get out of the rain for a while."

"Yeah? It rains a lot there?"

"Well, you know how Seattle is famous for having a lot of rain? It rains five times as much in Quinault. It's literally a rainforest."

"Huh. I'm from L.A., that actually sounds kinda cool to me."

"Well, the hunting is good."

"I bet it is."

She seems about to leave, but has a second thought and says, "Have you guys in Quinault heard about everything happening in New Orleans? With the rougarou and all?"

I nod, a curious feeling of dread coiling around my stomach. "We've heard some."

"It's wild, isn't it?"

"I guess."

"It's thrown all the packs into a tizzy. I don't really get the big deal myself. They're in New Orleans, we're in Los Angeles, you're in Quinault, we're hundreds of miles apart from each other, right, so why does it matter? But I guess the rougarou pack is supposed to be important or something. Everything's online now too. And I feel like all that Olvenar business is turning my little brother into a real asshole."

I nod, slowly, sense of dread coiling tighter. "Yeah, I don't like the Olvenar."

"Well, you wouldn't, would you? They hate guys like you almost as much as they hate girls like me."

"True." I think about what she said. "Guys like you." Another werewolf would notice that I smell female even if I look male, so she's probably assuming I'm a trans guy who isn't doing hormones or anything.

Yeah, the Olvenar hate guys like me.

She says, "I just hope it's all over soon, you know? I mean, all the conflict. Things will settle down eventually. After…" She trails off, shrugging. "You know."

"After the Abomination is dead, you mean?" I don't know why I said it like that. It comes out low and harsh.

She frowns. "Well, I wouldn't put it that way. They're not really planning to kill her, you know, that's just internet tough guy talk."

"That's what you think?" It comes out as a growl. Okay, I'm losing my cool here, I need to leave. I'm not here to make trouble, right? So I can't make any trouble. "Sorry. I just… really hate the Olvenar."

She nods. "I get that. They're pretty hate-able." A moment of awkwardness. "I'll tell my grandma you're just here to eat, no problem."

"Yeah, thanks."

She turns to go. I turn to go as well. I thought I was starving, but all of a sudden my appetite is completely gone.

28

MARTINI'S

After a brief, angry walk back to the main casino area of the Mesopotamian, my appetite comes back and I settle for a small bar in the center of the casino floor. Manhattans are on special and I get one of those, plus a "Mesopotamian plate" of lamb skewers, tabbouleh, humous, babaganhoush, and pita bread.

In my hand, a free ballpoint pen from one of the churches we went to, doodling on a paper drink coaster that shows the Mesopotamian logo, a picture of the Spire rising up out of the Ziggurat. In real life this didn't strike me as looking particularly phallic, but in the logo it sure does. I flip it over to doodle on the other side.

I'm staring, vague and unfocused, at the elevator in the center of the casino, the one that goes up and down the Spire, making note of who gets on and who gets off. Who seems like they won a lot at gambling, who seems like they lost too much? What couples seem like they're hooking up for the first time, and who seems ready to split up? Who's having an adulterous affair? Who wishes they hadn't brought the kids? Who's celebrating a birthday, anniversary, graduation? Who's never been in Las Vegas before? Who comes here all the time?

My grandmother used to do this: people-watch. She always had a notebook with her and would write down her observations, usually in shorthand, which I am apparently the last person in North America who knows how to read. I learned it in the cult, in anticipation of using it to provide "helpmeet" services for my hypothetical future husband. For just a second, I experience a moment of pure happy relief: no matter what terrible things happen to me in the future, at least I'm no longer trapped in the New Harmony cult, searching in vain for a way to believe all the things Father Wisdom taught, because I was afraid the alternative was eternal damnation.

In shorthand, I write: the one true way to be saved from hell is to stop believing in it.

A couple of women step out of the elevator and rivet my attention, before I've figured out why they're so riveting. Attractive, short skirts, but that describes a lot of women in Las Vegas. A second later I figure it out: they're dressed just like the cocktail waitresses at the Azphokite bar in Baton Rouge, where I played one of them as part of Leon's plan to get revenge for the murder of his mother. Short black dresses identical to each other in style, makeup rendering their faces pale and mask-like, hair pulled back into smooth, tight buns. But most importantly, their necks have light red marks, impressions of thick jeweled collars. They make the girls drop them off in a safe at the end of their shift, but I left wearing mine, and Babette ended up with it.

The Spire has an Azphokite bar. Of course, why wouldn't there be one in Las Vegas? But it seems to change everything, in my thinking. The Azphokites might be involved in the attempts on my life. In fact, now that I've thought of the possibility, I'm almost sure of it. They must be involved.

Gripped by a sense of urgency, I throw my cash on the table, slam the remainder of the Manhattan, head to the elevator. The top floor, 53, announces itself to be TOP OF THE SPIRE with a little brass plate. I'm sure that's it. The

Azphokite bar in Baton Rouge was at the top of the office tower, even though it was only thirteen floors. But when I press the button, nothing happens. The elevator continues to sit there.

A couple gets in the elevator and sees me poking at the button. The man laughs. "You need to swipe a card to get up to the top floor," he says, pressing a button for floor 42. "Members only club, sorry."

"Oh," I say. "Thanks."

"The bar on floor 50 is pretty good if you just want a view of the city." He points to the brass plaque next to the button for 50, which says HANGING GARDENS.

"Thanks." But I'm impatient now that I'm stuck riding all the way up to floor 42 and then back down again. Each person who gets on the elevator makes it take longer. I need to talk to those women, find some way to get to Top of the Spire.

When I finally get back to the casino floor, their scent trail is still fairly fresh. It leads through the same kind of neglected-feeling empty corridors that led to the buffet, then eventually down one floor and through a door marked EMPLOYEES ONLY. Nobody challenges me. Down another few corridors, through some kind of industrial tunnel, up again to emerge at street level next to what looks like an abandoned retail center. Another couple of blocks off the Strip, to a bar called Martini's.

A bar that belongs to a guy named Martini? Or a bar where somebody thought "Martinis" takes an apostrophe?

The bar is loud and raucous, and the flashing neon sign declares that it's open 24 hours 7 days a week. The two women have swapped their short skirts for leggings, tank tops, and denim jackets, and they've released their hair to hang loose around their shoulders. No drinks in their hands yet. I take a deep breath. Men chat up women in bars all the time, don't they? And Abe looks okay right now, doesn't he? Almost normal? I can do this. Make it seem natural. I just need a thing. A conversational in.

I stand among the bar crowd, near the two women, until I hear something promising: one of the women says the word "Martinis" or "Martini's" to the other. I sidle a bit closer and make eye contact, with a slight smile. "Sorry, I didn't mean to eavesdrop, but can you tell me something? Is this bar owned by a person named Martini, or by a person who doesn't know how to use apostrophes?"

The women glance at each other, then back at me, burst out laughing. "Nobody knows," says the one with lighter hair. They look very similar to each other, and the first difference I'm able to get a handle on is that one is fully blond, while the other has mostly brown hair with blond streaks. They're about my size, too, which makes me think maybe there was a reason I could pass so easily as one of them: the Azphokite cocktail waitresses are of a type, and I happen to be that type. Well, Abby's that type. Abe not so much.

"Can I buy you both a drink?" I ask.

"Sure, let's go to a table," says the blonde, linking her arm in my arm. "I'm Tanya, and this is Shanielle."

"Abe."

Shanielle takes my other arm. "Nice to meet you, Abe."

The two women steer me to a small booth and skootch in, so that I'm trapped between them. It's not unpleasant, but it feels calculating. Are they planning to rip Abe off in some way? That would be kind of a Vegas thing to happen.

Tanya says to me, "Do you have cash?" I nod. "Give me forty bucks and I'll get our drinks, the bartender knows me, she'll make 'em stronger if I order." I give her two twenties. She goes up to the bar and comes back with three drinks in small rocks glasses, but served up, without ice.

"I got us special martinis," she says, emphasizing the word "special." One glass has three olives on the spear and she puts that in front of Shanielle. Two olives, in front of me. One olive remains in her hand as she sits down.

Shanielle nods slightly and sips from the glass. "Thanks."

I hold the two-olive glass to my lips and pretend to sip, set it down. Something is definitely wrong here, and I'm not drinking anything until I know what it is. "Thanks for getting the drinks. What makes these martinis special? Served in the wrong kind of glass?"

She laughs. "Wrong? Don't be so judgmental, Abe." She clinks glasses with me and sips from her own drink.

"What's the gin?" I sniff. The alcohol smell is very strong, but I don't even know what the chemicals for roofie-ing somebody would smell like.

"Tanqueray," she says.

A lyric from an Amy Winehouse song pops into my head, *sniff me out like I was Tanqueray…*

It's not Tanqueray. I'm pretty sure it's Gordon's. Best gin for the buck, half the price of Tanqueray, and bartenders know that.

"It's good," I say. I might as well look like a rube who can't tell Tanqueray from Gordon's. Whatever they're planning, they should do it soon. I sense the two women exchanging looks behind my back.

Shanielle leans in from my left, close, very flirty. "So, Abe. Oh, nice cologne," she says, as if surprised, and strokes the arm of my leather jacket.

"Thanks. It's actually a beard wash called Scruffy."

She strokes the arm of the leather jacket again. It's a nice jacket, so I guess I don't blame her, but it still seems a little weird since we just met. "What brings you to Las Vegas, Abe?"

"Business."

"And what do you do?" Tanya leans in from my right. I could feel claustrophobic, but I try to squelch the feeling.

"Entertainment. I'm crew on the Angels of Rock show."

"Angels of Rock? Oh my God, you're part of that?" Shanielle recoils, with a look of horrified fascination. "I can't believe they're doing that festival again."

"Are you referring to the incident twenty years ago?"

"The incident." Shanielle makes a disgusted noise. "Ten people died and they call it 'the incident'."

"Ten people? I heard four people."

She makes a dismissive gesture. "Oh, they covered it up. If they didn't die on site, they claimed it was unrelated to the festival, but what do you think, if you go to a festival all day and then you die in the car on the way home?"

Tanya says, "Well, it was a car accident, nobody knows what causes those a lot of the time."

"Drinking. That's what causes car accidents. There wasn't even supposed to be any drinking at the festival but people were sneaking in the booze left and right because they basically didn't have any security. They had almost twice as many people in 2001 as they did the previous year, because of that guy—Tanya, you know the guy—"

"Travis Trapper," she says, obviously bored. She pulls out her phone and starts looking at it.

"Right, that song! Just a minute." Shanielle pulls out her own phone and during the moment where both women are deep into their phones, I play around with the garnishes. Two to one, one to three, three to two. It's like that game with the cup and balls. I pick up the one that now has two olives, wipe off the lipstick prints, take a sip, put it back down. It's definitely not as strong, but is it also not as doctored with something illicit? We'll see what happens.

"This song." Shanielle holds her phone up to my ear and plays about thirty seconds of it.

I recognize it, have a flashback to a truck driver, singing along, the dog Buddy on my lap, and all of a sudden, for one deep and painful moment, I miss Buddy more than anything. I think about him in Marysburgh with Antonia, picture her taking him for a walk, and I hope they're both happy. I hope Toni has a new girlfriend. And the new girlfriend has a dog. And they walk their dogs together.

"What's wrong, Abe?" Shanielle noticed that I got upset.

"Nothing. Just thinking about the people who died."

"Shanielle, we don't have to rehash the whole thing right now," Tanya says. She puts her phone away and smiles eagerly in my direction. "It was twenty years ago and I'm sure Abe here is making sure they don't have any of the same problems."

Shanielle says, "I don't remember, I was too young, but that guy was so huge right then, that exact time. Early October 2001. You never hear about him now. And it was so hot. The festival was in California and they had that Satan wind, you know the one I'm talking about."

"Santa Ana," Tanya says. "Santa Ana winds. The wind comes down through the canyon where it gets super-heated. They happen in the autumn, usually."

"Are you from Los Angeles?" I ask her.

She reaches for a drink, frowns briefly at the rearranged olives, takes the one that was originally mine. "Not L.A. Santa Ana is in Orange County. That's where I'm from. Anaheim."

"Disneyland," Shanielle says, laughing. She reaches for her own drink, gets a similar frown, takes the one that originally belonged to her friend. "Okay, so the show was in Anaheim, and it was really windy and really hot and there were twice as many people as they were expecting, so there wasn't enough of anything. Not enough staff, not enough port-a-potties, not enough free water. And people were bringing in alcohol and other drugs. They hardly had to sneak it in, because there wasn't enough security."

Tanya has apparently given up trying to get her friend to talk about something else and just starts helping her tell the story.

"It's true, there were problems all day long, people

fainting from heat stroke, women getting groped, fist fights. The final act was Travis himself, and everything was absolute chaos by that point. When he went on stage there was a huge crowd surge. Things got crushed, knocked over—one of the things knocked over was a couple of port-a-potties, if you can imagine how bad that smelled. So Travis goes on stage and tries to do a normal show. But something had damaged the sound equipment and only about half the speakers were working. So the crowd starts getting kinda angry, because they can't hear, you know? And they start chanting 'Red, White, and Brave! Red, White, and Brave!' Like they wanted him to just do the song and then they could go home. So he does it. But then some really drunk guy climbs up onto the stage, and knocks over a tower of stage monitors, and they fall right on his head. He gets killed right away. Smashed his head in, all bloody. So now people are screaming and running away from the stage, there's a real stampede. And when the whole crowd gets cleared out, finally, three people were dead. Crushed. Suffocated. They don't even know when it happened."

I picture what it would be like to get crushed to death in a crowd like that, with a knocked over port-a-potty spewing raw sun-baked sewage all over the place.

It would feel like hell. Like you were literally in hell.

Tanya sighs, drains the glass that originally had two olives. The one meant for me. "You're not a rich businessman, are you, Abe?"

"No, I'm a junior roadie." I frown. "Did I say I was a rich businessman?"

Shanielle does a double take. "What? No way!" She strokes my arm. "That's a really nice coat for a junior roadie."

"Yeah, but I got it used. Tanya, why did you say that about me being a rich businessman?"

She sighs. "We know you followed us from the casino, we're not stupid."

"No? What does that have to do with being a rich businessman?"

She gives me a weary look. "We're not stupid," she repeats. "We know we work at Top of the Spire. And you should know you're not getting up there. Even if you were a rich businessman, you still have to have a connection on the inside, they don't accept just any old guy with money." She stops. Inhales deeply, frowning, like maybe the drink is hitting her harder than she expected. "Anyway, forget it, you're not getting to the Top of the Spire."

"Well, either way, thanks for the info." I make a kind of cheers gesture with my drink and go to drink it. Tanya puts a hand on my arm.

"I wouldn't drink that, if I were you."

I put it down on the table, give her a serious look. "Really. Why not?"

She rolls her eyes. "It's doctored. You figured it out, I think. That's why your drink is still full while we've finished ours."

"Why was my drink doctored?"

"We're not stupid," she says, again. But it's almost like she's not so sure of that anymore. She wipes her forehead. "We've had guys follow us from the casino before."

"And you drug them? That seems dangerous."

"It's not," she says, but looks worried. "It just makes you go to sleep."

"Oh, good," I say. "I hope you're right about that."

"What?" She's looking at my drink. "You didn't even drink it." Her voice already has a notable drunken slur. "Why didn't you drink your drink?"

"You mean the one that was served with two olives? I swapped the olives around. You drank that one."

Her face goes pale. "You did what?"

"Switched the olives. Whatever you meant for me to drink, you're the one who drank it."

"Shit. I knew it tasted stronger than I was expecting."

Shanielle laughs. "You roofied yourself, Tanya!"

"What are you going to do?" She gives me a panicked look. "You can't do anything. Shanielle won't let you."

"I won't let him?" She gets mad, snaps. "What do you think I'm gonna to do to stop him?" She gestures at me.

"Come on, Shani, he's tiny, you're pretty tough, you could take him!"

"I'm not fighting some dude, no matter how tiny he is, just because you screwed up! Look, I'll take you home and make sure you don't get into too much more trouble, but that's it. I told you this was going to happen. Didn't I? I told you that you were going to fuck it up."

I say, "I wasn't trying to hurt you. I hoped I was wrong." I'm starting to feel guilty. I assert: "I didn't put anything in anybody's drink."

"Yeah. Okay. I guess." She looks grumpy for a moment, then turns drunk-happy. "This is boring, you want to go dancing?" She turns to Shanielle. "When was the last time we went dancing, Shani, we should go dancing."

"We should go home," Shanielle says, firmly.

"Okay." Tanya drops her hands to the table, her head to her hands. One snore.

Shanielle stands up. "Tanya." She pokes her shoulder. "Come on, Tanya, stand up. Please?"

She snores again. Shanielle tries picking her up from the table, but she's so limp, it doesn't go well. She grimaces and looks at me. "Can you help me get her home? Please? I'll call a car."

"Sure."

We walk/carry Tanya out to the main road. She seems to wake up briefly, looks me in the eyes. "Wait, who are you again?"

"I'm Abe."

"Hi, Abe. What are we doing? We were going dancing?"

"Shanielle and I are taking you back to your place."

"Oh, hey," she says. Smiling. "Fun. We have a nice place."

"We share an apartment," Shanielle says. "Not too far, a lot of the time we walk home, but tonight…"

"If you call a car I'll pay for it but it has to be cash," I say. In spite of everything I feel like this is my fault, even though I'm not the one who introduced roofies into the equation. "Honestly, I wasn't trying to hurt anybody, I just…"

She sighs, shakes her head. "I don't blame you, she asked for it. I've tried to get her to knock it off, I knew something was gonna go wrong. Although what I pictured was more like she would drug some old guy where it interacted badly with his medication or something and we had to call 911. This is probably better than that. At least she's not gonna go to jail."

The car comes. Takes us to an apartment complex a couple of miles off the Strip. I note that the car offers a cheaper "cash only" rate and pay it. We get Tanya up the stairs and to their couch, where she collapses, snoring.

Shanielle pours us both a drink, Maker's Mark, bourbon whiskey, plops into a chair. "God. I'm just glad it was you and not some genuine creep."

I sip the drink. If this one is roofied I'm out of luck. But I watched her pour them both straight from the bottle. "I'm glad you don't think I'm a genuine creep. But how do you know the difference?"

She laughs. "You know, I'm not too sure. It's just a vibe, I guess."

"Do you meet genuine creeps at Top of the Spire?"

"Oh yeah. I've served drinks to guys who made my skin crawl. But we're not even supposed to date guys from the club so it's good. I mean, sometimes the guys get drunk and try it, but we're not supposed to let them."

"No. I've been to an Azphokite bar, I remember that."

"Azphokite?" She frowns at me. "Who told you that word?"

"Is it not the right word? I'm sorry, I thought—"

"No, it's the right word. It's just, most people don't even know the name unless they're already a member."

"I was a guest once. My father was a member, he got me in, but we had a falling out after that. So I never finished the initiation process."

"Oh, yeah, okay." She nods. "So why do you want to get into Top of the Spire anyway? I know it has this mystique, but if you've been to a different Azzie club you know it's really just a bar. The only thing that makes it special is that they won't let you in. It's all hype."

"The one my dad took me to was a really nice bar." I sip the whiskey. Try to figure how to play this. I have a feeling, and I can't even say why, that she actually does know a way to get me in, but she's not going to just come right out with it. Maybe I could flash her? But that feels wrong. Using freaky werewolf powers would make me the kind of creep she worried I was.

"It is a nice bar, you're right about that. There's an outside deck with a spectacular view, but this time of year it's really cold out there. Anyway, I'm sick of talking about where I work."

"Okay. What do you want to talk about?"

"I don't know. Literally anything else. What about where you work? Are you worried about a repeat of the incident?"

"Well, now I am. The people on the tour told me about it, but they made it sound less serious than you did."

"They would." She nods, knowingly. "There was a thing on the local news, that's how I know."

"Do you like living in Las Vegas?"

"It's okay. It's like living anywhere, I guess. I grew up here, though. Tanya comes from Orange County, she misses the ocean sometimes."

"I miss the ocean when I've been away too long."

"Yeah? Where did you grow up, Abe?"

"Seattle."

"Oh, huh, they got the ocean there?"

We talk for a while about nothing in particular, while the alcohol hits her. And I feel bad for noticing this, for thinking about using her drunken state to get information about how to get up to Top of the Spire. It feels less wrong than flashing her, but still feels exploitive. I already know I can drink any non-werewolf under the table and beyond.

"I'm getting myself a refill, what about you?" She stands up.

"Sure." I hand over my empty glass.

She says, "You need to stand up and have a glass of water first. Vegas rules. Every round of drinks, you have to stand up and you have to drink a glass of water."

"New Orleans rules too." I nod. "Nobody does it, but those are the rules."

She laughs. "Yeah, nobody does it here either." She pours water from a cooler, two glasses, hands me one. "Cheers."

We drink the water in a single long gulp. Then she refills our glasses with bourbon.

She says, "New Orleans, huh? I've never been, what's it like?"

"It's really not like anywhere else. Imagine you took the party atmosphere of Las Vegas and…concentrated it? Added a lot of history. And lots of…moisture."

She bursts out laughing. "Moisture? That doesn't sound good. You're kinda funny, Abe. You know that? I mean you seem super serious at first but you're actually kinda funny."

She stares at me intently for a moment, and I get a slight jolt of sexual interest.

Oh. This could get tricky. I stand up, stretch, yawn. "What time is it?"

"About three a.m. But things go all night here. If you want food or something. Breakfast?"

"Sure, you want to go out for late night breakfast?"

"Oh, shoot, I don't want to leave Tanya alone. I mean, just in case she stops breathing or something, you know? I'm a little worried."

"Me too. When I switched our drinks it seemed like the right thing to do, but now I regret it. I should have just kept on not drinking my special martini."

"That's because you're a good person, Abe." She says this and moves in as if to kiss me. I step back.

"Hey, Shanielle, you've been drinking, are you sure about this?"

She moves in again, but this time she reaches out to touch my chest first thing. Which means she touches the binder. "What is that, a bulletproof vest...oh. *Oh.*"

"Sorry." I step back again, watch closely for her reaction. If she freaks out about it I will flash her, I don't think I have a choice.

Instead she smiles, gives me a little wink. "Hey, you know what they say, what happens in Vegas stays in Vegas." She gives me a one-armed hug of camaraderie. "You do make a nice-looking dude, I have to say. I love that jacket."

"Yeah? You want it?"

"What?" She looks taken aback. "Why would you give me your leather jacket?"

"If I give you the jacket will you get me into Top of the Spire?"

She laughs. "Oh, Abe, really?"

"But will you?"

She looks amused. "Okay, you got me. I have a couple of high roller's chips that I can give out. We get one per quarter as a bonus. But that's only, like, four a year, you know?"

"What do you usually do with them?"

"Well, one time I used one to impress a guy I wanted to date. And last year Tanya saved them up and got her dad and brothers in over Christmas. But sometimes we sell them. You can sell them for a lot of money if you find the right buyer.

There are dudes willing to pay thousands of dollars for one night at Top of the Spire, just so they can say they were there. You know?"

"So, you're telling me that a used leather jacket, no matter how much you like it, is a lowball offer?"

"Maybe." She sips, stares at me. "Can I try it on?"

"Of course."

I take my things out of the jacket pockets, transfer them to the back pocket of my jeans. She puts the jacket on. It looks good.

"I guess we really are around the same size, huh?" She strokes the leather. "It smells like your cologne."

"I wasn't lying, it's called Scruffy and it's a beard wash. I don't have a beard, obviously, but I use it on my head."

"But...you're not...you know, you're not doing the hormones and all that? Because I have a friend, he started taking the hormones and he grew a great beard, but then he started to lose his hair. Guess you can't have everything, right?"

"I don't think male-pattern baldness runs in my family, so I'm good there. But no, I'm not taking hormones."

"Well, you can get them here in Vegas. If that's what's worrying you. I know a lot of places, you can't get them anymore. But you can get them here in Las Vegas."

She strokes the leather again, seems to make up her mind. She goes to a drawer and pulls out a red poker chip that says HIGH ROLLER on it. She hands it to me. "Okay, what you do is, you give that chip to the front desk and they give you the key card you can use in the elevator. There's a dress code. Jacket and tie. Have you got a three-piece suit?" I nod. "Well, you should wear that." She squeezes my hands. "And Abe, be careful. They're serious about the men-only thing and they do mean cis men. If they discover what I discovered..."

"I'll be careful. Thank you."

"Yeah. Okay." She sits back down again with her drink.

"So now we've gotten that out of the way. Say, do you want a coat or something to wear back to your hotel? I had an ex-boyfriend who left a jacket here. It's kind of ugly but it's designer so I couldn't bring myself to just throw it out."

"Sure."

She fetches the jacket, which is, as promised, not very attractive. It's puffy and sort of patriot-themed in red, white and blue. It does have an inner pocket, though, and I transfer my items to it. I don't really like carrying things in my back pocket, I can't stop feeling like they're going to fall right out.

We continue to talk for a while, but then the sky starts getting light and I can't stop yawning. Tanya has been sleeping peacefully, regular breathing, and we're not so worried about her anymore. Shanielle hugs me as I leave. I step out into the chilly morning, glad of the jacket, no matter how unattractive.

All in all, the night worked out pretty well for me. Score one for Sin City.

29

THE APPEARANCE OF IMMORALITY

Back at the hotel, when I emerge from the elevator on floor 22, several of the men from the tour are gathered in the seating area. They're chatting in a subdued way, but when they notice me they fall silent and all eyes swivel in my direction. As if they were waiting for me.

"Hey guys." I wave, casual. "What's up?"

"Abe, were you out all night?" Luke says.

"Things go twenty-four hours in Vegas, I just lost track of time."

"That's not the jacket you were wearing when you left."

"No, it's not." I yawn hugely. "I swapped jackets with somebody, it seemed like a good idea when I thought of it."

Andrew snickers. "Was she cute?"

Luke says, "Was it a girl, Abe? Were you really out all hours, swapping clothes with a girl you just met?"

"It's not what you're thinking. Her friend got way too drunk and I helped them both get home. That's it. We sat up talking for a while making sure her friend was okay. Then I noticed the sky getting light and came back here. That's it."

Luke folds his arms. "And where did you meet these girls? Was it a bar?"

"Yes, I met them at a bar." I really want to go to sleep now and I'm starting to get irritated. "I went to the bar and I had one drink in the bar. Is that not allowed? Drinking in moderation was fine when we went to that brew pub."

"I'm just worried about you."

"Well, you don't have to worry about me. Okay? I'm going to bed."

Luke sighs. "Check your phone once in a while. I sent you half a dozen text messages."

He did. But I'm too tired to worry about it right now.

I drop off to sleep without bothering to get undressed, wake up a few hours later, shower, put on the complementary robe, go back to sleep for a few more hours. When I wake up for good it's already late in the day again, shadows long in the golden light, neon sputtering to life.

Today's the day I plan to go to Top of the Spire.

I get dressed carefully, in my three-piece suit and tie, spend some time fussing over my hair. I'm more nervous than I thought I would be. But I'm excited too. After all this time, am I finally going to find out who's really behind the attempts on my life?

I check the time. Seven p.m. Too early for the club. I need to go when it's crowded and I don't want to spend too long there. I'm guessing the likelihood of getting found out goes up with every moment I'm there. Between nine and eleven strikes me as the right window.

Restless, but too nervous to eat, I decide to just wander up the Strip, spend some time people-watching. It's not quite as much fun in Las Vegas as it is in New Orleans, but it's a distraction. And it's different. New Orleans has any kind of busker you can imagine, but the default is a musician. The default busker in Las Vegas seems to be a sleight-of-hand magician. I stop and watch a few of them. The illusion really works. It looks like the coin vanishes, and like the playing card magically appears in the tourist's pocket. I know, in a general way, how these tricks work, and none of them are designed to fool a werewolf nose, but the skill to pull them off is still impressive. There's a practiced dexterity that's really fun to watch.

After a while I decide I'm hungry in spite of the nervousness and make my way to the Mesopotamian casino, where I get the same food plate I ate yesterday, and an Old Fashioned with a giant branded ice cube in the center. It's good. When I finish eating, I get a second Old Fashioned and wander the casino floor with it.

I spend some time trying to figure out the appeal of gambling. It looks like a great way to lose ridiculous amounts of money very quickly. Weirdly, nobody looks happy to be doing it. They mostly wear expressions of grim and settled determination.

At the blackjack table, my eye is caught by a young Asian-American woman who reminds me, fleetingly, of Deena's Goth friend Claudia. Her Gothic look isn't as intense, but she does have dramatic eye makeup, dark lips, and a black dress with white lace at the cuffs and collar. She seems very focused and serious in her play, but makes modest bets, small wins and small losses. Then, after a point, she perks up, starts betting higher, and damn if it doesn't pay off. Bigger bets and bigger wins. She flushes with excitement as her pile of chips grows fairly large, as if she's on her way to becoming a real high roller.

Someone else has noticed her. Halfway across the casino floor, a white man in a dark suit is looking right at her, nostrils flaring. But he's no werewolf, not unless he's semi-wolfy like Edison. His sweat is entirely human. And excited, in the manner of a predator going after prey.

I don't like it. He reminds me of the Olvenar, even if he's not wolfy. Those cops who tried to kill me the first time weren't wolfy either. I don't know why the Olvenar would be targeting this young woman, but if he's Olvenar, I'm on her side.

He starts moving toward her, not rapidly, not looking at her too intently, trying to maintain a casual appearance. Maybe he knows rapid movement would alert her to his presence. Similarly casual, I get right in his way and pull out my phone.

He swerves to avoid me and swears under his breath.

I inhale deeply, pick an approach. He seems like a guy who likes to intimidate others, so I gather my wolf. Let the growl creep into my voice.

"Excuse me?" I say to him, aggressively putting myself in his way, planting my feet wide apart. "Do you have something you want to say to me?"

He frowns. "No, sir, sorry, sir. I just—"

I flash him. "What are you doing?"

"That woman, I think she's counting cards, I need to stop her." He frowns. "Why am I telling you this?"

I pitch my voice low and aggressive. "I don't know. Why *are* you telling me this?"

He takes a step backward, almost involuntary. Then he frowns, draws himself up, takes obvious note of our height difference. "Would you just get out of my way, buddy?"

I'm genuinely mad now. "Out of your way? Buddy. Look around you." I take a step forward and he takes one of those involuntary steps back. "It's a big casino floor. Why don't you get out of *my* way?"

He has a brief fear reaction, then one of confusion and annoyance. "Buddy, it's a casino, you cannot pick a fight with me in a casino, I don't care how tough you are. We can just kick your ass out onto the street."

"A fight?" I pretend to be offended, step back, take a sip of my drink. "My word, what are you accusing me of?"

"Nothing. Fine. Nobody's picking a fight with anybody. Just—" He looks for the woman, wilts when he can't spot her.

"Never mind." He turns away from me and walks rapidly one way and then the other, craning his head around in universal "looking for something" body language.

I travel the other way, circle around the casino a couple of times, find the woman's scent trail. It leads out of the casino, into the bar of a different casino. A fancy bar all decked out with draperies of white strands. It seems to be called the Chandelier Bar and it feels like being inside a giant spiderweb made of crystal. The woman sits alone at the bar. I gesture at an empty seat next to her.

"Mind if I sit here?"

"Be my guest." She has an odd, flat accent, maybe Boston? She barely glances at me, her attention focused on using one of those little golf pencils to make notations in a pocket-sized notebook. Then she does a double take.

"Wait, I know you. You're the guy who distracted that casino detective. You did it on purpose, didn't you?"

I shrug, slight grin. "Maybe."

"Why? We don't know each other, do we?"

"It was an impulse. You reminded me of an old friend and he reminded me of an old enemy."

"Hey yeah?" She grins. "I guess I oughta thank you."

I study the cocktail menu. "You could buy me a drink, the cocktails are expensive here."

"Wicked expensive. But they're really good is what I hear." She thinks for a moment, nods. "Sure, I'll buy a round. But this can't turn into a whole thing, okay? Like a date or anything? I'm here with my family."

"Of course. I have an appointment later myself."

"Well. Okay then." She nods, and we spend a few moments ordering from the bartender. I get something called Smoke and Mirrors and she gets a Oaxacan Old Fashioned.

"What's your name?"

"Abe. Dave Abernathy. You?"

"Katy Cheung."

"What brings you to Las Vegas?"

"Family. We get all the different branches of the family together in Vegas every New Year. Boston Cheungs, Vancouver Cheungs, San Francisco Cheungs, Hong Kong Cheungs."

"Is that fun?"

"In a way. If you can take all the fussy Hong Kong aunties who always want to know why I'm not engaged and why I dress like this. What about you? What brings you to Vegas?"

"I'm a junior roadie with the Better Angels tour."

"Better Angels? The Christian band? What are you doing here?"

"Here in Vegas? We have a show. Here at the bar? Drinking and hoping none of the guys from the tour see me."

She laughs. "Yeah, those super Christian types don't approve of cocktails much, do they?"

"No. Not much." Pause while our drinks arrive. Her drink is just a drink, looks and smells good, but mine is a big production as the bartender sets down a mirrored tray covered with a glass dome filled with swirling smoke. She pulls off the dome and the fragrant cherrywood dissipates, leaving behind a Scotch-based cocktail that smells wonderful. Smattering of applause. The bartender smiles, leaves.

I take a sip. It tastes even better than it smells. "Was that man right, were you counting cards?"

"I'm not allowed to say." Grin. "Eh, I'm going to MIT, card counting is a tradition. And no matter what they say, it's not illegal. It's not cheating. But you can't make any real money doing it anymore. I'm surprised they even bothered sending that detective guy after me."

"How does card counting work?"

"It's a blackjack thing. Most Vegas games have no memory, right? A spin of the roulette wheel, always an independent event." She pauses. "Do you know anything about probability?"

"I was home schooled, so the answer is no." I was trying to make it sound like a joke, but it comes out sounding genuinely bitter. I try to smile. "I know how it works in general. Flip a coin, 50-50 chance. But I'm sure there's a bunch of math to it hat I don't know."

"Well, the one thing you really need to know isn't math so much. It's just truth, right? A coin flip is always a 50-50 chance, it doesn't matter what the previous ten flips were. You could get heads 76 times in a row like in *Rosencrantz and Guildenstern Are Dead*. You ever see that movie?"

"No. Is it good?"

"Pretty good, yeah. So the thing is, blackjack works a little differently. It has memory, right? You play a card and now that specific card is out of the deck, so it won't come up again until they shuffle the deck."

"But when I see the dealers, they've got a little box and they're obviously dealing from more than one deck."

"Yeah, that box is called a shoe. And it does increase the house odds, you're right about that. But you can still increase player odds by card counting, just not as much, see? That's what I meant when I said you can't make any real money doing it anymore."

A pause, while we sip our drinks. "You're going to MIT? That's Boston, right?"

"Guilty." She laughs. "What gave me away, was it the accent? It was the accent, wasn't it? I've been told I have a wicked strong accent." She makes a disgusted face. "Usually by people who expect me to sound Chinese or something. Where you from?"

"Seattle."

"Yeah? I've been to Vancouver BC but never Seattle, what's it like?"

"A lot like Vancouver, I guess. What's Boston like?"

"I duno, kind of a weird town. All this patriotic history

stuff, all these colleges, and all these Irish pubs. A lot of sports, too. People are really into sports there."

Another sip. And then—

"Shit, it's my boss." I drain the rest of my drink, but hold it in my mouth for as long as possible.

"What, for real? From the Christian band?"

I nod. Luke comes into the bar and stands behind me, smoldering.

I turn around to face him. Finish swallowing. "Luke."

"Abe. What are you doing here?"

"Having a drink with Katy and talking about blackjack."

"Blackjack, Abe? Really?"

"Talking about it, not doing it." I turn to Katy, smile apologetically. "Sorry. This is going even worse than I expected. Thanks for the drink."

She nods and makes a cheers gesture with her own cocktail. "Yeah, my pleasure. Maybe see ya round."

Luke is shaking his head with a pained expression. "I just don't know what's gotten into you, Abe. We're in Las Vegas one night and all of a sudden you're drinking, and gambling, and staying out all night with scantily clad women—"

Now I'm genuinely mad and make furious, sizzling eye contact, hiss out, "Don't. You. Dare." He goes blank. I take him by the arm. "Come on, we've got to go."

I steer him out of the bar and to a slightly dark corner, a little out of the main thoroughfare. At first I'm very surprised to see an actual cigarette machine, vintage it looks like, then I realize it's been repurposed to sell tiny pieces of art. The charm of this brings my anger down ever so slightly and I manage to smile at Luke. "Come on, you know better than to judge a woman harshly because she's wearing a short skirt. I thought you knew better than that. And right in front of her face too. What were you thinking?"

He shakes his head. "This is Las Vegas."

"I'm well aware of that."

"It's just not like anything you've experienced before. It really is a hotbed of vice and temptation. I'm not just being an old fuddy-dud. I've spent quite a bit of time here, and I've seen young people like you… I've seen them fall."

"Maybe so, but I'm not as naive as you seem to think. I'm not gambling, Luke. I'm not even tempted to gamble. I was curious about it, so I asked a young woman who seemed to know what she was doing. Turns out she's from MIT. We were having an interesting conversation about math. That's all."

"Conversation, huh?" He frowns for a moment, then tries a different approach. "Abe, if that's all it is, why are you dressed up in your best Sunday suit? I think maybe because of your scars you don't have a concept of yourself as an attractive young man. Maybe these women flatter you with their attention."

"What? Oh, screw you." He winces at the almost-swearing, and I like him, so I wince a little myself. But I'm too mad to stop. "How dare you? Luke, I'm dressed up for the evening. I thought I might go somewhere nice for dinner." I gesture at the chandelier decor. "And the woman I was talking to was the same. She was dressed up for the evening. Maybe to go somewhere nice. It is not the fault of any woman alive that dressed up for a man looks like this," I gesture at myself, at the three-piece suit, "and dressed up for a woman looks like that." I gesture back at the chandelier bar, where it's not hard to observe that it's chock full of women in short skirts and high heels. Way more women than men, actually, now that I think about it.

"Look at that. All those women dressed up and having a girls' night out. And you're going to stand here and judge them for that? You think you can't have a conversation with a cute girl like you'd talk to any other kind of person? That is so low. That is so disrespectful to these women."

He chews on his words for a moment, then says, "Aren't you being disrespectful? Abe?"

"How?"

"You're not going to date them."

"No! I'm not! And that's my point. One of the women I met last night actually did try to flirt with me, but I turned her down, she accepted it with no problem, and we talked for the rest of the night anyway. Just. Talking."

He sighs. Inhales deep and long.

"And you don't think she was trying to change your mind?"

"No, I do not. I can tell when people are flirting with me, Luke. I know I seem like a naive little baby to you, but I know flirting when it happens."

He inhales. Exhales. Thinking. Then he says, "Abe, it's not just about what happens. It's also about the appearance of immorality—"

Those words.

Those exact words.

All right.

There it is.

The moment I've been braced for this whole time.

"Luke? You don't have to worry about this anymore. I quit."

"What? No, Abe, no, you—where will you go?"

"Oh, I don't know, maybe I'll move in with one of those scantily clad women you're so worried about."

I walk off. Flounce off, if I'm being honest. But I need to get my head together before the rest of the night. I need to be cool about it, and apparently "being cool" is the thing in all the world I find most difficult.

30

ANGELS OF ROCK

I walk around the Strip at a rapid pace for a while, start to feel a little more calmed down. I'm walking fast enough that I start to feel too warm in the three-piece suit and take off the jacket. Walk around some more until I feel cold enough to put the jacket back on. How do men do it? A three-piece wool suit is really, really warm, and they wear them indoors all day.

Check the phone: 9:10 p.m., time to go to the club. Back inside the casino and up to the man at the concierge desk, where I show my poker chip. "I'm Dave Abernathy. They said this would give me a one-night pass to Top of the Spire?"

"Do you have a reservation?"

"You need a reservation?"

Deep sigh. "On Fridays and Saturdays after nine p.m. Don't you guys ever look at the website?"

"Sorry. I didn't know." I'm so completely thrown that I'm not entirely sure what to do. "Can I…make a reservation? For later?"

"No."

"What? No? That's it, no?" Panic puts the edge of stress into my voice and he recoils a little, gives me a warning look.

"Yell at me and you don't get in at all, my dude," he says.

He holds up a card with the Top of the Spire logo in gold on black. "You might have that chip but it's still my discretion whether I hand over the key."

Sigh. Close my eyes. Tilt my head back. "Sorry, I'm just thrown. And having kind of a bad day. Why can't I make a reservation for later?"

"Friday and Saturday are completely full up already, and for Sunday you don't need one." He smiles. Smugly. He enjoys this part of his job way too much.

"So, are you telling me to come back on Sunday?"

"I am." He pauses. There's an unspoken "unless..." rolling somewhere behind the pause. Wait, he wants a bribe, doesn't he? A little high roller's largesse could probably get me in here tonight. Well. Damn.

"Sorry, man," I tell him. I pull out a couple of twenty-dollar bills, just in case that helps. "I can't tip you a hundred or anything, I'm not really a high roller, I just traded my leather jacket to one of the cocktail waitresses for her chip."

He chuckles. "Must have been a nice jacket."

"It was."

He takes the twenties out of my hand. "Well. If you want a little advice, Mr. Dave Abernathy, you don't really want to go up to the club on a Friday or Saturday night anyway. It's too crowded, makes it feel like all the other bars in town. On a Sunday evening, though? Around seven? You get the experience the way it was meant to be. Everything is extremely civilized and you feel like you're in a gentlemen's club in London in the 1920s."

"Yeah? The kind of place where men smoke cigars and spin a sepia-toned globe while they discuss the expedition to look for the forbidden artifact?"

"Exactly the place."

"Thank you. I'll be back on Sunday around seven."

I turn away, letting my smile collapse. Deflated. I feel like I want to sink right into the ground. It shouldn't matter this much, but it still feels bad, like the worst kind of rejection. Like nothing at all is going to work out for me ever and everyone obviously hates me and they're probably right to hate me, because objectively I suck.

I wander the Strip with no goal or purpose, just trying to distract myself from that feeling of crushing rejection. I have to come back on Sunday, that's all, it's not the end of the world. But I feel so low that I start to think about not coming back on Sunday after all. What am I really hoping to find out? I'm going back to New Orleans either way, aren't I? I'm going to confront Leon no matter what, aren't I?

No. No, I have to go through with it. I gave up my leather jacket for this. I really liked that jacket.

Maybe I'm just afraid. Is that it? I'm afraid of what's going to happen if the Azphokites figure me out? Because if they figure out I'm a girl, they'll probably just kick me out, but if they figure out I'm one specific girl, Abnegation Verreaux? They might toss me off the balcony of the 53rd floor. Something like that could be fatal even to a werewolf.

My thoughts spin around in dark circles and keep leading me back to the same place.

After a long night of aimless meandering, eventually I collapse in my hotel room, feeling defeated, when the fight hasn't even started yet.

o ⚜ o

POUNDING, POUNDING, POUNDING ON THE DOOR. DOOM IS coming.

Destiny, says a voice somewhere to my right. *Time to wake up.*

I hop to my feet, instinctively in a combat crouch, but the person on the other side of the door is Luke and I relax. I remember being mad at him but my dream-clogged brain isn't serving up the details quite yet. Instead I make sure my robe is tied securely and open the door.

"What?" I yawn.

"You weren't answering your phone."

"No." Pieces of yesterday start coming back to me. "I quit, remember? The phone is yours." I find it, hand it to him.

"Abe, please." He hands the phone back to me. "I'm here to apologize."

"Yeah?" I yawn again. "Real apology or fake apology?"

"Fake apology?"

"Something like, 'I'm sorry you're upset' and then you act like I'm the one being unreasonable?"

Small laugh. "I got you. Real apologize. I prayed about it, Abe. And this morning everything seemed crystal clear. I've been judging you with the world's eyes. Didn't our Lord Himself befriend women who were scorned by society?"

"Yeah, there's a lot of stuff Jesus did that would upset people if you did it today."

He nods, knowingly, and opens up his arms in a kind of supplication gesture. "Today's the last day of the festival and the Better Angels are playing their big show." He holds out my lanyard with the "CREW" badge. "I would feel a lot better if you were there. Not working your usual job. Just, out there in the crowd as a kind of roving, low-key security?"

Something about the way he says it gives me pause and I frown. "Is there a particular reason you want me there?"

"You'll think it's silly."

"Try me."

"I had a dream. I don't remember all the details, exactly, just that you were there and somehow the fact that you were there prevented a bad thing from happening."

I shrug. "It's not silly. I listen to my own dreams."

He nods. "Okay. Okay, that's good. Anyway, the way I figure, there's no harm, right? In having you there?"

"There's no harm." I pause, think about it. "No, I can't see any harm."

We hug. I guess we make up, and I'm glad. I didn't want us to part on bad terms. I wasn't wrong in most of the things I said to him, but I was still wrong to lose my temper.

As I'm going through the grooming ritual of one of my last times getting dressed as Abe, I start to have a peculiar feeling of nostalgia. I liked him. I'm going to miss him. He feels almost like a part of my childhood that I'm leaving behind.

I dress up in all my Better Angels gear: T-shirt and sweatshirt and knit cap, wear it all with the blue jeans. Check my look in the big full-length mirror. Just your typical mildmannered Better Angels fan. Do I manage to have that squeaky-clean evangelical look, like my brother Justice used to have? I don't think so, but I'm not sure why not. Vibes, I guess. Body language. The look in my eyes. Whatever it was that Father Wisdom always saw in me, the thing that made him think I needed to be punished, that's still there.

A couple of hours later, I'm at my first-ever music festival. I always assumed I would go to one eventually, but I thought the first one would be Jazzfest, and I kinda thought I'd be going with Steph's father.

His loss hits me like a punch in the gut, so strong I have to stop and collect myself. I've been trying to avoid crying, as Abe. I'm worried tears will strike people as feminine. But maybe it doesn't matter now.

When I arrive at Clean Skies Arena, none of the stages have any music going, but the food booths are in business, serving up some of the carnival food I remember from Rodeo Days. Something called "deep fried butter" intrigues me so much that I get one. How do you deep fry something that turns to liquid when it gets hot?

Wrap it in a lot of dough, it turns out. The idea seems to be that the butter melts inside a kind of pastry, which sounds like it should be delicious, but it's too much of the wrong kind of fat or something, and it strikes me as cloying.

A young woman sees me staring dubiously at the remainder of the deep fried butter stick. "Yeah, it's a bit much, isn't it? I got one yesterday."

"It goes against my nature to throw food away, but…"

"It's okay. I give you absolution." She makes a gesture like a cross and then pauses. "I'm sorry, I was raised Catholic."

"No, it's fine. I like Catholics." I laugh. "I'm sorry, that came out weird. You know what I mean."

"I do." She smiles, and I pick up a vague glimmer of sexual interest and, no, I've got to shut that down pretty quick.

"Well." I point to my crew badge. "Thanks for the absolution, gotta keep moving."

She nods, understandingly. And I move on.

I get a large iced tea, walk around with it, observing the crowd. One thing about the outside world that still seems a little weird to me is the way people always want to put ice in their drinks no matter how cold it is outside. I first noticed this in New Orleans, so I thought it was a New Orleans thing. But it's just as true here in Las Vegas.

Music starts coming from one of the tents and I duck inside. Find myself in what turns out to be the "revival" tent. Singing, praying, clapping, but more like a drum circle, no featured performer. A young man next to me tries to get me into the singing and clapping, and I shake my head, duck out again.

Another young man notices me when I duck out. He approaches with a kind of aggressive manner, holding out a pamphlet. "Have you heard of the Real Truth Revival? It's an important new youth in faith movement."

I ignore the pamphlets, point to my badge. "No, I'm a roadie on the tour."

He nods but his demeanor changes, darkens. "They say

Matthew of the Angels isn't even really a Christian anymore, is that true?"

"It's not true. He's a Christian. I've been to church with him several times."

"But is he *really* a Christian?"

I give him a puzzled frown. "That's for God to sort out, don't you think?"

He sighs. "Fine. You're right. I guess. But you know—" He pauses for a long time. "You should know there are rumors."

"If you think Matthew is such a heathen, why are you here?"

Long pause. Slight grin. "Well, I still like their music."

The first band on the main stage starts up. Four women who call themselves Daughters of Men and do a kind of minor-keyed, gritty, folk-influenced faith music involving banjos that I end up liking quite a bit. I didn't grow up with much music at all, because Father Wisdom didn't like it, but I did sometimes hear faith music at outside churches. After I ran away I certainly experienced the entire gamut of music, which sometimes included Gospel or other faith music. Even Night of a Thousand Dollys included a little faith music, because Dolly Parton did it.

As I'm bopping along, I realize something: I can be moved by the faith of the singer, or the songwriter, without thinking it has anything to do with me. The person who hurt me the most in my life, Father Wisdom, and the people who helped me the most, Steph and Luke, would all three tell you that they were motivated by sincere Christian belief. And they were! That's the crazy thing.

I murmur out loud to myself. "I don't care what you say your faith is. I care what it leads you to do."

A young man to my right startles, turns toward me. "What did you say?" he demands, with an unnerving intensity.

I hesitate before answering. "I said, I don't care what your faith is, I care what it leads you to do."

Now he turns weirdly angry. "Why would you say that?"

"Because it was a thing that occurred to me as I was listening to the music."

"Do you believe that?"

"That's why I said it."

"No," he says, emphatically. "No. Absolutely not. Certain deeds in the service of the true faith are no crime. No. You know not what you speak. No."

He doesn't wait for me to respond, just stalks off toward the edges of the crowd.

"Well. That was weird," I say, out loud, and a couple of people nearby nod in agreement.

So weird that I call up Luke.

"What's going on, Abe?"

"I just had a disturbing encounter with a young man out here, very hostile."

"You think he's going to make trouble?"

"It's possible. We should keep an eye on him."

"Will do. What does he look like?"

Looks, right. Non-werewolves need a visual description. "Average looking, medium-toned white guy, no freckles, short brown hair, brown eyes. Really sullen and glowering. That's the thing you would notice about him. Oh, he was wearing a Crusaders T-shirt. I don't know if that's one of the bands. It was black and had a Middle Ages warrior guy on horseback, plus a red cross."

"Not one of the bands. Crusaders is a Christian movement. Offshoot of the Right Path. Fundamentalist evangelicals. I'm surprised he's here. Right Pathers don't approve of Christian rock. They don't really approve of music, period. A lot of them are followers of John Wise, who preached that all music carries a false spirit, even traditional praise music and hymns."

My stomach flips over a couple of times. "I'm sorry, did you say John Wise? As in, New Harmony John Wise?"

"The very same. You've heard of him?"

"My father. He was a, a follower. Of John Wise. We didn't get along."

"I'm sorry, Abe. I'm familiar with John Wise. His child-rearing books about breaking the will? It's a harsh way to live."

"It is." Deep breath. I feel dizzy, like I'm going to faint. "I need to go. If you see the sullen guy in the Crusaders T-shirt, keep an eye on him."

"Will do."

I get some more iced tea, and for the first time the coolness of the ice seems soothing against the inside of my throat as I swallow. Nervous, I explore the arena in systematic detail, map it out more fully in my head. Where are the hallways, the hiding places, the weird little overlooked corners?

I'm following the sullen guy's scent trail, but not too closely. I don't want him to notice me.

Leon is the last person I want to think about right now, but his voice pops into my head anyway, as I remember something he told me about being a bodyguard: that our real gift, as werewolves, is the ability to shut down threats early, before there's any actual violence. Notice the person in the audience who's extremely stressed out. Notice the person carrying a gun when they're not supposed to have a gun. Notice the person hyped up on some drug. Notice the body language that doesn't fit the situation. Follow around that one guy who seems really off.

But, after a couple of hours, he hasn't done anything more menacing than go to the Speaking Tent, where a series of semi-famous theologians and religious writers are giving talks all day.

I leave him in the tent and get distracted by other things. People see my crew badge and ask questions or request small favors. "Where's the nearest bathroom?" "Is anybody selling earplugs?" "Could you hold my baby for a second?"

"Can you take a picture of us in front of the giant festival poster?"

The illusion that we're outdoors is really effective. The digital sky simulates a fiery sunset, the lights come on, the air conditioning gets just a little bit colder. Time for the Better Angels to take the stage.

For the first time during one of their performances, I'm not on hook to monitor the set list in order to know when to hustle onto the stage and bring Matt a freshly tuned guitar right before "Walk Through the Valley," or grab Peter's saxophone for when he does that clapping thing during "Rise Up." So I just listen. And here's the thing about The Better Angels: I do like them. I just don't like them *that* much. Which is actually pretty okay for being on the crew. I'm not tortured hearing their music all the time, but also I'm not starstruck.

They finish "Every Morning," one of their bigger hits, and while the applause is just starting to die down, a wave of excitement and surprise moves through the crowd as somebody new comes out onto the stage. A woman about Matt's age. Shouts of "SUSAN!" from the audience become a chant, "SUSAN! SUSAN! SUSAN!" Wildly enthusiastic applause.

The woman smiles, and makes a kind of quiet down gesture with her hands. The crowd shuts up.

"Hi everybody," she says, voice magnified, echoing off the edges of the stadium. I notice that people who were sitting in the stands are starting to flow down to the floor, trying to get closer to the stage. This must be the same Susan who was with the band in their earliest incarnation. Matt's ex-wife. He never talks about her at all, I had no idea this was going to happen. Did other people know? Luke must have known.

Susan speaks, "Some of you have been fans of ours for a long time, and you remember the story. About how Matt and Mark and I met in Bible college, and we formed a rock band, which was considered a little rebellious at the time."

Laughter from the audience.

"Matt and I got married while the band was still pretty new. We were spending so much time together practicing and writing music, we figured we had to get married to avoid the appearance of immorality."

More laughter.

"Some of you know the rest of that story. We picked up James and then Thomas to finish out the band, went to Nashville, won that gospel music contest, got signed to After the Flood Records, had a couple of albums that sold mostly in the Christian rock world. Then we released *To Hell and Back*."

Wild applause. Some people call out "Blood River!" People have called that out before, I think it's one of their songs, but Matthew always ignores it.

"'Blood River,' right. That was on the *Hell and Back* album, our big secular crossover success. Produced by the same guy who did U2 records, and we had three pretty big hits from it, two of which you already heard tonight, and one you haven't heard. The biggest one, kind of inescapable in the autumn of 1996, 'Blood River.'"

Applause, cheering.

"But none of you know the real story behind it, because Matt and I never talked about it publicly. Until now."

An expectant hush falls on the crowd. "Some of y'all knew that I wrote the song, even though I made Matt sing lead on it, and you guessed that it might be about a miscarriage. You were right."

The crowd murmurs but doesn't cheer or applaud. Maybe they sense it would set the wrong tone.

"What you don't know, because we've never talked about it, is that Matt and I were both kinda relieved when the miscarriage happened. It made us realize that we weren't ready to be parents, which made us realize that we weren't ready to be married, either. And that was all mutual, that was both of us. But for me specifically, it also made me start questioning my faith. Because I'm going to tell you a secret. A big secret. I prayed every night for that miscarriage."

Gasps of shock ripple through the crowd.

"See, once I found out I was pregnant, I knew I didn't want to be. And I would have thought an abortion was wrong, but—" her voice breaks. "I thought if I prayed for it, then it was God doing it. And if God himself chose to end my pregnancy, then it couldn't be wrong. Could it?" Dramatic pause, as the stadium goes nearly silent for a long moment.

During this dramatic pause I realize something. I got so caught up listening to Susan's story that I wasn't focused on scanning the audience for threats. And during that time, the situation has changed. There's nobody sitting in the higher seats anymore, everyone has moved as close to the stage as possible. The crowd in front of the stage is now very densely packed, dense enough to make crowd crush a worry.

But also, even though the upper seats are mostly empty, there's still movement up there, in the section just behind the stage. A person, where nobody's really supposed to be sitting anyway.

It could be one of the crew. It's probably one of the crew. But it won't hurt if I get up there and make sure.

It's so crowded that I find it challenging to push through and get to the stairs leading up into the stadium seats. I have to be a little more forceful than I'm comfortable with. When people give me dirty looks I just point to my badge. While I'm doing this, Susan continues her story.

"I got exactly what I prayed to God for. I should have been relieved and grateful, right? And I was, in a way. But I also felt guilty and confused. I was in a lot of pain. And there was so—much—blood."

That's the cue for the music to start up again, and the crowd whistles and cheers. It's a good song. Dark and mournful, but also instantly catchy.

For half a second I'm tempted to stop and just listen, but

that moment of temptation is overwhelmed with a feeling of fearful urgency, as if a voice just behind my head is shouting

!!!GET OVER THERE NOW!!!

Ancestors or something else, I don't stop to analyze, I just use werewolf speed to get over to where I saw the movement.

It's that guy. The sullen guy. Of course it is. I knew. Somehow I knew. And he's got a gun. I don't know how he got it into the stadium, but this is America, right, it's easier to find a gun than to find a Starbucks, and I don't stop to think about any of it, I just shout "HEY" so that he points the gun at me instead of the crowd, and then I tackle him.

The gun is one of those automatics or semi-automatics, and he gets off maybe half a dozen shots before I bring him down, but the bullets go into the seats, they don't hit me or anyone else.

Now he's subdued, beneath me, the gun well away from his hands. Crisis over, I hope.

And it's the weirdest thing. Nobody seems to have heard the gunshots over the music and the crowd all singing along. Below me, behind me, the festival goes on, the crowd is still happy, singing along to this Better Angels song they haven't done in concert for more than twenty years.

We can stop the trouble before it starts.

We can.

I did.

While the crowd sings, I'm kneeling my full weight on this guy's chest, using one hand to close off the circulation to his head and knock him out, using my other hand to call Luke.

"Luke, we have a situation here. I'm in the stands, section four, top row. Bring as many people as you can, and handcuffs or something like that."

"Got it, Abe. Is it the sullen guy?"

"It's the sullen guy."

Below me, the shooter passes out. I remain kneeling on his chest until Luke arrives, with several of the bigger crew dudes along with him: Jonas, Nick, and John. Nick has plastic zip ties. He doesn't ask questions, just binds the shooter's hands and feet. Jonas uses a cloth to pick up the gun.

"Oh no," he says. "This is bad, this is a—this is illegal, this is a military weapon. How on earth did he get it up here?"

Below us, the song ends. Wild applause. The concert is nearly over.

Luke says, "Abe, you're hurt."

"I am?" I look down and realize that some of the bullets went into my chest after all. My Better Angels tour T-shirt has three big, bloody holes ripped in it, and through those holes, oh no, through those holes you can very clearly see the binder, which also has three bloody holes in it. I zip up the sweatshirt. "I have to go. You guys have got this?" They all nod, and I take off, get back to my hotel room as quickly as possible.

When I get there, the bullet holes in my flesh are already closed up, but the binder is ruined forever.

31

TOP OF THE SPIRE

"Abe?" Luke is outside my door, knocking. Morning. Everything from the previous day comes flooding back to me and I groan out loud. Why is he here?

I open the door a little. "What do you want, Luke?"

"Can I come in? I got breakfast." He holds up a tray with two large coffees and a couple of breakfast sandwiches.

"Sure." Sigh, open the door all the way. He steps inside, and I close the door behind him. "What happens now?"

"We have breakfast." He sets the tray on the small table, sits down, makes a gesture toward the other chair like he wants me to sit. I do. In spite of everything I am hungry, and I do like coffee.

"The tour is over," he says. "But we've got all our rooms through tonight. There's going to be a wrap party this afternoon, after everyone's done with church."

"I'm not going to church with you, Luke."

"No? I guess I didn't think you would."

"Do they even have churches in Vegas? I thought it was all casinos."

Small half-laugh. "They definitely have churches. But I'm not sure, maybe the churches have a casino in the lobby."

For a while we eat and drink in silence. Then Luke says, "You performed a miracle last night."

"Really? A miracle?" I give him a skeptical look, try to make a joke. "I know I'm pretty awesome, but I still think 'miracle' is overstating it."

"You prevented a massacre. And you took bullets into yourself with no apparent harm."

"Huh. Does that count as a miracle?"

"I know what you are, Abe."

"You do?"

"Shortly after you joined the crew, the rest of us had a conversation about you. Some of the guys thought you were a trans person, but they disagreed about which direction. Then one of them, maybe it was Nick, said it was obvious. You were a eunuch, probably because of the accident. And everything seemed to fall into place. But now I think that wasn't right either."

"No?" I'm not sure how I feel knowing they all talked about me and concluded that I was a eunuch. I'm sort of annoyed and amused at the same time.

"You're a messenger of the Lord. An angel of some kind."

My sip of coffee goes down wrong and I start coughing. "I'm sorry, what did you say?"

He smiles. "I know you won't admit it. But I know what I saw. The bullets didn't harm you."

Deep breath. Blow it out slowly. "I suppose that's true."

"I don't know where you're going to go next," he says. "But anything you need from me, just ask."

"You already gave me what I needed. A sandwich and a safe place to sleep, when that had the power to save my life."

He looks embarrassed. "It's what any Christian would do."

"Come on, Luke, you know better than that. Maybe it's what any Christian ought to do, but most of them don't."

"Was it a test?" He looks at me, earnest, a little scared. "To come to us like you did? Scarred, and broken, and—and—"

"Ugly? I think that's the word you're trying not to say."

"No, I wouldn't." He looks hurt. "That's not a word I would use. But you did change. Over the last few weeks. Your scars, they're not as obvious as they were."

"No. They're not." Silence, while I consider telling him the real truth, decide there's no reason to do that. "It wasn't a test. Not unless every day is a test."

"Maybe every day is a test." He looks thoughtful.

"Maybe it is. Every day, a new chance to pass or fail."

I stand up. Put a hand on his shoulder. "Luke. I have one more thing to do here before I leave town. But when I leave, you'll probably never see me again."

"That's what I figured."

"But you've been really good to me, and I thank you."

He nods, gets a little teary-eyed. "You too, Abe. You prevented a massacre."

We talk for a little while longer, then he leaves to go to church and I decide to try to go back to sleep for a while, setting the phone alarm for six p.m. I suppose I'll give the phone back to him when I check out. Or should I take it to Top of the Spire? No, I don't think I want anything like that with me, in case I have to go full wolf and leave everything behind.

Sleep turns out to be impossible. My brain won't stop racing with questions and worries and hypothetical scenarios. Instead I decide to get dressed as Abe, probably for the last time.

I count my cash. Enough to get me to New Orleans, if I'm frugal. I put most of it in a slim pouch attached to an elastic harness that I designed, which I hope will stay put if I go to wolf form. But I haven't had a chance to test it. I leave out a handful of twenties to keep in my pocket for easy access.

The binder seems okay, in spite of the bullet holes, and does an adequate job of smashing down my boobs. It'll do for one night, anyway.

I go out wandering the Strip, watching people, trying to get my head in the right space. I watch the sleight-of-hand buskers, the take-your-picture-with-a-showgirl costumed women, the gamblers, the families, the little girl riding on her dad's shoulders who gets extremely excited when she sees a real duck paddling around in one of the fountains.

It's one of those days where I feel like a ghost, where it seems as if people are always moving to get away from me, without consciously registering that I'm even there. Maybe I stink or something. I did my usual shower and grooming ritual, but maybe there's some werewolf-related thing going on. Our sense of smell is incredibly powerful, but we have a hard time smelling our own selves, just like anybody.

After my success preventing the massacre yesterday, it seems like I should be on a high, but I'm not. Instead I'm feeling alienated, melancholy, when I go back to the concierge desk at the Mesopotamian. The guy at the desk recognizes me, nods.

"Dave Abernathy."

I hand over the poker chip and another couple of twenty-dollar bills.

He scans the chip with an electronic device, nods. "It's legit." Gives me a tight smile. Puts the chip into a drawer, pulls out a key card and a tie pin. "The key card will get you up in the elevator. You need to wear the tie pin the whole time, it tells them you're there as a high roller."

I accept both with a smile but my heart sinks. A tie pin that tells them what kind of membership I have? That means they'll all know I'm not really one of them. When I acted as one of the cocktail waitresses, they talked in front of me freely, as if I couldn't even hear them. But I doubt they'll do the same to a high roller.

The elevator keycard must be tied to my name somehow, because the instant the doors open I'm pounced upon by an attractive young woman in a diamond choker who calls me "Mr. Abernathy."

"Welcome to Top of the Spire." She takes my arm, steers me to the left. "Right this way, Mr. Abernathy."

So. It's even worse than I thought. The real Azphokite bar and the high rollers club aren't even the same room.

This whole plan is so ridiculous, maybe I should just abort the mission now. Claim illness?

No. I have to try, at least. Remember, I traded my favorite coat for this.

The woman in the diamond choker leads me to a bar decorated to look like a gentlemen explorers club from the 1920s: dark leather chairs, globes, bookshelves, artifacts. The concierge guy was not lying about that.

There are even a couple of regular Azphokite men in this section. I'm not sure why I'm so sure they're regular members. Lack of tie clip, maybe? But also something about their demeanor.

Babysitters. They're here to make sure we have a good time and leave with a glowing review of the legendary Top of the Spire club, keep the mystique going. But we won't see or hear anything we're not supposed to. It's all staged.

I'm not going to find out what I want. It's a bust. I should leave as soon as it won't draw attention. Shouldn't I?

"What would you like to drink, Mr. Abernathy?" asks my personal waitress, even as my heart is sinking.

I take a deep breath, remember to drop my voice into its lowest possible register. "Sazerac, please."

"Perfect choice, Mr. Abernathy, right this way." She steers me to a particular seat, gently but firmly. "Just wait here while I get your Sazerac for you, Mr. Abernathy."

She keeps saying my name in a way that feels unnatural. Is it supposed to make me feel welcomed, at home? It doesn't. It makes me feel weird. I think it would make me feel weird even if "Mr. Abernathy" really was my name.

Still, I make a point of sinking deep into the chair, giving the body language of somebody relaxing. It is a nice chair. Dark brown leather, well-aged, padding soft but not too soft.

I've been dropped into a conversation grouping of six chairs, three of which are occupied. I give them what I hope is a friendly but masculine smile, remember to drop my voice. "Evening, gentlemen." For some reason, this comes out in kind of a British accent. What the hell, brain? I guess I'm committed now.

"Good evening," says one of the men I've pegged as "babysitters." "My name is Marcus, Richard Marcus, and you are?"

"Abernathy. David."

He shakes my hand in a hearty way and I make sure to give it a tiny bit of extra squeeze, but not too much. "And what brings you to Las Vegas, Mr. Abernathy? Business or pleasure?"

"Both, actually. I'm here as a travel companion to my wealthy dowager aunt, but she tends to retire early." Shoot, did I use dowager correctly here? Is my accent consistent?

"And you got lucky at the tables?"

"Well, my aunt did. I don't gamble, myself."

Slight smile. "Really. Here in Las Vegas, you still don't gamble?"

"Don't much see the point. If I just wanted to lose a large amount of money very quickly, I would prefer to light hundred dollar bills on fire and toss them over the balcony. At least then I'd get to watch them burn." I'm channeling Alan Rickman for the accent, and worried it's making me sound like a bit of a jerk. But Marcus looks amused.

"Well," he says. "We do have a rather nice balcony for the purpose, and I have a lighter you could borrow." He flicks open a brilliant gold-plated lighter and for a moment we all just stare at the flame. Then he flicks it shut.

"I shall consider it," I say, with the tiniest smirk. There's a moment of silence and I hold my breath, wondering if I should say something, wondering if I'm caught after all. The moment stretches out, unbearable. But then the diamond waitress returns with my Sazerac.

"Thank you so much," I say, gratefully. Then, under my breath, "I'm terribly sorry, but I do seem to recall being told that in the club no money changes hands?"

She smiles tolerantly, as if she gets this question a lot. Come to think of it, she probably does. "That's right, Mr. Abernathy," she says, keeping her voice similarly low. "Your evening's membership in the club covers everything. All drinks and tips."

"Marvelous, thank you."

She smiles, scans the men in this little circle, asks one of them if he needs a refill. He orders an Old Fashioned.

"The Old Fashioned." Marcus gives us all an aloof smile. "This season's Manhattan, wouldn't you say?"

The man who ordered it looks confused. He doesn't realize Marcus is making fun of him for being trendy. I jump in, to keep the conversation going. "Well, the bars do like to show off their advanced ice cube technology." I hold up my Sazerac, which has been served with a single giant ice cube, branded with the Top of the Spire logo.

Marcus makes a cheers gesture toward me. "And what are you drinking, Mr. Abernathy? Not an Old Fashioned?"

"Sazerac. Official cocktail of New Orleans."

"Have you been there?"

"New Orleans? Many times. My aunt enjoys it."

"Does she? Your aunt travels a lot?"

"She does."

"And you always travel with her?"

"For the past few years, since getting out of school." Shit, why did I do the accent? I've never been to England. They're going to catch on and throw me out a window or something. Like in Mob days.

"I been to New Orleans one time," says one of the other men. By his voice, he's kind of drunk. I wonder what happens here, if you get too drunk. Do they escort you home? Take you to another room and let you sleep it off? "It was before Katrina. Great town for a party. We went all night. I don't know what it's like now. Great town though. Yeah."

"My aunt says the post-Katrina landscape has been significantly shaped by what you would call gentrification." This is something my Aunt Vivienne really has said.

General nodding, as if everyone knows exactly what I'm talking about. Marcus leans toward me with unnerving intensity. "I've been to New Orleans once," he says. "It was a memorable night, although I remember very little of it."

Laughter. Maybe I've got this. If we're just talking about drinking experiences in New Orleans, I have some good ones that do not implicate me as either a girl, or a werewolf. Like that time I had a drinking contest with Edison's friend Brad who ended up in the hospital getting his stomach pumped. Or that time I got into a bar brawl with members of the Russian mafia. Same night, in fact. Or that time we went to a Goth club that turned out to have a secret BDSM dungeon speakeasy. Also the same night. It was quite the night.

But I never have the chance to tell any of those stories, because one of the other men, a fellow high roller, says, "I'm sorry if this makes me sound like a total horndog, but, aren't there any women in this club? Other than the waitresses, I mean?"

Marcus laughs. "Of course, my friend. Just a moment." He stands up and makes a gesture like he's calling somebody over, but I don't see anybody in the correct line of sight. Still, a moment later, a couple of beautiful women in evening gowns, one with golden hair and one with dark hair, stroll over to us from the direction he signaled.

"Jillian, my friend here—what did you say your name was?"

"Bruce James," the man stammers, standing up, jaw dropped in a look of pure starstruck awe. "Aren't you Tawny Duncan?" he asks of the dark-haired woman.

"Jillian," she says, with a tolerant laugh. "But yes, you know my face because I played Tawny on *Curious Angels*."

"And I played Sabrina Doyle on the same show." The blond woman perches on the arm of my chair, smiling at me.

"Lovely." I smile politely. "I'm so terribly sorry, *Curious Angels* was a television program? Movie series?"

She laughs. "You didn't get *Curious Angels* in England?"

"Our loss," I say, making a cheers gesture with my drink.

She leans in with a confidential air and murmurs, "That's all right. It wasn't really that good. But it was popular, thanks to our costuming." Brief pause. "There was very little of it."

We both laugh. She nods her head and says, "You see that dark-haired young man over there?"

"The one with the exceptionally well-tailored suit in cream-colored linen?"

"The very same. That's the Crown Prince of Saudi Arabia."

"You don't say. What's he doing here?"

"He's a bit of a black sheep. Rumor is the family is going to cut him off, because he loses so much money gambling."

We chat for a while. I start to feel more confident of the accent the longer I spend doing it. It's not just an accent, it's a whole persona. Dry wit, measured disdain, precise articulation. My glass spends a few moments empty before my diamond waitress returns. I order a Japanese single malt, neat. Marcus nods with almost imperceptible approval.

A moment of silence, and I start filling it with a story borrowed from Edison's bandmate, Nora, who was originally from London.

"You know, I met the King of England once. I say 'met' but of course I was merely one person on a very long receiving line. He took my hand and smiled at me for a fraction of a second and then moved on.

"I was struck by a thought: this man is wealthy and powerful. He rules over millions of people. He has lived his entire life in a series of mansions. He commands armies. But he's really just an old man who smells of Brussels sprouts and lavender water."

"Brussels sprouts, really?" Bruce James is fascinated. "Had he spilled them on himself?"

"I have no idea. He didn't look mussed."

Marcus asks me, "And how did you come to be shaking the hand of the King of England, Mr. Abernathy?"

"It was something my aunt had done. She'd given a lot of money to a building restoration fund. This particular building was very important to the King for some reason. He hosted a thank you luncheon and she was able to bring a plus one, me." I pause. "This was a few years ago and he wasn't the King yet. Just to be clear."

A pause. Marcus says, "Well. Lucky you. Meeting the future King."

"It's not as if he would remember me. The food was quite good, though."

My Japanese single malt arrives. "Thank you, my dear." A sip. It's good. But all of a sudden I'm way too hot in this woolen three-piece suit. I need air. "Do you know the way to the outdoor balcony?"

She nods, points. "Just out those glass doors. But it's cold this time of year."

"Exactly what I'm looking for, thank you."

It's a small balcony, but nice. Each segment of the rambling Top of the Spire has its own balcony. Where I'm standing, I can hear men talking on the next balcony over, although I can't see them.

Wait. The next balcony over is the bar for the real Azphokites.

I inhale, hold my breath for a moment, listening carefully. But the men are talking about nothing. Football. Thanks to Edison I know a handful of things about football, but I've only seen a couple of games and most of what they're talking about means nothing to me.

Well, it's cold but not too cold, I can hang out here for a while. I lean on the balcony, contemplate the city lights, sip the single malt slowly.

A few men trickle out and have brief conversations, mostly about how cold it is, although they also give each other stock tips and occasionally complain about their families and girl-friends. Very similar to what they talked about when I was a waitress in the Baton Rouge Azphokite bar, come to think of it. And I have the same sense of growing contempt: these men are greedy, self-centered, cruel sometimes to the point of sadism, and they see all the people in their lives as nothing more than tools to be used and resources to be exploited.

I do pick up a few tidbits that seem interesting. They mention a man called "Epperton" who seems to be very high up in their organization. They mention a city, "Miami" and a place in or near Miami, an island resort called "Babylon." This is talked about as if there's going to be an event there.

"Are you going to Epperton's thing in Babylon?"

"No, not this year, the guest list is even tighter than usual. I hear he's got something special planned."

Flint Savage was from Miami, and it was just after my brother Roman went to Miami to settle his affairs that all this trouble started. So it seems intriguing and I perk up for a while, hoping someone else will go into more detail. But it's still mostly stock tips and I start to get bored as well as cold.

Then, Bon Dieu, Marcus comes out onto the balcony. He must know why I'm out here.

"Abernathy," he says.

"Cheers." I hold up my drink. "It's a bit chilly, but the view is spectacular."

"It is indeed."

Shit, the men on the other balcony can probably hear us talking. They won't say anything interesting if they know they can be overheard. That's the point. He really is babysitting me.

"You Brits are used to the cold, I suppose," he says.

"We are, although the cold here is quite dry compared to London."

"Do you enjoy the Las Vegas weather?"

"I don't mind it." I shrug. "Truthfully, I don't mind the weather most places. Dress appropriately. That's the secret. I'm wearing one of my heavier wool suits, on the advice of my aunt." I make a show of pulling the collar of my shirt away from my neck, give what I hope is a British-sounding self-deprecating laugh. "Which means I roast a bit when I'm indoors."

He nods thoughtfully. "Of course. But your drink's empty and you will need to go inside to get another one."

"I suppose that's true."

And then he takes my arm, leans in, says, "I know what's going on, Mr. Abernathy."

And my heart nearly stops.

This is it, he's about to tell me that he knows exactly what I am. Exactly who I am. And then he's going to lead me somewhere private, where they can chop off my head in peace.

But then he continues, "You're overwhelmed. First-timers often are. And, if I read you right, you're a bit of an introvert?"

Small shrug. "I'm British, we're all like that."

In return, he gives a small courtesy laugh. "Of course. So you wanted somewhere to be alone for a while. But if you spend your entire time here alone on the balcony, later, you'll feel as if you wasted a precious opportunity. Don't you think?"

"Hmm." I give him a thoughtful look. "You seem to know what you're talking about."

"I do, Mr. Abernathy. This is not, as they say, my first rodeo."

I think about my first rodeo, earlier this year. I think about the way the calf screamed as they were roping it. I feel like that calf, as I allow him to steer me back inside.

I'm not sure how long I was out on the deck, maybe fifteen or twenty minutes, but during that time the bar has really filled up with people. Mostly men but also a few more of those stunningly attractive women in evening gowns who I should probably recognize but don't.

Somebody has put out snack trays, little stacked canapés, an exotic crudité platter. No dips. The vegetables have already been tastefully dotted with whatever the high end version of ranch dressing is. Everything is meant to be a single morsel that can be picked up with the fingers and eaten without making a mess.

Another Japanese single malt in hand, I locate an untouched platter of sushi. Good but unsurprising. A fairly drunk man in a high roller's pin comes up near my elbow, says, "You like that sushi? That raw fish stuff?"

I give him what I hope is a British-y scornful look. "Obviously," I say, but then fail to eat the spicy tuna maki role that's in my hand. Because a bitten wolf has just entered the room.

We make eye contact from across the room. He's wearing a high roller's tie tack on a cheap-looking but brand-new suit in an unpleasantly greenish shade of gray. He smiles eagerly and comes right over to me.

"I didn't know I'd find anyone like us here."

He says this is a chummy way and I'm not sure what to make of that. Is he Olvenar? He can't be Olvenar. Did he notice I'm female? He wouldn't be so friendly if he had noticed, would he? But maybe if he's not Olvenar he doesn't care? He said "us," so he must think I'm the same as him, whatever he is. A werewolf, obviously, and maybe that's all he means.

I make a gesture toward the other man, who is trying the sushi and giving us a perplexed look. "Not here."

"Oh, right. Yeah. Sure. I'm Harry Dillon."

"Abernathy. David."

He shakes my hand eagerly, giving it a little bit of wolf strength, which I match without exceeding.

"Wow, you're strong for such a little guy," he says, in a joking way.

"You sound surprised, Mr. Dillon. You shouldn't be."

Slightly awkward pause while he fails to interpret my meaning. He fingers his tie tack. "How'd you get your pass? I got one at the Hammerfit in Cleveland. Savage Fitness, I mean." He grins. "What do you think about the rebrand?"

"I'm sure I don't have the faintest clue what you're talking about."

He literally takes a step backward. "You don't? Don't you have Hammerfits in England? England? Is that right?"

"England is where I'm from, that's correct. And, to the best of my knowledge, we don't have anything there called a 'hammerfit.'"

"So how did you…" He gestures at me. "You know, how did you get bitten?"

"Not here, Mr. Dillon," I say.

"Oh, right, sorry." He leans toward me in a conspiratorial way, whispers. "But I thought this was a safe place for our kind."

I take a deep breath, work harder than ever at channeling Alan Rickman-y disdain. "Our…kind?"

"The brotherhood. You know."

"I'm afraid I really don't have the slightest idea what you're talking about, Mr. Dillon." I finish my drink and sigh deeply. "Perhaps, if you circulate a bit, you'll find one of those brothers you're searching for. Now, if you'll excuse me, I have other business to attend to."

"Yeah, okay, see you later," he says, nodding.

I head out to the balcony, trying to make it look casual, breathe in the cold night air with relief. He talked about "the brotherhood." That means this guy is not only Olvenar, he's really obnoxious and pushy about it.

But what is he doing here? He mentioned thinking this was a safe place for "our kind." I assume he means were-wolves, but why does he think that? Maybe Harry from Cleveland knows exactly what I want to know? How the Olvenar and the Azphokites are connected? I would need to flash him to get the whole story, I think. But I have his scent now, I can track him anywhere.

Maybe this is it. I've gotten what I came for. I should leave as soon as possible, before it all goes, as the Brits say, completely pear-shaped.

Then I hear the now-familiar sounds of the doors on the other balcony beginning to slide open. Hold my breath in anticipation.

The men on the other balcony start speaking.

"But what is he doing *here?*" one of them says, voice low and urgent.

"You heard what he said to Abernathy. He got a token from one of those Hammerfit clubs, excuse me, Savage Fitness." Both men laugh scornfully.

"But when all this started, I thought we were going to keep things completely separate. That Lupercius would be acting on his own with no direct contact from the parent organization."

"Don't panic, Bernard. We don't know that he's here for any reason other than the high reputation of the club. You saw that appalling suit he was wearing. Like a used car salesman."

Both men laugh.

While they're still laughing, behind me, the door slides open. I spin around to see Harry from Cleveland coming out onto the balcony. I make hard eye contact, hiss, "Quiet."

He goes blank and still. Behind him, I slide the glass door closed as smoothly and quietly as possible.

Did the men on the other balcony hear any of that? They've stopped laughing.

I hold my breath again, waiting. The first man speaks again.

"Maybe, but two of them in one evening? That can't be a coincidence."

"Two of them?"

"That Brit Abernathy. The new guy pounced on him right away, nostrils flaring, greeted him like they knew each other, tried to talk shop. It was fairly obvious why." Chuckle. "Although Abernathy wasn't having any of it. To his credit, I think. Now, his suit is old, but it's a nice one. And tailored to fit him properly."

"I'm sorry, I'm still not sure what I'm hearing. Abernathy is one of them? The little guy?"

Deep sigh. "When they attack on the full moon, they don't first check to see how tall you are."

"All right, but, if he was bitten in England, he's not one of *them*. He might be a mutt, but he's not one of the brotherhood. They aren't recruiting overseas. Why would they? The bitches are here."

"Are they, though? Why haven't they been caught yet?"

"Well, the sexy bitch has a motorcycle gang of female werewolves guarding her." Another chuckle. "At least that's the rumor. It sounds a bit like the premise for a Russ Meyer film, don't you think?"

Another shared chuckle. "But what about the little bitch? The one they call the Abomination? How could one tiny girl avoid us for so long? What kind of resources does she have?"

"Hm." He makes a small grunting noise like an audible shrug. "She doesn't have any resources at all, that's the problem. After the incident in Atlanta she dropped out completely. Went feral, you might say. She never touched the spending accounts, didn't try to contact her old allies. She didn't even check her email. Which is why the organization thought the brotherhood sounded like a good idea in the first place. To catch a hound, you need a bigger hound."

He continues, "Although, if that man in the appalling suit is representative of the general caliber they're recruiting, I wouldn't trust him to find his own asshole with both hands and a flashlight."

More shared laughter. "I must say, Haldeck, you have almost reassured me."

"Almost?"

"I still think he's trouble. We can't let the brotherhood start to think they're, you know, *members*."

"Oh, no, of course not. But I don't think we need to worry about that too much. Most of them know their place."

"Do they, though? I've heard rumors…never mind."

"No, what've you heard?"

"Just that senior leadership is disappointed with their performance and thinking of shutting the whole thing down if they don't produce results fairly soon."

"That doesn't mean they don't know their place. That means they're incompetents."

Another shared chuckle.

"So what do we do with them?"

"It's not our call. Senior leadership is going to decide what to do about the brotherhood."

"No, not them-them. The other them. Abernathy and the one in the terrible suit."

"Oh, those two? We don't have to do anything. Bore them into going home early, I suppose, if you're really that worried about it." Pause, and when he speaks again there's a smile in his voice. "Unless you want to lock them both in a big room and watch them fight? I hear it's pretty enter- taining to watch their kind fight each other. Extremely violent."

"Heh." A reluctant laugh. "You know, if they did fight, my money's actually on Abernathy to win."

"Oh yeah, mine too." A chuckle that dies out. "Well, it's cold, are you reassured enough to go back inside?"

No verbal response, but I hear the door slide and the men walk back inside.

Bon Dieu. A moment of giddy thrill as I realize I got exactly the information I was looking for. The Azphokites themselves are the ones ultimately behind the attacks on me. Leon and the twins are doing their bidding. The entire Olvenar Brotherhood is basically, from their perspective, a little side project.

And then my moment of giddy triumph is swamped by the most crushing despair: when my enemy was Leon I had, at least, a little bit of a chance at beating him. If my enemy is the entire Azphokite organization, what possible chance do I have?

Harry is giving me a stricken look and I realize he must have come out of his daze in time to hear some of what the other men were saying.

"Abernathy, did you hear that?" he says. "They don't want people like us here."

"I did hear them," I say, cautiously. "Although I'm still not entirely sure what they were talking about."

"But they—the brotherhood—this is terrible."

"Is it? I suppose they did imply that our next round of drinks might be a bit slow in coming."

"No, it's…you're not one of the brotherhood, you don't understand."

"I suppose I don't."

He finishes his beer and erupts into a sudden blazing rage, tossing his empty glass to the granite paving stones so that it shatters violently. "They have been using us. The higher-ups. The big men. Using us!"

"Using you to do what?" I ask, mildly, but he's too far

gone. He starts hyperventilating, hulking up his posture in the way that werewolves sometimes do before a fight.

"They think we're *tacky*." He explodes, with a growl and an eye flash. Slides the glass door open so hard it shatters, stalks into the party on fire with aggression and violence, overturning snack trays and knocking drinks out of people's hands, maximum chaos. People scream and begin to scatter.

He marches straight into the other room, the room connected to the balcony where the real Azphokites are hanging out, easily tossing aside the men who initially try to restrain him.

Well. I don't know what he's planning to do over there, but this seems like my cue to leave.

Everyone else is leaving too. Most of them seem to be heading toward the elevator. I head toward the stairs, the emergency exit. After a few floors I start to feel impatient, take off my slippery men's dress shoes and put on werewolf speed.

Even so, it's fifty-two floors and takes me a while to get down. I'm nearly at street level when I hear the distinctive howl of emergency vehicles approaching.

Push my way through an emergency "alarm will sound" exit door, and wow, what do you know, an alarm starts wailing, and a bright light starts flashing.

I move away from it quickly, toward where I see a huge crowd gathering. Even from this distance I can smell the blood and death. Harry Dillon from Cleveland, and I'm pretty sure he "fell" from the balcony of the club.

One of my questions answered: it's not something a werewolf can survive.

I run the other way.

32

THE LAS VEGAS STRIP

Nervous and keyed up, I walk the Strip at a rapid pace, no particular destination, just trying to process everything that's happened and plan what comes next.

If my real enemies are the Azphokites, maybe I shouldn't go to New Orleans after all. New Orleans could be a trap. But where should I go? Where *can* I go?

Months ago, a lifetime it seems, Robbie asked me, "Are you just going to run forever?" I didn't have an answer. It sounded like a bad idea. Like not much of a life. But now that I know who my enemies really are, the "run forever" option seems even worse. It seems pointless. One of the most wealthy and powerful secret organizations in the world is after me. They tried something, the Olvenar, which hasn't worked (yet), but if it keeps on not working, they're going to try something else. And they're going to keep trying new things until something works.

Unless I find a way to defeat them, they're going to destroy me, just like they destroyed my grandmother. But how can I possibly take on an enemy like that? Maybe, if Leon is doing their bidding unwillingly, he could be turned into an ally?

Maybe, if it's true that Babette is leading an all-female werewolf motorcycle gang, we can team up? Or maybe I can ride off into the sunset with them? Maybe you really can run forever, if you do it as part of a badass werewolf motorcycle gang.

Or, do the Azphokites have a headquarters somewhere? And what would happen if I actually went there? I'd probably just get killed. But what if I went there with a small army of werewolves?

I'd probably get all of them killed.

My thoughts whirl around like the winds of a hurricane, never resting anywhere. I just keep walking, trying to stay with the crowds, stay anonymous.

At a corner, while I'm waiting for the light to change, a black limousine pulls over to the side of the street. The back door opens up.

"*There* you are," says a woman, in a chipper, crooning voice, the kind of voice you'd use with a pet dog, but she's making eye contact with me. "Come on, girl, get inside, there's a good girl. I've got those boots you like to chew on, come on now." And she shakes them toward me.

Grandma's boots.

The woman shaking them at me is Opal. My half-sister. The Frat Boy Killer.

I climb into the back of the limo, take the boots, cradle them against my chest.

"Why shouldn't I just rip your head off right now?" I growl at her. The last time we saw each other she nearly got me and Edison both killed.

She smiles. "Because I've got something you want."

"The boots, sure. I don't know how you found them, but you already gave them to me."

Her eyes light up. "Better than the boots. Sister, I've got a plan to take out the head of the Azphokites."

"The head. That means there is a head? Like, one guy in charge of the whole thing?"

"There is," she says, with a big grin. "A man named Jeffrey Epperton."

"Epperton. I've heard the name. The men at Top of the Spire were talking about him."

"They would. Not everyone in the organization knows he's the head of it, but they've all heard of him. He's incredibly rich and incredibly corrupt. You would not believe the terrible things he's gotten away with. Especially the terrible things he's done to young women just like you." Pause. Evil smirk. "Well. Not *just* like you. They *looked* like you, though. And that's the heart of my plan." She pauses. "Bikini espresso you, I should mention, not Dave Abernathy you. Nice suit, though. How fast can you heal the remaining facial scars?"

"I don't know for sure, but I think I'm strong enough for a full moon transformation, and that should do the trick."

"Okay, good, that's soon enough. So. Are you in?"

Am I in? Bon Dieu. Opal is a killer, and liar, and I don't trust her at all. But I also know the kind of men she likes to kill, and how she likes to kill them. The Frat Boy Killer's signature move was to set things up so that a wealthy, arrogant man, who had previously gotten away with sexual assault, would die in a way that looked entirely accidental. Like the result of his own foolish choices. Falling down the stairs head-first while drunk, or doing too much cocaine during a New Orleans summer and dying of dehydration.

That means I believe her in this: she does have a plan to kill Jeffrey Epperton. And it does have a chance of working. Small chance, maybe, but do I have a better plan?

I don't.

I flash back to the cops who originally tried to kill me, and a nervous rage churns deep in my gut. I let it. This isn't assassination, this isn't killing for money. It's the opposite. The ancestors should be with me. This is their will, isn't it? Grandma told me so. Stop the Olvenar, which means stopping the Azphokites.

I hug Grandma's boots to my chest, inhaling deeply.

"All right, Opal. Tell me your plan."

ACKNOWLEDGMENTS

Thank you to people who helped me get this book into production:

My dad, who provided computer equipment and moral support.

Carol, my beta-reader, for keeping the story on track.

Shannon, my editor, for making sure things held together as a coherent whole.

Paul, my proofreader, who worried that he didn't find more typos.

And to my mom, who wasn't here anymore by the time it was finished, but I read it to her anyway. I hope she liked it.

ABOUT THE AUTHOR

Julie McGalliard is a writer, data scientist, and occasional cartoonist. She lives in Seattle and has traveled to New Orleans a lot.

Follow her adventures at https://www.gothhouse.org/author/juliemcgalliard/

Photo by Andrew S. Williams

ALSO BY JULIE MCGALLIARD